"Jonathan Maberry is a writer whose works will l
years to come." —**Ray Bradb**

"Maberry has the unique gift of spinning great stories in any genre he chooses. His [Pine Deep] vampire novels are unique and masterful."
—**Richard Matheson**

GHOST ROAD BLUES

Winner of the Bram Stoker Award (Best First Novel)

"Reminiscent of Stephen King . . . Maberry supplies plenty of chills in this atmospheric novel. This is horror on a grand scale." —*Publishers Weekly*

"Jonathan Maberry is one of the brightest new lights in contemporary horror. In *Ghost Road Blues* and now *Dead Man's Song*, Maberry proves that he has the chops to craft stories at once intimate and epic, real and horrific, and to create the kind of fiction that should bring disaffected readers back to the fold." —**Bentley Little,** author of *Gloria*

"Every so often, you discover an author whose writing is so lyrical that it transcends mere storytelling. Jonathan Maberry is just such an author, and his writing is powerful enough to sing with poetry while simultaneously scaring the hell out of you." —**Tess Gerritsen,** author of the Rizzoli and Isles novels

"If I were asked to select only one new voice in horror fiction to read today, it would be Jonathan Maberry. *Ghost Road Blues* jumps so easily out of his blend of words, images, and characters, you hardly realize you're reading a novel rather than watching a movie." —**Katherine Ramsland,** author of *Confession of a Serial Killer*

"A fun, fun read and creepy as hell. Jonathan Maberry serves up scares like pancakes at a church social." —**Gregory Frost,** author of *Rhymer*

"I read as much horror fiction as I can get my hands on, and it's been a LONG time since I've read anything that I've enjoyed as much as *Ghost Road Blues*." —**Stephen Susco,** screenwriter of *The Grudge*

"*Ghost Road Blues* rocks. From the first page to the last, Jonathan Maberry displays the sure hand of a master of the craft. I can't wait to see what this new king of horror has in store for us next." —**Bryan Smith,** author of *Deathbringer* and the *House of Blood* books

"This haunting, complex, terrifying, and deeply humane novel is a heady feast for those who've been looking for something new and lyrical in horror." —**Gary A. Braunbeck,** author of *There Comes a Midnight Hour*

"Jonathan Maberry delivers a perfect suspenseful, edge-of-your-seat tale that will keep you riveted! I've "Glimpsed" the future and no one tells it better than Jonathan. Jonathan Maberry is always my go-to author for awesome!" —**Sherrilyn Kenyon**, #1 *New York Times* bestselling author

"Award-winning author Jonathan Maberry channels the best of Stephen King and Peter Straub to create a harrowing story of a mother and a lost child who are besieged by dark forces shadowing their pasts and futures. Raw and beautiful, detailed and explosive, here is a story that will haunt you long after you close the book." —**James Rollins**, *New York Times* bestselling author of *The Seventh Plague*

"Jonathan Maberry has crafted an extraordinary novel that transcends genre. He has created characters we long to know and touch and a plot that twists and turns with each engrossing page. A must read for those who love suspense and horror—or, just a remarkably excellent work of fiction!" —**Heather Graham**, *New York Times* bestselling author

"Maberry consistently delivers delightful dread, and *Glimpse* is his scariest yet." —**Scott Signer**, #1 *New York Times* bestselling author

"So scary I wished I could close my eyes as I read it—but I didn't want to miss a word. The brilliant Jonathan Maberry—evocative, chilling and somehow terrifyingly knowledgeable about the dark necessities of the human heart—will grab you by the throat and not let go. Fair warning— leave the lights on." —**Hank Phillippi Ryan**, Agatha Award, Anthony Award, Mary Higgins Clark Award, and thirty-two-time Emmy Award-winning author

DEAD OF NIGHT

"This has to be one of the best traditional zombie tales I've ever read . . . This is a zombie book for the ages." —*Seattle Post Intelligencer*

"Jonathan Maberry has created an homage to death itself and an homage to the undead that is as poetic as it is terrifying. It's a brand new and in-triguingly fresh slant on the zombie genre that we all love!" —**John A. Russo**, co-screenwriter of *Night of the Living Dead*

INK

"A brilliant and supremely scary novel." —*Booklist*

"Maberry is a master of dark fiction, and *Ink* is an impressive, enthralling addition to his already impressive oeuvre." —*Locus Magazine*

KAGEN THE DAMNED

"Maberry's first venture into sword-and-sorcery fiction employs powerful imagery to tell a classic tale of revenge and blood which fans of Howard, Moore and Wagner will relish! And if you love Lovecraft, you're in for something very special!" —**Michael Moorcock**, World Fantasy Lifetime Achievement Award winner

"Jonathan Maberry is definitely channeling Robert E. Howard, H.P. Lovecraft, and L. Sprague De Camp, this is a great novel with sharp swords, elder gods, mythical cities, and heroes who will become legends." —**Kevin J. Anderson**, *New York Times* bestselling author of *Dune: House Atreides* and *Spine of the Dragon*

"*Kagen the Damned* is the best sword-and-sorcery book I have read in the last ten years. Fans of Joe Abercrombie, Pat Rothfuss, Mark Lawrence, and Robert E. Howard are going to love this." —**Weston Ochse**, author of *Seal Team 666*

"*Kagen the Damned* is a gloriously nuanced, exceptionally brutal epic fantasy crossed with cosmic horror that manages to mine new material out of a very familiar space. It's thoughtful, beautiful, awful, fresh, and very, very welcome." —**Seanan McGuire**, *New York Times* bestselling author of *When Sorrows Come*

"This book is violently honest and honestly violent about the horrors of war. Unrelenting action plunges the reader into the world. The ending is satisfying, but readers will still want more of Kagen. Kagen combines the characters of Conan and Elric into a believable melancholy hero." —**Robin Hobb**, *New York Times* bestselling author

ROT & RUIN

"Maberry's thoughtful, postapocalyptic coming-of-age tale is in turns mythic and down-to-earth. This intense novel combines adventure and philosophy to tell a truly memorable zombie story, one that forces readers to consider them not just as flesh-eating monsters or things to be splattered, but as people." —**Publishers Weekly**, starred review

"Horror fans will appreciate the gorge-raising descriptions of the shambling zombies, while zombie-apocalypse aficionados will cotton to the solid world-building and refreshingly old-school undead." —**Bulletin of the Center for Children's Books**

"This is a romping, stomping adventure. Anyone with a pulse will enjoy this novel, and anyone with a brain will find plenty of food for thought inside." —**Michael Northrop**, author of *Gentlemen*

THE JOE LEDGER THRILLERS

"An enjoyable read, and one that's hard to set down." —*Fangoria*

"Heated, violent, and furious . . . as palatable as your favorite flavor of ice cream. [A] memorable book." —**Peter Straub**, *New York Times* bestselling author

"A fabulous new series. Joe Ledger and the DMS have my vote as the team to beat when combatting terrorist threats on a grand scale!" —**David Morrell**, *New York Times* bestselling author of *First Blood* and *Creepers*

"Brilliant, shocking, horrifying, it puts the terror back in terrorist." —**James Rollins**, #1 *New York Times* bestselling author of *The Judas Strain*

"Breakneck pacing, nonstop action, and a subtle sense of humor, this is an utterly readable blend of adventure fiction, suspense thriller, and horror." —**Publishers Weekly**

"A fast-paced, brilliantly written novel. The hottest thriller of the New Year! In The King of Plagues, Jonathan Maberry reigns supreme." —**Brad Thor**, #1 *New York Times* bestselling author of *The Athena Project*

"Joe Ledger and the DMS are back in their most brutal tale yet as they face off against a diabolical organization who is always one step ahead. As the sinister plot is exposed and the body count rises, *The King of Plagues* is impossible to put down. Be prepared to lose some sleep." —**Jeremy Robinson**, author of *Threshold* and *Instinct*

"Maberry unleashes a runaway brain of a thriller plot turbocharged with a depraved spirit of invention. Next to Joe Ledger, Jack Bauer, Fox Mulder, and Jason Bourne are rank amateurs." —**Javier Grillo-Marxuach**, Emmy Award-winning writer/producer, "Lost," "Medium," "The Middleman"

"Get ready to have your mind boggled." —*Booklist*, starred review

"A blend of SF, horror, technothriller, and crime novel, this is one of the best adrenaline reads out there." —*Library Journal*, starred review

"An action-packed read that sets hearts pumping and fingers quickly turning those pages . . . enjoy this thrilling roller-coaster ride of a book." —*San Francisco Chronicle*

"Maberry has done it again." —*Suspense Magazine*

"If you want a smart story, dripping in testosterone. The type that leans smarts over brawn, until brawn is needed. That and if you like kernels of horror in your espionage. You should grab *Rage* and thank me later." —*Ain't It Cool News*

EMPTY GRAVES

"If you're looking for tense excitement and walking dead meat, welcome to the world of one of the masters of the zombie tale. Maberry could give a haint the willies." —**Joe R. Lansdale**, *New York Times* bestselling author, ten-time Bram Stoker Award winner, Edgar Award winner, World Horror Convention Grand Master Award winner, and Raymond Chandler Lifetime Achievement Award winner

"A horror triumph . . . just razor-sharp stuff. Maberry grabs you by the heart—then smashes you with rabbit punch prose. Each story explodes off the page." —**Max Brallier**, *New York Times* bestselling author and Emmy Award winner

"Stephen King, eat your heart out. Jonathan Maberry stands tall beside you as a master of horror." —**Judith O'Dea** (Barbara in the original *Night of the Living Dead*)

"If Ernest Hemingway wrote about the undead, you would have something approaching these brilliant, surgical excursions into zombie lit by Jonathan Maberry in his new collection, *Empty Graves*. Action packed, character-driven, disturbing as hell, and excruciatingly humane, these stories stick with you, and will live alongside the best of the genre. Highest recommendation!" —**Jay Bonansinga**, *New York Times* bestselling author of *The Walking Dead: Return to Woodbury*

"A big, meaty feast of classic zombie thrills." —**Isaac Marion**, *New York Times* bestselling author of *Warm Bodies*

"Don't be deceived. Maberry's graves are full of nasty surprises, and his storytelling is immaculate." —**Mike Carey**, bestselling author of *The Girl with All the Gifts*

"Sometimes it can seem like there's nothing new to say about zombies, but somehow, Jonathan Maberry always finds the words. Even when working with established tropes, he's always fresh, exciting, and deliciously upsetting." —**Seanan McGuire**, *New York Times* bestselling author of *Alien: Echo*

LONG
PAST
MIDNIGHT

LONG PAST MIDNIGHT

JONATHAN MABERRY

KENSINGTON
PUBLISHING CORP.

www.kensingtonbooks.com

KENSINGTON BOOKS are published by

Kensington Publishing Corp.
119 West 40th Street
New York, NY 10018

Compilation copyright © 2023 by Jonathan Maberry

"Property Condemned" © 2012. Originally published in *Nightmare Magazine*, issue 1; "Material Witness" © 2011. Originally published online as a free bonus story; "Long Way Home" © 2013. Originally published in *Halloween: Magic, Mystery, and the Macabre*, edited by Paula Guran, Prime Books; "Three Guys Walk into a Bar" © 2014. Originally published in *Limbus Inc, vol. 2*, JournalStone Publishing; "On Lonely Roads—A Poem" © 2022; "Mister Pockets" © 2013. Originally published in *Dread*, edited by Anthony Rivera and Sharon Lawson, Grey Matter Press; "Whistlin' Past the Graveyard" © 2013. Originally published in the Bram Stoker Awards Weekend souvenir program book; "The Trouble" © 2015. Originally published in *Darkness on the Edge of Town*, published by Blackstone Audi; "A House in Need of Children" © 2016. Originally published in *Beneath the Skin*, published by Blackstone Audio; "Ghost Creepin' Blues" © 2023.

All Kensington titles, imprints, and distributed lines are available at special quantity discounts for bulk purchases for sales promotion, premiums, fund-raising, educational, or institutional use.

Special book excerpts or customized printings can also be created to fit specific needs. For details, write or phone the office of the Kensington Sales Manager: Kensington Publishing Corp., 119 West 40th Street, New York, NY 10018. Attn. Sales Department. Phone: 1-800-221-2647.

The K with book logo Reg US Pat. & TM Off.

ISBN: 978-1-4967-4393-0 (ebook)

ISBN: 978-1-4967-4392-3

First Kensington Trade Paperback Printing: September 2023

10 9 8 7 6 5 4 3 2 1

Printed in the United States of America

This is for Anne Walsh, who always knew the secret shadows of October

And, as always, for Sara Jo

Contents

Foreword by Josh Malerman   xv

Author's Introduction   xix

Property Condemned   1

Material Witness   28

Long Way Home   65

Three Guys Walk into a Bar   91

On Lonely Roads   201

Mister Pockets   209

Whistlin' Past the Graveyard   235

A House in Need of Children   266

The Trouble   298

Ghost Creepin' Blues   334

Acknowledgments   371

Foreword

Jonathan Maberry has many sandboxes.

I picture his imagination as an enormous yard, fanning far beyond his oft-photographed office, beyond the place he calls home with his beloved Sara Jo. I can see the numerous sandboxes, numerous sites of work and joy, both ever-present in all he does.

Sandboxes . . .

Maybe you first met Jonathan by way of his *Rot & Ruin* series. You might've seen him out amongst the zombies, his zombies, Maberry bravely walking the Rot and Ruin, beyond the fence, a trading card of his own likeness in hand, though I don't imagine he'd be a hunter. Or maybe you first encountered Jonathan Maberry through Joe Ledger, his cussing detective/captain fighting biological warfare (and much more) across numerous books, short stories, and tie-ins (he's in the very book you're reading right now). It's just as likely your virgin sighting of the author was in the pages of *V-Wars* (spectacular stuff, this, but it's all spectacular), his vampire-infested graphic novels and comics. If it was through *Kagen the Damned*, his newest, then welcome to a whole wonderful world of . . .

. . . sandboxes.

Yes.

Wherever you met the man, he had some sand on his hands. When he shook your hand, you felt it. When he showed you his pen, you saw it. And when he turned to get back to writing (which he does, often), you witnessed a cloud of sand rising, enveloping him like the mists, vapors, and fog that permeate his incredible body of work. And it *is* incredible. The quality, the quantity, the breadth of ideas and . . .

. . . sandboxes.

The thing is, if you're a man of many, there must also have been *the first*. The first sandbox you built out in that yard of the imagination, back when nobody yet knew your name. And maybe (it's likely) that first box was built differently than the ones to come. Maybe the four sides of the wood framing were gathered in four distinct locales. Possibly the sand was a darker hue; I bet the box was huge. It's bizarre to think there was once a point in time when Jonathan Maberry had only one (fictional) sandbox to play in. But aren't those beginnings just the best? And isn't an author's first sandbox legend in light of all to come?

For Maberry, his legend began with the Pine Deep Trilogy.

And oh, what a castle he's built in that sand.

More than *Ghost Road Blues* winning the Stoker for best first novel (it did), the book broke down the door for him, introduced him to legions of (blood) thirsty fans, put him on the very real map in the very real sandbox of the horror genre. With *Ghost Road Blues* (and its totally vibrant/haunting conceit), Jonathan Maberry planted his flag in the sand. He was here to stay. And so was Pine Deep, PA. And, dead or not, so were Morse and Griswold. To put this in some perspective: the book in your hands is not only a collection of stories of this world, his first world, but it bookends a career thus far (and who knows what Jonathan has up his sleeve for the future). With *Long Past Midnight*, Maberry is directing us back to that starting line, *his* first, and framing for us all that he's done.

And what better way to do that than to give us some of the main players of his powerful trilogy (Crow, Val, Terry) back when they were kids, tempted by the allure of a local haunted house (but everything is haunted in Pine Deep, isn't it?)? Here's a passage I loved from the first story, "Property Condemned":

"There was a sound. It wasn't the smash of mirror glass, and it wasn't the bang of a pistol. It was something vast and black and impossible, and it was the loudest sound Crow would ever hear. It was so monstrously loud that it broke the world."

And a couple stories later, "Long Way Home," we're now in Pine Deep *after* the events of the Pine Deep Trilogy.

See? Bookends. Or, the wood framework of a workhorse's sandbox. His first.

Did you meet Jonathan Maberry by way of his lengthy exploits in nonfiction?

Possibly it was with one of the anthologies he's edited: it's likely Jonathan's edited one or several of the anthologies you've read. Anthologies in which I myself have had stories.

Which brings me to possibly his coolest sandbox. One he plays in often. It's way out at the edge of the yard:

Jonathan Maberry supports the hell out of other writers. From mentoring to advising, editing or inviting, from talking shop at conventions, seated behind tables displaying books of his own and other writers, to giving speeches and hosting the Stoker Awards, where he has a tendency to be as honest as anyone you've ever seen speak. Add this all up, the work, the joy, the teaching, the honesty . . . and there's a huge lesson to be learned.

Here's what Jonathan Maberry's shown me:

Work because you love it and work because you should. Respect the craft and respect those who do it. Mean what you do and find meaning in what you do.

And while you're doing all this?

Have fun.

Play.

In your sandbox. And when one box isn't enough? Go play in another. Then another. But never lose sight of the ones you've already called home. And, who knows, maybe one day, if you're really lucky, you'll have entire worlds decorating that yard, a million hats to wear, all so different but still all so you.

And us readers are lucky Jonathan Maberry has done this and continues to do this now.

Read *Long Past Midnight.* Return to Pine Deep and love every second of it, but just know this:

This world, this town, this sandbox was Jonathan's fictional first. And for that, we all owe Pine Deep a visit.

We all owe it a stay.

We all owe it a lot.

Josh Malerman
Michigan
Fall 2022

Author's Introduction

A Long Time Ago in a Cornfield Far, Far Away . . .

So, there we all were. In a cornfield.

A half dozen teenage guys, all of us from the inner city, where the only green we ever saw was mystery meat in the back of the fridge. We were all from Frankford High. At fifteen I was both the youngest and the biggest. Six-two by then, built like Sasquatch, and sporting a full beard. Puberty did not so much 'hit me' as run me down with a truck. So naturally I was the one who could go into liquor stores and get beer. Which we drank in very odd places.

Our usual spot to hang out, talk about girls, drink, talk about girls, complain about school, talk about girls, bitch about our folks, and talk about girls was a graveyard about eight blocks from school. No joke. We'd sneak over the walls and find a crypt or a grave with a marble slab, pop the tops on tepid beer, and talk. Sometimes we sang. Most of us were in choir—even those of us who boxed and played sports. A few of us did shows at our school and—because of the whole 'girls' thing—at the local Catholic girls' schools. And some of us were in rock bands. Very bad but very loud rock bands.

We did not sing loud enough to wake the dead. Not because we were actually *afraid* of raising the dead, but it was an inner-city cemetery and there were cops. So, in those dark nights, we sang some of the quieter stuff. CSN, James Taylor, Tom Waits, Leonard Cohen. Like that.

But the cops got hip to us anyway and chased our asses out of there time and again.

So, we spent a lot of time just walking and talking. Back then, kids walked. A lot. Everywhere. It was a thing. We walked and talked. Sometimes solving the problems of the world. Sometimes bitching even *more* about school or our parents. Mostly talking about girls.

And then on one of those walks, my buddy Roberto said, "Hey, you guys want to hang out in a cornfield?"

It was such a weird question that it stopped us.

"A cornfield?" asked Tom. "Like where they actually grow corn?"

Bear in mind . . . city boys in an era way before the Internet.

"Yeah," said Roberto.

"You shitting us?" asked Chuck.

"Serious as a heart attack."

"A freaking cornfield?" said Mark.

"Yeah."

I said, "Hell yeah."

They all looked at me. Roberto, I knew, already understood. He knew I was a little weird anyway. My grandmother was a spooky old lady who'd taught me to read tarot cards when I was eight, filled my head with tales of monsters from cultures around the world, and—just to be even cooler—was born on Halloween. And, it was clear, Roberto had already been to a cornfield.

Chuck asked, "Why?"

"It'll be cool," I said.

"How?"

"No cops to chase us out," said Roberto. "At night, there's no one out there."

"Out where?" asked Jamie.

"New Hope," he said.

And everyone went, "Ahhhhh!"

Roberto should have led with that. It's all about context. Location, location, location.

New Hope was north of Philly. It was a suburb, but back in the '70s, it was as different from the city as you can get. There was the town itself, known for its long history of strange events and frequent hauntings going all the way back to colonial days. *Newsweek* once labeled it "the most haunted town in America."

New Hope seemed incredibly distant, and it was at least an hour's drive. There was no highway that took you there. It seemed like everything was a back road, and in that part of Bucks County, none of the small farming towns was wasting tax dollars on things like streetlights.

New Hope was where the hippies had all these cool, weird little galleries and head shops. They had harvest festivals and Halloween midnight horror movie triple features at the drive-in.

New Hope was creepy in the coolest possible way, and cool in the creepiest possible way. The folks there *knew* they had that rep, and they made it the center of their tourism.

So . . . we went. Roberto drove. He had an old rust bucket of a car that was so comprehensively beat-up that I could not then, or now, tell you what make or model it was. It was a car, and we piled into it the following Friday night, chipping in a couple of bucks each for gas money and beer. He knew where to go and how to get find a farm access road in a way that would not alert anyone in the farmhouse.

If you've ever been to New Hope in the last thirty years, you won't recognize the version of it we saw. Now it's all suburban sprawl and infill, with nary a farm to be seen. Back in '74, the cornfields stretched into a green forever. Vast oceans of slowly swaying stalks and the constant hiss of stiff leaves brushing against one another. Between the cornfields were pumpkin patches, and those were edged with oak trees whose mighty arms stretched wide to support canopies of leaves so dense that no moonlight poked through. And dark? Hell, on an overcast night there was no light at all. Nothing. Not even light pollution from the little town of New Hope. It was too far away, and there were hills and trees and . . . nothing.

We hiked into the center of a field, and to this day I can't tell you how we ever found our way out. Roberto always managed. We followed like trusting sheep. If this was the 1980s and we were in a movie, Roberto would be the first to die, because the guy who knew how to escape never made it out of the first act. The rest of us would have been picked off one by one.

As for what we actually did out there . . . we told ghost stories. That was Roberto's plan, and he knew I'd aid and abet. Understand, we were poor kids from the least attractive parts of the inner city. Life was tough. Some of us were getting knocked around—or worse—at home. Some of us didn't even have much of a home at all. Our families were dysfunctional in all the ways that don't make for happy stories. But with all that, or perhaps *because* of it, we thought we were tough as nails.

And we could make a case for it. I was already a second-degree black belt in jujutsu and was working toward Golden Gloves in boxing. Roberto had been in his share of street fights and was dealing weed in the ghetto. Chuck wrestled and was known to beat on anyone who said something about his mom or sisters. Guys like that. Nothing scared us, because life had already scared us. Scared but had not killed, and so we made the wrong assumptions. We thought we were not only tough, but tough enough. We thought nothing could scare us because we'd already looked into the shadows at home and saw real monsters. Alcoholic parents, abusive relatives, uncles who were in and out of jail, older brothers who'd come back from 'Nam with heads full of ghosts.

So, sitting in the dark, passing cans of beer, in the middle of some farmer's field wasn't going to rattle out cages. Sometimes we'd bring an old metal bucket and use it to build a small fire. Not once were we chased away by cops or farmers. Not once. It occurred to us later that if something actually happened—a werewolf or a mad axe murderer or whatever—no one would come to investigate our screams. Not until farm workers found our corpses next day. That thought was one I had and didn't share. Maybe it was a little too scary.

It was Roberto who started the ghost story thing. He'd read a book about ghostly sightings in New Hope. He knew those stories by heart and embellished them to work his audience. And he knew how to tell a story. He had pacing and timing; he had the voice for it.

But his stories weren't really all that scary. Sure, we might have each gotten goosebumps, but in the dark your buddies couldn't see them.

When it came my turn to talk about the things going bump in the dark, I had a bit more game. All those school shows I was in gave me some dramatic chops, too. But it was the stuff my grandmother—Nanny, we called her—that gave me the edge. When I talked about vampires, it wasn't Bela Lugosi, Christopher Lee, or even Jonathan Frid. No. The vampires Nanny told me about were really strange. No suave guys in tuxedos. There were monsters with iron teeth who hung from the branches of trees. There were mermaids who were gorgeous right up until they dropped their glamour spells and showed their real faces. There were were-creatures who turned into cats or black roosters or swarms of spiders. There were ghouls who dug up the newly buried and ate their rotting flesh. And I'd pad out my repertoire with a sprinkling of urban legends, which were not as well-known back then and easier to sell as true stories I'd heard from a friend or a friend of a friend.

Yeah . . . I scared the bejeezus out of my buddies.

Couple of the guys were really freaked. Made me happy.

By that autumn, we were bringing girls out there with us. Nothing like stark terror to create those romantic moments. Well . . . at least that was the plan. Girls, being consistently more practical than me and my Neanderthal buddies, were not above getting up and walking the hell back to the car. Sometimes.

Most of the time, they stayed and listened. And sometimes told spooky stories they'd heard.

Without a doubt, the Pine Deep novels were born in that cornfield. There in the endless dark of the New Hope nights. There amid the corn and the pumpkins and the autumn moon and the strange noises we heard and were never able to identify.

Years later I understood what was going on. And maybe it was an old Neanderthal or Cro-Magnon gene firing, filling our minds with race memories of nuts huddled around a fire in the mouth of a cave while outside, the wheel of night turned with malicious slowness. No doubt they told stories, too. Maybe they were about saber-toothed cats or maybe gods and demons. Maybe ghosts.

There is a charm to it, but on some level, I think we believe some of that. Or at least believe the possibility that the world is a much larger and darker place than we know. It's easy to be skeptical in the heart of a city, with cold stone and cracked asphalt and streetlights. It's harder to doubt when it's dark as the pit and you can't see ten feet into the walls of darkness that keep trying to close around you.

Years later, in the late '90s, I was working at one of those cubicle jobs that don't matter enough for me to describe it. One of the women at work said that there was a terrific Haunted Hayride attraction in Upper Black Eddy, a town just north of New Hope. A bunch of us went on a Friday night after work. Six days before Halloween. The hayride was brilliant, and I later used it as the basis for the one that opens *Ghost Road Blues.* It was genuinely scary, and I wish I'd gotten to know whoever designed the damn thing. I'd love to have written him into one of my books.

It was while we were on that hayride—a flatbed being pulled slowly by a tractor along roads that snaked and switched and got lost in a vast cornfield—that I started having ideas about a story I'd like to tell one day.

At the time—pretty sure it was 1997—I was writing nonfiction exclusively, and that only part-time. But a writer's brain is a writer's brain. If a story plants a seed, you can't help but water it through speculation, daydreaming, and even making a few notes. The first book on spooky stuff I wrote, though, was a nonfiction book called *The Vampire Slayers' Field Guide to the Undead,* written under the pen name of Shane MacDougall. I did a ton of research, using all the things Nanny had told me as launching points. It was a huge, thick exploration of supernatural predators from around the world and throughout history. It was insanely fun to research and write.

Writing it sparked an interest in me to find horror fiction that used the folkloric versions of monsters rather than their often wildly watered-down versions found in pop culture. At the time the horror genre was in a real slump, and it was incredibly difficult to find novels like that. So my wife, Sara Jo, got tired of hearing me bitch about it and said, "Why don't you just *write* the damn thing. Get it out of your system."

Until then, honest to god, I was not at all interested in writing fiction. But . . . I tried it. Just, as she said, to get it out of my system. It took nearly four years to learn the elements of the fiction craft and generate a complete novel. And I liked it. The process, though difficult and not without setbacks and frustrations, was soooooo satisfying. I even scared myself a couple of times with the things I came up with.

The story was set in a fictional town called Pine Deep, but anyone who knew New Hope from back then, or ever went to Upper Black Eddy for the Hayride, will recognize the territory.

I decided it was, at very least, good enough for me to try and find a literary agent. But I frontloaded that process by saying that if I didn't get an agent in eighteen months, I'd take it as read that the book was only something I'd ever like. However, I got an agent in less than two months. And she sold it to the second publisher who read it. That book—*Ghost Road Blues*—and its two sequels, *Dead Man's Song* and *Bad Moon Rising*.

Then the book got nominated for two Bram Stoker Awards—the Oscars of the horror genre. I lost "Novel of the Year" to some cat named Stephen King. And, hey, if you're going to lose an award like that, lose to Steve. Plus, it was for *Lisey's Story*, and that is one hell of a great book.

I won the other Stoker, in the category of Best First Novel.

Somehow, I had become a novelist.

I wonder what that kid in the cornfield would have thought had he been able to see the future. Maybe he'd have started writing fiction sooner. Who knows?

Since then, I have written more than forty-five novels. Probably forty-eight by the time this book is in print. I've also written close to 150 short stories. A lot of them are horror stories. And there are a bunch set in Pine Deep. This bunch. The ones here in this book.

These tales are set in and around Pine Deep. They're set before and after the events of those first novels, which are collectively known as the Pine Deep Trilogy. I even wrote another Pine Deep novel, *Ink*, which is set fifteen years after the end of the trilogy. I expect to continue telling stories about that creepy, unfortunate, dangerous, weird little town. Stephen King has his Castle Rock and his Derry. I have Pine Deep.

Some of the stories included here are crossovers with other novels I've written. In two cases, they involve my ubiquitous action hero, Joe Ledger. Others focus on characters from the trilogy. Some relate directly to the events in the trilogy, which became known as The Trouble. Others stand alone. None require that you've read my first three novels. That wouldn't be fair. But if you *have*, then there's an extra layer, a deeper peek into the shadows.

I hope you enjoy these tales. If you've ever gone to a haunted hayride or haunted house, if you've ever walked in farm fields or country roads at night, or if you ever just wondered what the hell just made that sound in a bank of nearby shadows, I think you'll find something with which to connect here.

I'll see you on the other side of midnight, my friend.

Jonathan Maberry
San Diego, California
Fall 2022

Property Condemned

1

The house was occupied, but no one lived there.

That's how Malcolm Crow thought about it. Houses like the Croft place were never really empty.

Like most of the kids in Pine Deep, Crow knew that there were ghosts. Even the tourists knew about the ghosts. It was that kind of town.

All of the tourist brochures of the town had pictures of ghosts on them. Happy, smiling, Casper the Friendly Ghost sorts of ghosts. Every store in town had a rack of books about the ghosts of Pine Deep. Crow had every one of those books. He couldn't braille his way through a basic geometry test or recite the U.S. presidents in any reliable order, but he knew about shades and crisis apparitions, church grims and banshees, crossroads ghosts and poltergeists. He read every story and historical account; saw every movie he could afford to see. Every once in a while, Crow would even risk one of his father's frequent beatings to sneak out of bed and tiptoe down to the basement to watch Double Chiller Theater on the flickering old Emerson. If his dad caught him and took a belt to him, it was okay as long as Crow managed to see at least *one* good spook flick.

Besides, beatings were nothing to Crow. At nine years old, he'd had so many that they'd lost a lot of their novelty.

It was the ghosts that mattered. Crow would give a lot—maybe everything he had in this world—to actually *meet* a ghost. That would be . . . well, Crow didn't know what it would be. Not exactly.

Fun didn't seem to be the right word. Maybe what he really wanted was *proof*. He worried about that. About wanting proof that something existed beyond the world he knew.

He believed that he believed, but he wasn't sure that he was right about it. That he was aware of this inconsistency only tightened the knots. And fueled his need.

His *hunger*.

Ghosts mattered to Malcolm Crow because whatever they were, they clearly outlasted whatever had killed them. Disease, murder, suicide, war, brutality . . . abuse. The cause of their deaths was over, but they had survived. That's why Crow wasn't scared of ghosts. What frightened him—deep down on a level where feelings had no specific structure—was the possibility that they might *not* exist. That this world was all that there was.

And the Croft house? That place was different. Crow had never worked up the nerve to go there. Almost nobody ever went out there. Nobody really talked about it, though everyone knew about it.

Crow made a point of visiting the other well-known haunted spots—the tourist spots—hoping to see a ghost. All he wanted was a glimpse. In one of his favorite books on hauntings, the writer said that a glimpse was what most people usually got. "Ghosts are elusive," the author had written. "You don't form a relationship with one, you're lucky if you catch a glimpse out of the corner of your eye; but if you do, you'll know it for what it is. One glimpse can last you a lifetime."

So far, Crow had not seen or even heard a single ghost. Not one cold spot, not a single whisper of old breath, not a hint of something darting away out of the corner of his eye. Nothing, zilch. Nada.

However, he had never gone into the Croft place.

Until today.

Crow touched the front pocket of his jeans to feel the outline of his lucky stone. Still there. It made him smile.

Maybe now he'd finally get to see a ghost.

2

They pedaled through dappled sunlight, sometimes four abreast, sometimes in single file when the trail dwindled down to a crooked deer path. Crow knew the way to the Croft place, and he was always out front, though he liked it best when Val Guthrie rode beside him. As they bumped over hard-packed dirt and whispered through uncut summer grass, Crow cut frequent covert looks at Val.

Val was amazing. Beautiful. She rode straight and alert on her pink Huffy, pumping the pedals with purple sneakers. Hair as glossy black as crow feathers, tied in a bouncing ponytail. Dark blue eyes, and a serious mouth. Crow made it his life work to coax a smile out of her at least once a day. It was hard work, but worth it.

The deer path spilled out onto an old forestry service road that allowed them once more to fan out into a line. Val caught up and fell in beside him on the left, and almost at once Terry and Stick raced each other to be first on the right. Terry and Stick were always racing, always daring each other, always trying to prove who was best, fastest, smartest, strongest. Terry always won the strongest part.

"The Four Horsemen ride!" bellowed Stick, his voice breaking so loudly that they all cracked up. Stick didn't mind his voice cracking. There was a fifty-cent bet that he'd have his grown-up voice before Terry. Crow privately agreed. Despite his size, Terry had a high voice that always sounded like his nose was full of snot.

Up ahead the road forked, splitting off toward the ranger station on the right and a weedy path on the left. On the left-hand side, a sign leaned drunkenly toward them.

PRIVATE PROPERTY
NO ADMITTANCE
TRESPASSERS WILL BE

That was all of it. The rest of the sign had been pinged off by bullet holes over the years. It was a thing to do. You shot the sign to the Croft place to show that you weren't afraid. Crow tried to make sense of that, but there wasn't any end to the string of logic.

He turned to Val with a grin. "Almost there."

"Oooo, spooky!" said Stick, lowering the bill of his Phillies ball-cap to cast his face in shadows.

Val nodded. No smile. No flash of panic. Only a nod. Crow wondered if Val was bored, interested, skeptical, or scared. With her, you couldn't tell. She had enough Lenape blood to give her that stone face. Her mom was like that, too. Not her dad, though. Mr. Guthrie was always laughing, and Crow suspected that he, too, had a lifelong mission that involved putting smiles on the faces of the Guthrie women.

Crow said, "It won't be too bad."

Val shrugged. "It's *just* a house." She leaned a little heavier on the word *just* every time she said that, and she'd been doing that ever since Crow suggested they come out here. *Just* a house.

Crow fumbled for a comeback that would chip some of the ice off of those words, but as he so often did, he failed.

It was Terry Wolfe who came to his aid. "Yeah, yeah, yeah, Val, you keep saying that, but I'll bet you'll chicken out before we even get onto the porch."

Terry liked Val, too, but he spent a lot of time putting her down and making fun of whatever she said. Though, if any of that actually hurt Val, Crow couldn't see it. Val was like that. She didn't show a thing. Even when that jerk Vic Wingate pushed her and knocked her down in the schoolyard last April, Val hadn't yelled, hadn't cried. All she did was get up, walk over to Vic, and wipe the blood from her scraped palms on his shirt. Then, as Vic started calling her words that Crow had only heard his dad ever use when he was really hammered, Val turned and walked away like it was a normal spring day.

So, Terry's sarcasm didn't make a dent.

Terry and Stick immediately launched into the Addams Family theme song loud enough to scare the birds from the trees.

A startled doe dashed in blind panic across their path, and Stick tracked it with his index finger and dropped his thumb like a hammer.

"Pow!"

Val gave him a withering look, but she didn't say anything.

"*. . . So get a witch's shawl on, a broomstick you can crawl on . . .*"

They rounded the corner and skidded to a stop, one, two, three, four. Dust plumes rose behind them like ghosts and drifted away on a breeze as if fleeing from this place. The rest of the song dwindled to dust on their tongues.

It stood there.

The Croft house.

3

The place even *looked* haunted.

Three stories tall, with all sorts of angles jutting out for no particular reason. Gray shingles hung crookedly from their nails. The windows were dark and grimed; some were broken out. Most of the storm shutters were closed, but a few hung open, and one lay half-buried in a dead rosebush. Missing slats in the porch railing gave it a gap-toothed grin. Like a jack-o'-lantern. Like a skull.

On any other house, Crow would have loved that. He would have appreciated the attention to detail.

But his dry lips did not want to smile.

Four massive willows, old and twisted by rot and disease, towered over the place, their long fingers bare of leaves even in the flush of summer. The rest of the forest stood back from the house as if unwilling to draw any nearer. Like people standing around a coffin, Crow thought.

His fingers traced the outline of the lucky stone in his jeans pocket.

"Jeeeez," said Stick softly.

"Holy moly," agreed Terry.

Val said, "It's *just* a house."

Without turning to her, Terry said, "You keep saying that, Val, but I don't see you running up onto the porch."

Val's head swiveled around like a praying mantis's, and she skewered Terry with her blue eyes. "And when *exactly* was the last time you had the guts to even come here, Terrance Henry Wolfe? Oh, what was that? Never? What about you, George Stickler?"

"Crow hasn't been here, either," said Stick defensively.

"I know. Apparently three of the Four Horsemen of the Apocalypse are sissies."

"Whoa, now!" growled Terry, swinging his leg off his bike. "There's a lot of places we haven't been. *You* haven't been here, either; does that make you a sissy, too?"

"I don't need to come to a crappy old house to try and prove anything," she fired back. "I thought we were out riding bikes."

"Yeah, but we're here now," persisted Terry, "so why don't you show everyone how tough you are and go up on the porch?"

Val sat astride her pink Huffy, feet on the ground, hands on the rubber grips. "You're the one trying to prove something. Let's see you go first."

Terry's ice-blue eyes slid away from hers. "I never said I wanted to go in."

"Then what *are* you saying?"

"I'm just saying that you're the one who's always saying there's no such thing as haunted houses, but you're still scared to go up there."

"Who said I was scared?" Val snapped.

"You're saying you're not?" asked Terry.

Crow and Stick watched this exchange like spectators at a tennis match. They both kept all expression off their faces, well aware of how far Val could be pushed. Terry was getting really close to that line.

"*Everyone's* too scared to go in there," Terry said, "and—"

"And *what*?" she demanded.

"And . . . I guess nobody should."

"Oh, chicken poop. It's just a stupid old house."

Terry folded his arms. "Yeah, but I still don't see you on that porch."

Val made a face but didn't reply. They all looked at the house. The old willows looked like withered trolls, bent with age and liable to do something nasty. The Croft house stood, half in shadows and half in sunlight.

Waiting.

It wants us to come in, thought Crow, and he shivered.

"How do you know the place is really haunted?" asked Stick.

Terry punched him on the arm. "*Everybody* knows it's haunted."

"Yeah, okay, but . . . how?"

"Ask Mr. Halloween," said Val. "He knows everything about this crap."

They all looked at Crow. "It's not crap," he insisted. "C'mon, guys, this is Pine Deep. Everybody knows there are ghosts everywhere here."

"You ever see one?" asked Stick, and for once there was no mockery in his voice. If anything, he looked a little spooked.

"No," admitted Crow, "but a lot of people have. Jim Polk's mom sees one all the time."

They nodded. Mrs. Polk swore that she saw a partially formed figure of a woman in colonial dress walking through the backyard. A few of the neighbors said they saw it, too.

"And Val's dad said that Gus Bernhardt's uncle Kurt was so scared by a poltergeist in his basement that he took to drinking."

Kurt Bernhardt was a notorious drunk—worse than Crow's father—and he used to be a town deputy until one day he got so drunk that he threw up on a town selectman while trying to write him a parking ticket.

"Dad used to go over to the Bernhardt place a lot," said Val, "but he never saw any ghosts."

"I heard that not everybody sees ghosts," said Terry. He took a plastic comb out of his pocket and ran it through his hair, trying to look cool and casual, like there was no haunted house forty feet away.

"Yeah," agreed Stick, "and I heard that people sometimes see *different* ghosts."

"What do you mean, 'different ghosts'?" asked Val.

Stick shrugged. "Something my gran told me. She said that a hundred people can walk through the same haunted place, and most people won't see a ghost because they can't, and those who do will see their own ghost."

"Wait," said Terry, "what?"

Crow nodded. "I heard that, too. It's an old Scottish legend. The people who don't see ghosts are the ones who are afraid to believe in them."

"And the people who *do* see a ghost," Stick continued, "see the ghost of their own future."

"That's stupid," said Val. "How can you see your own ghost if you're alive?"

"Yeah," laughed Terry. "That's stupid, even for you."

"No, really," said Crow. "I read that in my books. Settlers used to believe that."

Stick nodded. "My gran's mom came over from Scotland. She said that there are a lot of ghosts over there, and that sometimes people saw their own. Not themselves as dead people, not like that. Gran said that people saw their own *spirits*. She said that there were places where the walls between the worlds were so thin that past, present, and future were like different rooms in a house with no doors. That's how she put it. Sometimes you could stand in one room and see different parts of your life in another."

"That would scare the crap out of me," said Terry.

A sudden breeze caused the shutters on one of the windows to bang as loud as a gunshot. They all jumped.

"Jeeeeee-zus!" gasped Stick. "Nearly gave me a heart attack!"

They laughed at their own nerves, but the laughs died away as one by one they turned back to look at the Croft house.

"You really want me to go in there?" asked Val, her words cracking the fragile silence.

Terry said, sliding his comb back into his pocket, "Sure."

"No!" yelped Crow.

Everyone suddenly looked at him: Val in surprise; Stick with a grin forming on his lips; Terry with a frown.

The moment held for three or four awkward seconds, and then Val pushed her kickstand down and got off of her bike.

"Fine then."

She took three decisive steps toward the house. Crow and the others stayed exactly where they were. When Val realized she was alone, she turned and gave them her best ninja death stare. Crow knew this stare all too well; his buttocks clenched, and his balls tried to climb up into his chest cavity. Not even that creep Vic Wingate gave her crap when Val had that look in her eyes.

"What I ought to do," she said coldly, "is make you three sissies go in with me."

"No way," laughed Terry, as if it were the most absurd idea anyone had ever said aloud.

"Okay!" blurted Crow.

Terry and Stick looked at him with a *Nice going, Judas* look in their eyes.

Val smiled. Crow wasn't sure if she was smiling at him or smiling in triumph. Either way, he put it in the win category. He was one smile up on the day's average.

Crow's bike had no kickstand, so he got off and leaned it against a maple, considered, then picked it up and turned it around so that it pointed the way they'd come. Just in case.

"You coming?" he asked Stick and Terry.

"If I'm going in," said Val acidly, "then we're *all* going in. It's only fair, and I don't want to hear any different or so help me God, Terry . . ."

She left the rest to hang. When she was mad, Val not only spoke like an adult, she sounded like her mother.

Stick winced and punched Terry on the arm. "Come on, numbnuts."

4

The four of them clustered together on the lawn, knee deep in weeds. Bees and blowflies swarmed in the air around them. No one moved for over a minute. Crow could feel the spit in his mouth drying to paste.

I want to do this, he thought, but that lie sounded exactly like what it was.

The house glowered down at him.

The windows, even the shuttered ones, were like eyes. The ones with broken panes were like the empty eye sockets of old skulls, like the ones in the science class in school. Crow spent hours staring into those dark eyeholes, wondering if there was anything of the original owner's personality in there. Not once did he feel anything. Now, just looking at those black and empty windows made Crow shudder, because he was getting the itchy feeling that there *was* something looking back.

The shuttered windows somehow bothered him more than the open ones. They seemed . . . he fished for the word.

Sneaky?

No, that wasn't right. That was too cliché, and Crow had read every ghost story he could find. Sneaky wasn't right. He dug through his vocabulary and came up short. The closest thing that seemed to fit—and Crow had no idea *how* it fit—was *hungry.*

He almost laughed. How could shuttered windows look hungry?

"That's stupid."

It wasn't until Stick turned to him and asked what he was talking about that Crow realized he'd spoken the words aloud.

He looked at the others, and all of them, even Val, were stiff with apprehension. The Croft house scared them. Really scared them.

Because they believed there was something in there.

They all paused there in the yard, closer to their bikes and the road than they were to that porch.

They believed.

Crow wanted to shout, and he wanted to laugh.

"Well," said Val, "let's go."

The Four Horsemen, unhorsed, approached the porch.

5

The steps creaked.

Of course they did. Crow would have been disappointed if they hadn't. He suppressed a smile. The front door was going to creak, too; those old hinges were going to screech like a cat. It was how it was all supposed to be.

It's real, he told himself. *There's a ghost in there. There's something in there.*

It was the second of those two thoughts that felt correct. Not *right* exactly—but *correct*. There was some*thing* in that house. If they went inside, they'd find it.

No, whispered a voice from deeper inside his mind, *if we go inside, it will find us.*

"Good," murmured Crow. This time he said it so softly that none of the others heard him.

He wanted it to find them.

Please let it find them.

They crossed the yard in silence. The weeds were high and brown as if they could draw no moisture at all from the hard ground. Crow saw bits of debris there, half-hidden by the weeds. A baseball whose hide had turned a sickly yellow and whose seams had split like torn surgical sutures. Beyond that was a woman's dress shoe; just the one. There was a Triple-A road map of Pennsylvania, but the wind and rain had faded the details so that the whole state appeared to be under a heavy fog. Beyond that was an orange plastic pill bottle with its label peeled halfway back. Crow picked it up and read the label and was surprised to see that the pharmacy where this prescription had been filled was in Poland. The drug was called Klozapol, but Crow had no idea what that was or what it was used for. The bottle was empty, but it looked pretty new. Crow let it drop, and he touched the lucky stone in his pocket to reassure himself that it was still safe.

Still his.

The yard was filled with junk. An empty wallet, a ring of rusted keys, a soiled diaper, the buckle from a seat belt, a full box of graham crackers that was completely covered with ants. Stuff like that. Disconnected things. Like junk washed up on a beach.

Val knelt and picked up something that flashed silver in the sunlight.

"What's that?" asked Terry.

She held it up. It was an old Morgan silver dollar. Val spit on her thumb and rubbed the dirt away to reveal the profile of Lady Liberty. She squinted to read the date.

"Eighteen ninety-five," she said.

"Are you kidding me?" demanded Terry, bending close to study it. He was the only one of them who collected coins. "Dang, Val . . . that's worth a lot of money."

"Really?" asked Val, Crow, and Stick at the same time.

"Yeah. A *lot* of money. I got some books at home we can look it up in. I'll bet it's worth a couple of thousand bucks."

Crow goggled at him. Unlike the other three, Crow's family was dirt poor. Even Stick, whose parents owned a tiny TV repair shop in town, had more money. Crow's mom was dead, and his father worked part-time at Shanahan's Garage, then drank most of what he earned. Crow was wearing the same jeans this year that he wore all last season. Same sneakers, too. He and his brother Billy had learned how to sew well enough to keep their clothes from falling apart.

So he stared at the coin that might be worth a few thousand dollars.

Val turned the coin over. The other side had a carving of an eagle with its wings outstretched. The words UNITED STATES OF AMERICA arched over it, and ONE DOLLAR looped below it. But above the eagle, where IN GOD WE TRUST should have been, someone had gouged deep into the metal, totally obscuring the phrase.

Terry gasped as if he was in actual physical pain.

"Bet it ain't worth as much like that," said Stick with a nasty grin.

Val shrugged and shoved the coin into her jeans pocket. "Whatever. Come on."

It was a high porch, and they climbed four steep steps to the deck, and each step was littered with dried leaves and withered locust husks. Crow wondered where the leaves had come from; it was the height of summer. Except for the willows, everything everywhere was alive, and those willows looked like they'd been dead for years. Besides, these were dogwood leaves. He looked around for the source of the leaves, but there were no dogwoods in the yard. None anywhere he could see.

He grunted.

"What?" asked Val, but Crow didn't reply. It wasn't the sort of observation that was going to encourage anyone.

"The door's probably locked," said Terry. "This is a waste of time."

"Don't even," warned Val.

The floorboards creaked, each with a different note of agonized wood.

As they passed one of the big, shuttered windows, Stick paused and frowned at it. Terry and Val kept walking, but Crow slowed and lingered a few paces away. As he watched, the frown on Stick's mouth melted away, and his friend stood there with no expression at all on his face.

"Stick . . . ?"

Stick didn't answer. He didn't even twitch.

"Yo . . . Stick."

This time Stick jumped as if Crow had pinched him. He whirled and looked at Crow with eyes that were wide but unfocused.

"What did you say?" he asked, his voice a little slurred. Like Dad's when he was starting to tie one on.

"I didn't say anything. I just called your name."

"No," said Stick, shaking his head. "You called me 'Daddy.' What's that supposed to mean?"

Crow laughed. "You're hearing things, man."

Stick whipped his ballcap off his head and slapped Crow's shoulder. "Hey . . . I *heard* you."

Terry heard this, and he gave Stick a quizzical smile, waiting for the punchline. "What's up?"

Stick wiped his mouth on the back of his hand and stared down as if expecting there to be something other than a faint sheen of spit. He touched the corner of his mouth and looked at his fingers. His hands were shaking as he pulled his ballcap on and snugged it down low.

"What are you doing?" asked Terry, his smile flickering.

Stick froze. "Why? Do I have something on my face?"

"Yeah," said Terry.

Stick's face blanched white, and he jabbed at his skin. The look in his eyes was so wild and desperate that it made Crow's heart hurt. He'd seen a look like that once when a rabbit was tangled up in some barbed wire by the Carby place. The little animal was covered in blood, and its eyes were huge, filled with so much terror that it couldn't even blink. Even as Crow and Val tried to free it, the rabbit shuddered and died.

Scared to death.

For just a moment, Stick looked like that, and the sight of that expression drove a cold sliver of ice into Crow's stomach. He could feel his scrotum contract into a wrinkled little walnut.

Stick pawed at his face. "What is it?"

"Don't worry," said Terry, "it's just a dose of the uglies, but you had that when you woke up this morning."

Terry laughed like a donkey.

No one else did.

Stick glared at him, and his nervous fingers tightened into fists. Crow was sure that he was going to smash Terry in the mouth. But then Val joined them.

"What's going on?" she demanded.

Her stern tone broke the spell of the moment.

"Nothing," said Stick as he abruptly pushed past Terry and stalked across the porch, his balled fists at his sides. The others gaped at him.

"What—?" began Terry, but he had nowhere to go with it. After a moment, he followed Stick.

Val and Crow lingered for a moment.

"Did they have a fight or something?" Val asked quietly.

"I don't know what that was," admitted Crow. He told her exactly what happened. Val snorted.

"Boys," she said, leaving it there. She walked across the porch and stood in front of the door.

Crow paused, trying to understand what just happened. Part of him wanted to believe that Stick just saw a ghost. He wanted that very badly. The rest of him—*most* of him—suddenly wanted to turn around, jump on the bike that was nicely positioned for a quick escape, and never come back here. The look in Stick's eyes had torn all the fun out of this.

"Let's get this over with," said Val, and that trapped all of them in the moment. The three boys looked at her, but none of them looked at each other. Not for a whole handful of brittle seconds. Val, however, studied each of them. "Boys," she said again.

Under the lash of her scorn, they followed her.

The doors were shut, but even before Val touched the handle, Crow knew that these doors wouldn't be locked.

It wants *us to come in.*

Terry licked his lips and said, "What do you suppose is in there?"

Val shook her head, and Crow noted that she was no longer saying that this was *just* a house.

Terry nudged Crow with his elbow. "You ever talk to anybody's been in here?"

"No."

"You ever know anyone who knows anyone who's been in here?"

Crow thought about it. "Not really."

"Then how do you know it's even haunted?" asked Val.

"I don't."

It was a lie, and Crow knew that everyone read it that way. No one called him on it, though. Maybe they would have when they were still in the yard, but not now. There was a line somewhere, and Crow knew — they all knew — they'd crossed it.

Maybe it was when Stick looked at the shuttered windows and freaked out.

Maybe it was when they came up on the porch.

Maybe, maybe . . .

Val took a breath, set her jaw, gripped the rusted and pitted brass knob, and turned it.

The lock clicked open.

A soft sound. Not at all threatening.

It wants us to come in, Crow thought again, knowing it to be true.

Then there was another sound, and Crow was sure only he heard it. Not the lock, not the hinges; it was like the small intake of breath you hear around the dinner table when the knife is poised to make the first cut into a Thanksgiving turkey. The blade gleams, the turkey steams, mouths water, and each of the ravenous diners takes in a small hiss of breath as the naked reality of hunger is undisguised.

Val gave the door a little push and let go of the knob.

The hinges creaked like they were supposed to. It was a real creak, too. Not another hungry hiss. If the other sound had been one of expectation, then the creak was the plunge of the knife.

Crow knew this even if he wasn't old enough yet to form the

thoughts as cogently as he would in later years. Right now, those impressions floated in his brain, more like colors or smells than structured thoughts. Even so, he understood them on a visceral level.

As the door swung open, Crow understood something else, too; two things, really.

The first was that after today, he would never again need proof of anything in the unseen world.

And the second was that going into the Croft house was a mistake.

6

They went in anyway.

7

The door opened into a vestibule that was paneled in rotting oak. The broken globe light fixture on the ceiling above them was filled with dead bugs. There were no cobwebs, though, and no rat droppings on the floor.

In the back of Crow's mind, he knew that he should have been worried about that. By the time the thought came to the front of his mind, it was too late.

The air inside was curiously moist, and it stank. It wasn't the smell of dust, or the stench of rotting meat. That's what Crow had expected; this was different. It was a stale, acidic smell that reminded him more of his father's breath after he came home from the bar. Crow knew that smell from all of the times his father bent over him, shouting at him while he whipped his belt up and down, up and down. The words his father shouted seldom made any sense. The stink of his breath was what Crow remembered. It was what he forced his mind to concentrate on so that he didn't feel the burning slap of the belt. Crow had gotten good at that over the years. He still felt the pain—in the moment and in the days following each beating—but he was able to pull his mind out of his body with greater ease each time as long as he focused on something else. How or why that distraction had become his father's pickled breath was something Crow never understood.

And now, as they moved from the vestibule into the living room, Crow felt as if the house itself was breathing at him with that same stink.

Crow never told his friends about the beatings. They all knew—Crow was almost always bruised somewhere—but this was small-town Pennsylvania in 1974, and nobody ever talked about stuff like that. Not even his teachers. Just as Stick never talked about the fact that both of his sisters had haunted looks in their eyes and never—*ever*—let themselves be alone with their father. Not if they could avoid it. Janie and Kim had run away a couple of times each, but they never said why. You just didn't talk about some things. Nobody did.

Nobody.

Certainly not Crow.

So, he had no point of reference for discussing the stink of this house. To mention it to his friends would require that he explain what else it smelled like. That was impossible. He'd rather die.

The house wanted us to come in, he thought, *and now we're in.*

Crow looked at the others. Stick hung back, almost crouching in-side the vestibule, and the wild look was back on his face. Terry stood with his hands in his pockets, but from the knuckly lumps under the denim, Crow knew that he had his fists balled tight. Val had her arms wrapped around her chest as if she stood in a cold wind. No one was looking at him.

No one was looking at each other. Except for Crow.

Now we're inside.

Crow knew what would happen. He'd seen every movie about haunted houses, read every book. He had all the Warren *Eerie* and *Creepy* comics. He even had some of the old EC comics. He knew.

The house is going to fool us. It'll separate us. It'll kill us, one by one.

That's the way it always was. The ghost—or ghosts—would pull them apart, lead them into darkened cellars or hidden passages. They'd be left alone, and alone, each one of them would die. Knives in the dark, missing stairs in a lightless hall, trapdoors, hands reaching out of shadows. They'd all die in here. Apart and alone. That was the way it always happened.

Except . . .

Except that it did not happen that way.

Crow saw something out of the corner of his eye. He turned to see a big mirror mounted on the wall. Dusty, cracked, the glass fogged.

He saw himself in the mirror.

Himself and not himself.

Crow stepped closer.

The reflection stepped closer, too.

Crow and Crow stared at each other. The boy with bruises, and a man who looked like his father. But it wasn't his father. It was Crow's own face, grown up, grown older. Pale, haggard, the jaws shadowy with a week's worth of unshaved whiskers, vomit stains drying on the shirt. A uniform shirt. A police uniform. Wrinkled and stained, like Kurt Bernhardt's. Even though it was a reflection, Crow could smell the vomit. The piss. The rank stink of exhaled booze and unbrushed teeth.

"Fuck you, you little shit," he said. At first Crow thought the cop was growling at him, but then Crow turned and saw Val and Terry. Only they were different. Everything was different, and even though the mirror was still there, nothing else was the same. This was outside, at night, in town. And the Val and Terry the cop was cursing at quietly were all grown up. They weren't reflections; they were real, they were here. Wherever and *whenever* here was.

Val was tall and beautiful, with long black hair and eyes that were filled with laughter. And she *was* laughing—laughing at something Terry said. There were even laugh lines around her mouth. They walked arm in arm past the shop windows on Corn Hill. She wore a dress, and Terry was in a suit. Terry was huge, massive, and muscular, but the suit he wore was expensive and perfectly tailored. He whispered to Val, and she laughed again. Then at the corner of Corn Hill and Baker Lane, they stopped to kiss. Val had to fight her laughs in order to kiss, and even then, the kiss disintegrated into more laughs. Terry cracked up, too, and then they turned and continued walking along the street. They strolled comfortably. Like people who were walking home.

Home. Not home as kids on bikes, but to some place where they lived together as adults. Maybe as husband and wife.

Val and Terry.

Crow turned back to the mirror, which stood beside the cop—the only part of the Croft house that still existed in this world. The cop—the older Crow—stood in the shadows under an elm tree and watched Val and Terry. Tears ran like lines of mercury down his cheeks. Snot glistened on his upper lip. He sank down against the trunk of the tree, toppling the last few inches as his balance collapsed. He didn't even try to stop his fall, but instead lay with his cheek against the dirt. Some loose coins and a small stone fell out of the man's pocket.

Crow patted his own pocket. The lucky stone was there.

Still there.

Still his.

The moment stretched into a minute and then longer as Crow watched the drunken man weep in wretched silence. He wanted to turn away, but he couldn't. Not because the image was so compelling, but because when Crow actually tried to turn . . . he simply could not make his body move. He was frozen into that scene.

Locked.

Trapped.

The cop kept crying.

"Stop it," said Crow. He meant to say it kindly, but the words banged out of him, as harsh as a pair of slaps.

The cop froze, lifting his head as if he'd heard the words.

His expression was alert but filled with panic, like a deer who had just heard the crunch of a heavy footfall in the woods. It didn't last, though. The drunken glaze stole over it, and the tense lips grew rubbery and slack. The cop hauled himself to a sitting position with his back to the tree, and the effort winded him so that he sat panting like a dog, his face greasy with sweat. Behind the alcohol haze, something dark and ugly and lost moved in his eyes.

Crow recognized it. The same shapeless thing moved behind his own eyes every time he looked in the mirror. Especially after a beating. But the shape in his own eyes was smaller than this, less sharply defined. His usually held more panic, and there was none at all here. Panic, he would later understand, was a quality of hope, even of wounded hope. In the cop's eyes, there was only fear. Not fear of death—Crow was experienced enough with fear to understand that much. No, this was the fear that, as terrible as this was, life was as good as it would ever be again. All that was left was the slide downhill.

"No . . ." murmured Crow, because he knew what was going to happen.

The cop's fingers twitched like worms waiting for the hook. They crawled along his thigh, over his hip bone. They found the leather holster and the gnarled handle of the Smith & Wesson.

Crow could not bear to watch. He needed to not see this. A scream tried to break from him, and he *wanted* it to break. A scream could break chains. A scream could push the boogeyman away. A scream could shatter this mirror.

But Crow could not scream.

Instead, he watched as those white, trembling fingers curled around the handle of the gun and pulled it slowly from the holster.

He still could not turn . . . but now his hands could move. A little and with a terrible sluggishness, but they moved. His own fingers crawled along his thigh, felt for his pocket, wormed their way inside.

The click of the hammer being pulled back was impossibly loud.

Crow's fingers curled around the stone. It was cold and hard and so . . . *real.*

He watched the cylinder of the pistol rotate as the cop's thumb pulled the hammer all the way back.

Tears burned like acid in Crow's eyes, and he summoned every ounce of will to pull the stone from his pocket. It came so slowly. It took a thousand years.

But it came out.

The cop lifted the barrel of the pistol and put it under his chin. His eyes were squeezed shut.

Crow raised his fist, and the harder he squeezed the stone, the more power he had in his arm.

"I'm sorry . . ." Crow said, mumbling the two words through lips bubbling with spit.

The cop's finger slipped inside the curled trigger guard.

"I'm so sorry . . ."

Crow threw the stone at the same moment the cop pulled the trigger.

The stone struck the mirror a microsecond before the firing pin punched a hole in the world.

There was a sound. It wasn't the smash of mirror glass, and it wasn't the bang of a pistol. It was something vast and black and impossible, and it was the loudest sound Crow would ever hear. It was so monstrously loud that it broke the world.

Shards of mirror glass razored through the air around Crow, slashing him, digging deep into his flesh, gouging burning wounds in his mind. As each one cut him, the world shifted around Crow, buffeting him into different places, into different lives.

He saw Terry. The adult Terry, but now he was even older than the one who had been laughing with Val. It was crazy weird, but somehow Crow knew that this was as real as anything in his world.

Terry's face was lined with pain, his body crisscrossed with tiny cuts. Pieces of a broken mirror lay scattered around him. Each separate piece reflected Terry, but none of them were the Terry who stood in the midst of the debris. Each reflection was a distortion, a funhouse twist of Terry's face. Some were laughing—harsh and loud and fractured. Some were weeping. Some were glazed and catatonic. And one, a single large piece, showed a face that was more monster than man. Lupine and snarling and so completely *wrong*. The Terry who stood above the broken pieces screamed, and if there was any sanity left in his mind, it did not shine out through his blue eyes. Crow saw a version of his best friend who was completely and irretrievably *lost*.

Terry screamed and screamed, and then he spun around, ran straight across the room and threw himself headfirst out of the window. Crow fell with him. Together they screamed all the way down to the garden flagstones.

* * *

The impact shoved Crow into another place.

He was there with Val. They were in the cornfields behind Val's house. A black rain hammered down; the sky veined with red lightning. Val was older . . . maybe forty years old. She ran through the corn, skidding, slipping in the mud. Running toward a figure that lay sprawled on the ground.

"Dad!" screamed Val.

Mr. Guthrie lay on his stomach, his face pressed into the muck. In the brightness of the lightning, Crow could see a neat, round bullet hole between his shoulder blades, the cloth washed clean of blood by the downpour.

"*No!*" shrieked Val. She dropped to her knees and clawed her father into her arms. His big old body resisted her, fighting her with limpness and weight and sopping clothes, but eventually Val found the strength to turn him onto his back.

"Daddy . . . Daddy . . . ?"

His face was totally slack, streaked with mud that clumped on his mustache and caught in his bushy eyebrows.

Val wiped the mud off his face and shook him very gently.

"Daddy . . . *please* . . ."

The lightning never stopped, and the thunder bellowed insanely. A freak eddy of wind brought sounds from the highway. The high, lonely wail of a police siren, but Crow knew that the cops would be too late. They were already too late.

Crow spun out of that moment and into another. There were police sirens here, too, and the flashing red and blue lights, but no rain. This was a different place, a different moment. A different horror.

He was there.

He was a cop.

He was sober. Was he younger or older? He prayed that this was him as an older man, just as Val and Terry had been older.

Older. Sober.

Alive.

However, the moment was not offering any mercies.

Stick was there. He was on his knees, and Crow was bent over him, forcing handcuffs onto his friend's wrists. They were both speaking, saying the same things over and over again.

"What did you do? Christ, Stick, what did you *do*?"

"I'm sorry," Stick said. "I'm sorry."

On the porch of the house, a female cop and an EMT were supporting a ten-year-old girl toward a waiting ambulance. The girl looked a lot like Janie and Kim, Stick's sisters, but Crow knew that she wasn't. He knew that this girl was Stick's daughter. Her face was bruised. Her clothes were torn. There was blood on her thighs.

"What did you do, Stick, what did you *do*?"

"I'm sorry," wept Stick. His mouth bled from where Crow had punched him. "I'm sorry."

Crow saw other images.

People he did not know. Some dressed in clothes from long ago, some dressed like everyone else. He stepped into sick rooms and cells; he crawled through the shattered windows of wrecked cars and staggered coughing through the smoke of burning houses.

Crow squeezed his eyes shut and clapped his hands over his ears. He screamed and screamed.

The house exhaled its liquor stink of breath at him.

8

Crow heard Val yell. Not the woman, but the girl.

He opened his eyes and saw the Morgan silver dollar leave her outstretched hand. It flew past him, and he turned to see it strike the mirror. The same mirror he'd shattered with his lucky stone.

For just a moment, he caught that same image of her kneeling in the rain, but then the glass detonated.

Then he was running.

He wasn't conscious of when he was able to run. When he was *allowed* to run.

But he was running.

They were all running.

As Crow scrambled for the door, he cast a single desperate look back to see that the mirror was undamaged by either stone or coin. All of the restraints that had earlier held his limbs were gone, as if the house, glutted on his pain, ejected the table scraps.

And so, they ran.

Terry shoved Stick so hard that it knocked his ballcap off of his head. No one stooped to pick it up. They crowded into the vestibule and burst out onto the porch and ran for their bikes. They were all screaming.

They screamed as they ran, and they screamed as they got on their bikes.

Their screams dwindled as the house faded behind its screen of withered trees.

The four of them tore down the dirt road and burst onto the access road, and turned toward town, pumping as hard as they could. They raced as hard and as fast as they could.

Only when they reached the edge of the pumpkin patch on the far side of the Guthrie farm did they slow and finally stop.

Panting, bathed in sweat, trembling, they huddled over their bikes, looking down at the frames, at their sneakered feet, at the dirt.

Not at each other.

Crow did not know if the others had seen the same things he'd seen. Or perhaps their own horrors.

Beside him, Terry seemed to be the first to recover. He reached into his pocket for his comb, but it wasn't there. He took a deep breath and let it out, then dragged trembling fingers through his hair.

"It must be dinnertime," he said, and he turned his bike toward town and pedaled off. Terry did not look back.

Stick dragged his forearm across his face and looked at the smear, just as he had done before. Was he looking for tears? Or for the blood that had leaked from the corners of his mouth when the older Crow had punched him? A single sob broke in his chest, and he shook his head. Crow thought he saw Stick mouth those same two terrible words. *I'm sorry.*

Stick rode away.

That was the last time he went anywhere with Crow, Val, or Terry. During the rest of that summer and well into the fall, Stick went deep inside of himself. Eight years later, Crow read in the papers that George Stickler had swallowed an entire bottle of sleeping pills, though he was not yet as old as he had been in the vision. Crow was heartbroken, but he was not surprised, and he wondered what the line was between the cowardice of suicide and an act of bravery.

For five long minutes, Crow and Val sat on their bikes, one foot each braced on the ground. Val looked at the cornfields in the distance, and Crow looked at her. Then, without saying a word, Val got off her bike and walked it down the lane toward her house. Crow sat there for almost half an hour before he could work up the courage to go home.

None of them ever spoke about that day. They never mentioned the Croft house. They never asked what the others had seen.

Not once.

The only thing that ever came up was the Morgan silver dollar. One evening, Crow and Terry looked it up in a coin collector's book. In mint condition, it was valued at forty-eight thousand dollars. In poor condition, it was still worth twenty thousand.

That coin probably still lay on the Croft house living room floor.

Crow and Terry looked at each other for a long time. Crow knew that they were both thinking about that coin. Twenty thousand dollars, just lying there. Right there.

It might as well have been on the dark side of the moon.

Terry closed his coin book and set it aside. As far as Crow knew, Terry never collected coins after that summer. He also knew that neither of them would ever go back for that silver dollar. Not for ten thousand dollars. Not for ten million. Like everything else they'd seen there—the wallet, the pill bottle, the diaper, all of it—the coin belonged to the house. Like Terry's pocket comb. Like Stick's ballcap. And Crow's lucky stone.

And what belonged to the house would stay there.

The house kept its trophies.

Crow went to the library and looked through the back issues of newspapers, through obituaries, but try as he might, he found no records at all of anyone ever having died there.

Somehow it didn't surprise him.

There weren't ghosts in the Croft house. It wasn't that kind of thing.

He remembered what he'd thought when he first saw the old place.

The house is hungry.

9

Later, after Crow came home from Terry's house, he sat in his room long into the night, watching the moon and stars rise from behind the trees and carve their scars across the sky. He sat with his window open, arms wrapped around his shins, shivering despite a hot breeze.

It was ten days since they'd gone running from the house.

Ten days and ten nights. Crow was exhausted. He'd barely slept, and when he did, there were nightmares. Never—not once in any of those dreams—was there a monster or a ghoul chasing him. They weren't those kinds of dreams. Instead, he saw the image that he'd seen in the mirror. The older him.

The drunk.

The fool.

Crow wept for that man.

For the man he knew that he was going to become.

He wept, and he did not sleep. He tried, but even though his eyes burned with fatigue, sleep simply would not come. Crow knew that it wouldn't come. Not tonight, and maybe not any night. Not as long as he could remember that house.

And he knew he could never forget it.

Around three in the morning, when his father's snores banged off the walls and rattled his bedroom door, Crow got up and, silent as a ghost, went into the hall and downstairs. Down to the kitchen, to the cupboard. The bottles stood in a row. Canadian Club. Mogen David 20/20. Thunderbird. And a bottle of vodka without a label. Cheap stuff, but a lot of it.

Crow stood staring at the bottles for a long time. Maybe half an hour.

"No," he told himself.

No, agreed his inner voice.

No, screamed the drunken man in his memory.

No.

Crow reached up and took down the vodka bottle. He poured some into a Dixie cup.

"No," he said.

And drank it.

Material Witness

1

Echo Team: Case File Report / DMS-ET 82fd1118
Events of August 16 / Prepared August 17, 11:30 a.m.
Team Leader: Captain Joseph Edwin Ledger

Preamble to the official statement of Dr. Rudy Sanchez:

I personally tested Captain Ledger and his men. Blood and urine, a full workup. There is no presence of alcohol or any controlled substance. Standard interview and psychological profiles demonstrate post-traumatic stress and nervous tension typical with recent combat, plus a degree of heightened nervousness that I believe should be ascribed to the unusual nature of the events as described by the members of Echo Team.

From the analysis of a voluntary polygraph test:

All three men were tested separately. I oversaw each test. Each man was given a number of unsequenced control questions as well as the set of questions prepared by Mr. Church. These questions were introduced randomly and without preamble. There is nothing in their responses or on the polygraph tape to suggest that any of them provided false or exaggerated answers. As disturbing and unlikely as it appears, these men believe that they saw and experienced everything exactly as described in Captain Ledger's after-action report and in the private interviews with Dr. Sanchez, Aunt Sallie and Mr. Church.

Handwritten note included in Mr. Church's private copy of Dr. Sanchez's psychological evaluation of Captain Joseph Edwin Ledger, First Sergeant Bradley Sims, and Staff Sergeant Harvey Rabbit. Note reads:

Per your question of earlier today . . . yes, I am certain that they believe that these events occurred. Please bear in mind the troubled history of that town. It has had far more than its share of troubles for many years. I respectfully but firmly decline your offer to go there and investigate matters for myself. No thank you! —RS

2

The Warehouse
Department of Military Sciences Baltimore Field Office
August 16; 8:19 a.m.
One Day Ago . . .

"God—*please!* They're killing me here. You got to get me out of this. Jesus Christ, you said this wouldn't happen."

I leaned forward to listen to the voice. Even with the distortion of a bad digital file, I could hear the raw terror, the urgency.

"When did this come in?" I asked.

My boss, Mr. Church, sat on the other side of the conference table. He was neatly dressed, the knot of his tie perfect, his face impassive. But I wasn't fooled. This had to be hitting him every bit as hard as it was me.

"That's the problem," he said. "This message is three days old."

"*Three days?* How the hell—?"

Church held up a hand.

I paused, dialing it down a notch. "How did this get missed? Burke's handler should have called us right away."

"The handler didn't get this until this morning."

"Then how—?"

"This message was left on the home phone of the Special Agent in Charge."

He let that float in the air for a moment.

"Wait," I said, "*home* phone?"

"Yes," said Church, "and isn't that interesting. Simon Burke would have no way of knowing who the AIC was, let alone having access to his home number."

"Did the handler get a call?"

Church opened a folder and slid it across the table toward me. "These are the phone records for the handler, Dykstra. The top page is the direct line to Burke's safe house. The next pages are Dykstra's cell and home numbers. The previous call from Burke was the routine check-in last week. Nothing since then. Nothing from a pay phone or from any other line that Burke could have used."

"The handler's cell . . ."

"No," said Church. "There is no identifiable incoming call on any line associated with the AIC or the handler that could have resulted in that message."

I frowned. "I don't understand. If Burke left a message, then there has to be a record."

Church said nothing. He selected a vanilla wafer from a plate of cookies which sat between us on the table. He nibbled off a piece and munched it thoughtfully, his eyes never leaving my face.

I said, "Then someone got to the records. Altered them."

"Mm. Difficult, but possible." He sounded dubious.

"Or . . . they have a way to erase their tracks, remove all traces of the call."

"Also possible, but . . ."

". . . even *more* difficult," I finished.

He said nothing. He didn't have to. There were very few computer systems in the world capable of the kind of thorough hacking like what we were discussing; and even then, there was only one computer that couldn't be fooled by any of the others, and that was

MindReader. That was *our* computer. It was a freak among computers, designed to be a ghost, to intrude into any other system and then rewrite its memory so that there was absolutely no footprint. All other computers left a bit of a scar on the hard drive. Not Mind-Reader. And Church guarded that system like a dragon. Not even the president had access to it without Church personally signing him in.

"Okay," I said, "could someone have gotten to the answering machine directly and recorded a message onto it from the AIC's house?"

"No. Dykstra uses a service provided by AT&T, and the messages are stored on their server. And if the call was made from Dykstra's home phone, there would be a record of that."

"And there isn't."

"No."

I reached over and took an Oreo from the plate. I can't come up with any good reason why a sane person would bother with vanilla wafers when the chocolaty goodness of Oreos was right there. It added to my growing suspicion that Church was a Vulcan.

"Who's looking for Burke?"

"The FBI has been looking for him since nine this morning. Except for us, no one else is in the loop."

"Local law?"

"They are definitely out of the loop. There have been some concerns about the police department there, though admittedly that was under previous management. The current chief has no strikes against him, but otherwise he's an unknown quantity. This matter was deemed too sensitive to be shared with him."

"Even now?"

Church pursed his lips. "Only with direct supervision."

"Which doesn't mean the FBI."

"No." Church ate more of his cookie. "We've backtracked to the a few hours before the call was left on Dykstra's voicemail and nothing. Burke has not used a credit card or made transactions of any kind under his own name. His car is still parked in his garage."

I sighed. "I'm not liking the spin on this one, boss. Burke's not a player. He might know in theory how to stay off the grid, but I can't see him managing it without making a mistake. Not for this long, not without help."

"Doubtful. And there's one more thing."

I waited, knowing that Church would save the kicker for last. "Burke's clever. His whole life is built around creating plots that his readers won't see coming. Apparently, he's used this same gift against his handler. We hacked the confidential reports between the handler and the AIC, and Burke's clearly gone missing four times previously. Not for long, a matter of a few hours each time. The handler eventually realized that Burke was using a bicycle to get into town or out of town via one of the two bridges. I had Bug do computer pattern sweeps on commerce records of stores within bicycle distance of the safe house. We've been able to establish that on the dates in question, and inside the window of time, there were purchases of six disposable cell phones. Burke has been making calls."

"Who's he calling?"

"Add this to the equation," Church said. "Interest in Burke and his unstoppable novel plot has increased substantially in the weeks following those purchases."

"Well, that's interesting as hell."

"Isn't it, though?"

"You think he's trying to sell it?"

"We have to be open to that possibility."

What Church didn't say out loud was: *In which case, Burke becomes a National Security liability.*

"We need to put this idiot in a bag," I said. "But we can't put out an APB. That would draw every shooter east of the Mississippi."

"Likely it would draw shooters from around the globe," said Church. "A dozen countries come to mind."

"What if he's already dead?"

He looked at me. Church wears tinted glasses that make it tough to read his expression. "Is that what you think?"

I thought about it and shook my head. "No. Considering how important Burke is, a pro would either be under orders to get him out of the country or get him to one of *their* safe houses. Or they'd want him splashed all over the headlines. Either way, the odds on him seizing the opportunity to leave a message is pretty slim."

"Agreed." Church took another cookie. Another vanilla wafer. Weird.

I nodded to the recorder on the table. "Play it again."

"This is Simon Burke . . . look, you jokers said you'd protect me. They're going to tear me apart. Look . . . I don't have much time . . . this is really hard. You got to do something. God—please! They're killing me here. You got to get me out of this. Jesus Christ, you said this wouldn't happen."

He played it three times more. It sounded just as bad each time, and Burke sounded just as terrified. I rubbed my eyes and stood up.

"He sounds genuinely scared," I said. "And outraged. I can't see him making that call *after* he's contacted potential buyers. It would make more sense for him to do that as a result of getting no action on this kind of a cry for help."

"Agreed. Which means we are short on answers and time is not our friend."

"Then I guess I'd better get my boys and get gone."

"Sergeant Dietrich is prepping a helo," said Church. He cocked his head at me. "Have you ever been to that town?"

"Pine Deep? Sure, but way back when I was a kid. My dad took me and my brother to the big Halloween Festival they used to have. That was before the Trouble, of course."

The *Trouble*.

Funny little word or something that stands as one of the worst disasters in U.S. history. More than eleven thousand dead in what has been officially referred to as an act of terrorism and insurrection by a domestic terrorist cell that had been formed by members of a local white supremacist organization. The terrorists dumped a lot of LSD into the town's drinking water. Had everyone convinced that half the town was turning into monsters.

"Terrible tragedy," said Church.

"I saw the movie they did on it," I said. "*Hellnight*, I think it was called. Hollywood turned it into a horror picture. Vampires and ghosts and werewolves, oh my."

Church chewed his cookie. "There was a lot of confusion surrounding the incidents. The *official* report labeled it as domestic terrorism."

I caught the slight emphasis he put on the word *official*. "Why, was there something else going on?"

He very nearly smiled.

"Have a safe trip, Captain Ledger."

3

Route A32
Bucks County, Pennsylvania
August 16; 4:22 p.m.

The chopper put us down at a private airfield near Doylestown, Pennsylvania, and a couple of DMS techs had a car waiting for us. It looked like a two-year-old black Ford Explorer, but we had the full James Bond kit. Well, I guess it's more the Jack Bauer kit. No oil slicks or changeable license plates. Mostly we had guns. Lots and lots of guns. The back bay was a gun closet with everything from Glock nines to Colt M4 carbines fitted with Aimpoint red-dot sights. And enough ammunition to wage a moderately enthusiastic war.

Bunny whistled as he opened all the drawers and compartments. "And to think I asked for a puppy for Christmas."

"For when you care enough to send the very best," he said, hefting a Daewoo USAS-12 automatic shotgun. "I think I'll call her 'Missy'."

"Freak," muttered Top Sims under his breath. First Sergeant Bradley Sims—Top to everyone—was a career noncom who had been in uniform nearly as long as Bunny had been alive, but for all that, he'd never cultivated the testosterone-driven shtick of idolizing weapons. To him they were tools and nothing more. He respected them, and he handled them with superior professional skill, but he wasn't in love with them.

Bunny—Harvey Rabbit, according to his birth certificate—looked dreamy-eyed, like a man going courting.

They were the only two members of Echo Team left standing after our last couple of missions. We had more guys in training, but Top and Bunny were on deck and ready to roll when this Burke thing came at us. Like me, they were dressed in civilian clothes. Jeans, Hawaiian shirts. Top wore New Balance cross-trainers that looked like they'd been spit-polished; Bunny had a well-worn pair of Timberlands.

I said, "Concealed small arms. We're here on a search and rescue. We're not declaring war on rural Pennsylvania."

Bunny looked hurt. "Damn, and here I thought it was redneck season."

Even Top grinned at that.

I looked at my watch. "Saddle up. We're burning daylight."

Even as I said it, I heard a rumble of thunder and glanced up. The sky above was bright and blue and cloudless, but there were storm clouds gathering in the northeast. Probably ten miles from where we were, which put the clouds over or near Pine Deep. Swell. Nothing helps a manhunt better than fricking rain.

We climbed into the SUV, buckled up for safety, and headed out, taking Route 202 north and then cutting onto the snaking black ribbon that was State Alternate Route A32. Top drove; Bunny crammed his six-and-a-half-foot bulk into the back, and I took the shotgun seat.

"So why's this Burke guy so important?" asked Bunny. "And since when do we screw around with Witness Protection?"

"Not exactly what this is," I said. "Simon Burke is a writer and—"

"I read his books," said Top. "Bit weird. Little paranoid."

I nodded. "He writes thrillers, and since the middle nineties, he built a rep for creating ultra-believable terrorist plots."

"Yeah, yeah," said Bunny, nodding. "I saw the movie they made out of one of those books. The one about terrorists introducing irradiated fleas into the sheepdogs in cattle country. Jon Stewart had him on and kind of fried the guy because a couple of meatheads actually *tried* to do the flea thing. Burke kept saying, 'how is that *my* problem?'"

"That's the story in a nutshell," I said. "Burke's plots have always been way too practical, and he likes showing off by providing useful detail. There's a fine line between a detailed thriller novel and a primer for terrorists."

"Hooah," murmured Top. That was Army Ranger-speak for everything from 'I agree' to 'Get stuffed.'

"Well, early last year, Burke was doing the talk show circuit to promote his new book—"

"—*A Predator Species*," supplied Top. "Read it. Give it four stars out of five."

"—and Conan O'Brien asks him about his plots. Burke, who's a bit of a jackass at the best of times, according to what I've been told and the interview transcripts I've read, starts bragging about the fact that he has a plot that is so good, so perfect that his contacts with Homeland 'strongly requested' him not to publish it."

"We know who that was in Homeland?" Bunny snorted.

"It wasn't Homeland," I said, "it was Hugo Vox, the guy who does all the screening for people getting top secret and above clearance. He ran the plot out at that counterterrorism training center he has in Colorado. Terror Town. Teams ran it six separate times and Vox said that the best-case scenario was a forty percent kill of the U.S. population. Low-tech, too. Anyone could make it work."

"Jeeeez-us," said Bunny.

"What was it?" asked Top, intrigued.

I told them. Top gave a long, low whistle. Bunny's grin diminished in wattage.

They considered it, shaking their heads as the logic of it unfolded in their imaginations. "Damn," Bunny said, "that's smart."

"It's damn stupid," countered Top. "Putting that in bookstores would be like handing out M16s at a terrorism convention."

"It was stupid for Burke to talk about it on Conan," I said. "Luckily, he didn't actually describe the plot on TV. Just enough to give the impression he really had something. You can probably guess what happened," I said.

Top made a face. "Someone made a run at him?"

I nodded. "Within a day of doing the show, he was nearly kidnapped twice. He must have realized his mistake, and he went straight to his lawyer, who in turn called the FBI, who called Homeland, who called us."

"And we did what?" asked Bunny. "Put a bag over him?"

"More or less. This is before we came on the DMS," I said, "so I'm getting this secondhand from Church. I drew this gig because I know Burke. Or, used to. He did ride-alongs with me and a couple other cops when I was with Baltimore PD. Bottom line is that Burke was set up in Pine Deep as a retired schoolteacher and widower. His handler's cover is that of 'nephew' who lives one town away. Place called Black Marsh, right over the river in New Jersey."

"So, it's just protective custody?"

"No. Homeland is cooking up some kind of scam thing where they'll eventually use Burke as bait to lure the cockroaches out of the woodwork. Get them to make a run at him so we could scoop them up, take them off for some quiet conversation, say at Gitmo."

"Well . . . that's pretty much what just happened, isn't it?" asked Top.

"I guess . . . but it wasn't on a timetable. They wanted Burke completely off the radar for a year or so to let things cool down. Homeland wanted to scoop up high-profile hitters, not bozos with suicide vests. The plan was to start seeding the spy network with disinformation this fall that Burke was willing to sell his idea for the right kind of money. Let that cook on the international scene for a bit, then set up a meet with as many buyers as we can line up. Then do a series of snatch-and-grabs. It's the kind of assembly-line arrests Homeland's been doing since 9/11. Doesn't put all their eggs in one basket, so even if they put four out of twenty potential buyers in the bag, they celebrate it as a major win. And I guess it is."

Top nodded. "So, what went wrong, Cap'n?"

"He disappeared."

"Disappeared? Did he walk or was he taken?"

"I guess that's what we're here to find out." I told them the rest, about Burke going AWOL a few times; and about the cell phones and the buzz overseas.

"Are we trying to find him and keep him safe," asked Top, "or put a bullet in his brainpan? 'Cause I can build a case either way."

I didn't answer.

We'd caught up with the storm clouds, and the closer we got to Pine Deep, the gloomier it got. I know it was coincidence, but subtle jokes of that kind from the universe is something I could do with-out. Luckily the rain seemed to be holding off.

We passed through the small town of Crestville, following the road so that we'd enter Pine Deep via a rickety bridge from the north. Both sides of the road were lined with cornfields. It was the middle of August, and the corn was tall and green and impenetrable. Here and there we saw old signs, faded and crumbling, that once advertised a Haunted Hayride and a Halloween Festival.

As we crossed the bridge, Top tapped my shoulder and nodded to a big wooden sign that was almost completely faded by hard sum-mers and harder winters. It read:

WELCOME TO PINE DEEP

AMERICA'S HAUNTED HOLIDAYLAND!

WE'LL SCARE YOU TO DEATH!

Somebody had used red spray paint to overlay the writing with a smiley face complete with vampire fangs.

"Charming," I said.

We drove down another crooked road that broadened onto a feeder side-street, then made the turn onto Main Street. The town of Pine Deep looked schizophrenic. Almost an even half of the build-ings were brand new, with glossy window displays and bright LED signs; and the other half looked to be at least fifty years old and in need of basic repair. Some of the buildings looked to have been burned and painted over, and that squared with what I'd read about the place. Before the Trouble, Pine Deep had been an upscale arts community built on the bones of a centuries-old blue-collar farming region. Even now, with its struggle to create a new identity, there were glimpses of those earlier eras. Like ghosts, glimpses out of the corner of the eye. But the overall impression was of a town that had failed. It wasn't dead, but it wasn't quite alive, either. Maybe the eco-nomic downturn had come at the wrong time, derailing the recon-struction of the town and the rebuilding of its economy. Or maybe the memory of all those dead people, all that pain from the Trouble, was like an infection of the atmosphere of this place.

"Damn," murmured Bunny. "They could film a Stephen King flick here. Won't need special effects."

"Town's trying to make a comeback," I said.

Top's face was set, his brows furrowed. Unlike Bunny and me, Top had read a couple of the books written about the town and its troubles. He shook his head. "Some things you don't come back from."

"That's cheery," said Bunny.

Top nodded to one of the buildings that still showed traces of the fire that had nearly destroyed Pine Deep. "That wasn't the first problem this place had. Even when I was a kid, *Newsweek* was calling this place the 'most haunted town in America.' Had that reputation going back to colonial times."

"Since when do you believe in ghosts?" I asked.

He didn't answer. Instead, he said, "Places can be like people. Some are born good; some are born bad. This one's like that. Born bad, and bad to the bone."

Bunny opened his mouth to make a joke, but he left it unsaid.

We drove in silence for a while.

Finally Top seemed to shake off some of his gloom. "We going to check in with the local police? If so, what badge do we flash?"

"That's where we're heading now," I said, as we pulled into a slanted curbside parking slot. "The FBI has been the public face of this kind of witness protection, but federal marshals are also involved. We're both. I'm FBI, you guys are marshals."

They nodded, and Top dug out the appropriate IDs from a locked compartment. We have fully authentic identification for most of the major investigative and enforcement branches of the U.S. government. The only IDs we don't have are DMS cards and badges, because the DMS doesn't issue any. We exist as far as the president and one congressional subcommittee is concerned.

We got out and headed toward the small office marked PINE DEEP POLICE DEPARTMENT. There were potted plants on either side of the door, but both plants were withered and dead.

4

Pine Deep Police Department
August 16; 4:59 p.m.

There were three people in the office. A small, pigeon-breasted woman
with horn-rims and blue hair who sat at a combination desk and dis-
patch console. She didn't even look up as the doorbell tinkled.

The two men did.

They were completely unalike in every way. The younger man, a
patrol officer with corporal's stripes, was at a desk. Early twenties,
but he was a moose. Not as big as Bunny—and there are relatives of
Godzilla who aren't as big as Bunny—but big enough. Six-four,
two-twenty and change. The kind of muscles you get from hard
work and free weights. Callused hands, lots of facial scars. A fighter
for sure. He had curly red hair and contact lenses that gave him
weirdly luminous blue eyes. Almost purple. Odd cosmetic choice
for a cop. Little triangular plaque on his desk read: CORPORAL
MICHAEL SWEENEY.

He remained seated, but the other man rose as we entered. He was
about fifty, but he had a lean build that hadn't yielded to middle age
spread. Short, slender, with intensely black hair threaded with silver.
He, too, had visible scars, and it was no stretch to guess that they'd
gotten them during the Trouble. And, strangely, there was also something familiar about him. I felt like I'd met him somewhere . . . or
heard something about him . . . whatever it was, the memory was
way, way back on a dusty shelf where I couldn't reach it.

The older man wore chief's bars and a smile that looked warm and
cheerful and was entirely fabricated. He leaned on the intake desk.
"What can I do for you fellows?"

I flashed the FBI badge. "Special Agent Morrison," I said. The
name on the card was Marion Morrison. John Wayne's real name.

His smile didn't flicker. I also noticed that it didn't quite reach his
eyes. "And your fishing buddies there?"

They held up ID cases, too, but I introduced them. "Federal Deputy Marshals Cassidy and Reid." Full names on the IDs were William Cassidy and John Reid. Hopalong Cassidy and the Lone Ranger. The guy at the DMS who does our ID needs a long vacation.

"Malcolm Crow," said the smaller man. "Pine Deep Chief of Police."

He offered his hand, which was small and hard, and we shook.

"So . . . again, what can I do for you?" he asked.

"Missing persons case," I said. "Confidential and high profile."

"Which means what? A special agent and two marshals? This a manhunt for a suspected terrorist or a missing witness?"

I shrugged, hoping he'd take that as a 'we're not supposed to talk about it' kind of thing. He ignored it.

"Can't help you if you won't share," he said.

I said nothing, giving him 'the look'. It usually makes people squirm. Chief Crow merely smiled his veneer of a smile and waited me out.

"Okay," I said, as if answering his question was the hardest thing I was ever going to be asked to do, "I can tell you this much. We had a protected witness living in Pine Deep. He's missing."

"Living here under what name?"

"Peter Wagner."

"Ah."

"Ah . . . what?"

"The writer."

I stepped closer to the intake bench. "And how would you know that?"

Behind Crow, Officer Sweeney stood up. He did it slowly, without threat, but there was still a lot of threat there. Unlike the chief, Sweeney's face was unsmiling. A good-looking kid, but one that you'd take note of, especially if he wasn't in uniform and you were both alone. Behind me, I heard the soft scuff as Top and Bunny made subtle moves. Shifting weight, being ready.

Crow seemed amused by all of this. To me he said, "You take a guy as famous as Simon Burke, give him a bad dye job and color contacts and you expect no one to recognize him? People in small towns *do* read, you know. And your boy is famous."

"Who else knows who he is?"

"Most people with two eyes and an IQ."

Crap.

"For what it's worth," said Crow, "people hereabouts know how to keep a secret." As if on cue, the thunder rumbled. It made Crow smile more. "Can I ask why a bestselling novelist is in witness protection?"

"National security."

"Ri-i-ght," he said, in exactly the way you'd say *bullshit*.

"Do you know where he is?" I asked. "Has he come forward and—?"

"No," Crow said, cutting me off. "I don't know where he is, but I suspect he's in some real trouble."

"Why do you suspect that, Chief Crow?"

He shrugged. "Because you're here. If he was out sowing some wild oats or getting hammered down at the Scarecrow Lounge, his handler would be on it. Or at most, he'd get a couple of kids right out of Quantico to help with the scut work. Instead, they send you three."

"We *are* the team sent to locate our witness."

"Ri-i-i-ght," he said again, stretching out the *I*.

"Would you like to see our credentials again?" This guy was beginning to irritate the crap out of me.

"Look," said Crow, leaning a few inches forward on his forearms. I could see the network of scars on his face. "You're about as close to a standard paper-pushing FBI agent as I am to Megan Fox. You're a hunter, and so are your pals. I don't care what the IDs say, because you're probably NSA at the least, in which case the IDs are as real as you need them to be and I'm Joe Nobody from Nowhere, Pennsylvania. But here's a news flash. Just about nothing happens in a small town without everybody hearing something. Our gossip-train is faster than a speeding bullet. If you want to find your missing witness, then you can do it the easy way, which is with my help; or the hard way, which is without my help."

I had to fight to keep a smile off my face. Guy had balls, I'll give him that much. The big red-haired kid was hovering a few feet behind him, looking borderline spooky with his fake blue eyes and unsmiling face.

"What do you suggest, Chief?" I asked.

Crow nodded. "Cut me in on the hunt. Give me some details, and I'll see what I can find."

I considered it. Thunder rumbled again, and the sky outside was turning gray. My instincts were telling me one thing, and DMS protocol was telling me something else. In the end, I said, "Thanks anyway, Chief. If it's all the same to you, we'll poke around on our own. I doubt the witness is in any real trouble. Not in a little town like this."

I meant it as a kick in the shins, but he merely shook his head. "You read up on Pine Deep before you came here, Agent Duke? I mean . . . agent Morrison."

Touché, you little jerk, I thought.

"Some," I said.

"About the troubles we had a few years back?"

"Everyone knows about them?"

"Well," he said, shifting a little. He glanced back at the redheaded kid and then at me. "Those problems were here long before we had our 'troubles'. I guess you could say that in one way or another, we've always had troubles here in Pine Deep. Lots of people run into real problems here."

I smiled now, and it probably wasn't my nicest one. "Are . . . you trying to threaten me, Chief Crow?"

He laughed.

Behind him, the redhead kid, Sweeney, spoke for the first time. "Just a fair warning, mister," he said. His voice was low and raspy. "It ain't the people you have to worry about around here. The *town* will help you or it won't."

Then he smiled, and it was one of the coldest, least *human* smiles I think I've ever seen. It was like an animal, a wolf or something equally predatory, trying to imitate a human smile.

Then Officer Sweeney turned away and sat back down at his desk.

Chief Crow winked at us. "Happy trails, boys."

I stared at him for a few moments as thunder rattled the windows in the tiny office. Then I nodded and turned to go. Just as Bunny opened the door for me, Crow said, "Welcome to Pine Deep."

I turned and met his eyes for a few long seconds. He neither blinked nor looked away. For reasons I can't adequately explain, we nodded to each other, and then I followed Top and Bunny out of the office. As we walked to the car, I could feel eyes watching me.

5

The Safe House
August 16; 6:28 p.m.

We got back in the car.

"Okay," said Bunny, "that was freaking weird."

No one argued.

"Want me to run him through MindReader?" asked Top.

"Yeah," I said. "I know him from somewhere."

"Cop thing?" asked Bunny. "You do a shared-jurisdiction gig with Pine Deep?"

"No."

"Something social? FOP weenie roast."

"Cute. But no. I don't think I've met him, but there's something banging around in the back of my brain about him. Crow. Could be a martial arts thing."

"He train?" asked Bunny.

"Yes," Top and I said together.

Top added, "Not karate, though. No calluses on his knuckles."

"Has them on his hands, though," I said, touching the webbing around my thumb and index finger. I had a ring of callus there, too. "Kenjutsu, or something similar."

"Kid uses his knuckles, though," Top said. "Hard-looking son of a bitch. Looks like he could go a round or two."

A few fat raindrops splatted on the windshield, and the glass was starting to fog. I hit the defrost and waited while Bunny called it in

to Bug, our computer guru at the Warehouse. Bug did a search
through MindReader and got back to us before we'd driven two
blocks.

"Plenty of stuff here," he said. "Malcolm Crow grew up in Pine
Deep. Medical records from when he was a kid show a lot of injuries. Broken arms, facial injuries . . . stuff consistent with physical
abuse."

"Anyone charged for that?"

"No. His mother died when he was little. He and his brother were
raised by his father, who has a loooong record of arrests for public
drunkenness, DUI, couple of barroom brawls. Sounds like he was
the hitter. Wow . . . get this. His brother was murdered by a serial
killer thirty-five years ago. Your boy was the only witness. Couple
dozen victims total before the killer went off the radar. Possibly
lynched by the townies, and the local police may have been involved
in that."

"Lovely little town," Top said under his breath.

"Chief Crow was a cop for a while," Bug continued. "Then was a
drunk for a long time. He sobered up and opened up a craft and novelty store and helped design a haunted hayride for a Halloween
theme park. All of this was before that Trouble they had there.
Crow was deputized by the mayor about a month before the Trouble, and—here's another cool bit—the deputation was because *another* serial killer was in town killing people. Thirty years to the day
from when Crow's brother was killed. Freaky."

"Damn," I said. "What else you got?"

"He's married. Wife is Val Guthrie-Crow. Hyphenates her last
name. And they have two kids. One natural—Sara—and one adopted,
Mike."

"Mike? What was his birth name?"

"Same as he's using now. Michael Sweeney. Never changed it."

"What else?"

"Crow, his wife, and Mike Sweeney were all hospitalized after the
Trouble. Various injuries. Their statements say that they don't remember what happened and they claimed everything was a blur,"
Bug said. "That more or less fits, because the town water supply was
supposed to be spiked with LSD and other party favors."

"Do we have *anything* linking Crow to the Trouble itself? Any involvement with white supremacist movements, anything at all?"

"No. Couple other guys on the Pine Deep police force might have been involved, though, including the chief at that time."

"But nothing that would connect Crow to it?"

"Nothing."

"What are his politics?"

"Moderate with a tilt to the left. Same for the missus."

"And Sweeney?"

"Registered independent but has never voted. Oh . . . hold on. Got a red flag here. Looks like Sweeney's adopted father—another asshole who liked to hit kids, if I'm reading this right—was one of the men suspected of orchestrating the attack on the town."

"What about the kid?"

"I hacked the Pine Deep P.D. files, and it looks like the stepfather filed a report for assault. The kid decked him and ran away."

I glanced at Top. "You read the kid as a bad guy?"

He shook his head, then nodded, then shrugged. "I really couldn't get a read on him, Cap'n."

I thanked Bug and told him to call us if he got anything else.

"So, what d'you think, boss?" asked Bunny. "Crow one of the good guys or one of the bad guys?"

"No way to tell. We're not even sure we *have* any bad guys in this. Burke could be shacked up with some chick."

"And doing what?" asked Top. "Making crank calls to the AIC?"

"*And* terrorists?" added Bunny.

I grinned. "Yeah, yeah."

We drove through the town, which takes less time than it does to tell it. Couple of stoplights. Rows of craft shops. A surprising number of cafés and bars, though most of them looked run-down. More for drinking than eating, I thought. The biggest intersection had the Terrance Wolfe Memorial Medical Center across the street from the Saul Weinstock Ball Field. The hospital looked new; the ball field was overgrown, and a hundred crows huddled in a row along the chain-link fence. Ditto for the hospital.

I noted it away and kept driving. The place was starting to get to me, and that was weird, because I worked a lot of shifts in West Baltimore, which is probably the most depressing place on earth. Poverty screamed at you from every street corner, and there was a tragic blend of desperation and hopelessness in the eyes of every child. And yet, this little town had a darker tone to it, and my over-active imagination wondered if the storm clouds ever let the sunshine down. Looking at these streets was like watching the sluggish flow of a polluted river. You know that there's life beneath the grime and the toxicity, but at the same time, you feel that life could not exist there.

We left town and turned back onto Route A32 as it plunged south toward the Delaware River. This was the large part of the township, occupied for the first mile by new suburban infill—with cookie-cutter development units, many still under construction, and over-built McMansions. More than three quarters of the houses had FOR SALE signs staked into the lawns. A few were unfinished skeletons draped in tarps that looked like body bags.

Then we were out into the farm country, and the atmosphere changed subtly, from something dying to something that was still clinging to life. Big farms, too, like the kind you expect to see more in the Midwest. Thousands of acres of land, miles between houses. Endless rows of waving green corn, fields bright with pumpkins, and row upon row of vegetables. A paint-faded yellow tractor chugged along the side of the road, driven by an ancient man in blue coveralls. He smoked a cheap pipe that he took out of his mouth to salute us as we went by.

"We just drive into the nineteen forties?" asked Bunny.

"Pretty much."

Mist, as thick and white as tear gas, was slowly boiling up from the gullies and hollows as the cooler air under the storm mixed with the August heat.

The GPS told us that we were coming up on our turn.

The lane onto which I'd turned ran straight as a rifle barrel from the road, through a fence of rough-cut rails, to the front door of a Cape Cod that looked as out of place here in Pine Deep as a sequined thong looks on a nun. Heavy oaks lined the road, and the big front lawn was dark with thick, cool summer grass.

"Okay, gentlemen," I said softly. "Place should be empty, and except for a brief walk-through by the handler, no one else will have disturbed the crime scene."

"Wait," said Top, "you want Farmboy and me to play Sherlock Holmes?"

"We're just doing a cursory examination. If we find anything of substance, we'll ship it off."

"To where? *CSI: Twilight Zone?*"

I rolled the car to a slow stop in a turnaround in front of the house. The garage was detached except for a pitched roof that connected it to the main house. A five-year-old Honda Civic was parked in that slot. The garage door was closed.

"Looks nice and quiet," Bunny said as he got out, the big shotgun in his hands. We split up. Bunny and Top circled around to the back and side entrances. I took the front door. We had our earbuds in place, and everyone was tuned into the team channel.

"On two," I said. I counted down and then kicked the door.

The door whipped inward with a crack, and as I entered, gun up and out in a two-handed shooter's grip, I heard the back door bang open, and then the side door that connected to the garage breezeway. We were moving fast, yelling at the top of our voices—at whomever might be in the house and at each other as we cleared room after room.

Then it was quiet again as we drifted together in the living room, holstering our guns and exhaling slowly. No one felt the need to comment on the fact that the place was empty. It was now our job to determine how it came to *be* empty.

"You take the bedrooms," I said to Bunny. "Observe first before you touch."

He was a professional soldier, not a cop. There were no smartass remarks when being given straight orders that could remind him how to do his job.

"Why don't I take the garage and around the outside," offered Top, and off he went.

I stood alone in the living room and waited for the crime scene to tell me its story. If, indeed, it was a crime scene.

The doors and windows were properly closed and locked from inside. I'd had to kick the door, and a quick examination showed that the deadbolt had been engaged. Same went for the side and back doors. I went upstairs and checked those windows. Locked. Cellar door was locked, and the windows were block glass.

Back in the living room, I saw a laptop case by the couch, and one of those padded lap tables. However, the case was empty. The power cable and mouse were there, but the machine itself was gone.

Significant.

The question was . . . was Simon Burke crazy enough to actually *write* his novel about the unstoppable terrorist plot?

I hadn't met him, but I read his psych evaluations. He had that dangerous blend of overblown ego and great insecurity that creates the kind of person who feels that any idea he has is of world-shaking importance and must therefore be shared with the whole world. They typically lack perspective, and everything I'd read in Burke's case file told me that he was one of those. Probably not a bad person, but not the kind you'd want to be caught in a stalled elevator with. Only one of you would walk out alive.

So . . . where was he?

My cell rang, and I flipped it open. The screen told me that it was an UNKNOWN CALLER.

That's . . . pretty unsettling. Our phone system is run through MindReader, which is wired in everywhere. There are no callers unknown to MindReader.

It kept ringing. Before I answered it, I pulled a little doohickey the size of a matchbox from a pocket, unspooled its wire, plugged the lead into the phone, and pressed the CONNECT button. Mind-Reader would race down the phone lines in a millisecond and begin reading the computer and sim card in the other phone. One of Mr. Sin's toys. He did not like surprises.

It rang a third time, and I punched the button.

"Hello—?" A man's name on a phone fuzzy with static.

"Joe?"

"Who's calling, please?"

"Joe? Is this Joe Ledger?"

"Sir, please identify yourself."

"It's me, Joe," he said.

"Who?" Though I thought I already knew.

"Simon Burke." He paused and gave a nervous little laugh. "Guess you've been looking for me."

"Where are you, Mr. Burke?"

"C'mon, Joe, cut the 'mister' stuff. Mr. Burke was my dad, and he was kind of a dick."

I looked through the window at the white fog that was swirling out of the cornfields. It was so thick you couldn't see the dirt. Between the black storm clouds and the ground fog, visibility was dropping pretty fast. That wasn't good. I said, "You told me that same joke the first time I met you."

"Did I?"

"Can you verify *where* we first met?"

"Sure," he said. "Central District police station on East Baltimore Street."

"Okay," I said, "good to hear your voice, Simon. You want to tell me where the hell you are?"

He laughed. "Too far away for you to come get me. At least right now."

I turned away from the window just as tendrils of fog began caressing the glass. "We need to get you back into protective custody, Simon."

"Joe," he said, "listen . . . I'm sorry for doing this to you."

"Doing what?" When he didn't answer, I said, "We know about the cell phones, Simon."

"Yeah . . . I guessed you'd figure it out. I just thought Church would send more people. I . . . I didn't know it would be just three of you."

My mouth went dry.

"Jesus Christ, Simon, what did you do?"

There was a sound. It might have been a sob, though it sounded strangely like bubbles escaping through mud. "Look . . . I was getting tired of waiting . . . and I knew that you'd be able to handle just about anything. So . . . I started reaching out to . . ."

"To *whom*?"

"Potential buyers."

"Oh . . . Christ . . . *why*?"

"I wanted to draw them in, just like the FBI said they were going to do. Only the feds were taking way too much time. I was wasting my life away in this crappy little town."

"Simon . . ."

"I offered to sell my plot. I . . . reached out to several buyers and told them that I had it all written down, and that they had to bring two million in unmarked bills. Don't worry, I'd have turned over the cash. I just needed it to look and feel real to them. And they bought it, too. They thought I was selling out."

"Who's bringing the money, Simon?"

"All of them."

"What do you mean? Damn it, Simon, how many buyers did you contact?"

"A lot."

"Simon . . ."

"Six," he said in a small and broken voice. "There are six teams of buyers. I told them to meet me at the house. I figured they'd get there and start shooting each other. It would be like a movie. I could sell that scenario. I could make a bestseller out of it . . . I could make a movie out of it . . ."

"Simon, when are the shooters expected here?"

"When? Joe . . . that's what I've been trying to tell you. That's why I was sorry it was just the three of you. They're already here. I . . . I didn't mean to kill you."

And the windows exploded in under a hail of high-caliber bullets.

6

The Safe House
Pine Deep, Pennsylvania
August 16; 6:41 p.m.

I dove for cover behind the couch.

It wasn't a good dive, and it wasn't pretty, but it got me low and out of the line of fire. Then I tried to melt right into the carpet. High-caliber rounds were chewing the couch to splinters and threads. The air above me was filled with thunder. Plaster and chunks of wall lath rained down on me.

The shots seemed to be continuous, so there had to be multiple shooters. They were firing full auto, and even with a high-capacity magazine, it only takes a couple of seconds to burn through the entire clip.

I shimmied sideways, trying to put the edge of the stone fireplace between me and the shooters. I had my Beretta out, but the barrage was so intense that I couldn't risk a shot.

Then the sound changed. There were new sounds. The hollow *pok-pok-pok* of small-arms fire and the rhythmic *boom* of a shotgun. Those sounds were farther away.

Top and Bunny returning fire.

The automatic gunfire swept away from me and split as the shooters focused on these two new targets. That gave me my moment, and I was up and running, pistol out. There was nothing left of the door except a gaping maw of splintered wood and glass through which the fog rolled like a slow-motion tide. I went through it fast, feeling the splinters claw at my sleeves and thighs. I was firing before I set foot outside.

In combat you see more, process more, and all of it happens fast. That's a skill set you learn quick, or you get killed. As I came out of the house, I saw five men standing in a loose shooting line in the turnaround. The fog was thick enough to cover them to mid-thigh. They were dark-skinned. Middle Eastern for sure, though from that distance, I couldn't tell from where. All four of them carried AK-47s with banana clips. Three were facing the garage, firing steadily at it; the other two were standing wide-legged as they leaned back to fire at the second floor.

I emptied my magazine into them. I saw blood puff out in little clouds of red mist as two of them staggered backward and fell, vanishing into the fog. Another one took a round through the cheek. Because he was shouting, the bullet went through both cheeks and left the teeth untouched. He was screaming louder as he wheeled around toward me.

I fired my last two rounds into his chest, and my slide locked back.

The remaining shooters opened up on me, and I dove behind the armored SUV. Their bullets pinged off of the heavy skin and smoked the window before ricocheting high into the sky.

The shooters wanted me so badly they forgot, in that one fatal instant, about Top and Bunny.

Bunny spun out of side door to the garage and fired three rounds with the shotgun, catching the left-hand shooter in the chest and face. Top leaned out of the second-floor window and put half a magazine into the last shooter.

As the last one fell, I swapped out the magazine in my Beretta and crept to the edge of the car. Simon Burke had said that there were six buyers. Five men lay sprawled on the bloody gravel.

Where was the sixth . . . ?

I tapped my earbud. "We have one more hostile," I began, but Top cut me off.

"Negative, Cowboy," he said, using my combat call-sign, "we have multiple hostiles inbound."

I turned and saw the fog swirling around two cars barreling down the long dirt road. Then there was a roar to my right, and I saw another pair of vehicles—ATVs with oversized tires—crashing our way through the cornfields.

"Where's this fog coming from?" demanded Top. "Can't see worth a damn."

"I got a team coming in on foot," called Bunny. "Behind the house, running along a drainage ditch. Can't make out numbers with that mist out there. No, wait . . . there's a second team farther back in the corner. Damn! A third at nine o'clock to the front door. Four men in black. Geez . . . Boss . . . we're under siege here. We need backup."

We needed an army, but we weren't likely to get one. The closest help was the Naval airbase in Willow Grove. Half an hour at least.

With a sinking heart, I understood the enormity of what Simon Burke had done. Not six buyers. Six teams of buyers. Conservative estimate—twenty men. Depressing estimate . . . thirty.

Coming straight at us.

7

The Safe House
Pine Deep, Pennsylvania
August 16; 6:46 p.m.

We needed five minutes.

With five minutes, we could have fitted out with Kevlar and ballistic helmets, strapped on vests heavy with fresh magazines, picked optimum shooting positions, and turned the whole farm into a killbox. We needed five damn minutes.

We had thirty seconds.

"Talk to me, Cowboy," said Top.

"Sergeant Rock and Jolly Green," I barked. "Converge on me. Living room. Now."

I spun around, yanked open the door of the SUV, ground the key in the starter, spun the wheel, and stamped down. The big machine took an awkward and ugly lurch, then found footing and rolled heavily away from the house. I went completely around the roundabout and then jerked the wheel over and put the pedal to the floor as I aimed it at the front door. The SUV punched a truck-sized hole through the shattered doorway, then it ripped across the living room floor and slammed into the stairs with enough force to rock the entire house to its foundations. I hadn't had time to buckle up for safety, so I got bashed forward and backward in my seat. I could taste blood in my mouth as I bailed out of the driver's seat and ran to the back.

"Sergeant Rock, coming in!" yelled Top as he pounded down the stairs. He had to vault the wreckage of the bottom steps, then run across the hood, up onto the roof, and then drop with a grunt into a squat next to me. He yelped in pain as his forty-year-old knees took the impact, but he sucked it up, forced himself up, and staggered over to me as I raised the back hatch.

"Coming in!" yelled Bunny, and then he was there, coming at us from the kitchen.

I clumsied open the gun lockers, and immediately, three pairs of hands were reaching for all the toys. I grabbed a bag of loaded magazines and an M4 and peeled away.

"Yo!" Top barked and tossed another bag to me. "Party favors!"

I snatched it out of the air and flashed him a grin. He grinned back. This was a total nightmare scenario, and only an insane odds maker would give us one in fifty on getting out of this. So . . . might as well enjoy it.

"Where, Boss?" asked Bunny.

"Kitchen. The fog might work for us. It'll confuse everything out there. Go!"

"On it." He shoved five drum magazines for the shotgun into a bag and slung it over his shoulder. Then he was gone, running back to the kitchen.

"Top," I said, "upstairs."

"Why you keep making the old guy run up and down stairs?"

We both laughed.

He grabbed his gear and climbed over the wreckage.

I glanced out through the broken window. The lead car was almost to the roundabout. It had slowed, though, and I figured that the converging teams were suddenly aware of one another. Who knows, I thought, maybe Burke was right. Maybe they'd slaughter each other while Top, Bunny, and I stayed in here and played cribbage.

And maybe tomorrow I'd wake up looking like Brad Pitt. About as much chance of that.

I heard voices shouting and car doors slamming.

Then gunshots.

The first rounds were fired away from us, off to my three o'clock, the direction of the team on ATVs.

Then three other guns opened up on the house.

So much for cribbage.

8

The Safe House
Pine Deep, Pennsylvania
August 16; 6:51 p.m.

It became hell.

A swirling surreal white hell, with the red flashes of muzzle fire filtered by thick fog, and all sounds muted to strangeness. Overhead the storm grumbled and growled, but no rain fell.

Maybe one of these days I'll look back on that ten minutes under the August sun in backwoods Pennsylvania and laugh about it. Maybe it'll become one of those anecdotes soldiers tell when they want to story-top the last guy. Or, maybe when I think about it, I'll get the shakes and go crawling off to find a bottle.

Everyone was shooting at everyone.

I've never seen anything like it. Don't ever want to see anything like it again.

One team was dead. That left five teams of shooters, sent by God only knows who. Three of the teams were Middle Eastern, I could tell that much, and that made sense. Then I heard someone yelling in Russian. Someone else was yelling in Spanish.

I was yelling in every language I could curse in . . . and I am fluent in a lot of languages.

I crouched down behind the open door of the SUV, reached around with the M4, and opened fire. I wasn't aiming. No-damn-body was aiming. But everybody was sure as hell capping off a lot of rounds. My hearing will never be the same. Ditto my nerves.

I think I even screamed for a little bit. I'll admit it, I'm not proud.

I fired the magazine dry, dropped it, slapped in another, fired, swapped it out, fired. The effort of holding the gun was rattling the bones in my arm to pieces, and I don't think I hit anything with the first four magazines. The mist was chest high now, and the men out there were crouched down. It was like trying to fight in the middle of a blizzard.

So, I set down the gun and dug into the bag for one of Top's 'party favors'. An M67 fragmentation grenade.

"Come to papa," I murmured.

The M67 looks like a dark green apple, but instead of juicy sweetness, the spherical body contains six-and-a-half ounces of composition B explosive. When it goes boom, the body bursts into steel fragments that will forever change the life of anything within fifteen meters. I lobbed one out through the gaping hole that had been the front wall of the house. I never heard it bounce, never heard it land.

Everyone heard it when it blew. A loud, muffled *whumph.*

And everyone heard the screams that followed.

Another thing I'm not too proud to admit. I enjoyed those screams. Part of me did. The Killer that shares my mind with the Civilized Man and the Cop. That's the part of me that's always waiting in the tall grass, face grease-painted green and brown, eyes staring and dead, mouth perpetually caught in a feral smile.

The Killer wanted more, so I popped the pin on two more party treats and threw them out. More bangs, more screams.

Then I was up, laying the M4 over the hinge of the open door. Hot shell casings pinged and whanged off of the SUV's frame, and smoke burned my eyes. All I could taste in my mouth was blood and gunpowder.

The smoke from the grenades wafted away on a breeze, and I could see one of the cars belonging to one ground sitting on flat tires, its sides splashed with blood, windows blasted out. Two ragged red things lay sprawled on the gravel, and a travel of blood led away toward the tall corn. The second vehicle was sitting askew in the ditch that lined the driveway, its windshield and driver's side polka-dotted with hundreds of bullet- and pellet holes.

"Hey, Cap'n!" yelled Top from upstairs. "I'm running out of wall to hide behind."

"I'm open to ideas," I yelled back.

I think I heard him laugh. Top's a strange guy. Like Bunny. Like me, too, I suppose. As much as the Civilized Man inside my head was cringing and whimpering, the Killer was totally jazzed. I'm kind of glad I didn't have Kevlar and a ballistic shield, or I might have done something stupid.

Luckily, someone *else* didn't do something stupid.

No, correct that—a bunch of people did a bunch of stupid things, and that's why I'm still here to tell you about it.

It spun out this way . . .

The team that came in on the ATVs were yelling something in Farsi and trying to cut their way to the house. No way to tell if the guys who came in the cars were their enemies, or simply business rivals. In either case, the ATV guys came rolling in, firing over the handlebars with their AKs, chopping the cars to pieces and ripping up the last three car guys. If this was a two-way fight, or even a three-way fight, they might have won. They were the biggest team. Eight men on four ATVs.

I leaned out and sighted on them and started to pick them off. I got both men in the lead vehicle with four shots, and the ATV twisted and fell over onto its side, slewing around with one of the men still in the saddle. The second ATV hit that one at about forty miles an hour, and the driver and passenger tried to leap to safety. 'Tried' wasn't good enough.

Suddenly a shooter stood up out of the mist and aimed a pump shotgun at me. He caught me flatfooted while I was watching the ATV wreck. He was twenty feet away, right outside the shattered wall, and I saw his face crease into a wicked smile as he raised the barrel.

Suddenly the fog around him changed color from a milky white to a bright red. The shooter's fingers jerked the trigger, and the double-ought buckshot blew downward harmlessly into the gravel. The man canted sideways and fell, and as he dropped, I saw another figure move like a dark shadow through the mist. It was small, and at first, I had the irrational thought that it was Simon Burke, but this figure moved with oiled grace.

I aimed my M4 at him. Whoever he was, he belonged to one of the teams sent to take Burke. I mean, thanks for saving my life and all that, but this is one of those incidents where the enemy of my enemy wasn't necessarily my friend.

I unloaded half a magazine at him, but the bullets swirled the fog without hitting anything. The figure had faded out of sight.

There was a crash behind me, and I spun to see Bunny come running in from the kitchen. A fusillade of shotgun blasts were tearing the back of the house to kindling. Bunny overturned the oak dining room table and crashed a breakfront down on top of that. It would give him a few seconds of cover, but these guys had enough firepower to chew through anything.

He threw me a wild grin. "America's Haunted Holidayland," he yelled. "We'll scare you to death."

I nodded to the SUV. "That's our last fallback. The armor should hold for a bit."

He made a face but nodded. A 'bit' wasn't much.

Bullets continued to hammer the house from all directions. But there were also occasional screams.

I cupped my hands and yelled, "You're my hero, Top!"

His face immediately appeared at the top of the stairs. "Not me, Cap'n. They're doing a good job on each other. Maybe we should try and wait this out."

Before I could answer, two men came charging in through the open doorway. Both were firing AKs, and I had done a diving tackle to save Bunny from the spray of bullets. We hit the floor and rolled over behind the couch. There was an overlapping series of shots, definitely from a different caliber, and I peered around the edge of the couch to see the two shooters sagging to their knees, both of them already dead from headshots that had taken them in the backs of their skulls and blown their faces off. As they fell forward, I caught another glimpse of the slim, dark figure vanishing into the fog.

Only this time, I saw the shooter's face.

Just for a moment.

"Hey, Boss," said Bunny, "was that . . . ?"

"I think so."

"He on our side, or is he with one of the teams?"

I shook my head.

We crawled out, and I hurried over to the crumbling wall to recover my bag of grenades.

Only it wasn't there.

The killer in the mist had taken it.

"He took the frags!" I yelled, and suddenly Bunny and I were scrambling back, ducking down behind the SUV. Bullets still hammered the back, and there was no cellar.

"Oh man," whispered Bunny, and now there was no trace of humor on his face. After a while, even the black comedy of the battlefield burns away to leave the vulnerable human standing naked before the reality of ugly death. We were screwed. Totally screwed, and we knew it.

When the first grenade blew, Bunny closed his eyes and clutched his shotgun to his chest, as if it was a talisman that would provide some measure of grace.

But the grenade didn't detonate inside the house.

The blast was close, but definitely outside.

There was a second. A third. A fourth and fifth, and between each blast, there were spaced shots. Not automatic gunfire. Spaced, careful pistol shots.

Men screamed out in the mist.

Men died in the mist.

I saw another shape move through the gloom. Not small. This one was big, but he was only a shadow within the fog. He turned toward me, and I expected to see blue eyes.

The blood froze in my veins.

The eyes that looked at me through the fog were as red as blood and rimmed with gold.

And then they were gone.

I blinked. My eyes stung from the gunpowder and plaster dust. Had I seen what I thought I saw, or were my eyes playing tricks?

I didn't want to answer that, but . . . my eyes don't play tricks.

We crouched down, weapons ready to make our last stand a damn bloody one.

But the battle raged around the house. Around us.

"Top!" I yelled. "Talk to me!"

"We got new players, Cap'n."

"What can you see?"

"Not a damn thing. No, wait . . . oh, holy—"

Three more blasts rocked the side of the house, and suddenly all the gunfire in the front ceased.

There was a moment of silence from the back, too, but then it started up again.

A voice called out of the mist. "In the house!"

I said nothing and waved Bunny to silence.

After a pause, the voice yelled again. "Hey . . . John Wayne . . . you got some rustlers on your six. You in this fight, or are you waiting for Roy Rogers?"

I looked at Bunny.

"Well . . . son of a bitch."

And that fast, we were on our feet and running back to the kitchen, firing as we went. The incoming assault was less fierce, and we made it to what was left of the brick wall. A bullet plucked my sleeve and chips of brick dust.

We saw them. Three groups left, but only a few of each. Two burly Russians behind a stack of hay bales over to the left. Couple of Arabs right across the back lawn, using a toolshed as a shooting blind. And three Latinos off to the left, firing from behind a tractor.

The voice called out of the mist. "Game on?"

I grinned. "Dealer's choice!" I yelled back.

I thought I heard a laugh. "You guys take scarecrow and Tim Allen. I got John Deere."

Bunny frowned at me for a moment before he got it. Scarecrows are stuffed with hay. Tim Allen's comedy is all about tools. John Deere makes tractors.

Bunny said, "Yippie kiyay . . ."

I swapped out for a fresh magazine. "Say it like you mean it."

He took a breath and bellowed it into the fog.

They had the numbers. We had the talent.

I saw muzzle flashes coming from two points in the mist, catching the tractor in a crossfire. Bunny and I turned the toolshed into splinters. Top emptied four magazines into the straw.

The white hell outside became a red desolation.

The thunder of the gunfire echoed in the air for long seconds and kept beating in my ears for hours.

The mist held its red tinge for a while, and then with a powerful blast of thunder, the rain began to fall.

When we went outside to count the living and the dead, we only found dead. Six teams. Thirty-two men.

There was no one else in the yard. No one else anywhere.

"Cap'n," said Top as he came back from checking far into the cornfields, "that was Chief Crow and that Sweeney kid, wasn't it?"

I said nothing.

The shapes had matched. One small figure, one big. The voice had matched Crow's. Even the John Wayne reference.

But we never found footprints. Not a one. I blamed it on the rain.

The bullets that were dug out of the bodies of the shooters did not match any weapon found at the scene. When the service weapons of Chief of Police Malcolm Crow and corporal Michael Sweeney were later subpoenaed for testing, the lands and grooves of their gun barrels did not match the retrieved rounds. Shell casings from a Glock similar to Sweeney's and a Beretta 92F like the one Crow carried did not match the test firings performed by FBI ballistics. Witnesses put Crow and Sweeney elsewhere at the time of the incident.

"I've never seen a cover-up this good in a small town," I said to Church ten days later.

Instead of answering me, he stared at me for a long three-count and ate another vanilla wafer.

Then he opened his briefcase and removed a manila folder marked with an FBI seal. He set it on the table between us, removed a folded sheet and placed it atop the folder, and rested his hand over them both.

"What's that?" I asked.

Still making no comment, he handed me the folded paper. It was a National Weather Service report for August 16. There was no report of a storm, no Doppler record of storm clouds or fog.

"So? Somebody missed it."

"When the forensics team took possession of the crime scene," he said, "their reports indicate that the ground was dry and hard. There had been no rainfall in Pine Deep for eleven days."

"Then we need new forensics guys."

Church said nothing. He handed me the FBI folder. I took it and opened it. Read it. Read it again. Read it a third time. Threw it down on the table.

"No," I said.

Mr. Church said nothing.

I picked up the folder and opened it. Inside were several documents. The first was a report from a forest ranger who found a body in the woods. The second was a medical examiner's report. It was very detailed and ran for several pages. The first two pages explained how a positive identification was made on the body. Fingerprints, dental records, retina patterns. A DNA scan was included. A perfect match.

Simon Burke.

He had been severely tortured. His wrists and ankles showed clear ligature marks, indicating that he had been tightly bound. There were also bite marks on his wrists consistent with his having chewed through the cords. His stomach contents revealed traces of fiber.

According to the autopsy, Burke had managed to free himself from bondage and escaped from a cabin where he was being held. He made his way into the forest and apparently became disoriented. He was seriously injured at the time and bleeding internally. Forensic analysis of the spot where he was found corroborated the coroner's presumption that Burke had collapsed and succumbed to his wounds. He died, alone and lost, deep in the state forest that bordered Pine Deep.

That wasn't the tough part.

I mean . . . I felt bad for the little guy. He'd become a character in one of his own books. The intrepid underdog who outwits the bad guys and manages to escape. Except that this wasn't a book. It was the real world, and the bad guys had already done him so much harm that it's doubtful he could have been saved even if Echo Team had found him.

But . . . that wasn't the reason Church sat there, staring at me with his dark eyes. It wasn't the reason that my heartbeat hammered in my ears. It wasn't the reason I threw the report down again.

The coroner was able to estimate the time of death based on the rate of decomposition. By the time he had been found on August 22, his body had passed through rigor mortis and was in active decay.

The estimated time of death was irrelevant.

It was the estimated date of death that was turning a knife in my head.

When the forest ranger had found him, Simon Burke had been dead for ten days.

Ten.

"No way," I said.

Church said nothing.

"Burke called the AIC on the thirteenth."

Church nodded.

"I spoke to him on the sixteenth."

Church nodded.

"It was him, damn it."

Church selected a vanilla wafer from the plate, looked at it, and set it down. The date of death written on the report was August 11.

Mr. Church closed the folder, sighed, stood, and left the room.

I sat there.

"God," I said.

My heartbeat was like summer thunder in my head.

Long Way Home

Author's Note: This story takes place several years after the events described in the Pine Deep Trilogy, of which *Ghost Road Blues* is the first volume. You do not need to have read those books in order to read—and hopefully enjoy—this little tale set in rural Pennsylvania.

1

Donny stood in the shadow of the bridge and watched the brown water. The river was swollen with muddy runoff. Broken branches and dead birds bobbed up and down—now you see 'em, now you don't—as the swift current pulled them past.

The river.

Jeez, he thought. *The river.*

He remembered it differently than this. Sure, he'd lived here in Pine Deep long enough to have seen the river in all her costumes. Wearing gray under an overcast sky, running smoothly like liquid metal. Dressed in white and pale blue when the winter ice lured skaters to try and cross before the frozen surface turned to black lace. Camouflaged in red and gold and orange when early November winds blew the October leaves into the water.

Today, though, the river was swollen like a tumor and wore a kind of brown that looked like no color at all. It was like this when Halloween was about to hit. You'd think a town that used to be built around the holiday, a town that made its nut off of candy corn and jack-o'-lantern pumpkins and all that trick-or-treat stuff would dress up for the occasion. But no. This time of year, the colors all seemed to bleed away.

The last time he had seen the river was on one of those summer days that made you think summer would last forever and the world was built for swimming, kissing pretty girls, drinking beer, and floating on rubber inner tubes. It was the day before he had to report for basic training. He'd been with Jim Dooley; he remembered that so clearly.

Jim was going into the navy 'cause it was safe. A red-haired Mick with a smile that could charm the panties off a nun, and a laugh that came up from the soles of his feet. You couldn't be around Jim and not have fun. It was impossible, probably illegal.

They'd driven twenty miles up Route 32 and parked Donny's piece-of-shit old Ford 150 by Bleeker's Dock. The two of them and those college girls. Cindy something and Judy something.

Cindy had the face, but Judy had the body.

Not that either of them looked like bridge trolls, even without makeup, even waking up in Jim's brother's Boy Scout tent in the woods at the top of Dark Hollow. They were both so healthy. You could stand next to them, and your complexion would clear up. That kind of healthy.

And with Jim around, they laughed all the time.

Nothing like pretty girls laughing on a sunny day, as the four of them pushed off from the dock and into the Delaware. Way up here, above the factories down south, way above the smutch of Philadelphia, the water was clean. It was nice.

On that day, the water had been slower and bluer. It hadn't been a dry summer, but dry enough so that in shallow spots you could see the river stones under the rippling water. Judy swore she saw a starfish down there, but that was stupid. No such thing as freshwater starfish. Or at least Donny didn't think so.

Didn't matter anyway. That was the last time Donny saw Judy. Or Cindy, or even Jim, for that matter. The girls went back to college. Jim went into the navy.

Donny went into the army.

It all seemed like a long time ago.

Way too fucking long.

It was no longer summer. October was burning off its last hours. Even if the river looked like sewer water, at least the trees were wearing their Halloween colors.

Donny stood by the bridge and watched the brown river sweep the broken, dead things away. There was some message there, he thought. There was at least a Springsteen song there. Something about how nothing lasts.

But Donny was no more a songwriter than he was a philosopher.

He was a man who had spent too long coming home.

Donny climbed up from the bank and stepped onto the creosote-soaked planks of the bridge. It was a new bridge. The old one had been destroyed in the Trouble.

He'd missed that, too.

He'd read about it, though. Probably everybody read about it. That shit was how most people first heard of Pine Deep. Biggest news story in the world for a while. Bunch of militia nutjobs dumped all sorts of drugs into the town's water supply. LSD, psychotropics, all sorts of stuff. Nearly everybody in town went totally apeshit. Lots of violence, a body count that dwarfed the combined death tolls of Afghanistan and Iraq. Eleven thousand six hundred and forty-one people dead.

So many of the people that Donny knew.

His folks.

His cousin Sherry and her kids.

And Jim.

Jim had come home on leave from the navy. He hadn't taken a scratch in boot camp, had been posted to an aircraft carrier, was halfway through his tour and filling his letters with jokes about how the worst thing that happens to him is the clap from getting laid in every port in the Pacific.

Jim had been stabbed through the chest by a drugged-out corn farmer who claimed—swore under oath—that he was killing vampires.

How fucked up was that?

The massacre in Pine Deep changed the world. Like 9/11 did. Made the great big American paranoia machine shift its stare from everyone else in the world to its own backyard. Domestic terrorism. No one was safe, not even at home. Pine Deep proved that.

Eleven thousand people dead.

It had happened ten years ago. To the day. The militia goons had used the big Pine Deep Halloween Festival as its ground zero. Thousands of tourists in town. Celebrities. Everyone for miles around.

If the militia assholes ever had a point, it died with them. The press called them "white supremacists," but that didn't make sense. Most of the people in Pine Deep were white. WASPs, with some Catholics and a handful of Jews. Except for a few families and some of the tourists, there wasn't enough of a black or Latino or Jewish or Muslim presence to make a hate war point. It never made sense to Donny. The people in town were just caught up in the slaughter. Either they wound up taking the same drugs, or the red wave of insanity just washed over them.

Donny had been in Iraq, midway through his second tour.

He'd been over there, killing people, trying not to die from insurgent bullets or IEDs, fighting to protect the people at home. But the people at home died anyway.

Donny never did figure out how to react to it, and standing here now on this new bridge didn't make it any clearer. The death of so many at home, neighbor killing neighbor, felt like a sin. It felt like suicide. Even though he knew that with all those drugs in the water no one could ever be held responsible for what they did. Except those militia dickheads, and Donny wished there was at least one of them alive that he could hunt down and fuck up.

"Damn it, Jim," he said to the air.

He stared across the bridge to the thick stands of oaks and maples and birch trees. From here, in the sun's fading light, it was hard to tell if the trees were on fire or if it was just the red blaze of dying leaves.

Donny adjusted the straps of his backpack and stretched out one foot. Somehow taking this step would be like crossing a line.

But between what and what, Donny had no idea.

He was no philosopher.

He was a soldier coming home.

2

It seemed to take forever to walk across the bridge. Donny felt as if his feet were okay with the task, but his heart was throwing out an anchor.

He paused halfway across and looked back.

Behind him was a million miles of bad road that led from here all the way back to Afghanistan and Iraq. He was amazed he'd made it this far home. Donny always figured he'd die on a cot in some dinky aide station in the ass-end of nowhere, way the hell out on the Big Sand. God knows the world had tried to kill him enough times. He touched the row of healed-over scars that were stitched diagonally from left hip to right shoulder. Five rounds.

Should have died in the battle.

Should have died in the evac helicopter.

Should have died in the field hospital.

Lost enough blood to swim home.

The dead flesh of the scars was numb, but the muscle and bone beneath it remembered the pain.

And beneath that suffering flesh?

A heart that had ached to come back home, when there was a home to come back to. Now that heart beat a warning tattoo as if to say, *this is not your home anymore, soldier.*

This isn't home.

All the way here, with every mile, every step, he wondered why, after all these years away, he was coming back here at all.

He closed his eyes and felt the river wind blow damp across his cheeks.

The house he grew up in wasn't even his anymore. Attorneys and real estate agents had sold it for him. His parents' stuff, his sister's stuff, and everything he'd left behind when he joined the army had either gone to the Salvation Army or into storage.

Donny realized he didn't know where the key was for that. A lawyer had sent it to him, but . . .

He gave himself a rough pat-down, but he didn't have any keys at all.

No keys, no change in his pockets, not even a penknife to pry open the storage bin lock.

Shit.

He turned and looked back as if he could see where he'd left all of that stuff. Did someone clip him on the bus? Was it on the nightstand of that fleabag motel he'd slept in?

How much was gone?

He patted his left rear pocket and felt the familiar lump of his wallet, tugged on the chain to pull it out. He opened it and stared at the contents.

Stared for a long time.

Donny felt something on his cheeks, and his fingers came away wet.

"Why the fuck are you crying, asshole?" he demanded.

He didn't know how to answer his own question.

Slow seconds fell like leaves around him.

A car came rumbling across the bridge, driving fast, rattling the timbers. Crappy old Jeep Grand Cherokee that looked so much like the one Jim used to drive that it tore a sob from his chest. Sunlight blazed off the windshield so he couldn't see the driver. Just as well. Maybe it meant the driver could see a grown man standing on the fucking bridge crying his eyes out.

"You pussy," he told himself.

The car faded into the sun glare on the other side, but Donny could hear the tires crunching on gravel for a long time.

Donny sniffed back the tears, shoved his wallet back into his pocket, took a steadying breath, and then raised his head, resolved to get this shit done.

He crossed the bridge, paused only a moment at the end of the span, and stepped onto the road.

In Pine Deep.

Home.

3

Donny walked along Route A32.

Unless he could thumb a ride, it was going to take hours to get into town. There were miles and miles of farm country between here and a cold beer. So far, though, no cars. Not a one.

As he passed each farm, he thought about the families who lived there. Or . . . used to live there. Donny had no idea who was still here, who'd moved out after the Trouble, or who hadn't made it through the war zone the militant assholes had created. He'd gotten some news, of course. The Tyler family was gone. All of them. And the Bradys.

The farm to his right, though, was the old Guthrie place. One of the biggest farms in town, one of the oldest families. Old man Guthrie had died before the Trouble. Or, maybe at the start of it, depending on which account he'd read. Guthrie had been gunned down by some gun thugs up from Philly. Donny couldn't remember if the thugs were hiding out in Pine Deep, or they broke down there, or whether they were part of the white supremacist nutbags. Either way, one of them popped a cap in Mr. Guthrie, and that was a shame, 'cause the old guy was pretty cool. Always ready to hire some town kids to pick apples and pumpkins and pay them pretty good wages. Always smiling, he was. Deserved better than what he got.

Beyond the rail fence, the late-season corn was high and green, the thick stalks heavy with unpicked ears. Two crows sat on the top bar, cawing for their buddies to join them, but the rest of the birds were way up in the air, circling, circling.

What was it they called a bunch of crows, he wondered? He had to think back to Mrs. Gillespie in the third grade. A pod of whales, a parliament of owls, and a . . .

A murder of crows.

Yeah, that was it. So, what was it when there were only two crows? Attempted murder?

Donny laughed aloud at his own joke and wished Jim were here.

Jim usually came up with clever shit like that. Jim would have liked that joke, would have appreciated it. Would have patted him on the back, fist-bumped him, and then stolen the joke for his own repertoire. Which was okay. Jokes are free, and everyone should take as many as they could, that's how Donny saw it.

Smiling, Donny walked along the rail fence. Up ahead he saw an old guy on a ladder wiring a scarecrow to a post. The scarecrow was dressed in jeans and a fatigue jacket, work gloves for hands, and a pillowcase for a head. Straw and shredded rag dripped from the sleeves and pants cuffs. Shoes were mismatched, a Converse high-top sneaker and a dress shoe with no laces. Donny slowed to watch the man work. The man and the scarecrow were almost silhouetted by the sun. The image would have looked great on a Halloween calendar. A perfect snapshot of harvest time in the American farm country.

He liked it and smiled.

"Looks great," he said when he was close enough.

The old guy only half-turned. All Donny could see was grizzled white hair and wind-burned skin above pale eyes. He nodded at Donny's fatigue jacket.

"Afghanistan?"

"Yes, sir," answered Donny.

"You left the war," said the old man.

"No, sir . . . I reckon the war left me. It's over. They're cycling most of us home."

The old man studied him for a few long seconds. "You really think the war's over?"

Donny didn't want to get into a political debate with some old fool.

"I guess that's not for me to decide. They sent me home."

"Did they?" The man shook his head in clear disapproval and said, "The war's not over. No sirree-bob, it's not over by a long stretch."

Donny didn't know how to respond to that, so he began edging farther up the road.

"Son," said the old man, "some folks join the army to fight and some join to serve. What did you join for?"

"To protect my home and my family, sir." It sounded like a bull-shit platitude, even as he said it, but in truth it really was why Donny enlisted. Ever since 9/11, he was afraid of what might happen here at home, on American soil. Donny knew that he wasn't particularly smart, and he was far from being politically astute, but he knew that he wanted to do whatever he could to protect those who couldn't protect themselves. In school, it had been Jim at his back, who kicked the asses of bigger kids picking on the geeks and dweebs. Donny hated a bully. As far he saw it, terrorists were just bullies of a different wattage.

"Gonna be dark soon," said the old guy, apropos of nothing.

Donny glanced at the angle of the sun.

"Yeah. In a while, I s'pose."

"We all got to do what we can."

With those words, the old man nodded to himself then turned back to his work. After half a minute, Donny realized that there was nowhere to go with that conversation.

Gonna be dark soon.

Yeah, well, sure. Happens a lot around nighttime.

Crazy old fuck.

Donny walked on.

When he was just at the end of the Guthrie fence, he heard a sound and turned to see a man riding a small tractor. Far, far away, though. Way on the other side of a harvested field. The tractor looked like one of those really old kind, the ones that looked a little like a 1950s hot rod. It chugged along, puffing smoke but not really making much noise. At least not much of it reached Donny. Only an echo of an echo.

He cupped his hands around his eyes to try and see who was riding it. But all he could see was a man in coveralls with hair that could have been white or blond.

Even so, Donny lifted his hand and waved.

The man on the tractor waved back.

Maybe another old guy, but not an old fuck.

It was a simple conversation between strangers a mile apart. Donny wondered if it was a stranger, though. Might have been another of the Guthries. Or it might have been someone working for them. Or, hell, maybe it was whoever bought the farm if the surviving Guthries sold it after the Trouble. Didn't much matter. It was just nice to see someone.

Anyone.

The Guthrie farm ended at Dark Hollow Road, and Donny lingered at the crossroads for a moment, staring down the twisted side road. Not that he could see much—certainly not all the way to the Passion Pit, where everyone went to get high or get laid—but it was down there. That's where he and Donny went with those two girls. Last place he went in town before he climbed onto a bus to go learn how to be a soldier.

That last good night and day. All those laughs, the snuggling, cuddling sex in the tent with Judy, while Jim and Cindy screwed each other's brains out in a sleeping bag by their campfire. A great night.

But then he thought about Judy. She hadn't written to him, not once in all the time he was away. He never heard from her after that night.

That was strange. It felt bad. For a long time, it made him wonder if he was lousy in the sack, but over time he realized that probably wasn't it. Judy had gone to college, and that was a different world than a war half a world away. Maybe the sex and the pot they'd smoked was some kind of close-one-door-open-another thing. Like he and Jim were doing with their last blast weekend before going to war.

Maybe.

He'd written to her, though.

Four letters with no replies before he got the idea that she wasn't ever going to write back.

In some way, he supposed she was as dead to him as his folks and town. And Jim.

"Jesus, you're a gloomy fuck, too," he told himself. He turned away from Dark Hollow Road and the dead memories, disgusted with himself for thoughts like that.

On the road, the traffic was still a no-show, so he drifted into the center of the two-lane, liking the sound his heels made on the blacktop. A soft but solid *tok-tok-tok*. The echo of it bounced off the walls of trees that divided one farm from another.

At the top of a hill, he looked down a long sweep, and the beauty of his town nearly pulled more tears from him. The farms were not the geometrically perfect squares of some of the agricultural areas he'd seen. Some were angled this way, others turned that, with hedgerows and fences and rows of oaks to create borders. Cornfields swayed gently like waves on a slow ocean. Pumpkins dotted green fields with dots of orange. Autumn wheat blew like marsh grass in the soft breeze.

High above, a crow cried out with a call that was so plaintive, so desperately sad that the smile bled away from Donny's features. With the distortion of distance and wind, it sounded like the scream of a baby. Or the banshee wail of a woman kneeling over the body of a dead child.

Donny had seen that image, heard that sound too many times. In Iraq, in Afghanistan.

He touched his shirt over the scars, remembering pain. Remembering all the dying that went on over there.

But it went on here, too.

While he was gone, his town died, too.

Except for the one car that crossed the bridge, there hadn't been a single vehicle on the road. A tractor in a field hardly counted. And only two old sonsabitches at the Guthrie place. All of the other fields and the whole length of Route A32 were empty. It was Halloween. The road should have been packed with cars. Jeez . . . had the Trouble totally killed the town's tourism economy? That would seriously blow. Just about every family in town had their income either tied to farming stuff like Indian corn and pumpkins or to attractions like the Haunted Hayride, the Haunted House, the Dead-end Drive-in, and other seasonal things. Had the Halloween Festival been revived? Could he have been wrong about the town starting to come back from the Trouble?

It was weird.

Donny felt suddenly scared. Where *was* everyone else?

Had the town died for real?

Had he come home—come all these miles—to a ghost town?

High above the far row of mountains, he saw a white cloud float between him and the sun. Its vast purple shadow covered most of the horizon line, and as it sailed across the sky toward him, it dragged its dark shadow below, sweeping the land, brushing away details with a broom of darkness.

The belly of the cloud thickened, turned bruised, and was suddenly veined with red lightning.

A storm was coming.

He hadn't noticed it building, but at the rate it was growing, it was going to catch him out here on the road.

He suddenly wondered if that's what the old guy on the ladder was trying to say.

Gonna be dark soon.

He looked over his shoulder at the road he'd walked. It was a black ribbon fading out of sight as the shadows covered it. Up ahead was eight miles of hills between him and a bar or a Motel 6. He chewed his lip as he debated his options. The breeze was stiffening, and it was wet. It was going to rain hard and cold. And soon.

Maybe he could go back and ask one of the guys at the Guthrie place for a ride into town. Or a dry spot on a porch to wait it all out.

He could have done that.

Didn't.

Instead, he let his gaze drift over to the thick wall of oaks and pines beyond the closest field. He could haul ass over there and stay dry under the thick canopy of leaves. Yeah, sure, you weren't supposed to stand under trees in a lightning storm, but you weren't supposed to stand out in a cold rain and catch pneumonia, either.

Thunder snarled at him to make up his mind. The first big raindrops splatted on the blacktop.

He cut and ran for the trees.

4

As he ran, he thought he saw the car again. The Jeep Grand Cherokee that looked like Jim's. It bumped along the rutted length of Dark Hollow Road, a dozen yards to his right, beyond the shrubs and wind-bent pines.

The car was heading the same way he was. Going away from the main road, following an unpaved lane that only went to one spot. The Passion Pit that had long ago been carved out of the woods by generations of hot-blooded teenagers so they could try and solve the mysteries that burned under their skin. Donny had lost his cherry there. So did most of the guys and girls he grew up with. Getting popped at the Pit was a thing, one of those rite of passage things. It was cool. It was part of being from this town. It was what people did.

That car, though; why was it heading here right now? Wrong time of day for anything but a quickie. Wrong weather for anything at all. No tree cover over the Pit. Rain would sound like forty monkeys with hammers on the roof of an SUV like that.

The car kept on the road, going slow like it was keeping pace with him.

Eventually it would reach the Passion Pit, and so would he.

How would that play out?

If it was a couple looking for privacy, they weren't going to be happy to see him. But Donny thought, if it was someone who took a wrong turn in a heavy rain, then maybe he could leverage a ride in exchange for directions.

Worth a shot.

But the car pulled out ahead of him, bouncing and flouncing over the ruts, splashing mud high enough to paint its own windows brown. Donny watched it go.

"Nowhere to go, brother," he told the unseen driver.

Donny angled toward the road, thinking that if the car was going to turn around at the Pit, then he wanted to be where he'd be seen.

He jogged through the woods, staying under the thickest part of the leafy canopy, sometimes having to feel his way through rain-black shadows.

When he got to the edge of the clearing, he jerked to a stop.

The car was there.

Except that it wasn't.

It was the wrong car.

Same make, same model. Same color. The muddy tire tracks curved off the road and ended right there. Those ruts were only just now filling with rainwater.

But it had to be the wrong car.

Had to be.

"What the fuck . . . ?" Donny said aloud.

The car sat there at the edge of the Pit.

Maybe not "sat." Hunched. Lay. Something like that. Donny stared at it with a face as slack as if he'd been slapped silly.

The car was old. Rusted.

Dead.

The tires were nothing but rags, the rims flecked with red rust. There were dents and deep gouges in the faded paintwork. Spider-web cracks clouded the windshield. The side windows were busted out, leaving only jagged teeth in black mouths. Creeper vines snaked along the length of the SUV and coiled around the bars of the roof rack.

The car was dead.

Dead.

Cold and rusted and motherfucking dead.

He didn't know what to do. He didn't know how to think about something like this. His mind kept lunging at shreds of plausibility and reason, but they were too thin and slippery to grab. This made no sense.

No goddamn sense.

He stood just inside the wall of the forest. It was thinner here, and rain popped down on him. Hitting his shoulders and chest and forehead like a big wet finger jabbing him every time he tried to concoct an explanation for it.

He turned and looked at the curving tire tracks. No chance at all that they belonged to any other car than this. He looked at the car. No way it had driven past him. He looked at the road. There was nowhere else to go. The Pit was the only destination on that road. The Pit was the only place wide enough to turn around and go back, and besides, Donny had been close enough to the road to have definitely seen something go past him.

It made no sense.

No sense.

No sense.

Donny didn't realize that he was crying until the tears curled past his lips and he tasted salt.

"Oh, man," he said as he sagged down into a squat, buttocks on heels, palms over his face, shoulders twitching with tears that wanted to break like a tide from his chest. His voice sounded thin, like it was made out of cracked glass. "Oh shit, oh shit, oh shit."

"Yeah," said a voice behind him. "It's all total shit."

Donny almost jumped out of his skin. He whirled, rose to his feet, fists balled, heart hammering, ready to yell or fight or run.

Instead, he froze right there, half up, bent over, mouth open, heart nearly jerking to a halt in his chest.

A figure stood fifteen feet away. He'd managed to come this close without making a sound. Tall, thin, dressed in a Pine Deep Scarecrows football shirt. The shirt was torn, with ragged cloth drooping down to expose pale skin beneath; the material darkened as if by oil or chocolate, or . . .

Donny felt his own mouth fall open.

The world seemed to fall over sideways.

The figure had a big shit-eating grin on his face.

"Hey, Donny," said Jim.

5

"What the fuck?"

It was all Donny said, and he said it five or six times.

Jim laughed.

"No," growled Donny, "I mean what the fuck?"

"Guess you're the fuck," said Jim. "Christ on a stick, you should see the look on your face."

"You can't," began Donny. "I mean . . . you just can't. You can't . . ."

"Yeah," agreed Jim. "But I guess I can."

"No."

"So can you."

"Can what, man?" screamed Donny. "This is crazy. This is totally fucked."

Jim spread his hands in a "what can I say" gesture.

Donny pointed an accusing finger at him. "You died, you stupid shit. You *died!*"

A shadow seemed to pass over Jim's face, and his smile faded a bit. Not completely, but enough.

Enough to let Donny know that Jim didn't really find this funny.

Somehow, in a way Donny couldn't quite identify, that realization was worse.

Tears burned on Donny's face. They felt like acid on his skin.

Jim stepped closer, and with each step, his smile faded a little more. He stopped a few feet away, the smile gone now. Donny saw that Jim's face was streaked with mud. His skin gleamed as white as milk through the grime.

"You died," Donny said again, his voice less strident but no less hurt.

"Yeah," said Jim, "I did. Kind of blew, too."

Donny said, "What . . . ?"

"The whole death thing? Blows elephant dick."

"What are you . . . ?"

"For one thing, it hurt like a bitch." Jim touched his throat. "Nothing ever hurt that much before. Not even when I busted my leg when I fell off the ropes in gym class and the bone was sticking out. Jeez, remember that? You almost hurled chunks."

Donny said nothing. He wasn't sure he could.

"They had to carry me out of school. I was crying and shit 'cause it hurt so bad."

"That was when we were kids," said Donny weakly. "Fourth grade."

"Yeah," agreed Jim. "Long time ago. Lot of ships have sailed since then, huh?"

Donny just looked at him.

"But the day I died? Man . . . that was something else. The pain was red hot. I mean red fucking hot. And all the time it was happening, I kept trying to scream." His voice was thin, almost hollow, and Jim's eyes drifted away to look at something only he could see. Memories flashing on the inside walls of his mind. It was something Donny understood, even if he could understand nothing else that was happening.

"Help me out here, Jim," said Donny slowly. "You remember . . . dying?"

"Sure."

"How?"

Jim gave him a half-smile. "I was there, dude. I was paying attention to that shit."

"No, assface, how do you remember dying? How can you remember dying? I mean, how's that even possible?"

Jim shrugged. "I just remember. The pain in my throat. How hard it was to try and breathe. The air in my lungs feeling like it was catching fire. Shit, there's no part of that I'll ever forget." He glanced at Donny and then away again. More furtive this time. "I remember how scared I was. I pissed my pants. Imagine that, man. Me dying and pissing my pants and even with all that pain, I think I felt worse 'cause I gave myself a golden shower. Isn't that fucked up? I mean, how pathetic is that? I'm dying, some motherhumper is tearing my throat out with his teeth, and I'm worried about what people will think when they find out I juiced my shorts."

Donny looked at Jim. At his neck.

"That's not how you died," he said.

"What?" asked Jim.

"That's not how you died. That's not what happened."

"Yeah," said Jim, "it is."

"The hell it is. I read about it in the papers, saw it on the Net. Heard about it from people in town who lived through that shit, the Trouble. Some drugged-out farmer stabbed you in the chest."

Donny jabbed Jim in the chest with a finger, right over the place where his friend's shirt was torn. He jabbed hard. Twice.

"Right there, man. They said you got stabbed with a big piece of wood right there."

Jim stepped back out of poking distance. There was a look on his face that Donny couldn't quite read. Annoyance? Anger? And what else? Shame?

"Oh," said Jim. "Yeah, well, there was that."

"That's how you—"

"No," Jim said, cutting him off. "It's not how I died."

"But . . ."

"When that happened," continued Jim, "I was already dead."

6

Donny said, "What?"

Jim touched the spot on his chest where he'd been poked. He tried to push the torn material back into place to cover it, but the shirt was too ragged.

"Um," he said, and strung that word out for as long as he could.

"What the hell are you trying to say?" demanded Donny. "You got to start making sense out of this shit."

"Sense? Damn, man, you don't ask for much." Jim shook his head. "I was killed, man, but not by that ass pirate with the stake."

"*Stake*," said Donny, tasting the word and not liking it one bit.

"It's all part of the way they look at us. They think that stakes and all that shit really works."

"W-what?"

"Stakes. It's just bullshit, man."

"What are you talking about? C'mon man, don't do this to me," pleaded Donny.

"Dude," said Jim sadly, "it's already done. I died when I got bit. I was already dead when I got staked."

"Already dead . . . ?"

Jim nodded.

Donny stared at him, his mouth forming words, trying to shape sounds out of broken echoes of what Jim had just said.

"You got . . . *bit*?"

"Bit, yeah."

"By . . . what?"

"The fuck do you think bit me? The tooth fairy?"

"But are you trying to say that you were killed by a . . . a . . . ?"

"Go on, man, nut up and say it. Put it the hell out there."

Donny licked his lips and tried it, forced the word out of his gut, up through his lungs, and out into the world. As he struggled to say it, Jim said it with him.

"A vampire."

"Yeah," said Jim, "I got bit by a goddamn vampire. How totally fucked up is that?"

They stood there staring at each other as the heavens wept and the trees shivered.

"Before you totally lose it," said Jim, "just think about it. All those stories about the Trouble? All that wild shit everyone was saying about how when everyone got stoned from the drugs the militiamen put in the water, they started seeing werewolves and ghosts and vampires. You read about that, right?"

Donny said nothing.

"Well, there really wasn't any white militia . . . not like the papers said. There was a jackass who was a racist prick, but he was working for someone."

"Who?" asked Donny in a ragged voice.

Jim shrugged. "Doesn't matter. A big bad mothergrabber from Europe somewhere."

"A vampire?"

"Oh yeah. He started killing people, turning 'em into vampires and shit. Then there was a big-ass fight, and people started killing each other, killing the vampires, vampires killing civilians. It was totally fucked up."

"And . . . you?"

"Oh, they got me like ten days before the shit hit the fan. I was home on leave, and I was on the way over to Jessie Clover's place. You remember her from school? Brunette with the ass? I started banging her the day I got home, and I was tapping that every night. I was on my way to her place for some pussy when someone grabbed me and dragged me over a hedge."

"A vampire?" asked Donny.

"Shit yeah it was a vampire, but here's the nut-twister . . . the vampire was that kid, Brandon Strauss. You know him, fourteen or fifteen, something like that. Hung out with Mike Sweeney all the time."

Donny nodded numbly.

"Kid's half my size, but he's got all these vampire superpowers and shit," said Jim. "I tried to beat the shit out of him, and I got some good shots in, too, but . . . like I said, he's got that strength and speed. That part of the vampire legend is true. Speed, strength. Hard to hurt. Hard to kill. And . . . always hungry."

Donny took an immediate step backward.

"Hey," said Jim, "no, man . . . don't be like that. You're my road dog. I'm not going to hurt you."

"You're a fucking vampire, man," said Donny.

"Yeah, well, that part sucks."

They stood there, cold and awkward as the rain fell. Donny pointed to his friend's chest.

"You did get stabbed, though, right?"

"Yeah, and that hurt, too. Hurt like a bastard. That's the thing . . . even being, um, like dead and all? We still feel pain. And that hurt. Not as much as Brandon killing me, but it was bad."

"What happened?"

Jim's eyes darted away again. "He was alive," he said. "Even though he was looped on drugs from the water, he was alive. I was hurt . . . and I was hungry."

"Oh, shit . . ."

"Yeah," said Jim. "It kind of blows. I mean . . . it's evil and all that, but for some reason, I don't really seem to give much of a shit about that. It's nasty. It's messy, and even though I have to kill, I really can't stand the fucking screaming. Oh, man, you think it's bad when you're like at a concert and everyone's yelling? For me, it's like that but like ten times worse. All that heightened sense of hearing crap . . . it sounds good, it sounds like superhero shit, but then when you actually hear a full-throat, balls-to-the-wall death scream, you go about half deaf. Your head wants to explode, and the pain drives you bat shit."

He stopped as if considering the kind of picture his words were painting.

He sighed.

"Long story short, man," he half-mumbled, "I only died that one time. And if I'm careful and smart and follow the rules, I won't ever die again."

Donny echoed those last four words. "Won't ever die again."

"Yeah."

"But you're killing other people?"

Jim looked momentarily surprised. "Oh, the vampire thing. No, man, that's yesterday's news. I don't hunt like that."

"What do you mean?"

"What I said. I haven't made that kind of kill in years, man. Not since right after the Trouble."

Donny narrowed his eyes. "You expect me to believe that?"

"Shit, man, you can believe what you want. But it's true. I can live off of animals. There's a whole state forest right here. As long as I feed every couple of weeks, I'm good to go. The taste blows, but I figure it's kind of like being a vegan. It may not taste good, but it's better for my health."

"Why? What made you stop?"

"The Big Bad got killed. That night when the town burned, somebody must have killed the vampire that started all this."

"Who?"

"Shit if I know. I wasn't there when it happened. I was, um . . . doing other stuff."

"Killing people?"

Jim looked away once more. "You don't understand how hard it is. The hunger? It screams in your head. Especially back then, especially when the Big Bad was alive. It was like he juiced us all, amped us up. You couldn't fight it. And when he died? Christ, it was like a part of me died, too. I wanted to die. Really, man, I wanted to kill myself."

"But you can't die."

Jim snorted. "Everything can die."

"But you said that you couldn't die."

"No, I said that if I was careful, I wouldn't die. Not the same thing."

Donny frowned. "You can die?"

"Sure. That night, when we had the Trouble? Couple of hundred of us died."

"There were that many?"

"Yeah. Would have been thousands if the Big Bad had his way. But we almost all died that night."

"Almost all? There's more like you?"

Jim didn't answer that, but that was answer enough.

"This is bullshit," grumbled Donny. Then he corrected himself. "This is nuts."

"It's the world, man. Bigger, weirder, badder than we ever thought. And lately it's started to get worse. There's more . . . of them, of people like me."

"Vampires," Donny supplied.

Jim flinched. "Yeah. More vampires and maybe something coming—something like the Big Bad we had—coming back. People . . . or something . . . are starting to hunt. Not animals, like we been doing . . . but humans."

"What do you mean something's coming? What's coming?'

Jim said, "Bad times are coming, Donny. Bad times are here. It's getting dark, and there's something coming. I . . . can feel it. I can feel the pull. It's Halloween, man. Stuff . . . happens on Halloween. Halloween kicks open a door. You're from here, you know that. Something's going to take a bite out of town."

"No," said Donny, dismissing all of this as if it were unreal.

His gaze drifted over to the rusted-out car. Jim followed his line of gaze.

"Is that yours?" asked Donny.

"Yeah. I miss that old heap. We had some fun with that."

"It's a wreck."

"Well, yeah. Been like that for years."

"But I saw you driving it."

Jim frowned.

"No, man."

"I did. On the bridge and then ten minutes ago."

"Really," said Jim, "that car's deader than me. It's *dead* dead, you know?"

"No, I don't know," snapped Donny. "None of this makes sense. I finally manage to get home, and you want me to just accept all this shit?"

Jim shrugged.

"It's bullshit," snarled Donny suddenly. "This? All of this? It's bullshit."

"It is what it is."

Donny stepped forward and suddenly shoved Jim. "Don't give

me that crap, Jim. We went to fucking war, man. We enlisted to fight for this, to protect all of this." He waved his arms as if to indicate the whole of Pine Deep and everyone in it. "And while we're out there fighting real bad guys—terrorists, the Taliban, Al-Qaeda and shit— you're trying to tell me that vampires came in and killed everyone I know? You want me to believe that?"

Jim spread his hands again.

Donny shoved him again. "No! I fought every day to get back home. I bled to get back home. Do you have any idea how many firefights I've been in? How many times I was nearly killed? How many times I got hurt? Do you have any idea what kind of hell I went through?"

"I know, man."

"No, you don't. You went into the navy, Jim. You played it safe. But I went to fucking war. Real war. I fought to protect . . . to pro- tect . . ."

Fresh tears ran down his face. They felt as cold as the rain.

Colder.

"And it's all for shit. There are more like you out there. They're going to keep feeding on my town. They're going to make a punk out of me because they'll just take away everything I fought for."

Jim looked at him, and there was a deep sadness in his eyes. "Donny . . . believe me, man, I do know what you went through. I know all about it. Everything."

"Oh yeah? And how the hell are you supposed to know that shit? You get psychic powers, too?"

"No, man . . . I read it."

Donny blinked. "Read it?"

"Yeah."

"Read it where?"

A single tear broke from Jim's right eye. It carved a path through the grime on his face. "I may sleep under the dirt, dude, but I do read the papers. I read all about you."

"What are you . . . ?"

"They did a whole big story on you. Donny Castleberry, Pine Deep's war hero." Jim shook his head. "Donny . . . I read your obit- uary, man."

Donny said nothing.

"They had the whole story. You saving a couple of guys. Getting shot. They played it up, big, too. Said that you killed four Taliban, including the one who shot you. You went down swinging, boy. You never gave up the fight."

Donny said nothing. What could he say? How could he possibly respond to statements as ridiculous as these? As absurd?

The ground seemed to tilt under him. The hammering of the rain took on a surreal cadence. None of the colors of the forest made sense to him.

He touched his chest, and slowly trailed his fingers slantwise across his body, pausing at each dead place where a bullet had hit him.

He wanted to laugh at Jim. To spit in his face and throw his stupid words back at him. He wanted to kick Jim, to knock him down and stomp him for being such a liar. He wanted to scream at him. To make him take back those words.

He wanted to.

He wanted.

He . . .

He fought to remember the process of recovering in the hospital in Afghanistan, but he couldn't remember a single thing about it. Not the hospital, not a single face of a nurse or doctor, not the post-surgical therapy. Nothing. He remembered the bullets. But it seemed so long ago. He felt as if there should be weeks of memories. Months, maybe years of memories. His discharge, his flight back to the States. But as hard as he tried, all he could grab was shadows.

After all, he couldn't remember how he came to the bridge that crossed the river to Pine Deep. None of it was in his head.

None of it was . . .

Even there?

"God . . ." he breathed. If, in fact, he breathed at all.

"I'm sorry," said Jim. "I'm so sorry."

Off away in the woods, there was a long, protracted shriek. It was female. Cold and high and completely inhuman.

It's getting dark.

"What is that?" he asked.

Jim shook his head. "I don't know. Not really. Whatever it is, it's not right, you know?"

Donny said nothing.

"When it screams like that, it means that it's starting to hunt."

"It's a vampire, though," said Donny hoarsely.

"Yeah," said Jim. "I think so. Some . . . kind of vampire. Something I haven't seen before. Something bad."

Donny turned and looked toward the road. "And it wants to kill Pine Deep."

"It doesn't care about the town. It just wants the people."

"No," said Donny. He wiped at the tears on his face. The wetness was cold on the back of his hand. As cold as ice. "I didn't fight and . . ."

He couldn't bring himself to say the rest.

Fight and die.

"I didn't come home . . . come *back* . . . just to see terrorists destroy my town."

"Terrorists?" Jim almost laughed. "They're not terrorists, man, they're . . ."

But his words trailed off, and it was clear from his expression that he was reevaluating the word "terrorists."

"Donny?" he asked.

"Yeah?"

"I don't have any inside track on this shit," Jim began, "but I wonder if that's *why* you're back."

Donny said nothing.

"What if the town needed you and you were . . . I don't know . . . *available*?"

Donny said nothing, but inside his head, something went *click*.

"You said that you can die," he murmured.

"Yeah."

"Can you tell me . . . how?"

Jim only paused for a single second. "Yeah," he said.

The scream tore the air again. Deep in the woods, hidden by the rain. But coming closer, angling through the darkened forest and the pounding storm, toward Pine Deep.

"Maybe you're right," said Donny. And as he said those words, he felt a smile force its way onto his mouth. He couldn't see it, but he knew that it wouldn't be a nice smile. Not pleasant, not comforting.

He turned to Jim.

"All bullshit aside, Jim, we both signed up to serve. To protect our homes and our folks and our town, right?"

Jim nodded.

"So . . . let's serve. Let's be soldiers," said Donny. "You tell me how to kill them, and I'll bring the fight right to them. Right fucking to them."

"Are you serious?" asked Jim.

A third scream slashed at the air.

Donny touched the dead places on his chest.

"Yeah," he said, and he could feel a small, cold smile form on his mouth. "Dead serious."

Jim looked at him, and his eyes filled with fresh tears. Not of pain, nor of fear. There was love there. And joy. And something else, some indefinable quality that Donny could not label.

"Okay," said Jim. "Dead serious."

The scream came again, louder and closer than before.

Donny stared in the direction of the approaching monster.

And he smiled.

A soldier's smile.

Three Guys Walk into a Bar

1

The card was tucked into the cleft of a crack in the vinyl of my old Ford Escape's dashboard. The car was locked, the alarm functional but silent.

Card was still there.

I hovered there in the open doorway of the car and looked at it. Whoever had placed it there crinkled the end, so the card folded back to make it easy for me to see what was printed on it.

LIMBUS, Inc.
Are you laid off, downsized, undersized?
Call us. We employ. 1-800-555-0606
How lucky do you feel?

"Balls," I said.

2

I plucked the card out and threw it on the shotgun seat, got in, fired up the old beast, and headed out of the parking lot of the medical offices of Dr. Frieda Lipschitz.

She's a great doctor, but seriously, no one should ever have a name like Lipschitz. I know it doesn't mean what it sounds like it means. Dr. Frieda—and I have to call her that, or I can't keep a straight face—makes a point of telling everyone that it's a bastardization of Leobschütz, the German name for the Polish town of Głubczyce. Okay, sure, fine, nice history lesson. Change your name. Go with Lefkowitz or Lipstick or anything.

I mean, if you're a proctologist, you have a certain responsibility to your clients. It's a thing. Go with it.

So, there's me, driving away from Dr. Frieda's office after her telling me that I need a colonoscopy because I'm looking at fifty close enough to read the fine print and guys my age who eat like I do and drink like I do and generally act like overgrown frat boys like I do need to have someone stick a hose and a flashlight up their ass. Not how she put it, but words to that effect.

I told her I'd think about it.

She then browbeat me for twenty minutes, and somehow, I wound up agreeing. But . . . I really don't know if I could or should do it. There are complications with guys like me going under general anesthesia. Those complications could be life-changing for anyone in the E.R. if I have a bad dream.

Funny thing is, the thing she harped on the most was my cholesterol.

"You eat too much red meat," she said.

I tried to make a joke and tell her that it wasn't by choice. She didn't get it and, let's face it, it's not like I could explain.

So, she stuck her fingers in my butt, told me my prostate was okay, and cut me loose with a date for the procedure and a prescription for stuff that would 'cleanse my bowels' the night before.

Given a choice between marathon pre-procedure bowel evacuation and, say, getting mugged by an entire hockey team, I'll take my chances with the hockey team. Sticks and all.

This is what I was thinking about as I drove.

The card was still on the seat next to me.

Still saying *Limbus* on it. Still reminding me of the last card with that name on it I'd had.

What was it now? Three years ago and change.

One of the nastiest cases I ever worked. Some psychopaths skinning young girls.

Yeah. Skinning.

Turns out, when I finally ran it down, the skinning wasn't actually the worst thing that was happening to those girls. I know, you're thinking, how could it get worse than that?

There are more things in heaven and earth, Horatio.

Some of those things come into my life dragging a lot of very ugly baggage.

That case haunts me.

Absolutely fucking haunts me.

Sometimes in the middle of the night, I wake up and see those dead girls standing around my bed. Naked of flesh, stripped of humanity, bloodless and lost.

I know I'm dreaming, but I think I'm awake. The things those girls say . . .

When I really wake up, I try to remember their words, but I can't. Not really. It's like the dead speak in a language that the living can't really understand. Can't, and shouldn't try.

What scares me the most is that the older I get, the more I think I'm starting to understand a few words of that language. It's becoming more familiar.

I leave night lights on now.

Me. Sam Hunter. Ex-cop, occasional bodyguard, working private investigator. Whatever else I am. Tough and scary.

A night light.

Shit.

The card refused to evaporate or fly out the window even though there was a breeze whipping through the car. As if it was anchored there. As if it didn't want to leave.

Limbus, Inc.

How lucky do you feel?

I stopped at a red light and watched a father cross the street while holding the hands of two little girls. Twins. Maybe four years old. Curly blond hair on one, curly red hair on the other. Otherwise, identical.

The little girls looked at me. Both of them.

They smiled at me.

I smiled back.

Innocent little kids. Pretty, happy. Their whole lives ahead of them.

The group of assholes I hunted for Limbus flayed the skin from girls only a dozen years older than these two. Girls who also expected to have lives, a future. Happiness.

Dead. Destroyed.

Consumed.

The father shepherded his daughters to the other side. The little redhead kept looking back at me.

And, as the light turned green, she gave me a single, silent nod.

It was such a weird thing. Not a kid thing. It was an adult gesture, and for a flickering moment, her blue eyes were filled with a much older light.

Then she turned away, and the guy behind me beeped his horn.

I hit the gas too hard and jerked the Escape forward, cursed, adjusted the pressure on the pedal, and drove away from the moment.

The card was still right there.

When I pulled into the slot outside of the creaky old building where I have my office, I left the card where it was. I didn't want to bring it inside. It would mean that I was at least considering giving them a call. No way that was going to happen.

I locked my car, went up into my office.

Read the mail.

Most of it was bills. Some of it was junk.

Some of it was threatening letters.

Usual stuff.

I made some calls. Did some Net stuff for clients.

Didn't think much at all about the card.

Except that's a lie.

I couldn't *help* but think about the fucking card.

I was thinking about the card when Stevie Turks walked in with two of his goons. Card went right out of my head at that point.

Here's the thing about Stevie. His real last name is Turkleton, and he's a six-and-a-half-foot-tall lump of ugly white boy with more biceps than brains. I was warned about him when I took a missing persons case last year. Stevie likes young chicks. Ideally fifteen or so. He gets them high, gets them naked, and videotapes them having sex with Stevie and some of his crew. The video files are uploaded to a server in the Netherlands and sold to foreign buyers. I found this out while looking for a ninth-grade girl who was last seen in Stevie's storefront business—a video gamer shop on Broad Street near Girard. The girl's mother let me look around the kid's room, and that allowed me to pick up her scent. Everyone has a distinctive smell. Even kids with good hygiene. Most people can't tell.

I'm not most people.

It took me a week to find the kid. Unfortunately, by then Stevie had spent way too much time with her. The kid was so far out on the edge of a heroin high that she didn't know what day it was. Barely knew her own name.

They'd been busy with her. Three video sessions a day. Different outfits. Schoolgirl clothes, cheerleader uniforms. Shit like that.

I am no prude. But I have a very clear set of rules. Rape is, to me, no different than murder. It kills a part of the victim's soul. I've seen it way too many times. As a cop in the Cities and as a P.I. in Philly.

And when it comes to the rape of a child? When it comes to white slavery? Sex trafficking? Forced addiction?

Well . . .

Stevie was in the hospital for three months. Did that without changing, either. Just me, a blackjack, and a lot of moral indignation.

Would have been worse if I'd let him see the real me, but I actually wanted him to stand trial.

He lawyered up, of course, and they're taking their sweet time getting the trial started. Jury selection is next month.

Honestly, though, I did not expect him to be stupid enough to come here, to my office. He thought he was being smart by bringing two guys who were as big as he was. The three of them looked like bridge supports. Muscles on top of muscles.

Stevie opened his jacket to show the gun tucked into his belt. One of the goons closed the door. It was after hours; there was nobody else in the building. Again, they thought they were stacking things in their favor.

I stood up from behind my desk.

Stevie pulled his gun and pointed it at me. "You don't want to fucking move, dickbag."

3

The killer moved through the shadows. Running low, running fast. The winding ribbon of the game trail twisted and turned, whipsawed and plunged down the backs of the hills. Night birds screamed and fled the trees, flinging their ragged bodies into the cold sky. The last of the season's crickets held their noise, their insect minds unable to process anything other than the concept of danger.

Of death.

A brown bear raised her head and sniffed the air. Then it pulled her cubs close and sheltered them with her bulk. The bear closed her eyes, not wanting to see what it was that passed so fast and so close.

The killer was aware of these things.

It drank in the intoxicating richness of sight and sound, of smell and taste. There was no drug that could match this rush. Not even the most powerful psychotropic pill or magic mushroom. Nothing came close.

It reveled in the thousand things that flooded in through its senses. The enormity of the information had been staggering at first.

At first.

Now . . .

Now it was greater than a sexual thrill. Greater than anything.

Almost anything.

There was one thing that sent an even more potent thrill through the killer's dark mind.

It raced toward that experience now.

With claws that tore the soft ground.

With teeth that gleamed as the killer smiled and smiled and smiled.

4

I stayed where I was. "You really want to do this, Stevie?"

"No, I'm still fretting over whether it's a good idea."

We both grinned at that. It was a good comeback.

"They already have my deposition. On video. I signed the transcript in front of witnesses."

He shook his head. "Don't mean shit. It's your word against mine. And that little slut isn't going to be worth shit on the witness stand. My lawyers will rip her a new asshole. Not that her last asshole wasn't good. I tapped that shit. Damn if I didn't. Tight? Holy shit was she tight."

"Stevie," I said quietly, "you'd do yourself a big favor to shut the fuck up right about now."

He chuckled. "Why? Thinking about that tight little brown-eye giving you wood?"

"Stevie . . ." I said.

"Fuck this guy, Stevie," said one of the two goons. He had a big nose that looked like it wanted to be punched.

"Yeah, fuck him," agreed his colleague, who had no noticeable chin. "Let's do him and get the fuck out of here."

Stevie shook his head. "I'm not in a hurry. I spent three months thinking about this. This asshole suckered me and stomped me when I was down, and I need him to appreciate the consequences of his actions."

"Who writes your dialogue?" I asked. "I'm serious. Joe Pesci couldn't sell lines like that. You sound stupid, Stevie. No, let me correct that, you sound cheap. You're a third-string kiddie porn asshole, and your father would have done the whole world a favor by jerking off instead of banging your mother. Now you come here and try to lay some tough guy *Goodfellas* rap on me like I'm supposed to go all knock-kneed. Are you kidding me?"

He brightened. "Wait, you think I'm putting this on? Really? 'Cause I think that you're going to realize just how wrong you are when I cut your dick off and stuff it in your—"

And that was as much of this bullshit as I could take. It wasn't a good day to begin with. Doctor sticking both hands and one foot up my ass. That damn card from Limbus. These assholes. The memories of the hurt in the girl's eyes when she was done with rehab and sitting with the cops to tell them what she remembered. A hurt I was sure would always be there, polluting her life, darkening her skies.

I know I said I wanted Stevie to go to trial.

I really did.

Past tense.

I jumped over the desk at him.

He wasn't expecting that.

Not a knock against him that he wasn't expecting it. The average person wouldn't be primed to make that kind of intuitive leap.

I was only a medium-sized, middle-aged man when I started the jump.

I was something else when I hit him.

I saw the way his eyes changed as he realized just how much trouble he was in. As he realized exactly what tough really was and how little judgment he possessed. As he realized that the world was so much different than what filled his limited understanding.

He'd come with superior numbers and overwhelming force to kill a man.

He did not bring enough of anything to kill the wolf.

5

A solitary headlight cut through the forest, and the killer stopped.

He froze into the moment, becoming absolutely still. The breeze blew past it, rifling hair, but the killer was now part of the vast and complex darkness of the woods. Beneath the canopy of oak and pine boughs, the floor of the forest was as impenetrable as the deepest part of the ocean. Not even a spark of moonlight fell through that ceiling.

But the headlights . . .

They moved along the serpentine fire access road, pushing the engine buzz in front of it.

The killer watched the light, amused by it like a traveler seeing a will-o'-the-wisp. The road the bike drove came from the southeast and curved around toward the northwest.

Toward where the killer waited.

The killer felt drool worm its way from between his lips, hang pendulously from his chin, and then fall. He could hear the release of the ropey spittle. Could hear the splash as it struck the grass. He could hear everything.

The sound of the motorcycle and the glow of its light ignited a burning hunger deep in the killer's mind. His mind, first. Then in his chest, and then in his stomach.

Always in the mind.

That's where hunger began.

That's where lust lived.

The killer turned, peeling itself out of the featureless black of the forest as it stepped onto the winding road.

To wait.

6

It takes a long, long time to bag three grown men.

Takes even longer to clean up the mess.

My office is prepped for it, though. Everything is waterproof. Everything is cleanable. I keep a bucket and mop, bleach, paper towels, rags, soap, sponges, and brushes in the closet. A big box of heavy-duty contractor black plastic bags. And a wheeled mail cart.

Took me nearly five hours to clean everything up.

Played Tom Waits and Steely Dan really loud while I did it. Sometimes you got to play loud music to distract you from what you're doing. And, yes, I have playlists for this sort of thing.

My life is complicated.

I killed two more hours driving to a landfill I knew of and dumping the bags, then driving back. Tried not to look at the card while I was driving. Still hoping it would blow out the window. Still didn't. Came back to the office, drank some beer. Watched a DVR of the All-Star Game and fell asleep on my couch.

I didn't start thinking about the card until I woke up. Took a poor-man's shower standing in front of the sink and washing myself with paper towels. Thought about coffee and decided to go find some.

The card was still in my car when I came outside at a quarter to seven in the morning.

Except it wasn't where I left it.

It should have been on the passenger seat. Instead, it was tucked into the cracked vinyl where I'd found it the first time.

But this time, it was turned backward so I could see what somebody'd written in blue ballpoint. One word.

Now.

I looked at the card.

I got out of the car and looked around the area. The usual suspects were doing what they usually do. Cars passed on Street Road, heading everywhere but where I gave a shit. No one was looking at me. No one looked like the kind of person who'd leave this kind of card.

I didn't want to call the number. They might as well have printed *nothing but trouble* in red embossed typeface.

I said, "Fuck."

I went back into my office.

And called the goddamn number.

7

The motorcycle rounded the curve in the road, and the light splashed its whiteness ahead. The pale light painted the figure standing in the road.

The driver tried to stop in time.

He swerved.

He braked.

The bike turned and began to slew sideways toward an inevitable collision. One that would break bone and burst meat and splash the landscape with blood that would be black as oil in the night.

The killer did not move.

Not right away, at least.

As the bike and its driver skidded and spun toward him, the killer rose up from four legs to two. He bared his teeth and with red joy reached out to accept the gift that was being given.

It was not just meat and blood that fed him.

He feasted on the screams, as well.

Oh, how delicious they were. And he made sure they lasted a long, long time.

8

The voice that answered did not belong to the beautiful woman who'd hired me last time.

The voice was male.

Nasal, high-pitched, fussy. If a Chihuahua could talk, it would be like that.

Funny and cute if it was a cartoon. Less so on a business call.

Instead of saying "Hello" or any of that shit, he picked up half-way through the second ring and said, "Mr. Hunter."

My name, not his.

"Who's this?"

"We're delighted that you called, Mr. Hunter."

"I'm not. Who is this?"

"Limbus," he said.

"No, your name."

A pause. "My name is Cricket."

"First or last?"

"Just Cricket."

"Jeez."

"And, as I said, we're delighted you called."

"Why?"

"My employers were very satisfied with the manner in which the last matter was, mmmm, handled."

The humming pause was for effect. He wanted me to know that *he* knew exactly how that case was handled. I had to use some irregular methods. Irregular for most P.I.s. Only semi-irregular for me.

"Can I speak with the lady who hired me before?"

"Mmmm, which lady would that be?"

"Don't jerk me off."

Another pause. "That person is no longer a part of this organization."

"What happened to her?"

"She is, mmmm, engaged in other work," said Mr. Cricket. "And before you ask, Mr. Hunter, I am not at liberty to discuss the matter."

"Balls."

To be fair, it was what I expected. I would have been genuinely surprised if I ever saw her again.

I sighed. "Okay, so what do you want?"

"Are you, mmm, familiar with the town of Pine Deep, Pennsylvania?"

"Sure. In Bucks County, on the river."

"Have you ever been there?"

"No. I heard it burned down."

"There was some trouble," Cricket said diffidently, "but that was a number of years ago. It has been, mmmm, substantially rebuilt."

"Big whoop. How's that matter to me?"

"We would like you to go there."

"Why?"

"To conduct an investigation."

"What would I be investigating?"

"There have been a series of, mmm, attacks."

"What kind of attacks?"

"Murders."

"Murders? Plural?"

"Five murders," he said. "And one person seriously injured."

"That's too bad. Correct me if I'm wrong, but don't even one-Starbucks towns in Bucks County have police departments?"

"They do."

"Maybe you haven't heard, but unless you're in a movie, it's pretty rare for anyone to hire a private investigator to go anywhere near a police matter. Cops, as a rule, take that sort of thing amiss."

"Amiss," he repeated, apparently enjoying the word.

I waited.

Cricket said, "You used to be a police officer."

" 'Used to be' is a phrase you should look at more closely."

"You're *still* an investigator."

"Private. And let me reiterate that P.I.s do not—I repeat *do not*—interfere with active police cases. Cops tend to get cranky about that. Cranky cops can make life very difficult for working P.I.s, even small-town cranky cops. If I interfered, I could get my ticket pulled."

"I do not believe that would happen in this case, Mr. Hunter."

"Why, are you cats going to pay for my lawyer?"

"Mmmm, no."

"Are you going to run inference between me and local law?"

"No."

"Then have a swell day."

"Mr. Hunter, the reason you won't have those kinds of problems is that the Pine Deep Police have requested our assistance."

I said nothing.

"They have, in point of fact, requested *your* help."

"Me?"

"Well, perhaps I should clarify . . . your actual name was not included in the request."

"Then what—?"

"Well, mmmm, through various channels, the chief of police in Pine Deep has been searching for an expert in a certain kind of crime."

"I'm no expert. More of a general practitioner. Jack of all trades, master of none," I said, trying and failing to make a small joke.

"Forgive me, Mr. Hunter, but we disagree with that assertion. You are exceptionally well qualified for this particular kind of crime."

"How so?

"Because of the unique nature of the murders."

That's when I got the first real tingle of warning. Small, but serious. The smart thing to do would have been to simply end the call. No goodbyes, no polite refusals, just hit the button, put the cell phone in the bottom drawer of my file cabinet, and go to the multiplex to watch a movie about things blowing up. Maybe get some Ben and Jerry's afterward.

That's what I should have done. I knew it then, and I sure as shit know it now.

Instead, I felt my mouth speak, heard my voice say, "What do you mean?"

I swear to Christ that I could *hear* him smile. Like a fisherman who knew that his last tug had set the hook.

"The victims," he said after the slightest pause, "were torn apart and partially, mmmm, consumed."

"Oh," I said.

"And at the scene of each crime, the forensics experts took castings of an unusual set of prints. Do you, mmmm, care to guess which kind of prints?"

I pinched the bridge of my nose. "Not really," I said.

"Just so," he said.

There was a very long silence on the line. Mr. Cricket did not seem interested in breaking it. He wanted me to jump out of the water into his little boat.

And, damn it, I did.

"Tell me the rest," I said.

9

The killer sagged back from the orgy of its feast.

Sated.

Swollen.

His mouth tingled from the hundreds of tastes present in fresh meat and blood.

His cock was turgid from the frenzy of the kill.

His eyes were glazed from the intoxicating beauty of it all.

He rolled over and flopped onto his back, letting the night breeze cool the blood on skin and mouth and hands.

Hands now. Not paws.

He lay there and stared up through the trees. They were sparser here above the road, and he could see a few stars.

He could see the moon.

It was a sickle-slash of white. So bright. So bright.

10

After the call was over, I sat slumped in my chair, staring a hole through the middle of nowhere.

Cricket hadn't told me much more, saying that the local law in Pine Deep would give me the whole story. He suggested I familiarize myself with that troubled little town. The story was readily available on the Net.

When we finally got to the question of my fee, Cricket made his mmmm-ing noise again and said, "Third drawer down."

After which the line went dead.

I pushed my wheeled chair back from my desk and looked at the bottom drawer. It was closed, the way I'd left it, and I hadn't checked it since getting back. The wall clock ticked its way through a lot of cold seconds while I sat there. I hadn't told Cricket I was taking the job. We had no formal agreement. And whatever was in that drawer did not constitute acceptance on my part. Not unless I put it in the bank.

So I could just leave it there.

Or I could mail it back to them.

Except that there was no address on the card. Just the number.

I drummed my fingers very, very slowly on the desktop.

The minute hand had time for two whole trips around before I opened the drawer.

The usual stuff was there. Yellow legal pads, box of disposable mechanical pencils, extra rolls of Scotch tape, plastic thing of staples, a dog-eared Jon McGoran thriller I was rereading.

And the envelope.

Placed very neatly and squarely in the exact center of the drawer's interior space. Fussy. Like I imagine everything was on Cricket's desk. I think he even straightened the stuff in my drawer.

"Mmmm," I said in acknowledgment.

The envelope was a standard number ten, off-white, with nothing written on the outside.

I could tell right away that it wasn't a check. Checks are flat. The contents of this envelope distorted its shape. Bulged it.

I sighed and reached for it. Hefted it, weighed it in my hand.

Heavy.

Heavy is nice. First nice thing about this matter.

I tried to judge how much would be in there. If it was fives, tens, and twenties, it could be five hundred. Half a week's income for me, on a good week.

I tore open the top and let the bundle of bills slide down into my hand.

The top bill was not a five, a ten, or a twenty.

Mr. Benjamin Franklin smiled at me with a smug awareness as if to say, "Yes, son, we all have a price."

I took a breath and folded down the corner of the top bill.

The next one was a hundred, too.

So were the next thirty-nine.

My scalp began to sweat.

The stack didn't end there, though.

There were six bills with the face of someone I'd never seen on a piece of paper currency. Read about him, but never actually looked at one.

William McKinley.

The denomination insisted that this was a five-hundred-dollar bill.

There were six of these.

Six.

I turned on my computer and did a search to see if these were even in circulation anymore.

They weren't. The last five-hundred-dollar bills had been printed in 1945.

These were all from 1934. All crisp and clean, as if they'd never been used.

I did a second search to see if they were still worth five hundred.

They were not.

Not even close.

I found auction sites that listed them, that sold them.

My scalp was sweating even more. So was every other part of me.

I called the number for one of the auction houses, a place in Doylestown. The receptionist transferred me to the rare coins guy. When I explained what I had, the man snorted and asked me if I was making a prank call. I assured him I was not.

"And you have *six* such bills?"

"Yes," I assured him.

"Would you mind reading the serial numbers to me?" The skepticism was thick in his tone.

I read the numbers. They were all in sequence.

He made a sound somewhere between a gasp and a growl.

"Please," he said, "assure me that this is not a joke."

"Not unless someone is playing one on me. But look, just tell me . . . are these still good? I mean, could I deposit them in my bank?"

He made that sound again. Much louder this time.

"Please, sir, do not even *joke* about that. If these are legitimate bills, and if they are in the condition you describe, then they have considerable worth."

"Yeah . . . I saw something on your site that they might be worth fifteen hundred or—"

"No," he said abruptly.

"Oh," I said, deflated, "then—"

"If these bills are real, then they are worth a great deal more than that."

"Like . . . how much more?"

"Do you have any understanding of rare currencies?"

"Not beyond that fact that it's rare for me to *have* currency."

He gave a polite little laugh. Enough to tell me that I wasn't as funny as I thought I was, or maybe that this was no time for jokes.

"Rarities of any kind are what drive the passion for collection. Art, coins, stamps . . . they have value based on a number of factors. Condition—even a scratch can take hundreds off of a rare penny, and—"

"Right, I understand that part."

"Condition is one factor in determining value. The actual degree of rarity is another. Take, for example, the 1933 Saint-Gaudens Double Eagle. When the Depression was in full swing, President Roosevelt took the country off the gold standard and recalled all gold coins for melting. About a dozen of that particular coin never made it back to the mint or were smuggled out again by enterprising government employees. One of those coins resurfaced in 1992 and was confiscated by the Secret Service but was not melted down. In 1933, it had a face value of twenty dollars; in 2002, it was sold at auction for over seven million dollars."

"Jesus Alexander Christ."

"Exactly."

"Now the third thing that can influence the value of an item is provenance. You know what that is?"

"Sure—who owned it, when they owned it, how it moved from owner to owner. Like that."

"Like that, yes. In the case of the 1934 five-hundred-dollar bills, there is a sequence of them that were part of a private collection of rarities. The entire collection, by the way, was appraised in 1973, and at that time valued at just under nine million dollars. It would be worth considerably more now."

"And these bills?"

"They are all from the missing sequence. There were ten bills in sequence. One turned up in Lambertville, New Jersey in 2006. The rest have remained completely off the radar since the owner of that collection died."

"Who was he and when did he die?"

There was a pause. "Excuse me, Mr. . . . ?"

"Hunter," I said. "Sam Hunter."

"Excuse me, Mr. Hunter, but would you be willing to engage our firm to handle any auction for these bills? I can assure you that no one else would be able to get you a higher price for them, or a quicker sale."

"If I decide to sell them," I said, "we can talk. Right now, I need to know more about the bills. That'll help me decide what to do."

"I understand."

"What's your name?" I asked.

"Milton Peabody," he said. It seemed about right. He had a Milton Peabody kind of voice.

"So, who owned the bills?"

"They were part of the private collection of a foreign gentleman who moved to Eastern Pennsylvania in the late nineteen sixties. His name was Ubel Griswold."

That name rang a very faint bell. Not a nice bell, either, but no matter how hard I scrabbled for details, there was nothing in my memory. I wrote it down so I could do a search later.

"And where did this Griswold guy live?"

Mr. Peabody said, "He lived in Pine Deep. And that is where he was murdered."

11

The killer got slowly to his feet. He stumbled once in the dark. The man could see less than the beast. He longed to revert, to stay in the other shape. Always.

Always.

Always.

But that other mouth was not made for speech, and he needed to speak.

He was naked, but around his neck was a small metal disk on a sturdy chain. The chain was painted a flat black so that it caught no light. The disk had a single button.

He caught it between thumb and forefinger that were sticky with blood. He pressed the button.

"I . . ." he began, then coughed and spat out a wad of clotted blood. "I need a cleanup team."

He did not speak in English.

12

So, yeah, I took the case.

Cricket told me that an email with some case details would be in my inbox. It was. Somehow, though, Cricket had blanked out his own return email address. Like most P.I.s, I know some tricks about tracing emails. I hit a dead end right away. Whoever these Limbus people were, they were very tech savvy. They left me nowhere to go.

So I opened the email. There was no text, just an attachment with five photos. I opened them and sat for a long time looking at the pictures. Five people. Two men, two women, one child.

They were all dead. They had all been torn up.

These were morgue photos rather than the more useful crime scene photos. Two of the victims were in pretty good shape—relatively speaking. They had massive chest and throat wounds but were otherwise intact. Whole.

The other three were not.

Whole, I mean.

Each of them had been torn to pieces. Actual pieces.

"This was no boat accident," I said in my best Richard Dreyfuss, but there was no one around to get the joke.

I zoomed in on the photos and studied the wounds. I'm no forensic expert, but I know how to read wound patterns. To guys like me, they tell a very clear story. Flesh torn by bullets and flesh torn by knives tell one kind of story. Friction injuries of a certain pattern can indicate a motorcycle accident or a fall down a mountain. There are distinct differences in dog bites, rat bites, and snake bites. You simply have to understand human tissue and bone, something of physics, something of anatomy.

What I was seeing told a very specific story. Maybe a coroner might have some problems with it because of the angle of certain wounds, the depths of the bite marks, the apparent bite strength needed to crush bones like the humerus and femur. Me? I could read this like a book.

Personal experience is a great teacher.

I saved the images to my computer and thought about the money.

The money would go into my bank, but not riding a deposit slip. Before I did that, though, I ran a high-res scan of each side of each bill and sent the files to myself via DropBox.

I also sniffed each bill.

I do that. I'm not weird the way it sounds. I'm weird in a different way. My sense of smell is better than most. Better than most dogs, if you want to make a point of it. Sniffing the bills told me a lot.

First, I could tell that they'd been handled by someone, but not recently. It was an old scent, just a trace. And that's really interesting, because it meant that no one had handled that money recently, and by recently, I mean in years. The scent was really old, barely there. How had those bills then been placed in the envelope? The hundreds were mixed bills, most of them relatively recent. Late nineties into the early 2000s. Stuff that's still in circulation. The same human scent was on them, too.

That scent and no other.

"Curiouser and curiouser," I said to the empty room. I did not for a moment believe that the scent was that of the mysterious Mr. Cricket. There was also no residual smell of latex from gloves. What had they used to stuff the envelope? Plastic tweezers?

I spent some time going over the envelope, but if there was anything to find, then not even my senses could pick it up. That was very disturbing.

And also . . . intriguing.

Before I left for Pine Deep, I spent a few hours on the Net reading up about Ubel Griswold and the troubles in the town. A lot of it was new to me. I used to live in Minneapolis, and Pine Deep is a rural suburb of Philadelphia. Griswold, according to the news reports, had been a foreign national who'd moved to America in the 1960s. His name was German, but one reporter implied that the man was either Russian or Polish. Or maybe from Belarus, from back when that little country was known as the Byelorussian Soviet Socialist Republic. Either way, Griswold moved to the States, bought some land, and set himself up as a small-time cattle farmer in a section of Pine Deep known as Dark Hollow. In 1976, the area was rocked by a series of particularly savage killings. There was a whole slew of them, and it was believed they were the work of one man, whom the papers nicknamed 'the Reaper.' Reporters love titles like that.

The manhunt for the Reaper was intense, and the leading suspect in those killings was an itinerant day laborer and blues musician named Oren Morse. Known locally as the Bone Man because he was as thin as a scarecrow.

Ubel Griswold vanished on a—you guessed it—dark and stormy night, and his body was never found. The locals apparently ran Morse to ground and lynched him. The killings stopped at that point, so it seemed pretty clear they'd killed the killer.

If the story ended there, it would be weird and sad enough, but there was a second part. Thirty years to the actual day of the Reaper killings, another psychopath came to town in the person of one Karl Ruger. He was a real piece of work. A former mob button man who'd gone way off the reservation into Hannibal Lecter territory. Apparently, Ruger had ties to a local group of radical white supremacist militiamen, and they put together a terrorist attack that still stands as the worst example of domestic terrorism on U.S. shores. You read about it in the papers, maybe saw the movie they did. Or read the books. The Trouble. That's what they call it.

Ruger and the other assholes spiked the town's water supply with hallucinogens during a big Halloween festival. Pine Deep was wall-to-wall with tourists. Everyone went apeshit nuts. Eleven thousand people died.

No matter how many times I read and reread that number, it still hits me in the gut.

Eleven thousand.

Three times that many were injured, and more than half the town burned down.

The Trouble.

According to the Net, the town was trying to come back. Some of it was already back, though it was no longer a Halloween tourist spot. It was settling back into being a blue-collar farming community with a scattering of craft shops and some galleries.

That's what I learned from web searches.

So, while I drove out there, I tried to make sense of those events—forty years ago and ten years ago—and how they might connect with recent murders. There was damn little about the new killings in the press, and every story I read suggested that each of the victims died in a violent car crash or farm-related accident. Not one word of anything criminal. The news stories didn't mention anything about animal attacks, either, which means either that was squashed, or the reporters out there are dumb as fuck. My guess was the former.

I hit Route 611 and turned north.

13

The killer watched the big man in the woods.

The man was dressed in dark clothes. Battle dress uniform, boots, a shoulder rig with a holstered pistol. A Beretta. A knife clipped to the inside of the right front pants pocket.

The killer crouched on the thick oak limb and leaned down to watch.

The big man walked around the wreck of the motorcycle. He touched nothing. He stood for long moments studying it. He walked the perimeter of the crash scene, then out to the road, then back.

Occasionally the big man spoke out loud, even though he was alone.

The killer strained to hear.

"Bug," the big man said, "looks like we got another one." He read the bike's license plate number. He gave a physical description of the driver. Or what was left of the driver. He stood as if listening. "No, tell Top and Bunny to check out that car crash in Lambertville. I'll call if I need them to come a-running."

He listened again.

"No. I think I'm going to have to talk to the locals on this. Yeah, I know the chief. Ornery little bastard. Okay. Cowboy out."

The big man suddenly straightened, as if he'd heard something. His gun was suddenly in his hand. It was like a magic trick. The man was fast.

So fast.

He crouched and turned, bringing the gun up into a two-handed grip, eyes tracking at the same time as the gun barrel. The man was sharp.

Very sharp.

He even looked up at the surrounding trees.

For one fragment of a moment, he looked directly at the killer.

But he did not see him.

The camouflage was too good, the intervening foliage too thick, the place of concealment too well chosen. So the narrowed eyes of the big man moved away. Reluctantly, though, as if the big man's instincts were not in harmony with his senses. As if his instincts were sharper, more primitive. Limited by the sensory awareness potentials of the modern human.

The killer smiled.

He could understand that.

He did not move at all.

But he watched every single thing this big man did. This was a dangerous, dangerous man. This was a killer in his own right. That much was obvious. His speed, the confidence he demonstrated as he turned to face the unknown. As if he'd faced—and fought—things that came at him from unexpected directions. Many times.

He had that kind of aura.

The killer in the trees watched the killer with the gun.
He wanted so badly to fight this man.
To battle with him in the most primal of ways.
To revel in defeating him.
To taste the blood of another predator.
To eat a warrior's heart.

14

Pine Deep is a triangular wedge of fertile farmland and mountains in Bucks County. It's bisected by Interstate Alternate Extension Route A32, lying hard against the Delaware River that separated Pennsylvania from New Jersey and framed on all sides by streams and canals. A32 wavers back and forth between the two states, across old iron bridges and up through farm country, and then plows right through the town. To the southwest was the much smaller town of Black Marsh, and above Pine Deep was the even tinier Crestville. A32 was the only road that cut all the way through those three towns. All other roads inside the triangle lead nowhere except someone's back forty or to the asymmetrical tangle of cobblestoned streets in Pine Deep's trendy shopping and dining district. Bigger and more prosperous towns like Doylestown, New Hope, and Lambertville were pretty close, but Pine Deep felt more remote than it was. Like a lot of farming towns in America, it covered an astounding amount of real estate for the number of people who lived there. Some of the farms had ten thousand acres of corn or pumpkins or garlic and maybe a dozen people living in the farmhouse and related buildings. Migrant workers did a lot of the labor.

I rattled across the bridge and drove into Pine Deep in the middle of an afternoon that was hotter than the weatherman said it would be. The trees were heavy with lush growth, and the brighter greens of spring had given way to the darkness of summer leaves. Towers of white cumulonimbus clouds rose like the pillars of heaven, but the distant western sky was softer, painted with cirrus clouds in brushstrokes of gray-white. There were birds up there, and at first, I thought they were hawks, but they were too big. Probably turkey vultures.

I slowed to a stop on the shoulder of the road and leaned out to look up at them. Counted them.

Thirteen.

I tried not to make anything of that.

Spooky town, meaningless coincidence.

I kept driving.

A32 rolls on for mile after mile, and I didn't see a single living soul. The corn was half-grown and stiff and tall. The pumpkins were only pale knobs. Way off in the distance, the farmhouses looked like toys from a Monopoly set. I drove past a tractor sitting at an angle in the middle of a fallow field, the engine rusted to a bright orange. A threadbare crow stood on the curve of the seatback, his head turning slowly to follow the passage of my car. Flies swarmed in the air over a dead raccoon whose head had been squashed flat by a car tire.

I turned the radio on to find some music to lighten the load. Couldn't get reception worth a damn except for some religious blood and thunder stuff. I dug a CD at random from the center console and fed it into the slot. Tom Waits began growling at me. Song about a murder in a red barn.

"Balls," I said, and almost turned it off.

Didn't though.

Drove on, listening to Tom's gravelly voice spin dark magic under the blue summer sky.

15

The highway wandered around between some hefty mountains and then spilled out at the far end of a small town. Kind of a Twin Peaks vibe to it. One main street. Lots of crooked little side streets. Low buildings, lots of trees. From the crest of the hill, I could look down and count all five of the streetlights.

I took my foot off the brake and let the car find its own way down the hill, coasting, in no hurry to get there. As I reached the main drag, I switched the CD player off and drove in silence through the center of town. There were people here and there, but you couldn't call it "bustling" without lying. Most of the houses and stores had been rebuilt or repaired, but here and there I could see some blackened shells. Even after ten years, the town still wore its scars.

Eleven thousand people.

Were there eleven thousand ghosts haunting these hills and this sad little town? I sure as shit wouldn't buy real estate here. Not at a penny an acre.

According to the Wikipedia page for the city of Pine Deep, there were currently two thousand one hundred and nine people living here. In town and on the farms. It was hard to believe. I'd have guessed maybe five, six hundred.

I tried to imagine what it must be like to live in a place like this. It had been devastated by domestic terrorism. It had taken a worse hit than New York on 9/11 in terms of deaths. Maybe worse still when you considered that it hadn't been done by enemies of our country or religious fanatics. This terror was homegrown. It was brother attacking brother. That's some hard shit to accept, hard to get past.

As I drove down the main street, I saw the haunted looks on the faces of the people of Pine Deep. Some looked furtively away, unwilling or unable to meet the eyes of a stranger. Fear, paranoia, shame. Hang any label on it you think will fit.

Others stared at me, their eyes dark and intense, their attention focused and unwavering as I rolled past. I don't think I saw a single smile. I don't think I could blame anyone for being that grim, that detached. I sure as hell would be if this were my town.

I passed the Saul Weinstock Memorial Hospital, but the place was only half-built. Creeper vines had crawled over the stacks of building materials, and there were no lights in any of the windows.

Halfway through town, I saw the sign for the police department. It was a storefront place with big ceramic pots and dead evergreens beside the door. I nosed my car into an angled slot and killed the engine.

The sign on the glass door read:

PINE DEEP POLICE DEPT.
CHIEF MALCOLM CROW

Turn around and go home, said a little voice inside my head.

"Too late for that," I murmured, and got out. As I did, a woman came out of the office. Tall, with short black hair and dark blue eyes. Slim and very pretty in a no-nonsense country way. Around fifty but fighting it and winning. A touch of make-up and a mouth that looked made for smiling, but which wore no smile. She stopped five feet in front of me and gave me an up-and-down appraisal. Impossible to tell what she read from my scuffle of brown hair, JC Penney sports coat over jeans, Payless black sneakers. Probably not much.

But something flickered in her eyes, and she half-turned, opened the door to the police office, and called inside. "He's here."

She left the door ajar.

I pasted on a friendly smile. "Are you with the police?" I asked.

A little smile flickered on her mouth. "I'm married to it."

"Oh. Then you're Mrs. . . . um . . . Crow?" I ventured.

"Val Guthrie. I kept my maiden name." She offered her hand, and we shook. Her hand was hard and dry and strong. She didn't go for a manly bully-boy handshake. She was strong the way women are strong. This one had zero interest in defining herself by comparison to a man. I liked that. I liked her.

"Sam Hunter," I said.

"You're the private investigator?"

"Yes, ma'am."

"Named 'Hunter'?"

"Yes."

"That a stage name or something?"

"No. It's a coincidence, but I've come to embrace the cliché."

That upped the wattage on her smile as she reappraised me. "You're a smartass."

"Says so on my business card. Sam Hunter, Professional Smartass."

She laughed. "You're going to get along fine."

She patted me on the shoulder and, still smiling, walked toward a parked Ford F-250 pickup whose bed was piled high with burlap sacks of seed. I watched her go, admiring both the straightness of her posture and the curves that went with the whole package. Smart, sexy, and powerful. Nice.

I turned to the open office door and wondered what kind of a husband a woman like that would have. My guess would be someone who looked like Thor from the *Avengers* movies. Some big, tanned Nordic son of a bitch with muscles on his muscles and maybe a bit of aw-shucks in his voice. Or one of those redneck giants who bench-press Hereford cows. Probably politically to the right of Sarah Palin. Rural Pennsylvania bears a lot of resemblance in attitude and culture to the less progressive back roads of Mississippi.

As I went in, the man I saw behind the desk was the precise diametric opposite of my guess.

He stood up to meet me, a wide grin on his elfin face. He was shorter than the woman who'd just left—call it five-seven and change. Slight build, curly black hair that had gone mostly gray, a sallow tan crisscrossed with white lines from old scars. His name tag said CROW.

"Mr. Hunter?" he asked, extending his hand.

16

The killer followed the big man back to the road, then hid behind a rhododendron while the man got into a black SUV and drove away. The killer noted the license number, but if this man was what he thought, that plate number would likely be a dead end.

That was fine.

The big man was hunting now.

Hunting him.

The killer wanted to make very sure that the big man found his prey.

17

"Sam Hunter, sir," I replied, taking the chief's hand. For a little guy, he had a good, strong hand. Shooter's callus on his index finger, and a ring of calluses all the way around to his thumb. Only other guy I know with those kinds of hands trained with those Japanese swords. *Katanas.*

"How can we help you?"

"I was asked to come here and—"

Still smiling, Crow interrupted, "Let's see your driver's license, P.I. ticket, and any other ID you'd like to show me. That's it, spread it all out on the counter."

I did as he asked, and he scooped it up and took it over to his desk. He did not offer me a chair. Cops have a right to ask private dicks to jump and to ask how high on the way up; and if we don't jump the right way, they can get a judge to pull our license faster than you can say Sam Spade. At best, P.I.s are an irrelevant fact of life to cops; at worst, we are flies to be swatted. I did not feel like being swatted.

I stood like a schoolboy in the principal's office while he studied my cards and then typed my information into his computer. Crow made a few calls, and I watched his face. He frowned, he grunted, his eyebrows arched. He'd be a lousy poker player. Finally, he sat there, lips pursed, for maybe fifteen seconds. I wondered if he was jerking my chain and decided he probably was. A wiseass comment struggled to get past my lips, but I clenched my teeth and kept it trapped inside.

"Okay," Crow said, rising and crossing to the counter that served as the intake desk. He placed my stuff down and slid it across to me. "No wants, no warrants."

I nodded and put the cards back into my wallet.

"I called Minneapolis P.D. and some buddies in Philly. You don't have a lot of friends out there."

"Hoping to make some here," I said.

He grinned. "Let's see how that works out."

We stood there and smiled at each other for a moment. Then

Crow waved me past the counter to his desk, nodded at the patched and creaking leather guest chair, and sank into a slightly bigger one on the other side.

"Chief," I said, "before we begin—"

"Crow," he corrected.

"Hmm?"

"Everybody calls me Crow. I don't like 'Chief' 'cause it makes me feel like I should be wearing feathers, and I don't like 'Mister' 'cause my dad was Mr. Crow, and he was kind of a dick. So, Crow."

"Fair enough. I'm Sam."

We nodded to seal that.

"Crow, before we begin, I'd like to understand why I'm here."

"Me, too," he said.

"Um . . . what now?"

He went to a Mr. Coffee and poured two cups, handed me one. "You go first. How'd you get here?"

I sucked my teeth for a moment, then decided to tell him the truth. Most of the truth. I left certain parts out, as I'm sure you'll understand.

"Limbus," he murmured, echoing the word.

"They said you reached out to them. That you were looking for some help on a case."

"Is that what they said?"

"More or less. They said the Pine Deep P.D. did. I guess that's you, right?"

"Mostly me. Couple officers hiding somewhere, sitting speed traps, generally fucking off. And my best guy's out at a crime scene."

"Related to this?"

"To be determined."

"Okay," I said, "but *did* you call Limbus or not? Didn't you ask them to bring in an expert?"

"Not exactly."

"Then what?"

He opened his desk drawer and removed a business card, looked at it for a moment, then handed it to me. I didn't need to read it. I already knew what it would say.

LIMBUS, Inc.
~~Are you laid off, downsized, undersized?~~
~~Call us. We employ.~~ 1-800-555-0606
How lucky do you feel?

However, someone had drawn neat straight lines through most of the text.

"Look on the back," he suggested, and I turned it over.

In very neat script, someone had written a note:

We can provide a consultant
familiar with matters of this kind.

Before I could ask, he opened his desk and removed a second card. And a third. They were identical, front and back.

"I found one of these near each of the crime scenes."

"Near?"

Crow studied me for a moment. "Near. One was in my cruiser, apparently placed there *after* I arrived on the scene. My cruiser was locked."

"Ah," I said.

"Ah *what*?"

I explained where I'd found mine.

He gave a sour grunt. "The others showed up pretty much the same way. I even had an officer watch my car. He did, and no one approached it that he could see."

"How sharp is your officer?"

"Sweeney?" Crow's smile was thin and wide and weird. "He's pretty sharp. Nothing gets past him."

"Except someone did."

Crow gave me a crooked smile. "That note on the back. Want to tell me what it means?"

I shrugged.

"Sorry, Sport," said Crow, "but I'm gonna need something more than a shrug. Explain to me how you are an expert."

"I never said I was an expert."

"You're here as a 'consultant,' though."

"Sure. Why not?"

"Exactly what do you consult *on?*"

That was the question I'd known was coming but didn't really know how to answer. I'd hoped that he would have been in some way clued in about me, but it was pretty clear he wasn't. Or maybe, in place of a good poker face, he was a bluffer. If so, I couldn't read him.

So, I reached into my jacket and produced a set of color prints I'd made from the email attachments Cricket had sent me. I spread them out on Crow's desk, neatly, side by side.

"The news reports say these were accidents," I said.

"So do my official reports."

I shrugged. "But we both know different."

He looked at me instead of the pictures. "And you're certain these were murders?"

"I am."

"What makes you so sure?"

"Because," I said, "I've seen these kinds of murders before."

Crow nodded, gathered the photos up and handed them back to me. "So have I."

18

The killer heard another car coming, and he faded deeper into the shadows as a police cruiser came bumping and thumping, trailing a plume of dust.

An hour ago, this same cruiser had been out here, but the officer had abruptly left minutes before the big man had arrived. The killer now understood. The big man had somehow lured the police officer away so he could have a few minutes alone at the crime scene. Now the officer was returning.

The killer shifted downwind so that he could not be detected and then climbed another tree. He settled in, drew his camouflage cape around him, and watched. The officer who got out of the car was not the same one who was here before. That first officer had been a red-neck with a beer gut. This new arrival was lean and hard-muscled. Very tall. With red hair and sunglasses that he never took off, not even when he walked through shadows.

The breeze was blowing past the crime scene toward where the killer hid, and that allowed him to take the officer's scent.

Suddenly all of the alarms inside the killer's mind began to ring.

This officer was not at all what he seemed.

He was something much more.

Something powerful.

Something very like the killer.

Very much like him.

19

Crow told me he wanted to take me to the most recent crime scene. We took his cruiser, which was a battered Ford Interceptor SUV that looked like it hadn't seen the inside of a car wash since Bush was president. As I got in, I peered at the side panel of the door.

"Is that a bullet hole?" I asked.

"Good chance," he said.

I got in. There was a hole on the inside, too. A through-and-through. "You didn't get it fixed?"

He shrugged. "Air conditioner's busted. Gives a nice cross breeze."

"Uh-huh."

As we drove, he talked about everything except the case. The Phillies and the Eagles—teams I didn't give a fuzzy rat's ass about since my heart belongs to the Twins and the Vikings. I said "Uh-huh" a lot. He talked about his wife's farm, which was now the fifth-largest independent garlic farm in Pennsylvania. I asked him if he had kids. He didn't answer and didn't say anything for a couple of miles. Then he started a new conversation about what he liked on TV. As if I hadn't asked the question.

So, fuck it, we talked about TV. *The Walking Dead. Game of*

Thrones. 24. We both liked typical man stuff. Monsters, guns, and boobs. Big surprise. He was a closet fan of *So You Think You Can Dance*. My dirty secret was *Downton Abbey*. Total tough guys.

For most of the drive, we were backtracking the route I'd taken to get to town, but then he made a turn down a small side road. I caught the name on the sign.

DARK HOLLOW ROAD

It was a name I'd seen in the news stories. There had been murders here. And that murdered rich guy, Ubel Griswold, had lived in Dark Hollow.

I asked him about Griswold.

And Crow goddamn nearly drove us off the road and into a tree.

20

The killer watched the big police officer.

The cop spent several minutes taking photographs and measurements.

Then the officer abruptly stopped, stiffened, and turned in a slow circle. It was very much like what the other man had done earlier.

Except the officer raised his head and sniffed the air.

21

The Ford slewed around and kicked up gravel and leaves, barraging a weathered fence and nearly knocking the slats out. He threw it in park and wheeled on me, took a fistful of my tie and jerked me forward so that we were inches apart.

"How the *hell* do you know about Ubel Griswold?" he snarled.

His face was insane. I mean it. Like bugfuck nuts. There was nothing in those eyes but a wild madness that scared the living shit out of me.

The moment stretched, and I could feel the heat of each of his ragged breaths.

When I didn't answer, he leaned an inch closer. "Listen, dickhead, this is not a game you want to play. Not with me."

"What the fuck?" I said. And I said it slowly.

Crow shoved me back against the door. His hand rested on his holstered pistol. "I'm going to ask once more. Real nice. And believe me when I tell you that this is not an opportunity for wiseass comments or calling for a lawyer. This is you and me here in this truck, and we are going to have an open and frank conversation, am I making myself crystal fucking clear?"

I held my breath.

I had an escape hatch for when things really hit the fan, but I didn't want to use it. Not on a stranger, not on a cop. And not on someone who might actually be an innocent. Not sane, by any stretch, but probably not a villain.

Besides, if the wolf came out to play, there was no way to ever reclaim the moment.

So I had that ace but knew I couldn't play it. I'd be alive but in jail, or in the wind, and I didn't want to live the rest of my life that way. On the other hand, he was a cop, a stranger, and clearly, a fucking lunatic. Or something close to it. He could mess up my entire life.

When I didn't answer, he snapped, "Do you understand me?"

I nodded. "Loud and clear. It's your game, man. Just calm down."

"I'll calm down when I have a reason to. And don't you tell me what to do. You're on the wrong side of the badge to do that. Now . . . let's try this one last time—how do you know Ubel Griswold?"

"I don't know him."

"How do you know *about* him?"

"From Google. I looked him up."

"Why? What's your connection to him?"

I said, "Limbus."

He frowned. "What?"

"Limbus. That's how I know about Griswold."

"No," he said, shaking his head. "Give me more than that."

You have to develop good instincts about people if you're going to shoot hoops in the kinds of playgrounds I frequent. My nerves were telling me this guy was half a keg short of a six-pack. My senses told me that he was scared out of his goddamn mind. And that he was primed to attack. I could smell the adrenaline. I could almost taste it.

My gut, though . . .

My gut told me he really was one of the good guys.

Call it instinct, call it whatever.

I held up my hands in a no-problem way.

"Okay," I said. "I'll tell you, but you're scaring the shit out of me with that gun."

He looked down at his hand, at the fact that he'd unsnapped the holster. He made a little grunting sound. Surprise at what his hand was doing while he wasn't watching.

"Fuck," he said.

"Fuck," I agreed.

Didn't snap the holster though. Instead, he laid his hand on his thigh. A token gesture that lowered my blood pressure by maybe half a point.

"Talk," he said.

I took a breath, and told him about Limbus, about Cricket, and about the envelope of money.

Crow didn't say a word the entire time. Didn't ask a question. Instead, he sat there and chewed on his lower lip and looked strange. Older. Confused. Tired. He took his hand off his lap and rubbed his eyes, then spent almost a full minute looking out the window.

"Shit," he said.

I cleared my throat. "Don't suppose you want to tell me what the hell's going on? 'Cause, Chief, I'm pretty sure I've never been this confused before."

"Welcome to Pine Deep," he muttered.

"Huh?"

"Nothing."

We sat there for another minute. Doesn't sound like a lot of time until you're peeling the seconds off one at a time while seated next to an armed crazy person.

Out of the blue, Crow asked, "What do you know about the Trouble?"

I shrugged. "What everyone else knows. Maybe a little less. I mean, sure, it was big news for a while. Domestic terrorism, over ten thousand people dead. Worst day in U.S. history. Got that. I didn't hear Ubel Griswold's name in any of that, though, except in a footnote about a coincidence. Him getting killed thirty years to the day before the Trouble here."

He nodded. "Yeah. You ever see the movie they made? *Hellnight?* Or read the book?"

"No. I read a review when it came out. Saw it on Redbox but didn't get it. I heard they changed the story around. Made something supernatural out of it."

"Something like that."

"So? Why are we talking about it?" I asked.

He looked out the window at the cornfields to the right side of the road and the deep, dark forest on the other.

"If you weren't here because of that Limbus card, I wouldn't be saying what I'm about to say," said Crow.

"Um . . . okay."

"The story about the white supremacists spiking the town's water, driving everybody crazy?"

"Yeah?"

"Kind of true."

"*Kind* of?"

"Kind of. It was a cover story."

"Wait," I said, "are you saying there was a government cover-up?"

Crow shook his head. "Not exactly. Not the way you're thinking. The feds *did* cover some things up, but there was a group of white supremacist dickheads operating in town, and they did, in fact, dump a bunch of hallucinogens into the water. Fritzed everyone out. They also planted bombs to blow up the bridges, knock down the cell towers, take out all phone and cable service, and generally turn the main part of town into World War III."

"I don't—"

"That happened," he said. "But the tricky thing is that all of that was itself a cover for something else."

"Wait, the white-trash dickheads were covering up for someone? Who? I don't understand. And, if that was a cover-up, why'd the feds use that story, too?"

He smiled at the windshield. No visible humor in it, though.

"Because the cover story was something everyone could sell. Domestic terrorism. White power. Racism. Drugs in the water. That's doable. That makes sense. That's something, scary as it was, tragic as it was, people could live with. The rest of the country, I mean. Maybe the rest of the world. They could live with that story, especially since all of those militia assholes died that night."

"You lost me a couple of turns back, man."

"No," he said, "I just haven't gotten to the part where it makes sense. Or maybe I should say I haven't gotten to the truth. 'Cause unless you're who or what I think you are, this isn't going to sound like the truth, and it isn't going to make any fucking sense at all."

"You are scaring the living piss out of me here," I said.

He nodded. "Yeah, being scared is absolutely the appropriate response. I was scared then. More scared than I've ever been in my life. But I have to tell you, Mr. Hunter, that I am starting to get that scared again."

"Why?"

"Because I'm afraid that what was happening then is happening now. That it's happening again."

"Okay . . . but what did happen back then? If there was a cover story, then what was it covering up?"

That's when he finally turned to me, and I saw all sorts of dark lights glimmering in his eyes. If he'd looked crazy before, then he looked absolutely lost now.

"The whole thing, the drugs, the violence, all of that was done to hide the fact that there were monsters in Pine Deep."

I had to take a moment on that. "When you say . . . 'monsters' . . . ?"

"I mean monsters. Vampires and . . ."

When he didn't finish, I pushed him.

"And what?"

He looked me right in the eye.

"And werewolves."

10

To which I said, "Oh shit."

To which he replied, "Yeah."

11

We sat there.

Talk about the elephant in the room.

I said, "You're looking at me funny."

He said, "I guess I am."

"Am I going to regret asking?"

"Depends on how this conversation goes," he said. "Could play out a bunch of different ways."

"You're making a lot of assumptions. You know how that usually turns out."

He shrugged. I noticed he'd placed his hand on his lap again. Very close to the gun.

Again.

Balls.

"I'm going to say a word," he said. "It's a word that the Limbus guy used. He didn't explain what it was. He figured I already knew. Which I do."

"Okay."

"I'm going to say it, and then you're going to tell me the first thing that comes to mind. Fair enough?"

"I don't like games," I said.

"Not a game."

I said, "Shit."

Then I said, "What's the word."

His hand moved an inch closer to his pistol.

Let's face it, I expected the word to start with a *w*.

Instead, he used a different word. A lot more precise. A word that changed the entire dynamic between us.

He said, "*Benandanti.*"

I looked at him, at his face, his eyes. At the expression he wore.

I took a breath and said, "Yes."

He closed his eyes.

And said, "Thank God."

12

Without another word, he turned in his seat, restarted the car, put it in drive, and hit the gas. We drove for maybe a mile before he said anything. I sure as hell wasn't starting any conversations.

Crow said, "Tell me."

"I don't talk about this with anyone."

"Tough. Tell me."

"You used the word," I said. "You know what it means."

"Sure," he said, "I know what the word means. 'Goodwalker.' I want to know what it means to you."

"I think you already know."

"That's not what I mean. I want some background on you. Because if the stuff that's happening is what I think it is, then there's only two sides. Black and white. No gray area at all."

I nodded. He was being very cagey about it. So was I. We were dancing around it because, hell, this really isn't the kind of conversation people have.

I mean, I do, but only at home, when I'm around my aunts and my grandmother and my cousin. They're like me. They're exactly like me. Families tend to keep secrets like this. I've always kept it to myself. Usually, the only people who find out about our family secret do so on their last and worst day.

On the other hand, I think I can say for certain that the people at Limbus—whoever or whatever the fuck they are—know. Why else would I be here? Cricket knew that I'd recognize the bite and claw patterns in those photos.

He was right.

"This has to go two ways," I said. "If I show you mine, you got to show me yours."

"You comfortable with the way that came out?" he asked.

"You know what I mean."

"Yeah. And . . . yes, this is a two-way street. Kind of has to be, don't you think?"

So, after another mile, I began talking. Trees whipped past. The sky above us was blotted out by the canopy of fall foliage.

"It's a family thing," I said. "Going back like . . . forever. My bunch is more or less Irish-English mutts. Been here since five minutes after the Mayflower. But we have roots in Italy going back to Etruscan times. Like six, seven hundred years B.C., you dig?"

He nodded.

"We weren't always what you'd call saints, but I guess in our own way, we've always been on the side of the angels. Not literally, 'cause that would be a little New Agey, even for me. But in spirit. White hats, no matter how battered and stained those hats were."

"Nice to know," he said, then threw me a curveball. "Any relation to Theiss?"

I took a moment on that, then figured in for a penny, in for a pound. "Direct descent," I said.

"Wow."

"Wow," I agreed. "Not sure which version of the story you heard. The one that makes the history books is that back in 1692, in Jurgenburg, Livonia, a *Benandanti* named Theiss was arrested and put on trial for being . . . well, for being what he was."

"Say the word," said Crow. He cut me a glance out of the corner of his eye. "Really . . . say it."

I sighed. "Okay. Theiss was arrested for being a werewolf."

He took a deep breath, held it, let it out; then he picked up the story I'd started. "Theiss's defense was that at night, he and the members of his order—"

"Family," I corrected.

"Family. Okay. He and the members of his family transformed into werewolves in order to fight demons and other kinds of evil. Witches, pernicious spirits. Like that. He was whipped for superstition and idolatry and let go."

"To paraphrase you," I said, "that's the story they sold to the press."

"And the real story?"

"He was tortured for a long damn time. They wanted him to confess to being an apostate of Hell and an enemy of God. But . . . Theiss was a tough old motherfucker. They tried it all on him. Thumbscrews, the rack, dunking. The church is nothing if not enthusiastic."

"They couldn't break him, though?" prompted Crow.

"No. In the end, they let him go, because they figured that he couldn't possibly endure all of the torture if he didn't have God's grace. Yada, yada, yada. So, they let him go. They even gave him a nickname. You seem to know the story. What'd they call him?"

Crow smiled thinly. "The Hound of God."

"Right. The thing is, a lot of the history books get it wrong. They don't always connect the *Benandanti* with werewolves. Mostly 'cause there are a lot of New Age lamebrains who use that name like the Celts use 'wicca.' There are plenty of *Benandanti* in Europe today who come in to bless a new baby or sage a new house. Like that."

"Don't mock," said Crow. "They might be doing something useful."

"Maybe they are, but that doesn't make them true *Benandanti*."

"Ah," he said, "pride goeth before a fall."

"Yeah, well, fuck you, too."

"Point taken."

We both smiled at that. Not sure what it meant, though.

"So," I said, "are you going to ask me the obvious question?"

"Do I need to?"

"I don't know. You tell me?"

"Sam," he said, "I knew what you were when you walked into my office."

"Why? Because Cricket told you?"

"Nope."

"Then how? I didn't wear my *I'm A Werewolf, Ask Me How* button today."

He didn't answer. We rounded a bend, and on the other side was a parked police cruiser, lots of crime scene tape strung between tree trunks, and a big kid in a deputy's uniform leaning against the fender of the car. Maybe twenty-two. He was massive. Six-four, with more muscles than is necessary on any human being. He had his arms folded over his chest, a kitchen match between his teeth, and a scowl as dour as a country parson at a peep show.

I took one look at him, and I knew why Crow knew what I was when he met me. This was his deputy.

And damn if he wasn't playing for the same team as me.

Shit.

13

The killer climbed another tree and hunkered down in the crotch, his body completely concealed by camouflage, his face painted green and brown. He had a pair of binoculars whose lenses were covered with a filter that would not reflect light. His clothes were daubed with a paste made from ground bird feathers, squirrel urine, owl feces, and insect larvae. Not even a bloodhound could smell him through that.

Not even one of his brothers could smell him.

Not unless they were very close, and the killer was six hundred feet away and fifty feet up a towering oak.

He watched the three figures below.

The smallest of the three men was strange. The killer knew him, had seen him many times in the town. Had read about him on the Internet. Chief of Police. Alcoholic. Husband to a farmer.

And, very likely, a killer, too. A man who was more dangerous than his size and age suggested.

The biggest of the three men was even harder to categorize. He was a monster, even by the killer's standards. Man, wolf, and some-

thing else. There was a darkness in him that ran all the way to the soul. The killer feared him for reasons he could not name.

The third man looked weak but wasn't. Middle-sized, middle-aged, thin, and haggard. He looked like a salesman, and not a successful one. He looked tired and frail.

But the killer could smell the wolf in him.

It was a strong wolf.

A true hunter.

The killer wanted to fight him. To see which of them was stronger. To see which of them deserved to live.

He would have to arrange that.

He knew, in fact, that he would have to face all of these men. And maybe the big man he'd seen earlier. He would have to kill them all.

He . . . and his family.

The slaughter would be so delicious.

14

We sniffed each other.

I'm not proud of it.

And don't get the wrong idea. We didn't sniff each other's asses. We're strange but we're not weird. We stood a few feet apart and took the air. His expression never flickered. Him I definitely wouldn't play poker with. If he was like me, he was cataloging everything he could from my smell. I sure as hell was.

He was bigger and stronger than me, but the wolf in him was younger. A lot younger. It was more savage than mine. Less controlled. I could feel it wanting to come out. The kid had some iron goddamn control, though.

"Okay, okay," said Crow, "you two are weirding me out. So cut the shit."

"He's the consultant?"

"Yes. Officer Mike Sweeney, meet Sam Hunter, and vice versa. Shake hands and mind your manners. Both of you."

He didn't budge, so I took the cue and offered my hand. Sweeney looked at it for a moment, then without haste, took it. And held it.

"Crow," he said, "this guy had blood on him. Been in a fight. Couple of different guys. No . . . three different guys."

My mouth went dry. No one's ever read me that way. The way I usually read people.

Crow came and stood beside Mike. "I won't ask if Mike's telling the truth," he said, "'cause Mike doesn't make those kinds of mistakes."

"Private matter," I said.

"Which you're going to tell us about," said Crow.

I shook my head. "I plead the fifth."

"No," said Crow.

"No," said Mike.

"Then we have a problem," I said. "I didn't come here to be blindsided by Sheriff Andy and Barney Fife."

"Who?" asked Mike.

Crow said, "Sam, I think it's fair to say that a lot of what's going on here isn't going to make it into any official report. If you're going to work with us, then it has to be by being straight up."

"You could arrest me."

"Pretend for a moment that I won't."

We stood there inside that moment, none of us budging.

"He killed someone," said Mike. "He changed and he killed someone."

Crow nodded. "Is that true?"

I shrugged.

"Did they need killing?" asked Mike.

I tilted my head to one side. "You hear about that case last year? Guy doping little girls and making rape porn?"

"I heard about it."

I shrugged again.

"There's not going to be a trial," said Crow, "is there?"

"Doesn't look like it."

Mike Sweeney took a step closer and sniffed again. Then he nodded and stepped back. "More than one guy."

"Even total assholes have friends."

"Had," he corrected.

"Had," I agreed.

He smiled then. A very small, thin smile. It was the kind of smile nobody—and I mean nobody—would ever want to see. There was no trace of humanity in it. No fragment of mercy.

"Fuck 'em," he said. "You're here as a consultant?"

"Yeah."

"Then consult."

With that, he turned his back on me and walked toward the crime scene.

Crow sighed.

"What was that all about?" I asked.

"Mike had a complicated childhood."

"I can imagine."

He shook his head. "No, I really don't think you could."

He turned to follow Mike, and I, feeling more awkward than I had since my first middle school dance, trudged along in his wake.

15

I ducked under the yellow crime scene tape and moved into a space that was dense with shadows. A motorcycle was wrapped around a tree. Front wheel torn open, gas tank ruptured, seat dislodged, headlight glass twinkling in a thousand pieces. There was dried blood everywhere, though for once I had to rely more on sight than smell because of the presence of the spilled gasoline.

Mike took an iPad from a briefcase he'd laid on the edge of a plastic tarp near the crash site, called up an image folder, and handed it to me.

"The body was transported last night. These are the photos."

I looked at them one at a time. High-res digital photography is very stark, very detailed. Artless and cruel. The body of a man lay partly atop the bike, partly on the grass. And partly fifteen feet away. He was literally torn to pieces. It was a very brutal kind of thing, and a very familiar kind of thing.

I tried my Richard Dreyfuss line again.

"This was no boating accident."

Crow chuckled. Mike didn't.

"Sam used to be a cop," Crow said to Mike. To me, he said, "Walk the scene. Tell me what you see."

I did. There were tire tracks that curved off the road and right into the tree. There was dead grass around the spilled gas. There was blood spatter. There was the ruined machine.

"This is bullshit," I said.

Crow and Mike exchanged a quick look.

"Walk us through it," said Crow.

We went back to the road, and I reconstructed it for them. "Here's what is supposed to have happened," I said. "It rained last night, right?"

"Until ten."

"Ten. Okay. And when was the crash?"

"Passing motorist called it in at ten-twenty-one."

"Uh-huh. So, the story is this. Guy's tooling down this black-as-fuck road in the middle of a rainstorm at night. Loses control, goes into a skid, wraps his bike around the tree at high speed, and goes splat."

Crow put a stick of gum into his mouth and began folding the little foil wrapper with great care. "Uh-huh," he said.

"Bike had to be going at high speed, and for some reason the driver didn't throttle down when he lost control."

"Uh-huh."

"To do that much damage, he had to be going at a hundred or better."

"Uh-huh."

I looked at him. "All of which amounts to a yard-high pile of total bullshit."

"Why?"

"Let's start with the road. Why would anyone be on this road at night? Does it even go anywhere?"

"It's a fire access road, and it's used by the forestry service," said Mike. "Kids come up here to make out."

"Not in the rain," I said. "And not on a bike. It's not a dirt bike, either."

"No."

"In the photos, the guy's wearing jeans and a sweatshirt. In the rain?"

Crow spread his hands.

"Where's his helmet?"

"He wasn't wearing one," said Mike.

"Again I say, in the rain?"

No one bothered to answer that. I squatted by the tire tracks. "No way these were made during the storm. Look at the ridges in the mud. Even if it was drizzling, they'd be smeared more than this."

They nodded.

"And over here," I said, moving from the road onto the dirt, to a point halfway to the impact point. "See how deep it is here? The bike accelerated right here. Right when the bike was lined up with the tree."

They nodded.

I went over to the bike now and bent over it, touching various points on the fractured frame. "This is all wrong. It looked like the bike was starting to tilt away from the line of impact, like the driver was trying to avoid collision by ditching sideways. That would be the natural thing, even if you lose control in the dark. But look at the underside of the frame, right here. That's crumpled the wrong way. It should be pushed up, but it's pushed in. That means the bike, while slewing sideways, was starting to stand back up."

"And what does that tell you?" asked Crow.

"It tells me that whoever was riding this bike jumped off right before it hit. Jumped off with a hell of a lot of force, enough to nearly stand the bike up while it was falling over. If that was the case, then the body should have landed over here. He wouldn't have been *on* the bike when it hit. At most, he'd have gotten a leg trapped under it, but he wouldn't have hit the tree hard enough to be splattered."

Crow said, "That's pretty good. What else?"

I bent over the bike again and spent some time with it. I've seen a lot of car and motorcycle accidents, accidental and criminal. I've also seen some faked accidents before. I've been in court plenty of times to hear expert testimony on the physics of high-speed vehicular impacts. What I was seeing here didn't square with my understanding of cause and effect. I said as much to them.

"This isn't something you probably want to put in your official report," I began, "but I think someone *bent* this bike around the tree."

"Bent," said Crow.

"Bent."

"That would take a lot of muscle."

"It would."

"Could *you* do it?"

I thought about it for a moment. "No. Under certain, um, circumstances, I could mangle it pretty good, but some of these bends . . . no. I couldn't."

"Which brings us to our problem, Mr. Consultant."

"Yeah."

"Mike and I walked this site together and we came up with the same read on it that you gave us. Nice work, by the way."

"Thanks."

"Once the forensics guys were gone, I asked Mike to see if he could duplicate those bends."

I stared at him. And at Mike, who continued to make his matchstick bob slowly up and down. "Well," I said, "that must have been interesting."

"It was instructive," admitted Crow. "Mike was able to bend it a little. But that was with the frame already fatigued and cracked. And trust me when I say this, Mike is a very, very strong young man."

"Knock it off, Crow," said Mike.

"I'm making a point here."

Mike looked at the trees and sighed slowly.

"So," continued Crow, "what I'm wondering is whether you and Mike working together—under, as you say, certain circumstances—could do that kind of damage."

It was an interesting question.

We all stood there and thought about it.

I shook my head first. Then Mike.

"No," I said, "not even together."

Crow nodded. "What I thought. But someone did. And either it was one very, very, *very* strong son of a bitch—someone way outside of the normal range. Or . . . whatever passes for normal with you guys."

I said nothing.

"Or we're dealing with something even worse. Something that's stronger than two werewolves."

I said, "Well, shit."

Mike Sweeney grinned. "Yeah, and isn't that interesting as all shit?"

16

The killer moved away from the kill site.

He was confused by the presence of two others like him. That was wrong. That made no sense. There should only be one wolf in these woods. The big, red-haired one. The one who seemed to belong here.

But now this other one was here.

The killer did not like it.

He wasn't afraid, though. Fear was not a factor in the killer's life. Not now, anyway. He was beyond that now.

He faded into the woods and vanished.

17

"The victim," I said. "The wounds in those photos . . . what's the coroner going to say about it?"

"Exactly what I want him to say," said Crow.

"He, um . . . knows?"

"He's the coroner for Pine Deep, Pennsylvania. He's come to accept certain realities."

"Shit."

"Tell me about it."

"But we all know those aren't injuries sustained in a crash."

"My guess," said Crow, "is that the body was torn up pretty good by whoever our Big Bad is, and then dropped off a roof. There are visible impact injuries."

"Unless they're stupid, they'd have to know that an autopsy would—"

"We can assume they didn't choose Pine Deep by accident."

"Meaning you can keep secrets?"

"Meaning we've had to keep secrets."

Mike snorted but didn't say anything.

I walked past the scene into the woods and stood there for a while, letting the smells and sounds tell me whatever they wanted to share. After a few moments, Crow and Mike joined me.

"Shame it rained so hard last night," Crow said. "No scent to follow."

I glanced at Mike. "You tried?"

He shrugged.

"Sure. Lots of scents, but they're all mingled. Rain, you know?"

I nodded. "Makes me wonder if the rain was part of an agenda. Not just to fake the slip-and-slide crash, but to wash away any useful spoor."

Mike grunted and nodded.

"What were the other crash sites like?" I asked.

"Similar," said Crow. "In each case, there was some kind of accident—car wreck, farm accident, house fire—but the details don't completely square. Especially the pathology. Someone's killing people and doing a slightly better than half-ass job covering it up."

"Yeah, but how would a regular police department be reacting to this?"

Crow nodded his approval. "I did some checking to see if there are any similarly troubled cases."

"And?"

"There were four suspicious fatal accidents in upstate New York last August, in the Finger Lakes district. All ultimately ruled accidental, but with notations about anomalies in the case files. Another two in Cape May, New Jersey in December. Same conclusions. And three out near Pittsburgh this past May. The pattern is the same. A couple of the investigating detectives have been sharing case information in hopes of getting somewhere, but there's so little conventional evidence that they keep hitting a wall."

"Because they don't have certain specialized knowledge," I suggested.

"Yup."

"This is interstate," I said. "That makes it federal. A serial killer?"

"Maybe."

"Shame there isn't really something like *The X-Files*. Fox Mulder would go nuts for something like this."

"Can't call him, can't call the Ghostbusters," he said. "If wishes were horses."

We stood there and looked at the huge forest. Oaks and sycamores and pines, with underbrush so dense it seemed impenetrable.

"What do you know about the vics?" I asked.

Crow fielded that. "No obvious connections. Not between the victims here in Pine Deep or between ours and those in other towns. I have someone doing background checks—a computer geek friend of mine—but so far, we got bupkis."

"Balls," I said.

"Balls," he agreed.

18

The killer ran through the darkening woods, exulting in the power that rippled through his muscles. The solidity of his bones. The song of hunger that shouted in his blood.

He would find something to kill.

Anything.

Animal.
Human.
Even a bear.
Anything that would scream.
Thinking red thoughts, he ran.

19

We spent the rest of the afternoon going over the crime scene, which yielded a lot of information, none of which seemed particularly useful. Then we went back to the station, and Crow walked me through the rest of the case file. Again, lots of forensic information—photos, hair and fiber samples, casts of tire tracks, coroner's reports, the works.

Bottom line?

Well, shit. We knew there was one or more werewolf killing people.

They were doing it in bunches and, apparently, moving on.

Motive? Unknown.

Identity? Unknown.

Anything of actual use?

Impossible to say.

"Have you reached out to the FBI about this?" I asked.

"I filed a report."

"And—?"

"You familiar with the word *obfuscation*?"

"Ah."

"What about your own investigation? Do you have any leads?"

"Beyond guesswork on the nature of the killers?"

"Beyond that, yes."

"Nope."

"Oh."

"But," he said, "I've been hearing about strangers in town."

"What kind of strangers?"

"Unknown. I have my people running that down right now. All I know is that there have been a few out-of-towners around. One of them was over at the Scarecrow Inn, asking questions about the accident. And either the same guy or a different guy asking questions at some of the farms."

"You have a description on him?"

"Big, blond guy. The one local I talked to said he looked 'mean.' "

"That's it?"

"Getting information from stubborn farm-country folk is like pulling your own teeth. You'll get it, but there's a lot of unpleasant effort involved."

"Ah. This guy flash a badge of any kind?"

"Not so far."

"You think he's a fed?"

"Maybe. Who else would be asking questions?"

I thought about it. "Could be another P.I., maybe hired by the family of one of the victims."

"Our vics were locals."

"A vic from another town."

Crow pursed his lips, nodded. "Maybe. I'll bet a shiny nickel it's a fed."

"There's another possibility."

"What's that?"

"Could be someone related to the killings, asking around to see what the locals know."

"Or suspect," he suggested.

"Or suspect," I agreed.

We poked at it for another couple of minutes and got nowhere. Then I suggested we retire to the local bar and drown our sorrows in some beers. Crow smiled and shook his head.

"Gave up drinking. I go to meetings now."

"Balls."

"Mike doesn't drink, either."

"He in the same twelve-step?"

"No. He's a purity freak. Organic foods, no drugs, no alcohol. Won't even take an aspirin."

"How come?"

Crow sucked his teeth for a moment. "He has some health concerns. He wants to make sure he stays ahead of them."

"Like . . . ?"

"Like it's his business and there's no second half to this discussion." He said it pleasantly enough, but there was a finality to it.

"Well, shit," I said. "*I* need a beer. Maybe six or eight of them."

I left him at his office and walked up the street until I found a place called the Scarecrow Inn. It wasn't exactly a dive bar. Dive is an active word. This was more like *dove*. Past tense. Dark as pockets. Bunch of little tables with old wooden chairs that didn't match. Visible ass-wear on the stools. Sawdust on the floor, like they do down south. Half the people were ignoring the NO SMOKING sign, including a table full of fat guys with cigars. A wooden bar that was probably two hundred years old, and a bartender who looked to have been here since the place was built. Tall, cadaverous, comprehensively wrinkled. Big jar of hard-boiled eggs by the beer taps. Country music on the jukebox. Travis Tritt, I think, but I'm not a country fan, so what do I know.

I found an empty stool, ordered chili and a schooner of Yuengling to go with it. Dug into a bowl of peanuts while I was waiting.

Crow let me take the case file, so I made my way through the chili and two beers while reading every single word. I had a few pages of notes, mostly outside-chance connections I'd run down when I was in front of a computer again. I'd brought my iPad, but—big surprise—there was no Wi-Fi in the Scarecrow Inn. Too modern for them. They're probably still grousing about those newfangled electric lights.

As I read, I became very slowly and subtly aware that I was being watched. At first I passed it off as the usual stranger-in-town thing, but then my spider sense really began tingling. So, I used taking a sip of beer to check the room out in the mirror behind the bar. Everyone was a stranger, so that wasn't very helpful. There were about two dozen people in the place, either dressed for work on a farm or in casual clothes.

Then I spotted the two people who didn't belong.

They were seated alone at tables on opposite sides of the place, and they were so totally different from each other that it looked like they were here to make a statement. White guy, black guy. White guy was big in a jock ballplayer way. Not big like Mike Sweeney or the goons I danced with yesterday. Muscular, mid-thirties, blond. All-American looks. Kind of like the guy who plays Captain America in the movies. Mean-looking son of a bitch, though. Could be a cop, could be a soldier. Could be a freelance shooter. Something very dangerous about him. I could tell that right off. Sat there with half a smile on his face, nursing a beer, using the same mirror I was using to watch the other guy and, every once in a while, me.

The other guy was a black twenty-something. Short, skinny, bookish, with thick glasses and a fringe of beard. Not the only black guy I'd seen in Pine Deep, but one of maybe three or four. Gave off a pop-culture geek vibe.

The Geek was looking at me; the Jock was looking at him. And me.

I adjusted the way I was sitting so my gun was a little easier to reach.

The Geek caught me looking at him and looked away.

Then he looked back.

He did that a couple of times, and I kept looking at him until he caught and finally held my stare. I nodded. After a long five-count, he nodded back.

So, I figured fuck it. I picked up my beer and walked over to his table. For a moment I thought he was going to bolt. He sat straight as a rake handle and looked up at me. I'm not that big, and I'm not what you'd call physically imposing. I've been told, however, that I give off a certain vibe. At times.

Like now.

He cut a look to the front door and then back at me. At close range, I figured him closer to early twenties.

But here's the thing.

At close range, I could tell something about him I couldn't tell from across a smoky bar.

The kid had a certain scent.

A familiar scent. The kind I spent a lot of time every morning, with shampoo, skin creams, and cologne trying to mask.

A smell most people can't smell.

Except guys like Mike Sweeney.

He looked up at me, and before I could even ask, he said, "I think we need to talk."

"Yeah," I said. "I think we'd better."

"Not here."

I nodded to the door. "Let's go."

20

The killer smelled the hitchhiker before he saw her.

She smelled young.

She smelled afraid.

He knew that she would taste wonderful.

He knew that she would scream.

The young ones always screamed. They have so much to lose.

He raced down a hill and up the other side, then down again to the road. This was a lonely stretch. A stupid place for anyone to hitchhike. She couldn't have known that, or she wouldn't have come this way.

21

I stood aside to let him go first. If this was some kind of elaborate setup, I didn't want to be the first guy through the door.

It wasn't.

The kid stopped in the middle of the pavement, hands in his pockets. He wore a long black coat over jeans and a T-shirt with the words OBSCURE POP-CULTURE REFERENCE stenciled on it. He looked nervous. Maybe scared.

"There's a park up the street," he said, and we began walking that way.

"Let's start with the basics," I said. "Name?"

He hesitated.

I said, "Would you rather I held you down and stole your wallet?"

"Antonio," he said. "Antonio Jones."

"Real name?"

"Sure. Why?"

"Sounds like a stage name."

He shrugged. "Antonio Jones."

"Fair enough. I'm Sam Hunter."

"You're a cop?"

"Not anymore. Private investigator," I said as we crossed the street. There were only two traffic lights in town, and they both blinked yellow continually. Either they were trying for a Twin Peaks thing, or all small towns are creepy like that. Yellow means *caution*, so I figured a subtext was implied. Besides, it was that kind of a day.

Antonio said, "Working for the cops, though?"

"Why do you want to know?"

"I saw you with Chief Crow and Iron Mike."

"'Iron Mike'?"

"That's what people used to call him. In school, I mean. When he was little. Before the, um . . ."

"Before the Trouble?"

"Before that, yeah."

"Why? Was he always a bodybuilder?"

"Huh? Oh . . . no. Mike used to be in his head all the time. Always dreaming up stuff. One day he'd be a Jedi, the next he'd be Sheriff Rick. Or Conan. Whatever. He spent a lot of time like that. Playing by himself. Daydreaming in school. Not sure if he started calling himself Iron Mike or the other kids did."

"You went to school with him?"

He shook his head. "Two years behind."

We crossed a side street and entered the park. Like most of the town of Pine Deep, the park was seedy, untended, and dark. Broken slats in the benches. Overflowing trash can. Beer bottles lying among the weeds. Indifferent lighting.

"Nice place for a mugging," I said to my new friend.

He stopped and looked at me. "I know," he said.

Which is when I felt the icy mouth of a gun barrel press into the base of my skull.

"Don't try anything funny," said a male voice. "And I'm pretty sure we both know what I mean by 'funny.'"

22

The killer stalked her because stalking was fun.

One game was to see how close to the edge of the woods he could get without the hitchhiker seeing him. Then to make small, odd sounds so that she became aware of something. *But unaware of what was in those shadowy woods.*

That game was fun.

Then he changed his own rules. He ran ahead and stepped out of the woods. Very briefly. Just long enough for the girl to see him. A quick glance; then he was gone.

The way her lithe young body stiffened was very appealing. She had long legs and long hair and tiny little breasts. She was maybe sixteen, but young for it. Bruises on her face. Running away from a heavy-handed father, perhaps.

The girl stood there, uncertain, without a plan and without a direction, staring in the direction of the big, dark thing that had watched her from the road ahead.

She turned around, considering the road she'd walked. It was empty, and it led back in a direction she could not go. Not if something had been bad enough to put her out alone on a road like this.

The girl waited for almost five full minutes, looking at the road, looking under the trees, seeing nothing because the killer allowed her nothing to see. Not even when she was looking directly toward where he crouched. She had human eyes, and they were so weak.

He waited until she began walking again. Hesitantly at first, and then at a rapid clip. The girl wanted to be past this stretch of road.

The killer circled around and came out of the woods behind her. He crept onto the asphalt and moved up behind her. Taking his time, waiting for that exquisite moment when the girl would inevitably turn to check behind her.

That was a new game.

He loved the way this one would end.

23

I stood absolutely still.

No matter how fast I can do the change, it's not fast enough to dodge a bullet. Besides, little known fact about werewolves. Head shots? Pretty much does it. Head shots will pretty much flip the switch on everything. Vampires, zombies, me.

So, no, I didn't try anything funny.

I stood there.

"You carrying?" the voice asked.

"Shoulder holster," I told him.

"Take it out with two fingers. Hand it to Antonio."

I did. Antonio took it like it was radioactive. He looked scared and nervous and embarrassed. If this was a mugging, it wasn't following the right pattern.

"What else?" asked the guy with the gun.

"Blackjack. Rear pocket."

"Okay. Remove it the same way. Ditto for your wallet. Hand them to the kid."

"Got thirty bucks in my wallet," I said, just to see how he'd react.

"Cute. See that bench? Put your hands in your pants pockets and go sit down. Do it real slow and we'll stay friends."

I did what he asked, and as I turned to sit, I got my first look at him. He was an All-American jock type. Six-two or so. Blond hair, blue eyes, white smile. Looked healthy, but there was something in his eyes. Like maybe there was something freaky going on behind them. Something crazy, something dangerous. Something very, very dangerous. I discreetly sniffed, but his scent was one hundred percent human.

Not a wolf, but definitely an alpha.

"What's the play?" I asked.

He ignored me and spoke to Antonio. "You sure this guy's playing for the same team as you?"

Antonio paused, sniffed the air in my direction, paused again. "Pretty sure."

"Check his ID."

The kid did that. "Sam Hunter," he said, reading my driver's license. "Oh, hey. He has a private investigator's license."

"Read me the numbers."

He did.

The guy with the gun held his Beretta 92F in a rock-steady hand. He looked at me, taking stock. "Okay, Mr. Hunter," he said, "we're going to have us a nice chat."

"Uh-uh," I said. "I showed you mine, now you show me yours. Who the hell are you?"

"What, you don't think this is a mugging?"

I snorted.

"What would you say if I told you I was a cop?"

I shrugged. "You look the type. I used to be a cop."

"Where?"

"Minneapolis."

"What happened?"

"Got kicked out."

"Why?"

"I don't play well with others."

"Other cops?"

I shrugged again. "It's possible a couple of perps got dented while resisting."

"What kind of perps? This a racial thing?" he asked.

"No," I said. "I don't like bullies. Not too crazy about guys who hurt women and kids."

I watched his eyes while I said that. You can tell a lot from the way a guy reacts. Dickheads tend to grin. Closet-abusers get self-righteous about due process. By-the-book cops are merely disapproving. Guys who've walked some dark streets tend to connect with you on a purely nonverbal level—but the connection is there. Even guys who are good poker players always have a tell in moments like that.

This guy did.

There was the tiniest thinning of his lips. Not a smile. Nothing like that. More like a predatory smile. There are different kinds of predators. There are the kinds who target the weak. And there are those with more of a Dexter vibe who don't lose sleep if a child abuser has a hard time on the way to the station.

"Any of this going to come up if I run a background check on you?"

"My dismissal letter makes for quality reading," I told him.

"Okay," he said, though he didn't lower the gun. "New subject. What are you doing in Pine Deep?"

"What does it matter to you?"

"Not a two-way conversation, Sparky. Answer the question."

"I'm here on a case."

"What case?"

"A police case. I'm working with local law on a series of unexplained deaths."

"Who's your contact here?"

"The chief of police. Malcolm Crow."

Keeping his gun pointed at my forehead, he tapped his ear. "Bug, you get all this?"

I didn't hear anything, but the guy did. "Copy that."

" 'Bug'?" I asked. "You wearing a wire?"

He ignored me and stood in an attitude of listening. I couldn't see his earbud or mike. Had to be high-tech stuff if it was that well-concealed. Which changed my estimation of him from cop to some kind of federal agent. FBI or higher. Which made some sense if someone in the Justice Department was taking these deaths seriously. If there was any evidence to link the kills, then it made this a federal case.

Didn't explain why he was holding a gun to my head.

"Okay," he said, "thanks, Bug. Hit me with anything else you dig up."

The jock looked me up and down for a few moments longer, then he lowered his gun. Lowered it, not put it away.

"You had a colorful career in the Cities," he said. "Samuel Theiss Hunter. How the fuck did you get hung with a name like that?"

"My parents read a lot," I said. "And they're a little weird."

"Uh-huh."

"You got my background that fast?"

"I have good people."

"How long have you been tailing me?"

"Since you left the Scarecrow."

"Why'd you pick me?"

He nodded to Antonio. "My friend tagged you."

"He wearing a wire, too?"

"Does it matter?"

I changed tack. "You want to tell me who you are and why you pulled a gun on me?"

He glanced around at the darkened trees, then shrugged and holstered his piece.

"Joe Ledger," he said.

"FBI?"

"Same league, different team."

"Care to tell me which team?"

"Not really." He grinned at me. Son of a bitch had great teeth. I wanted to punch them down his throat.

"Can I have my gun and wallet back?"

"Antonio," said Ledger, "give the man his wallet."

The kid handed it to me, and I slipped it into my pocket. I held my hand out for the gun.

"Let's pretend you don't need it right now," said Ledger.

I lowered my hand.

"Okay, Mr. Mysterious. How about you tell me what in the fuck is going on."

"You first," he said, "why don't you tell me why you're here in Pine Deep."

"I already told you."

He gestured to the bench. "You gave me a headline, now give me the story."

We sat, the two of us. Antonio stood a dozen feet apart, my gun in his pocket. He fidgeted and looked like he wanted to be anywhere else but here.

I looked at Ledger. "The chief said there was someone asking questions around town. That's you?"

He shrugged.

"If you're already looking into these deaths, then you must know what's going on. You know about me. Not about my background, but, you know . . ."

"You get weird and fuzzy," he said, "yeah, I know. Still borderline freaked out about it, but I know."

"Which means the government knows?"

"Some parts of it do. Most don't."

"Am I about to get myself onto some kind of watch list? You guys have an *X-Files* thing for real?"

"*X-Files* is fiction, and it's FBI," he said. "I personally don't give a rat's hairy nuts about the things that go bump in the night unless those bumpy things have a political agenda."

"I don't."

He touched his ear. "So I'm told. You're a lapsed Independent. You haven't voted since you left Minneapolis. Never been arrested at a rally. You're not a person of interest in any way that matters to guys like me."

"So why this setup? You had Knick-Knack here lure me to where you could blindside me. Very slick, and I fell for it. But as your mysterious Bug must have told you, I'm not a player in anything political. I don't even watch the debates. I think everyone in Washington needs a good foot up their ass, but I don't have any aspirations to be the one doing the kicking. Is there any chance you're going to stop being Mr. Cryptic and get to the fucking point?"

Ledger laughed. "Fair enough. This clandestine shit always makes me feel like a jackass."

"See it from my side."

He nodded. "But this isn't a discussion, Sam. This is me interrogating you. This is you cooperating without reservation. This is me—much as I hate to do it—waving the Patriot Act in your face and not having to play quid pro quo. Sorry, but life's a bitch like that."

"Why don't you just go ask the fucking chief of police?"

"I will. But he's lower priority. And, he's kind of a dick," said Ledger.

"You know him?"

"We've met. Besides, he's an ordinary guy. You're not. You're definitely not, if Antonio is certain."

"Absolutely," said Antonio. "He's like me."

"I'm neither short nor black," I said.

We all laughed.

Ledger said, "So, I want you to tell me why a werewolf private investigator—and I'm having a hard time saying those actual words—is in Pine Deep, Pennsylvania. I want to know what you know about the person or persons who committed these murders. I want to know if you have any connection to them, because I'm pretty damn sure you're all members of the Hair Club for Weirdos. So, talk."

"I think this conversation would make more sense if we included Chief Crow," I said.

"I don't."

A voice behind him said, "I do."

And there was the unmistakable sound of a pump shotgun being jacked.

24

The girl turned around.

She saw the killer.

Of course, she did. It was what she was meant to do.

He was fifty feet behind her, moving on all fours, grinning with all his teeth.

She screamed.

She screamed so loudly.

A shrill, piercing note that the killer was positive would live within his personal treasure trove of superb screams. It was a girl scream. A girl-woman scream. Filled with all of the dark imaginings of the child. And all of the understanding of the adult. It was as perfect as she was, this girl on the edge of womanhood. She, in all of her desperate, bruised beauty. Her defiled innocence. Her ripeness.

She ran.

Of course, she ran.

He would have been disappointed, crushed, if she had not.

She dropped her backpack and her cheap little purse and ran.

He let her run.

Another fifty feet. A hundred.

Two hundred.

And then he ran after.

25

Joe Ledger turned. Slowly, without real concern.

Malcolm Crow stood twenty feet behind him, a Remington pump snugged into his shoulder.

Ledger smiled, got up, walked over, bent and picked up an unfired shell from where it had landed on the grass.

"Much as I appreciate the dramatics of pumping the shotgun—it's a real nut-twister—it's done purely for effect. You wouldn't have come out here without a shell being already in the breech. Which means you had to eject one to make your entrance."

He reached past the barrel and tucked the shell into the chief's pocket.

Crow sighed and lowered the gun.

"It scares the piss out of most people," he said.

"Hey," said Ledger, "I'm not saying it didn't work on me. I'll

probably have a pee stain on my Joe Boxers. Just making an observation. You see that on TV?"

"Yeah."

"They always do it on TV. Saw one episode of *The Walking Dead*
where a guy racked his gun twice."

"Nice."

They smiled at each other.

"Howdy, Chief Crow," said Ledger.

"Howdy, Duke."

I said, "Duke?"

Crow nodded. "First time we met, he introduced himself as Marion Morrison. John Wayne's real name."

"Oh."

"Flashed an FBI badge."

Ledger shrugged. "It was convenient."

Crow pushed past him and walked over to Antonio. He held out
a hand and waited as the kid looked for and received a nod from
Ledger. He handed my gun to Crow, who exhaled through his nose
and handed it to me.

I considered how much fun it would be to pistol-whip Ledger,
but frankly didn't like my chances. Not without changing. He
looked like a happy-go-lucky dumb jock, but there was something
behind that façade that troubled me. I had the feeling he could turn
mean as a snake if he wanted to. I didn't want him to.

Crow turned back to the agent. "We are going to have a frank
conversation, Agent Whateveryournameis."

"Joe Ledger."

"Agent Ledger. Fine. We're going to have a powwow, and if I get
even a whiff of obstruction—"

"Or obfuscation," I amended.

"—I will kick your ass out of Pine Deep. And before you ask, yes,
I think it can be done, and no, I don't give a cold shit what kind of
federal juice you have or which agency you belong to. Am I making
myself clear?"

"Crystal," said Ledger, though it was also clear he was amused.

"Good. Let's all go over to the Scarecrow."

"Not your office?"

"No. The coffee sucks moose dick. Artie at the Scarecrow makes the best coffee in town."

I said, "You don't mind that it's a bar?"

"Son," he said, giving me a weary, pitying smile, "everyone I've ever met in this town drinks like a fish. Seeing it isn't going to knock me off the wagon. This is Pine Deep. Besides, you two ass-clowns could use a few beers. Maybe it'll help wash off the testosterone."

"I'm in," I said.

We all looked at Ledger.

"First round's on me."

Crow nodded to Antonio. "You want to do me a favor?"

"Um . . . sure."

"You know Mike Sweeney?"

He swallowed and nodded.

"Go find him. Tell him where we are."

Then Crow laid the barrel of his shotgun over his shoulder and nodded toward the lights of town. "Gentlemen, shall we—?"

26

The killer ran at half speed most of the way.

He didn't want to catch her.

Yet.

Where would the fun be in that?

He loped along, watching her legs pump, watching her hair bob. Watching her.

Aching for her.

Hungering.

In other times, in older times, he would have taken her a different way. Like he'd done in harbor towns throughout Southeast Asia. Like he'd done when crossing this country. Like he'd done more times than he could remember. Back then, when it was his old flesh that he wore and his weaker senses that he used, he still loved the chase, the catch, the tearing of clothes, the tearing of skin, the tearing of screams from young throats. Screams of fear. Screams of desperation. Screams of despair when they reached that critical moment when all fight and all flight were clearly failing. Screams of use. Screams of invasion. And screams filled with pleading as they tried to hold on to the bottom rung of life.

That had been different. Good for what it was, but not what it was now.

Now the killer wanted something different. Sex was fine, but it no longer thrilled him. It was too easy to get and too shallow a thing. No, what he wanted was the blood. The meat. The crack of bones between his teeth. The taste of all of the several parts that made up a human life. Oils of different pungencies. The flavor of skin on the hand and how different it was than the flavors of thigh and breast and hip and throat.

She ran so hard. She tried so much to be part of her own future.

But she could not run that fast.

Because he could run so much faster.

27

So, three guys walk into a bar.

Pint-sized badass of a town cop. Scary jock government agent. And me. Werewolf ex-cop P.I.

Life has gotten very strange.

Even by my standards.

28

We took a table in a corner that was so dark, I needed my cell phone light to read the menu. I ordered a Philly cheesesteak, fries, and a beer. Ledger liked that and asked for the same thing. Crow had a Diet Coke.

"Okay," said Ledger, "cards on the table time."

"That'd make a refreshing change," observed Crow. "Let's start with your real name and official status."

There was no one seated within earshot, but even so, Ledger lowered his voice. "Captain Joseph Edwin Ledger," he said. "I work for a specialized group operating under executive order."

"Name?"

"If I told you I'd have to kill you." Ledger smiled as he said it.

"Not joking here," said Crow. "I'm a half-step away from arresting you. I don't care if you could squeeze enough federal juice to beat an obstruction of justice charge. I'm the chief of police, and you have to identify yourself."

Ledger nodded. "I used to be a cop," he said. "In Baltimore. Worked homicide and then I was attached to Homeland. Mostly sitting on my ass working wiretaps. Then I caught the tail of something, and when we yanked on it, there was a dragon at the other end. I was in on the bust, which went south, and everyone thought it would be fun to be stupid with guns. After that I was scouted by a group called the Department of Military Sciences."

"Never heard of it," said Crow.

"You wouldn't. We fly pretty much below the radar."

"Part of Homeland?"

"Parallel. A lot smaller, less red tape and bullshit. We target groups with cutting-edge bioweapons and other tech. Designer pathogens, man-portable nukes, that sort of thing."

"Mad scientists?" said Crow, amused.

"The maddest."

"So," I said, "you're James Bond."

Ledger shook his head. "No laser-beam cufflinks. No ejector seats. And I prefer lagers to martinis."

Crow sipped his diet pisswater. "Which doesn't explain why you're here. Again. Last time you were here, you pretended to be FBI, and you brought two thugs with you who claimed to be federal marshals. Which they weren't."

"Not as such, no."

"You brought a lot of bad people to my town. You turned a farmhouse into the Battle of Bull Run."

"I didn't deal that play. We had a guy in witness protection who did something very stupid. Tried to reach out to some very bad people in hopes of uncovering some terrorists on American soil. Brought a lot of cockroaches out of the woodpile. Things got creative, and the good guys rode their horses into the sunset." Ledger paused. "I never did thank you for stepping in on that."

Crow ran his finger around the rim of his glass. "I had no official involvement in that case. There was, I believe, no evidence of my ever having been there. Perhaps you're mistaken."

"Uh-huh," said Ledger. "Your nose grew two full inches when you said that."

They sat there and looked at each other, and I had the impression that there was a lot I didn't know about them. Not sure I actually wanted to know. I was already creeped out and probably way out of my depth here.

"Guys . . . going on the assumption that I have no idea what the fuck you two jokers are talking about, how about we circle around to the matter at hand?"

Crow leaned back in his chair, effectively breaking the connection. "All cards on the table," he said.

"All cards on the table," echoed Ledger. "Tell me about your investigation, and then I'll tell you why I'm here. I think we'll find we're working two ends of the same case."

Crow nodded and went through it all. The murders in other towns, the deaths here. The lack of any visible federal investigation. Ledger said nothing. He ate his cheesesteak and listened. I noticed Crow glossed over the part about who and what Mike Sweeney was. When he got to the part about Limbus, Ledger began asking questions. He wanted to know everything either of us knew about that organization. Unfortunately, we didn't know much.

When it was my turn, I told them about my previous case with the mysterious organization. Naturally, I omitted a few details—namely the nature of the real enemy in that case. I was still having nightmares about that.

I had my Limbus card with me, and he used his phone to photograph it and send the picture to his office. His contact there—presumably the 'Bug' he'd been talking to earlier—got back to him, and Ledger relayed the information to us. We didn't like it.

"The number is fake. My guys traced it, and it dead-ends. Understand something," Ledger said, "we have some pretty nifty toys, and we can trace darn near anything. We can't trace that number. And it's not re-routing tech. Our pingbacks tell us that there is nothing at the end of that line. Database searches on Limbus came up empty, too. There are some obscure references to various groups using that name going back more than a hundred years, but so far, we can't tie any of it together."

"You got all of this that fast?" asked Crow.

"Like I said, we have nifty toys. My people will continue to work on it. Maybe we'll come up with something. We have to assume, though, that your office is bugged, Crow. And maybe this Limbus group has some informants in town."

It was the logical answer, but Crow shook his head. "I don't think so," he said.

"Has to be," insisted Ledger.

Crow shrugged. "Not sure it does."

Ledger let it go for now. The fact that he did made me wonder if he'd run up against other stuff that was equally weird. I sure as hell have. Ever since I went into business as a P.I., I've found that this world is a lot bigger, darker, and stranger than I ever thought. Werewolves are far from the only thing going bump in the night. And in my day, I've met things I don't understand and things that terrify me.

Crow had that look, too.

So did Ledger.

The three of us lapsed into a brief silence. We ate, we drank, we avoided each other's eyes.

Finally, Ledger said, "Super soldiers."

Crow paused, his glass halfway to his lips. "What now?"

"Super soldiers."

"That's what we think this is about."

"Super soldiers," repeated Crow.

"Super soldiers?" I asked.

"Super soldiers," said Ledger.

And when he said it, I could see it.

"Jesus Christ," I said.

29

The killer dragged the girl into the woods and ate her.

Not all of her.

Just the good parts.

He nearly wept for the beauty of it.

30

"We inherited this case," Ledger said. "The first attacks happened in a small town near Saskatoon, Saskatchewan. Local law was called in when a couple of joggers running back roads to prepare for a marathon smelled something nasty. Mounties checked out an abandoned warehouse and—"

"Seriously?" I asked. "An abandoned warehouse?"

"I know. It's cliché, but you have to respect the classics. Anyway, they found two bodies pretty much torn to beef jerky. Been there about a week. Back door was open, so the locals had to conclude that the corpses had been bitten post-mortem by animals."

"Let me guess which *kind* of animal," said Crow dryly.

"Wolves aren't entirely unknown in Canada," I said. "Even if they're not exactly common is Saskatoon. The coroner's report, though, cited blunt force trauma as the cause of death. Murder weapon unknown, but presumably heavy and soft."

He looked at me. So did Crow.

"What?"

"If you wanted to arrange a crime scene in a way that would muddy the investigation, how would you do it? Specifically, you."

I felt my face getting hot. I don't like to be put on the spot, and I have never once in my adult life had anyone call me out for being what I was. Ledger was doing exactly that. It was so fucking weird. What was weirder still was that neither of these guys looked particularly freaked by this line of questioning. They weren't spooked by it. I was.

So fucked up.

I cleared my throat. "Um . . . well, I guess I'd, you know, *change*, and you know, maybe, um, hit the guys and, well . . ."

Crow and Ledger burst out laughing. They howled. Ledger slapped his thighs. Crow put his face in his hands, and his whole body shook. My face was actually burning now.

In a creaking, wheezing voice, Crow said, "He's embarrassed by being a were . . . were . . ."

The rest of it dissolved into laughter.

Joe Ledger began singing "Werewolves of London," and Crow joined him for the "Wahoooo" chorus.

"I am going to kill both of you," I said.

That made them laugh harder.

"Seriously. Headshots. Bury you out in the country."

There were tears on Crow's cheeks.

I glared at them.

"Yeah, well . . . fuck you."

Then I was laughing, too.

31

The killer heard something, and he raised his head. He'd been cradling the girl's head, sniffing her hair, but now there was a sound in the woods.

The killer tossed the head into the bushes and rose to smell the breeze. He was covered in blood, and the smell of the girl's life was like strong perfume, blotting out most of what was exhaled on the forest's breath.

He moved away from the kill, going deeper into the woods, following the sound. Smelling the air. He changed halfway so that he had arms but still had claws, and he climbed a tree.

There.

Way over there, a mile away or more, was the big red-haired policeman.

The local wolf, he thought.

Coming this way.

The killer shimmied down the tree, turned away from the half-eaten girl, and ran.

Was this local wolf blunted to the subtleties of the hunt? He wondered that as he ran.

He dared the wolf to pick up his scent. He dared him to follow.

He dared this pup to find him.

32

Eventually Ledger got back to his story. More beer was involved. The other patrons at the Scarecrow moved even farther away from the three loud, obnoxious crazy people in the corner.

"Anyway, anyway," said Ledger, bringing it all down to earth, "there was a second set of murders in Manitoba. A third on Prince Edward Island. In each case, there were two or more corpses. All mutilated. Each one in situations where there was another *convenient* possible cause of death. Industrial accidents, car crashes. You get the picture."

"Who put it all together?" asked Crow.

Ledger smiled. "A computer. We have a great pattern-recognition software package. It trolls interagency databases. Mostly used to scout for terrorist activity, but every once in a while, it coughs out something that's simply weird."

"Even so," I said, "what was the connecting factor? There are a lot of strange, violent deaths."

Ledger nodded his approval. "Location, location, location. In each case, the deaths occurred within twenty miles, give or take, of a known—or suspected—lab."

"What kind of lab?" I asked.

"Bioweapons research."

Crow shook his head. "Then your computer is wonky, 'cause there's nothing like that in Pine Deep. Nothing even remotely like it."

Ledger gave him a long, hard look. "How much of your pension would you like to bet on that?"

"Wait," said Crow, "what?"

"Yup, there is a bioweapons R&D facility in your own little slice of rural heaven."

"Run by whom?"

"That's a different question. It's sure as hell not run by the U.S. government. I know that for a fact."

"Are you talking about a private lab?" I asked. "Something attached to a pharmaceutical company?"

"No. We don't have those here, either," said Crow, who was getting very angry now.

"Then what?" I asked. "Private sector working on something they want to sell to Uncle Sam?"

Ledger shook his head. "I wish. No, gentlemen, I think what we have here is a clandestine and highly illegal lab. Probably funded by a terrorist group. And one that's highly mobile. I think it's been moving around North America doing research on the fly."

We digested that, and it was a hard pill to swallow.

"How sure are you?" I asked.

"Pretty sure."

"Based on what evidence?" demanded Crow.

"Based on a shitload of supposition and some negative reasoning," said Ledger. He drank the last of his beer and signaled for another. "Let's look at the facts, shall we? We have a series of murders in rural areas. Each murder has been orchestrated to look like an accident. Because of the nature of the injuries, they haven't been able to totally sell it, but enough so that no one in authority has been enthusiastic enough to start an international or even interstate investigation. Right now there's too much room for doubt."

Crow and I reluctantly agreed.

"Whoever these folks are, they have access to, or have somehow created, lycanthropes."

"Look at you using technical words," said Crow.

"I went to college," said Ledger. "We can suppose that they have more than one, because of the nature of the crime scenes. There's signs of evidence tampering that could not have been done in the absence of hypernormal physical strength."

"How did you make the jump from that to, um, *lycanthropes*?" I asked.

Ledger smiled. "Rumors in the pipeline." When it was clear that Crow and I wanted more than that, he explained, "There's been talk about this for a while now. Ever since Dr. Broussard found the lycanthropic gene and—"

"Whoa!" I said immediately. "Doctor who found what?"

"Ah," he said, "I would have thought that someone of your kind would have known about that. No? Okay, well, Broussard is a French molecular biologist working with a team in Switzerland. They've been indexing the genes that are known in the tabloids as 'junk DNA.' Turns out, they're not junk. You guys up on your genetics? No? I'll try to flatten it out for you. In genomics, they've found that about ninety-eight percent of our DNA is what they called 'noncoding.' Some of this noncoding DNA is transcribed into functional noncoding RNA molecules, while others are not transcribed or give rise to RNA transcripts of unknown function. Follow me?"

"I have no idea what the fuck you just said," I admitted.

"Lost me on the first curve," said Crow.

Ledger grinned. "Yeah, a couple of years ago I didn't understand any of this shit. It's become a kind of job requirement."

"Weird job," I suggested.

"You have no idea. Anyway, the amount of this noncoding DNA varies species to species. Like I said, ninety-eight percent of the human genome is noncoding, while only about two percent of, say, a typical bacterial genome is noncoding."

"I think I almost understood that," said Crow.

"At first, most of the noncoding DNA had no *known* biological function—emphasis on *known*—and someone hung the nickname 'junk DNA' on it. But there are teams all over the world working to unlock the secrets of those genes. Dr. Broussard's team has been working on chimeric genes and—"

"On what?"

"Chimeric. Genes that change their nature, or that change what they code for. They're a brand-new branch of evolutionary science. Broussard's pretty much ready to prove that a lot of theriomorphic phenomena in world folklore—and that means things that change shape—"

"I know." Crow and I said it at the same time.

"—are not part of some weirdo supernatural shit," continued Ledger, "but are evidence that genetics is a much, much bigger field than we thought. It's Broussard's belief that werewolves are a genetic offshoot of good ol' *homo sapiens sapiens.*"

We said nothing.

"And, before you ask, there are other examples of chimeric genes. I had a tussle a couple of years ago with *Upierczy.*"

"That's a kind of Russian vampire," said Crow quietly.

"*Homo vampiri,*" said Ledger. "Now fully documented, though we haven't released that to the press yet. The *Upierczy* are some nasty fucks. They call themselves the Red Knights and even though they're not supernatural, they are still every damn bit as scary."

"You don't believe in the supernatural?" asked Crow.

"Not really," said Ledger, but his tone was mildly evasive. It was clear he didn't want to travel down that side road.

"How does that connect to an illegal bioweapons lab in my backyard?" asked Crow.

Ledger shrugged. "Most of the labs doing illegal bioweapons research tend to be either offshore or hidden."

"Hollowed-out volcanoes?" I suggested.

"Close enough. A few are on ships in international waters. Or hidden in oil refineries. Places where they can hide science teams, where people come and go, and where large shipments of supplies are routine. We busted one in a container yard in Baltimore last year and another on a freight train operating out of the Pacific Northwest. We've found mini-labs in RVs, in mobile homes, and in your generic abandoned or short-leased warehouses. Computer and lab equipment is getting more compact every day, and it's easier to have a grab-it-and-go lab than before. And there are what amounts to virtual labs, where everyone is networked through Wi-Fi, so they don't all have to be in the same physical location. I think that's what we're hunting for here. Someone is messing around with lycanthrope DNA. Your basic *homo sapiens canis lupis*. Broussard's term, not mine."

"Even so, how'd you get to werewolves?" asked Crow.

"Hair and fiber recovered from victims. We, um, *hijacked* some of the lab reports and sent it to Broussard's people for sequencing. Rang all the right bells. And the genes show clear sign of after-market manipulation. Transgenics, gene therapy, all sorts of stuff." He leaned forward and rested his elbows on the table. "Our theory is that someone is trying to build a better werewolf. I don't know about you gents, but that pretty much scares the shit out of me."

33

The killer ran, and the local wolf ran after.

They chased each other through the woods for long minutes, and then the killer broke and ran through a stream and shed his pursuer like a snake sheds a skin.

After ten full minutes of running, the killer stopped and went to high ground. He searched in all directions for the local wolf. For the pup.

And found nothing.

He sneered in contempt.

A wolf that could not follow a living scent was no wolf at all. He deserved to be gutted and left to rot.

The killer made a mental promise to see that done.

34

"Why the fuck would someone want to do that?" I demanded.

"Two words," said Ledger. "Super soldier."

"Like Captain America with fur?" suggested Crow.

"More like Captain Russia or Captain North Korea, or something like that," said Ledger. "But in broad terms, sure. Why not? If you can make the science work, and if that science isn't all that expensive—and if you're starting with actual werewolves, it wouldn't be—why not give it a shot? Of course, it's more cost-effective and logistically sound to do something like this, to draw from the local populace of your enemy. If you can find lycanthropes within a target country and recruit them, then it reduces the likelihood of political fallout. It's always easier to disown a traitor than explain away a spy. Plus, given that there actually *are* werewolves, then imagine the psychological and religious implications. That kind of thing would do real harm. Actual monsters."

Crow and I sat there and chewed on that. Kind of choked on it going down.

It also made me review some of my own encounters with what I've always thought were supernatural elements. Was Ledger right? Were these things really part of a much bigger version of 'natural science'? Like the way physics has had to expand to embrace both Einstein's relativity and Max Planck's quantum physics and was being stretched further to take in chaos theory, string theory, and other crazy shit that I can't even begin to understand.

Vampires? Sure, the ones I met didn't turn into bats or command storms. None of that nonsense. And me? The phases of the moon didn't mean dick to me. Maybe it was all evidence that Mother Nature was a freaky bitch.

Demons and ghosts? Jury would have to deliberate a little longer on that. And that wasn't a topic I wanted to float with Ledger. Or Crow, though I was beginning to suspect that he knew more about this than all of us.

"What about that kid, Antonio?" I asked. "Is he part of this mad science bullshit?"

Ledger shook his head. "No. He's a friend of a friend."

Crow made a twirling motion with his index finger, indicating that he wanted more of an answer than that.

"One of the guys that works with me, a computer super-geek, travels in some of the same circles as Antonio. When the Broussard thing came up, this friend of mine did some covert Net searches. Very much on the DL, and based on message board posts, Facebook searches, and other data, he made a list of people who might actually be lycanthropes hiding within regular society."

"More NSA spy shit?" asked Crow, but Ledger ignored that.

"How many names?" I asked.

"A few," said Ledger, but he wouldn't go any deeper into that. All he said was, "Antonio Jones popped up on the list, and it happened to be that my friend knew him from some sci-fi and horror conventions. The kid's Facebook photo was of him in full make-up as a werewolf, except—"

"Except it was real?"

"Yup."

"That's nuts," I said, but I found it funny, too. "Hiding in plain sight."

Crow grunted. "Kind of makes you wonder."

"Yes, it does," Ledger agreed.

"So where does all this leave us?" I asked. "I mean, I can kind of buy this werewolf super soldier thing, and I've seen firsthand the kind of damage these assholes are willing to do, but . . . what now? We have a theory and no facts. Do you *Mission: Impossible* cats have any leads?"

Ledger sighed. "Not yet. I was kind of hoping you fellas could help with that."

"Why us?" asked Crow.

"'Cause, you got a werewolf working for you."

"Meaning me?" I asked.

"Meaning your deputy," said Ledger. "Meaning Officer Michael Sweeney. Meaning your adopted son."

Crow said nothing. His expression was completely blank. He hadn't mentioned Mike Sweeney.

So I asked. "What makes you think that?"

"Antonio," said Ledger.

"Balls," said Crow.

"Funny old world," said Ledger.

Which is when Crow's cell phone rang. He looked at it and made a face.

"It's him."

He held up a finger for silence as he took the call. Mostly, he listened.

Then he said, "Stay right there. Don't do anything. You hear me, Mike? You stay right where you are and wait. I'm bringing plenty of backup. No, I don't mean Otis and Farley. Don't worry, we'll be there in a hot minute."

He closed the phone and got to his feet.

"What is it?" Ledger and I both asked.

"Mike thinks he found them."

35

Ledger's car was right outside. A Ford Explorer that had gotten some kind of upgrade. The engine was quiet as a whisper, but the fucking thing could move. Crow rode shotgun; I was in the back.

"Buckle up, kids," said Ledger. He wasn't joking. He drove it like a getaway car.

"I only have two spare magazines," said Crow.

Ledger laughed at that. "I got enough shit in the back to invade Iran. Now tell me about Sweeney. What exactly did he find?"

Crow said that Mike was hunting the woods, trying to pick up the trail of the werewolves who'd wrecked the bike. He picked up a fresher scent, and for a while thought he was going to run another wolf to ground. Didn't happen that way, though, and he followed that to a blockhouse in the woods that was sometimes used by the

EPA when they sent their teams in. Some universities leased it for use, too. There's some oddball flora and fauna in the woods near Pine Deep.

"Mike said that the trail led to a shed attached to the blockhouse, and he thought that the rear wall might be phony. That's when he backed out and called me."

"You know this blockhouse?" asked Ledger.

"Sure." Crow gave him precise directions out of town, then began calling turns onto small side roads. Pretty soon we were driving roads so narrow and overgrown that weeds and branches brushed both sides of the car.

"I bet the last guy to use this road wore feathers," complained Ledger.

We went deep into the state forest and way off the grid.

As we drove, Ledger caught my eye in the rearview. "This lycan-thrope thing is pretty much new to me, and I'll be the first to admit that it's freaking me out."

"Doesn't show," I said.

"Feels it on the inside. My nuts crawled up inside my chest cavity and they don't seem to want to come down."

"You afraid of me?" I asked.

"Of course I am, you freak. You're a fucking werewolf. I have a fucking werewolf in my car. I am driving to meet *another* fucking werewolf who is waiting to lead me to a nest of fucking super-soldier werewolves. So, yeah, I'm afraid. I'd worry about anyone who said they weren't scared."

I grinned at him.

"Don't do that," he said. "You look like Hannibal fucking Lecter."

"Sorry."

"Tell me something," Ledger continued. "When you do that, um, change . . . how much of you is you and how much is the wolf?"

"One and the same."

"That's not enough of an answer, man. I need to know if I have to keep an eye on you. I mean, do I need to worry about you looking at me and thinking I'm on the menu?"

For some reason I couldn't adequately explain, I found that to be moderately offensive.

"No," I said.

"You're sure?"

"I'm sure."

He gave me another look. A hard one. "*Be* sure."

We drove the rest of the way in silence.

36

Crow had Ledger pull off onto a side road that ran fifty feet and dead-ended in the woods.

"It's a mile from here," he said. "Best if we go in on foot."

We all agreed to that.

Ledger popped the back of the Explorer and opened a big, flat metal box. Inside there were handguns, rifles, shotguns, boxes of rounds, and even some grenades.

"Party favors," said Ledger.

"Sweet mother-of-pearl," said Crow as he selected a bandolier fitted to hold a dozen loaded magazines. His sidearm was a Glock 40, and there were plenty of magazines for him. Ledger put one on, as well, with mags for his Beretta. He also took an A-12 combat shotgun with a big drum filled with buckshot and Frag-12 fragmentation grenades.

"For when you want to send the very best," said Ledger. I saw him check the spring of his rapid-release folding knife, too. Then he glanced at me. "What about you?"

I had my gun and two magazines, but that was all I needed. "Less I carry, the less I have to go back later and find. But . . . any chance you have an extra pair of sweatpants or something?"

"I have BDU pants. My size, but you can roll up the cuffs. Why?"

"Because I tend to ruin my clothes when I change, unless I strip out first. And if we walk away from this, I doubt you want me going commando on your back seat."

He grinned, took the rolled-up extra pants, and tucked them into the back of his belt.

We moved off into the woods. Crow texted Mike to let him know we were coming. Ledger was good in the woods. Fast and silent, like me. Crow knew how to move through nature, too, but he had a limp. We had to slow down to let him keep pace with us. Even so, a mile was nothing, and it fell away in a few quick minutes.

I smelled Mike before I saw him.

But he was closer than I would have liked. He was smart enough to come at us downwind. I turned a split second before he deliberately stepped on some dry grass. A moment later, Crow and Ledger turned, too.

Mike waved us down behind some dense bushes. Beyond it, built into a downslope of a long hill, was a box made from cinderblock. Boring, utilitarian, and stained by forest rains and insect slime. The structure was sixty-by-ninety, with a small shed built onto the east corner. Mike pointed to a clump of pines, and in the shadows, we could see three cars. An SUV and two sedans. Then he dug into a pocket and produced a handful of important-looking wires. Those cars weren't going anywhere.

The young officer nodded to the building. "I picked up a scent in the woods and followed it. Lost it a couple of times because I think he knew he was being followed. He went into the stream for a while, but I found him again. Stayed downwind and tracked him here. Saw him go inside the shed, but when I checked, he wasn't there. It's rigged to look like a toolshed, but the back wall's a dummy. Couldn't find the lock or handle, though."

Ledger nodded. "That's good police work, kid."

Sweeney gave him a stony go-fuck-yourself look. Crow patted him on the shoulder.

We watched the building for a few minutes.

"Don't see any security cameras," I said.

"Could be hidden," mused Ledger. "But I don't think so. I think this is a temporary setup. The fact that it's half a mile from No-fucking-Where is their security system. It'll be different inside. Guys like this always have lots and lots of guns."

"So do we," said Crow.

"They also have super soldiers."

"So do we."

Ledger nodded. He cut a look at Sweeney and at me. "And people wonder why I drink."

"Okay, coach," I said to Ledger. "This seems to be your ballgame. What's the play?"

Before he could answer, there was a sound behind us. Very small. Very furtive.

We spun around, guns coming up. The wolf that lives inside of me nearly jumped out. Must have been the same with Sweeney.

A small figure staggered out of the brush behind us.

Antonio Jones.

And he was covered in blood.

He reached out a hand toward us. His mouth worked as he fought to speak. Then his eyes rolled up and he pitched forward.

37

Ledger and Sweeney moved at the same time. They closed on Antonio so fast, it was like they blurred. With Mike I could understand the speed. The wolf was right there beneath his skin; it glared out through his eyes all the time. Ledger was just a man but moved with a speed and economy of motion that called to mind an expression I once read in an article about Jesse Owens. Oiled grace.

He reached Antonio first and caught the kid as he fell and lowered him to the ground. We all huddled around him.

"Jesus," I breathed.

The kid was a mess.

Someone had beat the shit out of him. They'd cut him up. There were long, ragged gashes in his face and chest and stomach. His hands were bloody, his knuckles visibly broken. Whatever had happened, he'd put up one hell of a fight.

Ledger wiped blood from the kid's eyes and mouth. Crow took his pulse. Mike pulled off his own uniform shirt and began ripping it into strips that I pressed against the worst of the cuts. Antonio's eyelids fluttered and opened.

"What happened, kid?" asked Ledger, bending close.

"I ... I ..." The young man's voice faltered. "I ... tried to ... stop ..."

He coughed, and blood bubbled at the corners of his mouth.

It took a while, but the kid mastered himself through an admirable effort of will. Sometimes you find strength in the strangest of places. This kid had some grit.

He told us that he saw the three of us leave the Scarecrow and was hurrying down the street to catch up, but we drove off. Then he saw two men hurry out of the bar, get into a car, and follow. Antonio didn't like the look of them. Or the smell. He got his scooter and tailed them. The car was well behind Ledger's Explorer, and once out in the country, it turned off and went up a logger's road. Antonio might have let it go, but he was positive that at least one of those men was a werewolf. So he followed. When he described the road, Crow and Mike nodded. The logger's road changed to a Forest Service road three miles outside of town and then crossed into the state forest. Antonio, thinking that these men might be heading for the hidden lab Ledger had told him about, kept following.

He lost the car twice, and when he found it a third time, not more than a mile east of where we all knelt, the men were in the process of hiding the car with boughs they cut from the trees. They heard the scooter, and before Antonio could turn it around and get the hell out of there, the two men changed into wolfshape and ran him down.

There was one hell of a fight.

Antonio was sure he injured one of them pretty badly, but he took too much damage to keep fighting. The other one—a big son of a bitch that Antonio described as "maybe Indian or Asian," was the one who took the kid apart. He slashed and bit him and beat him nearly to death. To get away, Antonio threw himself down a steep hill, fell into a river, and damn near drowned. The men gave up the chase, probably figuring him for dead. Antonio managed to get to the bank. When he climbed up the hill on the other side to try and find a road, he saw Ledger's car drive past with us in it.

He followed and found us here.

We exchanged looks. This was one impressive young man. Tougher than he looked, with big, clanking balls.

Antonio, spent from telling his tale and nearly ruined by the fight with the other werewolves, passed out and lay silent.

Ledger leaned close to me. "You know this lycanthrope stuff, Sam. Aren't you guys supposed to be able to heal fast? Some kind of hyperactive wound-repair system? Or is this kid going to die on us here?"

I hesitated. We *Benandanti* have a lot of specialized knowledge. Things about who we are and what we are. My mother, grandmother, and aunts were all very specific about keeping that information confidential. About sharing it with no one outside of the family. Not even with other werewolves.

So naturally, I had to give that a little thought before I answered. I glanced at Mike.

He shook his head. "I never had anyone to teach me how this all works," he admitted. "I've been hurt a few times. I know how fast *I* heal, but I'm not the same as Antonio. Or you."

His eyes were a strange and artificial blue. He reached up and pinched his eye, removing a contact lens. Then another. The eyes that were revealed were no human eyes at all. Nor were they werewolf eyes. They were as red as blood and ringed with gold.

Joe Ledger said, "What the fuck?"

I didn't say shit. Not sure I could have. Whatever he was, Mike Sweeney was a lot more than a werewolf. I was damn sure he wasn't even remotely human.

Ledger edged back, shaken and pale. "What in the wide blue fuck are you?"

Sweeney smiled. A rare thing for him. It was not the kind of smile you ever want to see. On anyone. Not even in a horror movie.

"What am I?" he asked, and for a moment, even the timbre of his voice was all wrong. Too deep. Too strange. "I have no idea."

Crow touched Mike's shoulder but looked at us. "Mike's family tree is moderately complicated. Maybe one of these days we can talk about it."

"Or maybe not," said Mike.

"Or maybe not," agreed Crow. "Right now, though, we got to help this kid. You have anything, Sam? *Benandanti* are supposed to be the secret keepers of the werewolves. Or something like that, am I right?"

"Something like that," I mumbled.

They all looked at me. I looked down at the kid.

Poor little bastard really put his ass on the line. Tried to make a difference.

"Sorry, grandma," I said.

"What?" asked Ledger.

"Nothing." I held my hand out to him. "Give me your knife."

He didn't hesitate, but instead reached for the rapid-release knife, snapped his wrist to lock the blade in place, and offered it to me, handle-first.

I took it and looked at my reflection in the polished steel. "Understand something," I said, "I'm going on what I've been told. I've never actually done this before."

"Kid's going to die," said Ledger.

"This is a gamble," I said. "This might kill him faster."

Crow shook his head. "A small chance is better than none at all."

Ledger and Sweeney nodded.

"Do it," said Ledger.

I put the edge of the knife against the heel of my left palm, took a deep breath to steady my nerves, and let the wickedly sharp blade do its work. Bright red blood welled from the small cut.

"Open his mouth," I said, and Mike put two fingers between the kid's teeth and then splayed them to push open Antonio's mouth. I clenched my fist to increase the blood pressure, and when the blood began rolling over my hand and down my wrist, I extended my arm and let the first fat drops fall. They splashed his lips, his teeth and then vanished into the darkness of his open mouth.

The old ritual says to use seven drops.

Seven, the number of heaven.

I gave him seven and one to grow on and then put my cut hand into my own mouth and sucked off the last drops of blood. When I removed my hand, the cut was already closed. Kind of freaky. Grandma hadn't told me about that part.

Ledger, who had gone pale earlier, went milk-white now.

"That," he said thickly, "is some weird-ass voodoo bullshit."

I grinned at him. I probably still had blood on my own teeth. "Welcome to my world."

Crow smiled, too. "Welcome to Pine Deep."

Mike Sweeney said nothing, but his red eyes burned into mine.

On the ground, Antonio Jones groaned once, twitched.

And died.

38

We tried everything.

CPR.

Mouth to mouth.

Everything.

But the kid's body settled into a terminal stillness. No pulse. No nothing.

I turned away and felt tears in my eyes. I balled my fist and drove it into the top of my thigh. Over and over again.

Son of a bitch.

Son of a motherfucking bitch.

This wasn't right.

It wasn't fair.

When I turned back, no one would meet my eyes.

Crow looked old and tired. Sweeney got up and walked back to the line of shrubs that separated us from the blockhouse. Ledger, he sat there looking down at the kid, shaking his head slowly.

He was the only one who said anything, though. "You tried, man. At least you tried."

Before I even knew I was going to do it, I grabbed a fistful of his shirt and pulled him halfway to his feet. "Fuck you, asshole. You should never have brought a kid into this. This shit is on you."

Ledger looked at me. If he was afraid of me, it no longer showed. He placed his hand on mine and pressed two fingers into nerve clusters. He did it without effort, and my hand popped open. Just like that. Ledger gently pushed me back.

"Don't ever do that again, Sam." His voice was very calm. It wasn't a request, and it was somehow more than a threat. He walked forward very slowly, which made me walk backward. Ledger got so close that his forehead and mine were touching. It might have looked like an intimate moment. Two close friends, two brothers, two mourners at a funeral.

But this wasn't that. This was alpha and wolf. His voice was very soft.

"You're letting emotions get in the way of your better sense. Don't. That's what happens to people when they get caught up in this kind of thing. They need to assign blame, and because the bad guys are usually out of reach, they lash out at whoever's close. The thing about that is—it's what those assholes want. They count on it. Terrorism isn't about overwhelming force. It's about fear. It's about grief. It's about confusion."

"This isn't terrorism—" I began, but he cut me off.

"The fuck it isn't. That's the *only* thing this is about. These sons of bitches killed that kid. They fucked us all up in doing it."

"It's not right!" I growled.

"Shh. Quiet now," he said. "No, it's not right. None of this is about right or wrong. None of it. It's about evil. It's about darkness. That's what this is about. These fuckers want to shut out all the lights. Everyone's lights. They want to be the boogeymen in the dark. That's what they do so they can feel powerful."

I said nothing. Ledger moved his head back a few inches so I could see his eyes. They were cold and they were hard, but I saw a bottomless pain there. Endless hurt. I could feel Crow and Sweeney watching us.

"Sam, the guys who did this are the same ones who killed the guy on the motorcycle and all of those other civilians. That's what they do. They don't have the balls to go to war with warriors, so they try to cripple us by targeting the innocent. The civilians. The ones who can't protect themselves. If you lose your shit, then that guarantees a win for them. Is that what you want?"

"No," I said hoarsely.

"No," he agreed.

"This . . . this isn't my sort of thing," I said.

"What *is* your sort of thing?"

"When I take on a client, it's like they become part of my . . ." The word stuck in my throat. I wanted him to understand. I didn't want to sound like an idiot. But I said it anyway. "When I take on a client, it's like they become part of my pack."

He studied me and nodded slowly. "And you'll do anything for your pack."

It wasn't a statement.

I nodded.

He took his wallet out, removed a dollar bill, and stuffed it into my shirt pocket. "Consider that a retainer from Antonio Jones. He's your client. When this is over, if we're both standing on our feet, you can bill me for the rest."

"I've already been paid."

"By whom?"

"Limbus."

"Fuck Limbus. They're not here. That kid is. You're working for him. And if there was ever a client who deserved to be in your *pack*, then he's it."

I shook my head, but even I didn't know if that was a denial of his words or a refusal to accept all of this bullshit.

"So what's the alternative?" asked Ledger. "We could fall back and wait for reinforcements and hope that these bastards don't slip away while we're waiting."

"No."

"Or we can cowboy up and go in there and *prove* to these mother-fuckers that they don't have a right to do these things. That they aren't allowed to do this. That there is punishment for it."

I cleared my throat. "We could be walking right into a trap. We don't know what's waiting for us in there."

Ledger smiled. His smile was every bit as alien and as awful as

Mike Sweeney's had been. "Maybe," he conceded. "But they don't know what's waiting for them out here."

It took me a few seconds, but then I felt a smile growing on my own face. I couldn't see it, but I was sure it wasn't one I'd want to look at in the bathroom mirror.

39

Ledger put a call in to his people and told them to come running. But best estimate was forty minutes. We couldn't risk that kind of time.

We decided to hit the place ourselves.

Ledger mapped out a plan. It was ugly, dangerous as hell, probably insane, and definitely suicidal.

We all agreed to it.

It had somehow become that kind of day.

40

We crowded into the shed.

Ledger took some goodies from his pockets and explained them as he set to work. The first thing was a pocket sensor that identified which wall of the shed had a door hidden behind it. That was easy. Finding the lock and door handle took a little longer, but Ledger found it. There was a knot in the wood of the back wall. It was phony and hid a pressure switch. Ledger produced a second gizmo that would let us know if the door was wired with bombs. It wasn't, which provided less of a relief than I would have thought. Then he took what looked like a Fruit Roll-Up from a metal tube, flattened it out, peeled off a plastic cover, and pressed it in place over the switch. He pushed a small electronic detonator into the putty-like material.

"Blaster plaster," he explained. "Very high-tech pressure-reactive chemical explosive." He held up a small trigger device. "Let's get out of Dodge."

We went outside and over the edge of the hill.

"Once I trigger it, we're committed. We go in hard and fast, and it's fuck you to anyone inside. Anything past that door is no longer American soil, and whoever's in there is to be considered an enemy combatant."

"Is that legal?" asked Crow.

"Do you care?" Ledger said.

"On the whole, not much."

Ledger nodded. "It'll get loud and smoky. Everyone keeps their shit wired tight. You check your targets. I do not want a bullet up my ass."

"What do we do if they want to surrender?" I asked.

"We let them," said Ledger. "We're not murderers, Sam. For right now, we're soldiers. Rules of engagement apply. You good with that?"

We all were.

We were all scared, too.

Even Mike, though it didn't show. I could smell it. Faint, but there.

Ledger was the coolest, but he had a fine sheen of sweat on his forehead. No doubt. After all, this wasn't a cell of Al-Qaeda. These were monsters. Scary monsters. Scarier than me, and I have my moments. Super-soldier werewolves. If there's a worse-case scenario that trumps that, please do not fucking tell me.

Ledger held up the trigger. "Good guys win, bad guys lose."

We nodded.

As the Bible says, we girded our loins.

He pressed the trigger.

The blast was impressive.

The shed stopped being a shed and became a rapidly expanding cloud of splinters and dust that blew over and past us. The door disintegrated, and a big chunk of the interior wall blew inward.

Ledger was up and moving before the first echo of the blast could bounce back at us from the surrounding trees. He had his pistol up, laser sight stabbing through the smoke. He bellowed through the thunder.

"Federal agents! Put your weapons down. Put your hands in the air. Do it now! Do it now!"

It was rhetoric. It was like saying hello.

None of us expected them to comply.

And, fuck it, they didn't.

41

We crowded behind him.

Crow and Mike Sweeney.

Me.

All of us with guns.

We ran into dense smoke and burst through into the blockhouse, none of us really knowing what to expect. I had a kind of Doctor Frankenstein thing in my head. Arcane science, secret experiments.

It wasn't like that.

There were two folding tables on which were laptops. And a third table crowded with some scientific junk. Open metal cases, high-pressure injection guns, alcohol swabs, IV bags. That was it. The whole shebang could have fit into the trunk of a midsized sedan. No exotic machinery, no bubbling vats or towering electrodes. This was twenty-first-century micro-science. Transgenics on the go.

But the equipment wasn't important to us. Not at the moment.

The occupants of the room were.

We were expecting two, maybe three of them. A handful at the outside. Some science geeks and a couple of their pet monsters.

Yeah, that's what we were hoping for.

Fuck.

There were fifteen people in the room.

Two of them were Korean. Both in lab coats. Both pencil-neck geeks. North Korean, as we later found out.

The others were homegrown. Twelve men, one woman. Americans and Canadians.

And every single one of them was a werewolf.

Every.

Single.

One.

Ledger put the red dot of his laser sight on the chest of the nearest man. A guy who looked like a baseball player. Fit, long-legged, rangy. The man was ten feet from Ledger.

"Hands on your head right now!" bellowed Ledger.

For just a split second, it all held together. A tableau. Them and us, with ghosts of smoke drifting around us.

Then the man grabbed the shoulder of one of the Korean scientists and hurled him at Ledger.

Not shoved him.

Hurled.

The scientist went flying into the air, well off the ground, arms pinwheeling, legs kicking, right at Ledger. The agent was able to twist out of the way, and the screaming Korean hit Crow. They went down hard.

Then all hell broke loose.

The crowd rushed at us, and even as I swung my gun toward the nearest, he stopped being a man and became a wolf. It was the fastest change I'd ever seen, and I've seen my grandmother do the shift. She could do it in the space of a finger-snap.

This guy was faster.

In a heartbeat, he stopped being a man and became a thing.

When I change, I usually go the whole way into pure wolfshape. Most werewolves do. We're faster as wolves. We have four feet and keener senses.

He did not.

None of them did.

They shifted into wolfmen. A horror-movie halfway point between man and wolf. He leapt at me and swatted the pistol from my hand. Claws like daggers dug into my chest, and if I hadn't begun the change as soon as he leapt, I'd have died as a man, right there and then. The man has more vulnerabilities.

He smashed me back and down, and immediately we were tearing into each other. Teeth and claws. Spit and blood.

I heard gunfire and didn't know who was shooting. Ledger, maybe.

Crow, too, if he could.

I doubt Mike Sweeney was still human.

There was a scream of fury that was higher and stranger than any wolf cry, and I knew at once it had to be him. It was almost the shriek of a jungle cat. What *was* he?

The wolfman who bore me to the ground was strong. Goddamn strong. He gripped my forelegs and tried to tear them apart. His grip alone was crushing. Pain exploded through my legs and shoulders. There was no way I was going to wrestle free. He was easily twice as strong as me.

Super soldiers.

What was it Ledger said? *Someone's trying to build a better werewolf.*

Yeah.

Shit.

So, fuck it, I stopped fighting a fight I couldn't win, and instead darted my head forward and bit his throat. I was in full wolfshape, and if my muscles weren't as powerful as his amped-up physique, my jaws were. Wolf jaws were always stronger than wolfman jaws. My family's genetics don't go back to *canis lupus.* Most werewolves do; we don't. We *Benandanti* are in a direct genetic line from *canis dirus.* The massive, prehistoric Dire Wolves. No canine predator in history had a stronger bite. And as werewolves, we get something extra added to the package.

He tried to tough it out, to muscle through my bite.

Fuck him.

He didn't.

His throat tore away between my teeth.

Blood exploded from him with fire hose pressure, smashing into my face, hitting the wall. The evil bastard died right there. His strength evaporated, and his powerful and scientifically enhanced physique became so much cooling meat. I threw him off of me and rose to four feet with bloody meat and fur hanging from my jaws.

The rest of the room was a madhouse.

Crow had his back to the wall and had Mike Sweeney's combat shotgun in his hands. He fired, pumped, fired, pumped, over and over again. I've been hit with shotgun shells before. Buckshot hurts. Bear shot will put me on my knees, but it won't kill a werewolf. Not unless you scored a headshot and blew apart the motor cortex or the brain stem.

The rounds in that shotgun were explosive.

He blew arms and legs off. He blew holes through chests.

Hard as balls to shake off a ten-inch hole through your sternum, supernatural or not.

Ledger didn't have his gun. It was somewhere on the floor.

Instead, he had his rapid-release fighting knife in his hand, and he was tackling two of the wolfmen at once.

He should have died. Right away. On the spot, end of story.

He was cut and bleeding, but damn it if that son of a bitch wasn't holding his own. He fought on the attack and with counterattacks. Nothing defensive. They came at him, and he went for them. He didn't stab. Stabbing is for suckers who want to die. Ledger used lightning-fast slashes, jabs, and picks to open up dozens of wounds in arms, legs, bellies, groins, and faces. The wolfmen were the ones on the defensive. Maybe it was their arrogance, maybe they'd never fought a warrior before, but they were losing what should have been a nothing battle.

It couldn't last, though. Ledger was human. He'd tire.

They wouldn't.

And even as I watched, I could see some of their wounds beginning to close.

This could only end one way.

I began making my way toward him. On the other side of the room, Mike Sweeney—or what had been Mike Sweeney—was fighting with the largest of the wolfmen. Two giants colliding. Both standing on two legs and slashing with clawed hands. Sweeney and the giant were well-matched, and there was no way to tell who was going to win that fight.

Before I could help him or Ledger, the only female werewolf in the room rushed at me. She was tall for a woman, and dishearteningly fast.

She laughed as she slashed at me.

If you haven't heard the cruel laughter of a werewolf, I hope you never do. It's so wrong in so many ways. There's no humanity in it. Just malicious glee and a red anticipation of what's to come.

She raked me from shoulder to hip as I tried to evade, the slashes burning like acid. I hissed and snapped at her, but she danced away, lithe as a dancer. Her riposte was a slash across my forehead that filled one eye with my own blood.

Bitch.

I darted in and she danced back, she slashed, and I jumped sideways. And that started our gavotte. She caught me more times than I evaded. I nipped her twice and did no damage at all. Unlike the first wolfman I'd fought, she used cunning and speed rather than relying on her strength.

She was faster than me. By a mile.

I needed to get close enough to use my bite strength.

She did not let me.

So I changed the game; I played hers.

As she lunged for a long slash, I shifted from wolf to wolfman. I pivoted and whipped out my hand and caught her wrist. Then I clamped my teeth around it as I shifted back to werewolf.

Bite strength, baby. Nothing beats it.

Bones collapsed, meat burst, and then I had her hand. She screamed so loud, I thought it would blow out my eardrums. I reeled, but it was all noise. She clutched her maimed arm to her body, trying to staunch the flow of blood that jetted from the stump. She backed away, the fight taken out of her.

I had other plans.

As she turned to flee, I hurled myself onto her back and slammed her down onto the floor. As we landed, I buried my fangs in the back of her neck. I could feel the vertebrae break apart. I could taste the cerebral spinal fluid as it filled my mouth. I could feel the life as it fled from her like steam from a ruptured pipe.

I almost howled. Like a wolf does after a kill. Almost.

But there was too much going on.

Ledger was being pushed back now. Bloody cuts crisscrossed his body. But amazingly, one of the wolfmen lay dead at his feet, the rapid-release knife buried to the hilt in the top of the creature's skull. Ledger had no weapon. All he had was speed and training and whatever angels protected him.

He was going to die, though. I could see that without question.

He was also fifty feet away, and I was never going to be able to get to him in time.

Crow was down on one knee, his whole side glistening red. The shotgun lay in pieces around him, but there were three dead werewolves, too. As I watched, Crow fumbled his pistol out of his holster and raised it. His hands trembled with pain and fatigue. And fear. I could see in his eyes that he thought he was going to die, too.

Maybe we all were.

I'd taken a hell of a lot of damage.

I started in his direction, but then my entire back exploded with searing, unbearable, blinding pain. I could feel nails rake across my spine and ribs. The force of the impact knocked me down and sent me sliding across the floor, riding a red carpet of my own blood. As my body spun, I saw a figure that I hadn't seen before.

A fourteenth werewolf.

Tall. Powerful.

He shifted back to his human aspect, standing there naked and indomitable.

With a face like an American Indian. High cheekbones, black eyes, straight black hair.

This was the werewolf who'd killed Antonio.

I was certain of it.

And, just as certainly, this was the alpha of this pack.

He exuded power.

Across the room, Mike Sweeney vanished beneath a pile of wolfmen. Blood geysered up around them, and screams filled the air.

My pistol was on the floor near his feet. He bent and picked it up, dropped the magazine to inspect it, slapped it back in, racked it. The round that had already been in the chamber went arcing over his shoulder. The man looked around the room. His mouth turned down in a frown. Not of unhappiness at how many of his people were dead. It was a sneer of contempt. Everything he saw—us, his own pack, all of it—was nothing to him. He was a monster among monsters. I could *feel* that. I knew it to be true. We werewolves have certain instincts. I knew that this man was as close to death personified as ever walked the earth. Maybe he was the pinnacle of the twisted research being done in this place. Maybe he was the superior soldier that they were looking for. An unstoppable force.

The pain in my back was excruciating, but I had to move. I had to try to fight. This wasn't just a bad guy, not some child abuser I was hunting, or a bail skip I was paid to nab. This wasn't the kind of scum I chased for small bucks as a P.I. This was the kind of evil I became a cop to oppose. Actual evil.

Was this what the people at Limbus wanted stopped? They'd put me in the path of a monster before, and I'd nearly died fighting it. This time, I was pretty sure that I *was* going to die. Limbus seemed so prescient, but as I struggled to get to my feet, I knew that their faith in me was badly misplaced.

The big man raised the pistol and pointed it. Not at me. He pointed it at Ledger. His mouth curled into a very small, very cruel little smile.

"No!" I snarled in a mouth that was not constructed for human speech. I flung myself at him. I tried to gut him with my claws. Tried to bite him with my teeth. But all I managed to do was bump against him and spoil his first shot. The round vanished into the smoke above Ledger's head.

The alpha grunted and clubbed me with the butt of the pistol. Once. Twice.

Again and again.

Beating me down. Breaking me.

Killing me.

And he wasn't even in wolfshape.

I collapsed onto the ground.

The man gave a single little nod and raised the pistol again.

This time, there was nothing I could do to prevent that shot.

Nothing.

42

I didn't have to.

There was a flash of movement. A blur, as fast as when Ledger and Mike had moved. Faster.

The hand holding the gun leaped into the air, trailed by rubies. The gun fired, but the barrel was pointing nowhere. The bullet struck the body of the dead werewolf woman, adding neither insult nor injury. Her flesh quivered but a little.

The alpha howled in agony. He spun around, and in doing so, changed from bleeding man to maimed wolfman. The thing that had attacked him, the creature that had taken his hand, landed ten feet beyond me. It whirled and bared its bloody teeth at the towering killer.

It was another werewolf.

Smaller than me. Darker fur. Eyes as hot as hell's furnaces.

It stood on four legs, claws flexing with such fury they scored the concrete floor. Hair rose along its spine; its ears were back. It was the picture of savage rage, of a total commitment to hate.

The killer looked into those eyes.

So did I.

I think we both recognized them.

I spoke the name.

"Antonio."

I didn't ask how. The blood. The old ritual I'd performed had done its work. Its magic. It had brought this young man back from the dark place. It had restored him, healed the terrible wounds that had been torn into his flesh. It had brought him to the peak of his feral power. Maybe to a greater peak than ever before.

Even maimed and bleeding, the alpha was still twice his size. He'd beaten this young man before. Easily.

He bared his teeth, and in that leer, there was a promise of even greater harm and humiliation. The alpha suddenly rushed at him, and though Antonio tried to dodge away, the killer was insanely fast. He struck Antonio with his stump, and it was like being smashed with a club. The younger werewolf yelped in pain and slammed into me so hard, we rolled over and over. Blood welled from his mouth and nose and splashed my face.

Then he scrambled to get off of me, slashing me by accident as he sought to evade the next blow. The alpha caught him on the hip and sent him slewing sideways.

I snapped at the alpha and caught his ankle. With all of my rage, I tried to bite hard enough to cripple him, but he squatted, twisted, and struck me on the side of the head hard enough to knock the world off its hinges.

Everything went dark.

I felt like I was falling from a great height. Falling through smoke for an endless time. I spun sideways and lay on the floor. Through shadows and blood, I saw the fight between Antonio and the alpha.

It was heroic, what that kid tried to do.

He gave as good as he got for as long as he could. Tearing and slashing. Leaping and biting. Fighting with fury. Fighting like a *Benandanti*. Had my blood given him that edge?

If so, it was not enough.

Not enough.

Which is a damn shame, because that was one hell of a comeback. One hell of an entrance. Heroism of that kind should be rewarded. Not pissed on.

I wished I could help.

I wished I had something left.

All I could do was lay there and feel myself die. I could feel Antonio's blood seep into my mouth. I could feel my own blood leak out. I could feel the coldness creep in.

Except . . .

Except that wasn't what was happening.

The taste of blood in my mouth was strange. It was his blood, but it tasted familiar. Like my own. It burned. It burned its way through the flesh of my mouth and into my blood. It burned through my blood.

It burned so goddamn bad.

And it burned so goddamn good.

The fire tore through me. It felt like there was acid in my veins. Lava. I screamed so loud, blood flew from my lips.

I was wolf.

I was a human.

I was both.

I screamed as I changed and changed and changed.

The alpha swatted Antonio aside and turned to see what was happening. He frowned again. This time in doubt. I changed and changed and changed and changed.

And all the time I burned.

I had no idea what was happening to me. It was ripping me apart. Burning me at the cellular level. Destroying me.

Except . . .

The burning stopped.

Like that.

Like a switch being thrown.

I collapsed onto the bloody floor, gasping, human, naked, covered in blood and sweat.

The alpha watched me with narrowed eyes.

Antonio, gasping on the floor, watched me.

In the reflecting surface of the pool of blood beneath me, I watched myself. I saw my human face. I looked for the cuts. The slashes. The exposed bone.

And I saw none of it.

What I saw was whole skin. Painted with blood, but no longer gaping, no longer bleeding.

On the floor, Antonio shifted back to human form. His eyes were bugged in amazement. But he was also smiling.

The alpha was not.

This was not the science he knew. This was not the work of some super-soldier formula. This must have looked like sorcery to him.

Magic.

Pretty much was like that for me.

Except that I understood it. As I lay there, whole once again, I understood it. Antonio's blood in my mouth. Somehow in performing the ritual on him, I'd changed his nature. From *canis lupus* to *canis dirus*. He was a Dire Wolf now. Not sure if that made him a *Benandanti*, but definitely a cousin. Enough so that his blood did for me what mine had done for him.

I rolled onto my hands and knees, and in doing so, raised my head to look up at the alpha.

"Surprise, surprise," I said. My voice was filled with ugly promise. Fine.

"You were dead," he said.

"Yeah, well, fuck it," I said.

And I launched myself at him.

It was the man who started that lunge; it was the wolf who buried his teeth in the alpha's throat.

He tried to change.

He tried to make a fight of it.

As the saying goes, that ship had sailed.

Beside me, I saw Antonio struggle to his feet. He shifted back into wolfshape and raced across the room to help Joe Ledger.

I killed the alpha.

God, did I kill that son of a bitch.

I tore him to pieces.

Pieces.

Never in my life had I ever felt that powerful.

Across the room, I heard a howl of agony. I looked up from the steaming corpse and saw a badly wounded Mike Sweeney struggling with two of the wolfmen. I saw Crow crawling toward a pistol that lay out of reach. Still alive, both of them.

There were more of the wolfmen in the room. The odds were still not in our favor.

And right then, at that moment, it didn't matter.

The wolf in me had never been this strong before. Maybe it never would be again. I threw back my head and howled. The howl of an alpha triumphant. It shook the walls. It knocked plaster from the ceiling. It shocked everyone and everything in that room into silence and stillness.

I howled again, louder still.

The alpha.

The master of this pack.

I screamed at them.

And one by one, the remaining wolfmen stopped their attacks.

One by one, they lay down on the bloody ground.

And goddamn it if they didn't roll to me.

In a pack, when the other wolves do that, the alpha bites them gently on the throat or belly, establishing dominance. Adopting them into the pack.

I came to them and bit them. One by one.

You couldn't, by any definition, call those bites *gentle.*

No, you couldn't.

When it was over, there were only five members of the pack.

Two of them were human.

Mike Sweeney and Antonio Jones looked at me. I lifted my head and howled.

And they howled with me.

43

Joe Ledger and Malcolm Crow were in bad shape.

We left Mike at the crime scene, but Antonio and I had to get them to the hospital, so we broke a lot of traffic laws doing it. We almost didn't make it in time.

While they were still in the E.R., a black helicopter landed in the parking lot, and three men came into the hospital. Two were clearly military, in unmarked black BDUs and wires behind their ears. One was a tall, blond-haired guy with lots of muscles. One was a black man in his early forties who looked like he ate crocodiles, uncooked. The third guy, though, was in his sixties, wearing a very expensive suit. Tall, blocky, with dark hair shot through with gray. Even at night he wore tinted glasses. He exuded a kind of personal power I have never before encountered. I would not have wanted to match my alpha status against his. No sir, I would not.

He introduced himself as Mr. Church. No badge, no ID.

He told me to wait for him, and he left the other two guys with me in the waiting room. Mike Sweeney was still at the crime scene. Antonio was in the waiting room with me.

The two military guys didn't say a fucking word. They stood

waiting. They exchanged a few looks. They studied me. One chewed gum, the other didn't.

After twenty minutes, their boss came out of the E.R. and motioned for his men and Antonio to leave. When the door was closed, Mr. Church sat down opposite me.

"Captain Ledger will survive," he said.

I let out a breath I hadn't realized I was holding. "How is he?"

"He's had worse," said Church. No trace of sympathy in his voice. No trace of anything.

"He's a good guy," I said. "But this wasn't his kind of fight."

Church eyed me. "And was it your kind of fight?"

I said nothing.

Church nodded.

"What about Chief Crow?"

"He'll have some challenging rehab, but they expect him to make a full recovery."

"Guess we got lucky."

"Apparently so."

I chewed my lip for a moment. "Did you talk to Ledger?"

"Briefly. He's been sedated."

"Did he tell you what we found?"

"He did."

"Tell me something, Mr. Church," I said. "I know this isn't my business, and you can pull rank and tell me to go piss up a rope. I'm Joe Nobody to you."

"Ask your question."

"That science . . . the, um, super soldier stuff?"

"What about it?"

"What happens to it? I mean, from what Ledger said, this is some kind of foreign terrorist thing."

"Multinational," agreed Church. "Funded covertly by North Korea."

"Okay. But it was terrorist science. What happens to it? I mean, does our government take it and start making its own monsters? Is that how it works?"

He leaned back in his chair, fished a small packet of vanilla wafers from his coat pocket, tore it open, and offered me one. I passed.

Never been a vanilla wafer fan. He took one and bit off a piece, chewed, and studied the remaining cookie for a long few seconds.

"What do you think we should do with it, Mr. Hunter? This is science that could put superior soldiers into battle against an enemy that is both relentless and determined to see America burn. That science could give us an edge. What do you think we should do with it?"

"Are you really asking or jerking me off here?"

"Asking."

I crossed my legs and stretched my arms across the backs of the seats to either side of me. "I think you should burn it. I think you should destroy whatever's in there. Burn it down and scatter the ashes. There are enough monsters in the world already."

"Not all monsters are the enemy, Mr. Hunter."

"Maybe not, but should we be in the business of making more?"

Church finished his cookie. He brushed a stray crumb from his tie, rewrapped the package, and put it into his coat pocket. Then he stood up.

"Wait," I said, "is that it? You never answered my question."

Church reached for the door handle, then paused. "Fifteen minutes ago, a Black Hawk helicopter fired four hellfire missiles at a blockhouse in the state forest. The news reports will all say that this was done to destroy a rogue laboratory making weaponized anthrax."

"That's bullshit."

"It's a useful story. And it will explain why that building and all of its contents have been reduced to hot ash." He opened the door but paused one more time. "The world has enough monsters already, Mr. Hunter."

"Wait," I said, rising to my feet. "What about this Limbus thing. They must have known about that lab and what was in it. You need to find them and find out how they know what they know. You need to find out who they *are.*"

His eyes glittered behind the tinted lenses.

He smiled faintly. "Thank you for your assistance in this matter."

And he went out.

An hour later, Joe Ledger was medevaced out of there. I knew that if I tried to find him or Mr. Church, I'd find nothing but shadows.

Antonio was in the hall, and we walked together to the doors to the E.R., then followed the gurney with Crow to his new room. We sat there all night. Crow's wife came in, glared at us, and went in to be with her husband. Hours passed.

We didn't say a word.

Not one fucking word.

The night seemed to last a million years.

In the morning, when Crow was awake, I said my goodbyes and left Pine Deep. All the way home, I blasted music, because I didn't want to listen to my own thoughts. As I neared the bridge out of town, I saw a police cruiser parked by the side of the road. Mike Sweeney leaned against it, big arms folded. He had bandages on his arms, his throat, his face. They did not make him look weak or injured.

He stared at me with eyes that burned like fire.

He nodded to me.

I nodded to him.

And I drove out of Pine Deep under a morning sky that was dark with clouds and offered nothing but the promise of coming rains.

On Lonely Roads

A POEM

I dreamed that I was dreaming.
    Or, at least, I thought I was.
    Driving through Pine Deep at night.
    Too many hours, too many beers past 'unsafe to drive'.
Coming back from a dirty bit of business out in the sticks.
    Blood on my hands.
    On my clothes.
    On my face.
    Red in my mind's eye. Coppery in my nose.
    Blood.

I don't remember stopping my car.
    Driving on autopilot, I guess.
    Half in the bag 'cause it had been a very bad day.
    The kind where even when you win, you feel like a loser. You
        feel lost.
Nobody wins on days like that.
    I mean, how could they?
    And it's worse doing what I do.
    Ghosts hire me.
    Their faces are inked onto my skin.
They whisper ugly things to me.
    Telling me how they died.
    Begging for answers.

I relive their deaths. That's how it works.
>	Once the ink is on me, that's what happens.
>	Making me feel everything that was done to them.
>	Every.
>>		Single.
>>>			Thing.
>	Some of them scream, too.
>	No one else can hear them, but I can.
Every single night.
>	Guy at the liquor store thinks I'm an alkie.
>	He has no idea.

Not the first time I fell asleep behind the wheel.
>	I have some scars from a sideswipe.
>	Nearly found Jesus that night.
Another time I woke up with splints and stitches and drains.
>	But this?
>	This was different.
Not even sure I could understand how.
>	Different.
>	For sure.

And, here's the twist—I wasn't even sure I was sleeping.
>	Sometimes being awake is its own kind of dreaming.
>	I could tell you stories. But . . . I expect you already know.
>	You get it.
>	You get me.

But here I was. My car in a cut-out near by the edge of the drop-off.
>	Way down below was Dark Hollow.
>	A moist, reeking cleft between three mountains.
Swampy down there.
>	Lots of flying things that buzz and bite.
>	Snakes and owls and roaches bigger than my thumb.
No one goes there because they want to.
>	Not anyone with their brains wired right.

You could say, "That place is haunted," and even the staunchest
   skeptic would say, "No shit," and without irony.
     It's like that down there.
     I was parked near the edge.
     Either dreaming it or waking up weird.
Either way it was me stopping on the wrong road.
     In the wrong part of the night.
     Last I remembered was listening to oldies.
     A playlist I made forever ago.
Lonely, plaintive stuff.
     Mostly Tom Waits and Leonard Cohen.
     Stuff they wrote on bad nights.
     After wrong turns and questionable decisions.
     Like the day I had.

Song that was playing now was another oldie.
     Another downbeat tune
     All about the comfort of darkness
     Hello, old friend.
     But I wasn't safe within a womb
     I was in Pine Deep
     On a back road I didn't know,

I don't remember coming here.
     Why or when, or by what route.
     A carve-out on a disused forest road.
     I know I sat there for a long time.
Engine on, headlights punching out through the shadows.
     Dark as fuck.
     I leaned out the window and looked up.
I remember seeing the stars.
     There at the outer range of my lights.
     Cut crystals on velvet
     Beyond reach
     That song still playing.
     Or looping. Not sure.

Maybe that's why I saw it.
    It.
    Maybe the song summoned it.
    Or woke it.
    However that works.
Or . . . is something in a dream.
    Was I even awake?
    Even now, I still don't know for sure.
I mean . . . most people don't see stuff like that when they're awake.
    But this was Pine Deep.
    So "most people" don't live here.
    The ones who do have their reasons.
    Whether they know it or not.
    I do.

At first, I didn't believe what I was seeing.
    Impossible thing.
    No way it was real.
    Didn't want to see nothing like that.
    Looked anyway.
    We're all braver in our dreams.
It rose up from the ground.
    I think it was part of the ground.
    Or maybe it hides that way.
    So you don't see it.
    Until it wants you to.
    Until it wants you to.

God damn it was big.
    Big as fuck.
    Bigger than a bear. Bigger than ten bears.
    Taller than a telephone pole.
    Not as tall as the trees.
    Except its horns.
Big rack of horns.
    God damn.
    Spreading out wide.
    Like an elk.

Too many points to count.
Big.

Built like paintings you see of minotaurs.
     All that chest and shoulders.
     I'm big, but I was a bug.
     It could close its hand around me.
     Crush me.
     And I wouldn't be able to do shit.
Headlights and fog painted it blue.
     Ghost blue.
     Except for those eyes.
     Those god damn eyes.
     White, like the sun at noon in August.
     White like the moon on bad October nights.

The worse part wasn't its eyes. Or size.
     The worse part was that it saw me.
     Me.
     Standing there beside my car.
     No idea when I got out.
     Just standing there.
While it towered over me.
     There's no meter to compare scale.
     Or strength.
     Or power.
     It was it, and that was enough.

I know my folklore and I know a lot about what's in the dark
     Behind shadows
     Out of the corner of your eye
     Behind you.
     But I didn't know this thing.
Not Sasquatch or Shampe or Mogollon or Hodag or Wendigo
     Not Katshituashku or Wechuge or Atakapa or Lofa
     Not Shíta or Uʿtlûñ'tä or Yé'iitsoh
     None of those.

Nothing, I suspected—knew, felt—that had a name
    Not a name a white man would know.
    Or a black man.
    Maybe if the colonists hadn't killed the people who lived here
    There'd be a name.
    Not now.
Nor did it need one.
    It was.
    And that was all it needed or wanted to be.

I didn't even try to run.
    I mean, how could I?
    Didn't even think about getting in my car.
    Why bother?
    It was right fucking there.
    Could have stomped my car flat.
So I stood there in the swirling fog.
    Looking up at it.
    Seeing it.
    Knowing that it saw me.
    Saw. You know?

I'm not normal. We both know that.
    Lot of people think I'm the scariest thing they ever saw.
    Mostly that's true.
    That's not about intent. It's about potential.
    But this thing . . .
    Jesus.
It took a single step toward me.
    Earthquake step.
    Trees shivered.
    Leaves fell.
    The nightbirds took flight and circled.
    But they didn't flee.
    No.
    That was something.
    That said something.

The thing looked down at me.
>I live in Pine Deep but I'm not from there.
>It was.
>I knew it. I could feel it.
>It's lived here longer than the trees.
>Maybe as long as the mountains.
>I'll never know.

It looked down at me.
>In me.
>Through me.
It shook that rack of antlers.
>I saw the muscles of its shoulders ripple.
>I watched its hands open and close.
>And open.
And then it paused.
>For just a moment.
>Considering me.
>Which is scary in its own way.
>To know it had that kind of awareness.
>To be the focus of its thoughts.

I saw the head nod.
>Not a bow.
>Hell no.
>Not to me. Let's be real.
>A nod, though, sure enough.
And I nodded back.
>Getting it.
>I lived in its town.
>I stood in its forest.
>It saw me and knew me.
>No. Maybe understood me really says it.
And I saw it.
>And understood it.

Then it turned away.
    Into the mist.
    Bending toward the ground.
    Not falling.
    Becoming.
    I can't explain it better.
    It's not something words were built to say.
    But I think you get me.
    Like I got it.
I stood in the headlight's glow.
    Feeling the cold and damp.
    Feeling the power beneath my feet.
    In the air. Everywhere.
    And knew I was home.
This was Pine Deep.
    My name is Monk Addison.
    I live here now.
    I got into my car and sat for maybe half an hour.
    Tom Waits whispering secrets to me.
Then I backed up, turned.
    Found the road again.
    And the night closed around me.
    Carrying me home.

Mister Pockets

1

There were towns like Pine Deep.
  A few.
  But not many.
  Luckily, not many.

2

The kid's name was Lefty Horrigan.
  Real name.
  His father was a baseball fanatic and something of an asshole. Big Dave Horrigan thought that naming his only son Lefty would somehow turn the boy into a ballplayer, ideally a pitcher with a smoking fastball and a whole collection of curves and breakers. Big Dave played in high school and might have made it to the minors if he hadn't screwed up his right shoulder in Afghanistan during the first year of the war. It wasn't a shrapnel hit from an IED or enemy gunfire. Big Dave had tripped over a rock and fell shoulder-first onto a low stone wall, breaking a lot of important stuff. When he got home and got his wife pregnant, he transferred his burning love of the game to Lefty. Papered the kid's room in baseball images. Bought him a new cap and glove just about every year. Took him all

the way to Philly to watch the Phils. Subscribed to every sports channel on the Net and had Lefty snugged up beside him from first pitch to last out.

Yeah, Lefty was going to go places. Lefty was going to be the ball-playing star of the Horrigan clan, by God so he was.

Lefty Horrigan hated baseball.

He wasn't entirely sure he'd have loathed baseball as much if his name had been Louis or Larry. Lefty was pretty damn sure, however, that being hung with a jackass name like that was not going to make him enjoy the sport. No way.

He was a small kid for his age. A little chubby, not the best-looking kid who ever pulled on a pair of too-white, too-tight gym shorts in the seventh grade. He had an ass, and he had a bit of a gut, and he had knocked knees. When he ran the hundred-yard dash, the gym teacher threw away the stopwatch and pulled out a calendar. Or so he said. Often.

When the other kids lined up to climb the rope, Lefty just went over and sat down. His doctor's note got a lot more workout than he did, and it had more calluses than his hands did. Nobody thought much of it. Fat kids didn't climb the rope. Fat kids sucked at gym class, and none of them went out for sports unless it was on a dare.

And it didn't much matter.

Nobody bullied Lefty about it. This was farm country, out beyond the suburban sprawl and infill of Bucks County, out where Pennsylvania looked like it did on holiday calendars. Not the gray stone towers of Philadelphia or the steel bridges of Pittsburgh, but the endless fields of wheat and corn. Out here, a fat kid could ride a tractor all day, or work the barns in a milking shed. Weight didn't mean much of anything out there.

So it didn't mean much in gym class.

Most that happened was people made certain assumptions if you were the fat kid. They knew you wouldn't volunteer for anything physical. They knew you were always a good person to tap for a candy bar. They knew you'd be funny, because if you weren't good-looking, you had to be funny to fit in. Lefty was kind of funny. Not hilarious enough to hang with the coolest kids, but funnier than the spotty lumps that orbited the lowest cliques in the social order.

Lefty could tell a joke, and sometimes he watched Comedy Central just to cram for the school days ahead. Stuff Jon Stewart or Stephen Colbert said was usually good for a pat on the back or a smile from one of the smarter pretty girls. If he made them laugh once in a while, he was part of the group, and all judgment pretty much ended there.

But his dad was still on him about baseball.

Fucking baseball, Lefty thought. What was the big freaking deal with baseball? A bunch of millionaires standing around in a field, spitting tobacco and adjusting their cups as if their dicks were crowded for room. Once in a while, one of them would have to run to catch a ball.

Shit.

Lefty worked harder than that pedaling his bike up Corn Hill. That was more of a workout than most of those guys saw in a whole game. And biking all the way across town or, worse, out to one of the farms, probably took more effort than playing a whole series. Lefty was sure of it. Just as he was sure that one of these days, puberty would kick in so that he grew tall enough to stretch his ass and gut into a leaner hide. Just like Mom said would happen.

So far, though, he had hair on his balls, hair under his arms, pit-sweat stink that could drop an elk at forty paces, and painful erections every time he saw either of the Mueller twins walk past. But he hadn't grown an inch.

At the same time, his dad was hoping that the growth spurt would somehow unlock the baseball gene that must be sitting dormant in him. Big Dave usually hovered between hopeful expectation and active denial about his son's views on the American pastime.

3

He saw someone cut in front of him and head across the street. Old Mr. Pockets, the town's only homeless person. What grandpa called a "hobo."

Mr. Pockets looked like he was older than the big oaks that lined the street. Older than anything. Even through the thick gray dirt caked on his skin, the hobo's face was covered in thousands of lines and creases. His brown eyes were so dark they looked black, deep-set as they were, and half hidden under bushy brows that looked like sickly caterpillars. Mr. Pockets wore so many layers of clothing that it was impossible to tell what was what. The only theme was that everything he seemed to wear—shirts, jackets, topcoats, aprons— had pockets. Dozens and dozens of pockets, into which he stuffed whatever it was he found in the gutters and alleys of town.

Lefty smiled at Mr. Pockets, and the old man paused halfway across the street and stared at him in the blank way he does; then he smiled and waved. Mr. Pockets, for all of his personal filth, had the whitest teeth. Big and white and wet.

Then he turned away and went trotting down a side street. Lefty rolled forward to watch him and saw that there was something going on half a block away. So, he pushed down on the pedals and followed the hobo, curious about what the cops were doing.

There was an ambulance parked halfway onto the curb outside of Colleen's Knit-Witz yarn shop. And two patrol cars parked crookedly, half-blocking the street and slowing traffic to a gawking crawl. Lefty pulled his bike as close as he could get, but all he saw was the chief and a deputy talking in the open doorway of the shop.

The chief of police was a weird little guy who walked with a limp. A long time ago, before the Trouble—and everything in Pine Deep was measured as being *before* the Trouble or after it—Chief Crow had owned a store right here in town. A craft store, where Lefty's cousin Jimmy used to buy comics. Jimmy was dead now. He'd been badly burned in the Trouble and hung himself six years ago.

Lefty only barely remembered the Trouble. He'd been five at the time. For him it was a blurred overlap of images. People running, people screaming. The state forest on fire. Then all those helicopters the next day.

In school they all had to read about it. It was local history. A bunch of militia guys dumped some drugs into the town water supply. Drove everyone batshit. People thought that there were monsters. Vampires and werewolves and things like that.

A lot of people went crazy. A lot of people died.

Every Halloween, the local TV ran the movie they made about it, *Hellnight*, in continuous rotation for twenty-four hours. Even though in the movie, there really *were* monsters, and the militia thing was a cover-up.

Lefty'd seen the movie fifty times. Everyone in town had. It was stupid, but there were two scenes where you could see tits. And there was a lot of shooting and stuff. It was pretty cool.

Chief Crow wasn't in the movie—the sheriff back then had been a fat guy name Bernhardt who was played by John Goodman, who only ever played fat guys. But the guys in school said that the chief had gotten hurt in the Trouble, and that was why he walked with a limp.

Now the chief stood with his deputy, a moose named Sweeney who nobody in town liked. Sweeney always wore sunglasses, even at night. Weird.

A friend of Lefty's broke out of the crowd and came drifting over. Kyle Fowler, though everyone called him Forks. Even his parents. The origin of the nickname wasn't interesting, but the name stuck.

"Hey, Left," said Forks. He had a Phillies cap on and a sweatshirt with Pine Deep Scarecrows on it.

"'Sup?"

They stood together, watching the cops do nothing but talk.

"This is pretty f'd up," said Forks. He was one of the last of their peer group to make the jump from almost cursing to actually cursing. Saying 'f'd up' was a big thing for him, though, and he lowered his voice when he said it.

"Yeah?" asked Lefty, interested. "I just got here. What's happening?"

"She's dead."

"Who's dead?"

"Colleen," said Forks. "I mean Mrs. Grady. Lady who owns the store."

"She's *dead*?"

"Dead as a doornail."

"How? She was old; she have a heart attack or something?"

Forks shook his head. "They don't call the cops out for a heart attack."

That was true, at least as far as Lefty knew.

"So, how'd she die?"

"Don't know, but it must be bad. They have some guy in there taking pictures, and I heard Sheriff Crow say something about waiting for a forensics team from Doylestown."

Lefty cut a look at him. "Forensics? For real?"

"Yeah."

"Wow."

"Yeah."

Forks started to say something, then stopped.

"What—?" asked Lefty.

His friend chewed his lip for a minute; then he looked right and left, as if checking that no one was close enough to hear him. Actually, there were plenty of people around, but no one was paying attention to a couple of kids. Finally, Forks leaned close and said, "Want to hear something really weird?"

"Sure."

Forks thought about it for another second and then leaned closer. "Before they pushed the crowd back, I heard them talking about it."

"About what?"

"About the way she died."

The way Forks said it made Lefty turn and study him. His friend's face was alight with some ghastly knowledge that he couldn't wait to share. That was how things were. This was Pine Deep, and stuff happened. Telling your friends about it was what made everything okay. Saying it aloud gave you a little bit of power over it. So did hearing about it. It was only *knowing* about it, but not talking about it, that made the nights too dark and made things move in the shadows. Everyone knew that.

Forks licked his lips as if what he had to say was really delicious. "I heard Sheriff Crow and that big deputy, Mike Sweeney, talking about what happened."

"Yeah?" asked Lefty, interested.

"Then that doctor guy, the dead-guy doctor . . ." Forks snapped his fingers a couple of times to try and conjure the word.

"The coroner."

"Right—then he showed up and started to go inside, but the sheriff stopped him and said that it was dark in there."

Lefty waited for more; then he frowned.

"Dark? So what?"

"No, look, all the lights are on, see?"

It was true, the Knit-Witz shop blazed with fluorescent lights. And, in anticipation of Halloween, the windows were trimmed with strings of dark brown and orange lights. All of the shadows seemed to be out here on the street. Underfoot, under cars, in sewer grates.

"Yeah, but the sheriff told the coroner guy that it was dark in there. And you know what the doctor did?"

"I don't know, get a flashlight?" suggested Lefty.

"No, dummy, he *crossed* himself," said Forks, eyes blazing.

"Crossed . . . ?"

Forks quickly crossed himself to show what he meant. Lefty made a face. He knew what it was; it was just that it didn't seem to fit what was happening.

Then Forks grabbed Lefty's sleeve and pulled him closer. "And Deputy Sweeney said, 'I think it's *them*.' He leaned on the word *them*, like it really meant something."

They stared at each other for a long time. It was Lefty who said it: "You think it's happening again?"

Forks licked his lips again. "I don't know, man, but . . ."

He didn't say it, but it was there, hanging in the air between them, around them, all over the town.

Like an echo of last summer.

Nine people died in the space between June second and August tenth. A lot of bad car crashes and farm accidents. In every case, the bodies were mangled, torn up.

It wasn't until the seventh death that the newspapers began speculating as to whether these were really accidents or not. That thought grew out of testimony and an inquest by the county coroner, who said he was troubled by what he called a "paucity of blood at the scene." The papers provided an interpretation. For all of the physical damage, given every bit of torn flesh, there simply was not enough blood at the crime scenes to add up to what should be inside a human body.

In August, though, the deaths stopped. No explanation, and apparently no further speculation by the coroner. It just ended.

They turned and looked at the open door of Knit-Witz.

I think it's them.

Lefty swallowed dryness.

It's dark in there.

"You know what I think?" asked Forks in a hushed voice.

Lefty didn't want to know, because he was probably thinking the same thing.

"I think it's the Trouble again."

The Trouble.

Lefty looked away from the store, looked away from Forks. He studied the sky that was pulled like a blue tarp over the town. It was wrinkled with lines of white clouds and the long contrails of jets that had better places to be than here. A single crow stood on the roof of the hardware store across from Knit-Witz. It opened its mouth as if to let out a cry, but there was no sound.

Lefty felt very small and strange.

Movement to his left caught his eye, and he turned to see Mr. Pockets five feet away, bending to pick through a trash can.

Lefty touched his jacket pocket. He had a Snickers bar, and he pulled it out.

"Here," he said, holding it out to the old hobo.

Mr. Pockets paused, one grimy hand thrust deep into the rubbish; then he slowly turned his face toward Lefty. Dark eyes looked at the candy bar and then at Lefty's face.

The smile Mr. Pockets smiled was very slow in forming. But it grew and grew, and for a wild moment, it seemed to grow too big. Too wide. Impossibly wide, and there appeared to be far too many of those big, white, wet teeth.

But then Lefty blinked, and in the same instant he blinked, Mr. Pockets closed his mouth. His smile was now nothing more than a curve of lips.

"May I?" he asked with the strange formality he had, and when

Lefty nodded, the old hobo took the candy bar with a delicate pinch of thumb and forefinger. Mr. Pockets' fingernails were very long, and they plucked the bar away with only the faintest brush of nail on flattened palm.

The hobo held the candy up and slowly sniffed the wrapper from one end to the other with a single continuous inhalation of curiosity and pleasure.

"Peanuts," he said. "Mmm. And milk chocolate—sugar, cocoa butter, chocolate, skim milk, lactose, milkfat, soy lecithin, artificial flavor—peanuts, corn syrup, sugar, milkfat, skim milk, partially hydrogenated soybean oil, lactose, salt, egg whites, chocolate, artificial flavor. May contain almonds."

He rattled off the ingredients without ever looking at the wording printed on the label.

Forks was watching the cops and didn't seem to notice any of this happening. Which was kind of weird, thought Lefty.

Mr. Pockets began patting his clothing, a thing he did when he found something he wanted to keep. His hands were thin, with long spidery fingers, and he went *pat-a-pat-pat-patty-pat-pat*, making a rhythm of it until finally stopping with one hand touching a certain pocket. "Yes," said Mr. Pockets, "this one has an empty belly. This one could use a bite."

And into that pocket, he thrust the Snickers bar. It vanished without a trace, and Lefty was so mesmerized that he expected the pocket to belch like a satisfied diner.

Mr. Pockets smiled and asked, "Do you have another?"

"Um . . . no, sorry. That was all I had."

The smile on Mr. Pockets' mouth didn't match the humor in his eyes. They were on a totally different frequency. One was friendly and even a little sad, but there was something really off about the smile in the old man's eyes. It seemed to speak to Lefty, but not in words. In images. They flitted through his head in a flash. Too many to capture, too strange to understand. Not shared thoughts. No more than looking at a crime scene was a shared experience.

"No," Lefty gasped, and he wasn't sure if he was repeating his answer or saying something else. "I don't have anything else."

Mr. Pockets nodded slowly. "I know. You gave me what you had.

That was so nice, son. Soooo nice. That was generous. How rare a thing that is. I thank you, my little friend. I thank you most kindly."

It was the most Lefty had ever heard Mr. Pockets say at one time, and he realized that the old man had an accent. Or . . . a mix of accents. It was a little southern, like people on TV who come from Mississippi or Louisiana. And it was a little . . . something else. Foreign, maybe? European or maybe just . . . yeah, he thought, *foreign.*

"You . . ." began Lefty, but his voice broke. He cleared his throat and tried again. "You're welcome."

That earned him another wide, wide grin, and then Mr. Pockets did something that Lefty had only ever seen people do in old movies. He winked at him. A big, comical wink.

The hobo turned and walked away, lightly touching his pockets.

Pat-a-pat-pat.

After a moment, Lefty realized that he was holding his breath, and he let it out with a gasp. "Jeez . . ."

Forks finally looked away from the crime scene. "What?"

"Man, that was freaking *weird.*"

"What was?"

"That thing with Mr. Pockets."

"What thing?"

Lefty elbowed him. "You blind or something? That whole thing with me giving him my Snickers bar and all."

Forks frowned at him. "What are you babbling about?"

"Mr. Pockets . . ."

"Dude," said Forks, pointing, "Mr. Pockets is over there."

Lefty looked where his friend was pointing. On the far side of the street, well behind the parked ambulance, Mr. Pockets was standing behind a knot of rubberneckers.

"But . . . how . . . ?"

Forks said, "Look man, it's getting late. I need to get a new calculator at McIlveen's and get home. I got a ton of homework, and besides . . ."

Forks left it unfinished. Nobody in Pine Deep ever needed to finish that sentence.

It was already getting dark.

"See ya," said Lefty.

"Yeah," agreed Forks, and he was gone.

Lefty pulled his bike back, turned it under him, and placed his right foot on the pedal, but he paused as he saw something across the street. Mr. Pockets was standing by the open alleyway, but he wasn't looking into it; instead, he was looking up. It was hard for Lefty to see anything over there, because that side of the street was in deep shade now. But there was a flicker of movement on the second floor. A curtain fell back into place as someone up there dropped it. Lefty had the briefest afterimage of a pale face watching from the deep shadows of the unlighted window. Someone standing in darkness on the dark side of the street. Pale, with dark eyes.

A woman? A girl?

He couldn't be sure.

Mr. Pockets turned away and glanced across the street at Lefty. He smiled again and touched the pocket into which he'd placed the Snickers. He gave the pocket a little pat-a-pat; then he walked into the alley and disappeared entirely.

Lefty Horrigan seesawed his foot indecisively on the pedal.

It was nothing, he decided. All nothing.

But he didn't like that pale face.

It's dark in there.

"Yeah," Lefty said to no one, and he pushed down on the pedal and drove away.

4

Lefty chewed on all of this as he huffed up the slope at the foot of Corn Hill, standing on the pedals to force them to turn against the pull of gravity. Aside from Lefty's own weight, his bike's basket was laden with bags of stuff he needed to deliver before dark. His after-school job was delivering stuff for Association members, and now he was behind schedule.

The sun was already sliding down behind the tops of the mountains. A tide of shadows was washing across the farmers' fields toward the shores of the town.

He rode on, fast as he could.

Pine Deep had a Merchants Association comprised of fifty-three stores. Most of the stores sold crafts and local goods to townsfolk and tourists. Lefty and two other kids earned a few bucks making deliveries for people who couldn't spare the calories to carry their own shit to their cars, their homes, or in some cases, to their motel units. On October afternoons like this, Lefty enjoyed the job, except for that fucking Corn Hill. In the winter, he called in sick a lot, and he never lost his job, because people always assumed a fat kid got sick a lot.

Lefty pumped his way up Corn Hill until he reached Farmers Lane, turned, and coasted a bit while he caught his breath. He had four deliveries to make today. The first was here in the center of town, and he made the stop to drop a bag of jewelry supplies—spools of wire and glue sticks—to Mrs. Howard at the Silver Mine. She tipped him a dollar.

A dollar.

Which bought exactly what? Comics were two-ninety-nine or a buck more. Even a Coke was a buck and a half. But he pasted on one of the many smiles he kept in reserve and made sure—upon her reminder—not to bang the door. She told him that every day. Every single day.

Then Mrs. Howard went back to gossiping with two locals about what was happening down at Knit-Witz. It seemed that the town already knew.

The town, he supposed, always knew everything. It was that kind of town.

As he climbed onto his bike, Lefty heard someone mention the Trouble, and the others cluck about it as if they were sure bad times were coming back. People threw out the Trouble for everything from a weak harvest to too many blowflies around a car-struck deer on Route A32. Everything was the Trouble coming back.

It's dark in there.

Lefty wondered if there really was something, some connection.

The town might know—or guess—but he didn't. And he didn't like the half-guesses that shambled around inside his head.

He turned around and found Corn Hill again and went three steep blocks up to the Scarecrow Inn to deliver some poster paint. They were gearing up for Oktoberfest and had two of the waitresses making signs. The bartender told one of the waitresses to give Lefty something. The girl, Katelyn, a seventeen-year-old who lived a few houses down from the Horrigans, gave the bartender's back a lethal stare and gave Lefty fifty cents.

Lefty stood there, legs wide to straddle his bike, holding the handlebar with one tight fist and staring past the quarters on his open palm to the girl's face. He didn't say anything. Anyone with half a brain could understand. She did, too. She understood, and she didn't give a wet fart. She waited out his stare with a flat one of her own. No, not entirely flat. A little curl of smirk. Daring him to say something.

Katelyn was pretty. She had a lot of red curls and big boobs, and she wore a look that told him that no matter what he said or did, this was going to end her way.

Hers. Never his.

Not now. Not ever.

Not just because he was a thirteen-year-old fat kid.

Not just because she had the power in the moment.

She gave him the kind of look that said that this was small-town America; he was fat and only moderately bright, living in a town that fed on fat and moderately bright people. They fueled the machinery, and they greased the wheels. Her look told him, in no uncertain terms, that when she was eighteen, she'd blow this town like a bullet leaving a gun.

She would. He wouldn't.

It was *always* going to be like this. She'd always be pretty. No matter what else he became. Even if he grew a foot and learned to throw a slider that could break the heart of a major league batter. She would always be pretty.

Here in Pine Deep, she had him by the nuts. And she fucking well knew it.

Lefty slowly closed his hand, feeling the coins against his skin.

Strangely warm, oddly moist. He shoved his hand into his pocket but didn't immediately let go of the quarters.

Katelyn still stared at him.

They both knew that he would break eye contact first. It was the way it was supposed to work. The universe turned on such immutable realities.

Lefty wanted to tough it out, but . . .

He lowered his eyes and turned away.

Katelyn didn't laugh, didn't even give a victorious snort. It wasn't compassion or manners. He simply wasn't worth the effort, and they both knew it. In two minutes, she would have forgotten the encounter entirely.

He knew he'd wear that moment when they put him in his coffin.

And that was the way these things worked, too.

He got onto his bike, holding it steady with one hand as he began to coast down Corn Hill. When he was far enough away, he put his sneakers down and let the tread skid him to a slow stop. Then he took the coins out of his pocket, unfolded his hand, and looked at two silver disks. Two quarters. A 1998—and didn't there always seem to be a 1998 coin in every handful of change?—and a 2013. Still new-looking, though it was a few years old now.

The coins were still warm. Warmer now for having been in his pocket.

He raised them to his face and peered at them.

Sniffed them.

And licked them.

He had no idea at all he was going to do that.

He immediately pulled his head back, disgusted, wincing, wanting to spit.

Except . . .

Except all of those were fake emotions, fake reactions, and he knew it. He played out the drama, though. He even went so far as to raise his left hand to throw the coins away.

And yet, after he sat there on his bike for another two or three minutes, he could still feel the coins in his fist, and his fist was in his pocket.

The taste of the warm, damp silver was on his tongue.

He had an erection that he didn't know what to do with.

Not out here, right here on Corn Hill, right here in front of the world.

Lefty felt sick. On some level, he felt sick.

He knew he should feel sick.

He wasn't *like* that. He wasn't no fucking pervert.

Lefty threw the coins away.

Except that isn't what he did.

In his mind, that's what he did, but the coins jingled in his pocket as he headed out of town to make his next delivery. With each pump of his legs, he pretended that he couldn't hear them.

5

Lefty's last delivery was all the way out of town, way out on Route A32. The Conner farm. The sun was fully behind the mountains now, and although the trees on the top looked like they were burning, the flat farmlands were painted with purple shadows.

"Shit, shit, shit," Lefty said aloud as he rode along.

The Conners weren't home, but there was a note on the door to leave the parcel on the porch swing-chair. He saw that they'd left him a tip.

An apple and a little Post-it that said, "Thanks!"

The note had a smiley face.

He picked up the apple and stared at it.

"Jesus Christ," he said, and threw the apple as far as he could. It sailed all the way across the yard and hit the garden fence.

Dad would have approved. A fastball with a nice break down and to the left. A batter would break his heart swinging at that.

"Fuck," he said, annoyed even that he'd thrown a good ball. Somehow it felt like an extra kick in the nuts.

He stomped down the steps and along the red brick walkway, then stopped when he realized he *was* stomping. He couldn't see himself, but the image of a disappointed fat kid stomping was disgusting. It disappointed him in his own eyes.

Lefty straightened, squared his shoulders, and walked with great dignity to where his bike leaned against the garden gate. A pair of Japanese maples grew on either side of the entrance, their pruned branches forming a leafy arch over the walkway. Lefty made himself stop and look at the trees for a moment, because he was still pissed off.

His eyes burned as if he was going to cry, but Lefty cursed aloud at the thought of tears.

"You're so fucking stupid," he told himself.

And he sniffed as he reached for his bike. He glanced up at the sky and then along the road. There was no way he was going to get home before full dark.

His heart beat the wrong way in his chest as the truth of that hit home. It was like being punched in the sternum.

It's dark in there.

It's dark.

"Yes," said a voice behind him, "it's dark."

6

Lefty jumped and whirled. He lost his grip on the bike, and it fell over with a clatter.

A woman stood behind him.

Tall.

Pretty.

Short red-gold hair snapping in the freshening breeze. Floral-print housedress flapping around her thighs.

Mrs. Conner.

She smiled at him with ruby red lips.

"I . . ." he began, but didn't know where to go with that.

"You didn't eat your apple," she said. "And it was so ripe."

He looked down at the apple. It had hit the fence hard and burst apart, the impact tearing the red skin to reveal the vulnerable white flesh.

But the apple was all wrong. The meat of the apple wasn't white; it was gray, and pale maggots writhed in it. Lefty recoiled from it, taking an involuntary step backward.

He bumped into the post and spun around.

It wasn't the fence post.

It was Mrs. Conner.

He yelped and spun around to where she should have been, to where she just was. But she wasn't there. She was here.

Right here.

So close.

Too close.

Much too close.

The top buttons of her housecoat were open. He could see the curves of her breasts, the pale-yellow lace of her bra. The blue veins beneath her skin.

"It looks delicious," she said. "Doesn't it?"

He didn't know if she was talking about the apple or about . . .

No.

He did know.

Of course he knew.

It's just that it wasn't right. Not in any moral sense. It wasn't right because it didn't make sense. This didn't happen. Not even in his wet dreams. This never happened. Probably not even to the hunky guys on the football team in high school. Not to thirteen-year-olds. Not to fat kids.

Not really.

Not ever.

Mrs. Conner moved a step closer, and he simply could not take his eyes off of her cleavage. The half-melon shapes of her breasts defined by shadows that curved down and out of sight behind the cups of her bra and the buttons that were still buttoned.

He stared at those breasts, looking at them, watching the rise and fall of her chest.

Except . . .

Except.

The breasts did not rise and fall.

Because the chest did not rise and fall.

Not until Mrs. Conner took a breath in order to speak.

"Ripe," she said. "Ripe for the picking."

Lefty slowly raised his eyes from those shadow-carved breasts, past that ruby-lipped mouth, all the way to the eyes of the woman who stood so close.

To eyes with pupils as large as a cat's.

Eyes that, he knew at once and for certain, could see in the dark.

In any darkness.

He felt himself growing hard. Harder than before with Katelyn. Harder than ever in any of his dreams. Hard enough to hurt. To ache like a tumor, like a punch. There was no pleasure in it, no anticipation of release. It hurt, and he knew, on every level of his young mind, that hurt—that *pain*—was the point of this. Of all of this. Of everything in his life and in this odd day. Hurt was the destination at the end of this day. He knew that now, even if he'd never even suspected it before.

It's dark in there.

And it was dark out here, too. And darkness called to him from the shadow beneath her breasts.

"So ripe," she said.

And he said, "Please . . ."

He was not asking for anything she had, not for anything she was. Not for those lips, or for those breasts. Or for any fulfillment of a fantasy that was too absurd even for his fevered midnight dreams.

"So, so ripe," said Mrs. Conner, as she reached out and caressed his cheek with the backs of her pale fingers.

He shivered.

Her fingers were as white and as cold as marble.

"And juicy," she said as she bent to kiss him.

With those red, red lips.

Lefty wanted to shove her away. Wanted—*needed*—to run as fast as his stubby legs would go. Wanted to get onto his bike and ride faster than the wind, ride faster than the sunset. Ride fast enough to leave the darkness behind.

That's what he wanted.

But all he could do was stand there.

Her lips, when she kissed his cheek, were colder even than her fingers. Her breath, colder still.

"Please," he whispered.

"Yes," she said.

Those were not parts of the same conversation, and they both knew it.

She kissed his cheeks, his slack lips. When he closed his eyes, she kissed his eyelids and delicately licked the tears that slid from beneath his lashes. Then she kissed his jaw.

And his throat.

Her tongue traced a line along his flesh, and whenever his heart beat, she gasped.

"Please," he said again, and his breath was so faint, the word so thin, that he knew that it was his last breath. Or maybe, he could take one more. A deep one, so he could scream.

He felt her lips part. Felt the hard sharpness of something touch his skin.

Two points, like needles.

"No," said a voice.

Mrs. Conner was still so close when she turned her face, that for a moment, she and Lefty were cheek-to-cheek. Like lovers. Like people squeezing into a booth to take a photo. The coldness of her flesh was numbing.

But more numbing still was the figure that stood behind them. Not in the road, but on the red brick garden path, as if somehow, he'd snuck over the fence so he could surprise everyone from behind.

A figure in tatters of greasy gray and the faded colors of countless garments.

A figure that smelled of earth and sewers and open landfills.

A figure whose lined and seamed face beamed a great smile.

Mr. Pockets.

7

Mrs. Conner said, "Go away."

Her voice was cold, sharp, without the sensual softness of a moment ago.

Mr. Pockets just stood there.

"This meat is mine," snarled Mrs. Conner. And with that, she jerked Lefty nearly off his feet, pulling him in front of her. Not as a shield but to put him on display. Her property.

Her . . .

What?

She'd called him *meat*.

Tears burned channels down Lefty's face.

The old hobo kept smiling.

"Get away," said Mrs. Conner.

He stood his ground.

Mrs. Conner pointed at him with one of her slender, icy fingers. "Go on now," she said in a voice much more like her own, without sex in it but still with passion. "Go on, *git*."

The wind gusted, and Mr. Pockets closed his eyes and leaned into the wind like he enjoyed the cold and all of the smells the breeze carried with it. Lefty thought the wind smelled like dead grass and something else. A rotten egg smell. Lefty wasn't sure if the wind already had that rotten egg smell, or if it came from the hobo.

Mrs. Conner tensed and took a single threatening step toward Mr. Pockets.

"Get your disgusting ass out of my yard, you filthy tramp," she growled. "Or I'll make you sorry."

"You'll make me sorry?" said the hobo, phrasing it as if it were a matter of great complexity to him. His speech was still southern, mixed with some foreign accent Lefty couldn't recognize. "What in the wide world could that mean?"

Mrs. Conner laughed. Such a strange laugh to come from so pretty a throat. It was how Lefty imagined a wolf might laugh. Sharp, harsh, and ugly. "You don't know what kind of shit you stepped in, you old son of a bitch."

"Old?" echoed Mr. Pockets, and his smile faded. He sighed. "Old. Ah."

Lefty tried to pull away, but the single hand that held him was like a shackle of pure ice. Cold, unbreakable. The fingers seemed to burn his skin the way metal will in the deep of winter.

"Let me go," he said, wanting to growl it, to howl it, but it came out as a whimper.

"Let him go," said Mr. Pockets.

"He's *mine*."

"No," said the hobo, "he's mine."

Mrs. Conner laughed her terrible bark of a laugh again. She shook Lefty like a doll. "You really don't get it, do you, shit-for-brains?"

"What don't I get?" asked the old man.

"You don't know what's going on here, do you? Even now, you don't get it? You're either too stupid or you've pickled what little brains you ever had with whatever the fuck you drink, but you just don't get it. I'm telling you to leave. I'm giving you that chance. I don't want to dirty my mouth on you, so I'm letting you walk away. You should get down on your knees and kiss the ground where I'm standing. You should pray to God and thank Him for little mercies, 'cause I—"

"No," said Mr. Pockets, interrupting.

"What?"

"No, my dear," he said—and there was less of the southern and more of the foreign accent in his tone—"it's you—and anyone like you—who doesn't understand. You're too young, I expect. Too young."

She tried to laugh at that, but there was something in Mr. Pockets' voice that stalled the laugh. Lefty heard it, too, but he didn't know what was going on.

Or rather, he did know and could not imagine how any thought he had, any insight he possessed, or any action he took could change this from being the end of him. The hardness in his pants had faded, and now he had to tighten up to keep from pissing down his legs.

The woman flung Lefty down, and he hit the gatepost, spun

badly, and fell far too hard. Pain exploded in his elbow and knee as he struck the red bricks, and as he toppled over, he hit the back of his head. Red fireworks burst in his eyes.

Through the falling embers of sudden pain, he saw Mrs. Conner bend forward and sneer at Mr. Pockets. Her face contorted into a mask of pure hatred. The sensual mouth became a leer of disgust, the eyes blazed with threat.

"You're a fucking idiot for pushing this," she said, the words hissing out between gritted teeth.

Between very, very sharp teeth.

Teeth that were impossible.

Teeth that were so damned impossible.

"I will drink the life from you," said Mrs. Conner, and then she flung herself at Mr. Pockets, tearing at him with nails and with those dreadful teeth.

Lefty screamed.

In stark terror.

In fear for himself and for his soul.

But his fear became words as he screamed. A warning.

"*Mr. Pockets!*"

However, Mr. Pockets did not need his warning. As the woman pounced on him, he stepped forward and caught her around the throat with one gray and dirty hand.

And with that hand, he held her.

She thrashed and spat and kicked at him. Her fingernails tore at his face, his clothes. Her feet struck him in the groin and stomach and chest.

He stood there and held her.

And held her.

Every blow that landed knocked dust from him. Lefty could feel the vibrating thuds as if they were striking him, the echoes bouncing off the front wall of the Conner farmhouse.

And Mr. Pockets held her.

Inches above the ground.

Then, with infinite slowness, he pulled her toward him. Toward his smiling mouth.

He said to her, "Oh, you are so young. You and those like you.

Even the ones you think are old. What are they, anyway? Fifty years old? The oldest living in these mountains, the one who came from far away and settled here, the one who made you, he isn't even three centuries old. Such a child. A puppy. A maggot that will never become a fly." As he spoke, spit flecked her face.

Mrs. Conner squirmed and fought, no longer trying to fight. She tried to get away.

Mr. Pockets pulled her close and licked the side of her face, then made a face of mild disappointment.

"You taste like nothing," he said. "You don't even taste of the corruption you think defines you. You haven't been what you are long enough to lose the bland flavor of life. And you haven't acquired the savory taste of immortality. Not even the pungent piquancy of evil."

"You don't . . . know . . . what you're . . . doing . . ."

Mrs. Conner had to fight to gasp in little bits of air so she could talk. She didn't need to breathe, Lefty understood that now, but you had to breathe in order to speak, and the hand that held her was clamped so tight. He could hear the bones in her neck beginning to grind.

Mr. Pockets shook her. Once, almost gently. "You and yours hunt these hills. You are the boogeymen in the dark, and I suspect that you feed as much off of their fear of you as from the blood that runs through their veins. How feeble is that? How pathetic." He pulled her close, forcing her to look into his eyes. "You think you understand what it is to be old? You call yourselves immortal because some of you—a scant few—can count their lives in centuries. You think that's what immortality is?"

Mr. Pockets laughed now, and it was entirely different from the lupine laughter of Mrs. Conner. His was a laughter like distant thunder. A deep rumble that promised awful things.

Lefty curled into a ball and wrapped his arms around his head.

"If you could count millennia as the fleeting moments of your life, even then you would not be immortal. Then, all you would be is old. And there are things far older than that. Older than trees. Older than mountains."

His hand tightened even more, and the soft grinding of bone became sharper. A splintery sound.

"You delight in thinking that you're evil," whispered Mr. Pockets. "But evil itself is a newborn concept. It was born when a brother killed a brother with a rock. And that was minutes ago in the way real time is counted. Evil? It's a game that children play."

He pulled her closer still so that his lips brushed hers as he spoke.

"You think you're powerful because monsters are supposed to be powerful. But, oh, my little child, only now, I think, do you grasp what *power* really is."

". . . please . . ." croaked Mrs. Conner.

Lefty's bladder went then. Heat spread beneath his clothes, but he didn't care.

"You think you understand hunger," murmured Mr. Pockets, as gently as if he spoke to a lover. "No. Not with all of your aching red need do you understand hunger."

Then Mr. Pockets opened his mouth.

Lefty watched him do it.

He lay there and watched that mouth open.

And open.

And open.

So wide.

So many white, white teeth.

Row upon row of them, standing in curved lines that stretched back and back into a throat that did not end. A throat of teeth that was as long as forever. Mrs. Conner screamed a great, terrible, silent scream. Absolute terror galvanized her; her legs and arms flailed wildly as Mr. Pockets pulled her closer and closer toward those teeth.

As Lefty Horrigan lay there, weeping, choking on tears, pissing in his pants, he watched Mr. Pockets eat Mrs. Conner. He ate her whole. He ate her all up.

He swallowed her, housecoat and shoes and all.

The old man's throat bulged once, and then she was gone.

The world collapsed down into silence. Even the crickets of night were too shocked to move.

Lefty squeezed his eyes shut and waited for everything he was to die. To vanish, skin and bone, clothes and all, like Mrs. Conner.

He waited.

Waited.

The cold breeze ran past and across him.

And he waited to die.

8

When Lefty Horrigan opened his eyes, the yard was empty.

Just him and his bike.

The rotten, shattered apple lay where it had fallen, visible only as a pale lump in the thickening darkness.

Mr. Pockets was gone.

Even so, Lefty lay there for a long time. He didn't know how long, but the moon was peering at him from above the mountains when he finally unwrapped his arms from around his head.

He got slowly to his feet. His knee and elbow hurt almost as much as the back of his head. The pee in his pants had turned cold.

He didn't care about any of that.

The wind blew and blew, and Lefty let it scrub the tears off his cheeks.

He limped toward the gate and opened it and bent to pick up his bike.

Something white and brown fluttered down by his feet, caught under the edge of one pedal. It snapped like plastic.

Lefty bent and picked it up. Straightened it out. Turned it over in his hands. Read the word printed in blue letters on a white background on a brown wrapper.

Snickers.

There was only the smallest smudge of milk chocolate left on the inside of the wrapper. Lefty looked at it; then he looked sharply left and right. He turned in a full circle. Waiting for the worst, waiting for the trick.

But it was just him and the night wind and the bike.

He looked at the wrapper and almost—almost—opened his fingers to let it go.

He didn't, though.

Instead, he bent and licked off the chocolate smudge. Then he folded the wrapper very neatly and put it into his pocket. He wasn't sure why he'd taken that taste. It was a weird, stupid thing to do. Or maybe it was something else. A way of saying something in a language he couldn't speak in words. And a way of expressing a feeling that he knew he would never be able to really understand.

He patted the pocket where he'd stored the wrapper. A little pat-a-pat.

Then Lefty Horrigan stood his bike up, got onto it, and wet, cold, sore, and dazed, he pedaled away. Through the darkness.

All the way home.

Whistlin' Past the Graveyard

Author's Note: This story takes place several years after the events described in the Pine Deep Trilogy, of which *Ghost Road Blues* is the first volume. You do not need to have read those books in order to read—and hopefully enjoy—this little tale set in rural Pennsylvania.

1

He had six different names.

It was Francesco Sponelli on his birth certificate, but even his parents never called him that. They called him Little Frankie most of his life. A kid's name that once hung on him made sure he'd never quite grow up. His father wasn't even Big Frankie. Dad was Vinnie. Big Frankie was an uncle back in Sicily, but who wasn't called Big Frankie *in* Sicily; just when people talked about him. Big Frankie never set a goddamn foot on American soil.

In school—from about four minutes after he stepped onto the kindergarten playground—he was Spoons. It was better than Little Frankie in about the same way that a kick in the balls was better than catching the clap. Not a holiday either way.

In the old neighborhood in South Philly—he was Frankie Spoons for all of the six months he lived there. And that's a cool name. Made him sound like a Made Man, which he would never and could never be, but it sounded great when he walked into the taproom and someone called out, "Hey, Frankie Spoons, come on and have a beer with the grown-ups."

Actually, no one ever said exactly that, but it was in his head. It's what he heard every time he walked into the bar. Especially when he saw one of the Donatellas there, who were third or fourth cousins. It was the kind of thing they said to each other because they *were* made men. The Donatella cousins worked a protection racket their family had owned since the sixties. They all had great nicknames, and they all said cool things to each other. Francesco just liked hanging out at that bar, because it made him feel like a man, like a tough guy.

Then he knocked up a girl from the 'burbs, and next thing, he was living in a crappy little town called Pine Deep in the inbred *Deliverance* backwoods of Bucks County. Near *her* folks and family, way too far from Philly, and although it was right over the bridge from New Jersey, it wasn't over the right bridge. Cross over the Delaware up there, and you're in fucking Stockton or Lambertville or some other artsy-fartsy damn place where they put boursin cheese on a son of a bitching cheesesteak, which is like putting nipple rings on the Virgin Mary.

Out there in Pine Deep, he was Spoonsie to the guys at the Scarecrow Lounge. Another stupid name that clung to him like cow shit on good shoes.

He longed to go back to Philly, but Debbie kept popping out kids like she had a T-shirt cannon in her hoo-hah. And any conversation involving "sex" and "condoms" became a long argument about a bunch of Bible shit that he was sure didn't really matter to God, Jesus, the Virgin, or anyone else. Four kids and counting. In this economy? On his pay? Seriously? God wants kids to grow up poor and stupid in a town like this?

As his Uncle Tony was so fond of saying, "Shee-eee-eee-ee-it."

But . . .

The nickname was only part of it. It was a splinter under the skin.

The kids? Well, fuck it. He did love them. Loved the process of making them, too, though he'd like to explore the option of stopping before he and Debbie turned their lives into one of those we-have-no-self-control-over-our-procreative-common-sense reality shows.

He suspected that she had some kind of mental damage. She seemed to enjoy being pregnant. Bloated ankles, hemorrhoids, mucus plugs, the whole deal. He was pretty sure that on some level, Debbie was—to use the precise medical term—batshit crazy.

But she was also the most beautiful woman he'd ever talked to. Even now, four kids in and a bigger ass than she used to have, Debbie could look at him from out of the corners of her eyes and stop his heart.

Even now.

So . . . he stayed in Pine Deep.

And he worked in Pine Deep.

That was something by itself. A lot of people in town didn't have jobs. The town was still recovering from the Trouble, and the economy blew. Sure, a few of the stores had rebuilt, and there was some out-of-town money to rebuild the infrastructure. Federal bucks. And after the town burned down, there was that big rock concert fundraiser bullshit. Willie Nelson, the Eagles, Coldplay, bunch of others, including some rappers Francesco never even heard of. It was on TV with that stupid nickname: ANTI-terror. With terror crossed out. All those middle-aged rock stars, none of whom had ever even heard of Pine Deep before those militiamen torched everything, singing about unity and brotherhood. Blah, blah, blah. If any of the money they raised ever actually reached the town, then it never made it into Francesco Sponelli's bank account.

All he got was an offer of free counseling for PTSD, which he didn't have, and a stack of literature about surviving domestic terrorism, which he didn't read, and a pissant break on his taxes for two years, which wasn't enough.

On the upside—which Francesco didn't think was really "up" in any way—the Trouble had kind of passed him by. He and Debbie and the kid—only one back then—were down in Warrington watching a movie at the multiplex when it all went down. They heard it on the news driving back. The news guys said that a bunch of shit-for-brains white supremacists put drugs like LSD and other stuff into the town's drinking water, and every single person went apeshit. What made it worse was that it was Halloween, and the town was totally packed with tourists. All those thousands of people went out of their minds and started killing each other. Worst day of domestic terrorism in U.S. history. That much was a fact. Francesco took Debbie and the kid to her sister's in Doylestown for a week. By the time they came back, Pine Deep looked like a war zone. Lot of people they knew were dead. Lot of the town was gone. Just freaking gone.

Lot of people out of work, too, because Pine Deep was built with tourist dollars.

One of the few businesses that didn't go under was the one he worked for. The one owned by Tom Gaines, Debbie's third cousin. Francesco's workload tripled, but he didn't get overtime. Gaines said he couldn't afford it because a lot of the customers couldn't afford to pay. Not right away. Some not at all.

But the job still had to be done.

And that was his life. Working for one of Debbie's family at shit for pay. Not exactly starvation wages, but it was a job with no future. Not really. Sure, he could have the job for as long as he wanted, but there was nowhere to go. There was no promotion possible. The whole company was the owner, Mr. Gaines, and him. And a couple of guys they hired by the hour to help with some heavy stuff. All of the rest of it was Francesco's to do.

Trimming all the hedges.

Pruning the trees.

Mowing the grass.

Digging the graves.

And . . . the other stuff.

The stuff he did at night.

So the graves wouldn't be messed with.

Mr. Gaines sometimes slipped him a couple extra bucks when things got bad. And he let Francesco drink as much as he wanted on the job.

He encouraged Francesco.

It was that kind of a job.

2

Before the Trouble, the job wasn't really that bad. Dead people don't complain; they don't give you shit. They don't dime you out when you go into one of the crypts to smoke a joint. He could get to a level, get mellow, and that would carry him through even the longest shift.

The job was quiet except for occasionally chasing teenagers out of the crypts who'd gone there to drink or light up. Once in a while, some prick vandal would use spray paint to tag a mausoleum or knock over a few headstones. But that happened in every cemetery, and everyone knew that, so Francesco adjusted to it as part of the job. The job was okay.

Even for a while after the Trouble, it was tolerable. He worked mostly days, and Gaines didn't go out of his way to be a prick. The boss was cheap, but not a cheap fuck. The difference mattered.

Then things started changing.

It started with people talking. The Scarecrow was one of the few bars that wasn't burned down, and it was a good place for a plate of wings and a schooner of Yuengling at the end of a day. But the flavor of the conversation there changed as the weeks and months went on. It really started after the cops and fire inspectors sorted out the last of the bones. It had taken a lot of sweat and elbow grease to put together a list of all the dead. The official tally was eleven thousand six-hundred and forty-one. Two-thirds of the whole town. Only the thing was that there weren't that many bodies. The count was short. Eighty-four short, and that's a lot of bodies to misplace.

They brought in teams of dogs to search the woods and the fields and under frigging haystacks. Still eighty-four missing.

The count stayed the same.

That's when the vandals started hitting the cemetery. Knocked-over headstones, grave dirt churned up, his toolshed broken into, beer bottles everywhere. Couple of times, he discovered that someone had pissed on a grave he'd just filled in. He mentioned all this to his cousins over a poker game. Near Danny was nodding before he finished describing the disturbances.

"Sure, sure, that makes sense," said Near Danny.

"It does?" asked Francesco, confused.

"Yeah," agreed Far Danny. "People are blowin' off steam. With all that shit happening—"

"All those people dying," added Near Danny.

"All that death and shit . . ."

". . . they're like obsessed with that death shit."

"Morbid."

"Morbid."

Francesco looked back and forth between them. "Okay, but why trash the cemetery?"

Near Danny and Far Danny said it at the same time. "Power."

Francesco said, "Huh?"

"Death came to that little fucking town and made everybody its bitch," said Far Danny.

Near Danny nodded. "And that boneyard—hell, that . . . what word am I looking for?"

"*Symbolizes*," supplied Far Danny.

"Yeah, that boneyard symbolizes death. So . . . of course someone who lost everything's going to go take a piss on it."

"Show death that *he's* alive, that he's nobody's bitch."

The two Dannys nodded.

"Wow," said Francesco.

Then Far Danny leaned across the card table and stabbed a finger at him. "But if any of these Mameluke bastards fucks with *you*, then that's different."

"It is?"

Near Danny grunted and gave him a hard sneer. "You're family."

"Nobody fucks with the family," said Far Danny. "No fucking body, you hear me, Frankie Spoons?"

"Any shit comes down you can't handle, you pick up the phone."

They sat there grinning at him like extras from a bad gangster film. Chest hair and gold chains, big gold rings, perpetual five-o'clock shadows. But they were the real deal. South Philly muscle who were tough on a level that Francesco could understand only from a distance. It was the kind of feeling you get looking at the big cats in the zoo.

Then the conversation turned to sports, as it always does. Could the Eagles do anything about their passing game, 'cause right now it was like watching the Special Olympics.

More weeks passed, and that's when people in town started talking.

Whispering, really. Real quiet, nothing out loud. Nothing in front of anyone. The whispers started over beers. At first it was late at night, before closing, guys talking the way guys do. Talking shit. Throwing theories out there, because that was the time of night for that kind of thing.

Even then, people talked *around* it. They didn't so much say it as ask questions. Putting it out there.

Like Scotty Sharp, who asked, "Do you think they really put drugs in the water?"

People said sure, of course they did. The Fed tested the water; they did blood tests on the people.

That's when Mike DeMarco said, "Yeah, well, my sister Gertie's oldest daughter goes out with that kid, you know the one. He's an EMT up to Crestville. And he said that only about one in four people tested positive for drugs."

Then some guy would say that was bullshit, and there'd be an argument. It would quiet things down. Until the next time it came back up.

Lucky Harris—and Francesco thought Lucky was a kickass nickname—asked, "Did you guys see that thing on the History Channel?"

They all did. A special about Pine Deep. Two thirds of it was the same bullshit you could get out of any tourist brochure, but then there was a section near the end when they interviewed a few survivors—and Francesco wondered if they deliberately picked the ones who looked like they were either half in the bag or half out of their minds. These "witnesses" insisted that the Trouble wasn't what the news was saying it was, that the white supremacist thing was a cover-up for what was really happening. And this is where the host of the show changed his voice to sound mysterious right as he asked what the *real* truth was about the Pine Deep Massacre.

"It was monsters," said the witness. An old duffer with white around his eyes.

"What kind of monsters?" asked the host.

"*All* kinds. Vampires and werewolves and demons and such. That's always been the problem with Pine Deep . . . we got monsters, and that night? Yeah, the monsters came to get us."

The host then condensed the eyewitness reports into a speculation that the white supremacists were really servants of a vampire king—like Renfield was to Dracula—and that the drugs in the water and all of the explosions were distractions, subterfuge.

Then there was a montage of jump shots that lasted only long enough for a dozen other witnesses to say the word *vampire*. The segment ended with the kind of dumbass tell-nothing questions those shows always have, accompanied by stock footage of old Dracula flicks and shots of Pine Deep taken with cameras tilted to weird angles. "Was Pine Deep the site of an attack by vampires? Do the dead really walk the earth? Have creatures out of legend begun a war against the world of the living? And what about the missing eighty-four? Authorities continue to search for their bodies, but there are some who believe that these people aren't missing at all and are instead hiding . . . and perhaps *hunting* during the long nights in this troubled little town. Government sources deny these claims. Local law enforcement refuse to comment. But there are some . . . who believe."

The guys at the Scarecrow had all seen that special. Just as they had all seen the headlines of the *National Enquirer*, which had supposed photos of vampires on the front page at least once a month.

Everybody knew about the stories. The conspiracy theories. As soon as the main shock of the tragedy died down, Jon Stewart and Stephen Colbert went ass-wild on the subject. They did bits about small-town vampires. Conan started a running segment with a vampire dressed in farmer's coveralls; at the end of each segment, the vampire would get killed in some funny way. He'd go out to harvest, forgetting he'd planted his fields with garlic. He'd trip over a chicken and fall on a convenient sharp piece of wood. The vanes of a windmill would cast a shadow of a cross on him. Shit like that. Making a joke out of it because it was stupid.

Vampires.

It was all bullshit.

Except that as the first year crumbled into the dirt, and the next year grew up dark and strange, it got harder and harder to call it bullshit.

Especially after people started dying.

There was a rash of car accidents in town. Accidents weren't all that rare with all the twists and turns on A32, but before the Trouble, it was mostly tourists who wrapped their SUVs or Toyotas around an oak tree they didn't see, or college kids driving too drunk and too fast with too much faith in underdeveloped decision-making capabilities.

But there was no tourism in Pine Deep right now. Maybe in another couple of years. Maybe if some outside group rebuilt the Haunted Hayride and the other attractions. Right now, State Alternate Route A32 was mostly empty except for farm workers coming and going to day jobs or farmers' wives heading into town to work shifts at the hospital or at one of the craft shops.

So, it was locals who started dying.

Linda Carmichael went first. Her six-year-old Hyundai went off the road, rolled, and hit a parked hay bailer that was sitting at the edge of a field. The papers said that she was so badly mangled that her husband had to confirm her ID by looking at a mole on what was left of her torso. Francesco didn't know if he believed that part, but when he drove past the accident spot on the way to work the next day, the car looked like a piece of aluminum foil somebody'd crinkled up.

It was a matter of discussion at the Scarecrow, but the Carmichaels weren't part of their circle, so the conversation moved on to sports.

The second accident was a bus full of Puerto Rican day workers. Nine dead because the bus skidded off the road and hit a panel truck. Both drivers were dead, too. There were no witnesses, but it must have been a hell of an impact to mangle everyone that badly.

"Yeah, maybe," said Lou Tremons, "but here's the thing, Spoonsie, there were no skid marks, and my cousin Davy heard Sheriff Crow say that it didn't look like a high-speed crash."

"Well, hell, son," said Scotty, "you can't kill that many people in a low-speed crash."

They all agreed that the sheriff, who used to be a drunk a long time ago, was probably drinking again and didn't know his ass from his elbow.

The conversation turned to sports.

But the deaths kept happening.

A mailman ran his truck into a drainage ditch and went halfway through the windshield in the process. Aaron Schmidt's son flipped his motorcycle.

Like that.

All violent accidents. Every body torn up.

Lots of blood on the blacktop.

Except . . .

Lou's cousin Davy heard Sheriff Crow tell his deputy that there didn't seem to be enough blood. In each case, there was less than you'd expect.

When Francesco dropped that little tidbit, the conversation at the bar stalled. Nobody talked sports that night. Nobody said much of anything that night. Even Francesco kept his thoughts to himself and watched the foam on his beer disappear, one bubble at a time.

The following summer was when the fires started. Everyone blamed it on the constant high temperatures, on global warming. But this was Pennsylvania, not Wyoming. There was a lot of water in the state, and even with the heat, there was plenty of rain. Francesco found it hard to buy that a drought killed all those people.

And a lot of people burned up, too.

Three of the Carter family went up while they slept. Only Jolene survived, because she was in the navy.

The guys all talked about that, and even though Bud Tuckerman suggested that it was more likely bad wiring because Holly Carter always had the air conditioners going full blast, and it had been a lot of summers since her husband had bought a new unit. The other guys mumbled agreement, but nothing sounded like enthusiastic support for that theory to Francesco.

The other fires? Five dead at the Hendrickson farm when the barn went up and cooked some kids from the horse camp.

The wiring at the camp was inspected twice a year. Scotty said so because that's what he did for a living, and he'd swear on a stack of fucking bibles that everything was up to code. Better than code, he said.

A lot of beers got drunk in thoughtful silence that night.

The weeks of summer burned away, and by fall, there were four more fires. Two business, one hotel, one house.

That last one was a ball-buster. That's where it hit home to the guys at the Scarecrow. It was Lou Tremons who got fried.

After the funeral, the guys met at the tavern in a missing man formation, with Lou's seat left empty and a glass of lager poured for him. The conversation was lively for most of the night as they all told lies about Lou. Tall tales, funny stories, some tearful memories. Francesco talked about the time he and Lou drove down to Philly to play cards with the Donatella cousins. Francesco described how Lou nearly busted a nut trying not to laugh at what everyone called the cousins. They were both named Danny, and as cousins they looked a lot alike, almost like twins, except that one of the Dannys—the one from Two Street—was really short, maybe five-seven, and the other Danny, the one who lived near Gino's Steaks, was a moose, six-seven. They looked like the same guy seen up close and far away, and long ago, the Don had nicknamed the big one Near Danny and the little one Far Danny.

Francesco warned Lou ahead of time not to laugh about it to their faces. Near Danny would break his arm off and beat Lou to death with it; and Far Danny carried a Glock nine and a straight razor, and he was a bad mamba-jamba. They worked the protection racket, and they were a pair of guys with whom you absolutely did not want to fuck. No sir, no way.

Francesco had a private motive for inviting Lou to the game. The Donatellas always called him Frankie Spoons, and he hoped Lou would pick it up and spread it to Pine Deep. But it didn't happen.

They had fun, though. Francesco caught the laughter in Lou's eyes all through the night, but Lou kept a plug in it until they were back in the car on I-95 heading north toward home.

"Then he totally lost his shit," said Francesco, and everybody had a good long laugh. Then they toasted Lou and tapped their glasses to his and drank. More than a couple of them had tears in their eyes.

Mike said, "Hey, Spoonsie, I saw a big bunch of flowers from the Donatella family. Was that the Dannys?"

"Yeah," said Francesco.

"Nice of 'em."

"Yeah. They're standup. They liked Lou."

The guys nodded. Everyone liked Lou. What wasn't to like?

"Far Danny called me," added Francesco. "After Lou . . . you know."

Everyone nodded.

"He said that he heard a lot of people been dying here in town."

More nods. Nobody said anything.

"Then he asks me if I thought there was anything hinky with Lou's death."

"Hinky," said Mike. Not a question, just keeping the word out there.

"Hinky," agreed Francesco.

"Why'd he want to know that, Spoonsie?" asked Joey the bartender, who was leaning on the bar, listening like he usually did.

"Like I said, he and Near Danny both thought Lou was okay. They told me they thought he was standup."

Nods.

"I thought you said those boys were wiseguys," said Joey.

Francesco shrugged. "Yeah, well . . . they're not bad guys."

Which was bullshit, and they all knew it, but they were Francesco's cousins, and when you're related to criminals—unless they were pedophiles or like that—then whatever they did wasn't so bad. Or as bad. Or something. None of them really looked too close at it.

"If it *was* something hinky, then maybe they'd have come up here, looked into it. They're like that. Lou was my friend, and he didn't shark them at cards, and they laughed at his jokes. So, I guess . . . you know."

They nodded. They knew.

"But I told them it was just an accident," said Francesco. "Just a string of bad luck."

They nodded at that, too, but no one met his eyes.

The only one there who was nearly silent all evening was Scotty, and eventually Francesco noticed.

"What's wrong, man?" he asked. Scotty was friends with Lou, but only here at the bar. They weren't really tight.

"I don't know, Spoonsie," Scotty began, fiddling with a book of matches. He'd pulled each match off and distractedly chipped off the sulfur with his thumbnail and peeled the paper apart layer by layer. He stopped and stared down at the pile of debris on the bar as if surprised that it was there.

"What is it?" asked Lucky Harris.

"It's just that . . ." Scotty began, faltered, and tried it again. "It's just that I'm beginning to wonder if your cousin Far Danny is right."

"About what?" asked Francesco.

"About there being something hinky."

"About Lou's death?"

"That . . . and everything else that's going on in town. You know . . . since the Trouble."

Everyone was looking at him now, and the intensity of their attention formed a little cone of silence around that end of the bar. Francesco was dimly aware of other people, other conversations, music, the Flyers on the flatscreen, but suddenly it all belonged to another world.

"What are you saying?" asked Mike.

"I don't know what I'm saying," Scotty said in a way that said he *did* know what he was saying. Everyone waited. He took a breath and let it out. "I was watching that show again. You know the one." They nodded. "And sometimes—not all the time, but sometimes—I wonder if it's all bullshit or if maybe, y'know, there's something there."

He suddenly looked around, trying to catch everyone's eyes, looking for someone laughing at him. Francesco followed his gaze, looking for the same thing. But nobody was laughing. Nobody was smiling. Most of the guys did nothing for a few moments, then one by one, they nodded.

That killed the conversation.

And it nearly stopped Francesco's heart from beating.

He saw Scotty say something completely under his breath. Francesco read his lips, though.

Scotty said, "*Jesus Christ.*"

3

Over the next few months, things in Pine Deep seemed to swing back and forth between a rash of new deaths and periods of calm. In a weird way, Francesco was more freaked out by the long spaces between the deaths. It was too much like calms before bad storms. And each one was a little longer than the last, so each time, it became way too easy to start thinking that it was over. This time it was over.

Except that it wasn't over.

The guys still met at the Scarecrow. They still talked about things, and all the time what Scotty said stayed with them like they'd been tattooed with it. But they didn't actually *talk* about it. Not out loud, not in words. But through eye contact? Sure. And with silences and with things that weren't said aloud. They all knew each other well enough to have those kinds of conversations. Francesco wondered who would pick up Scotty's conversational ball and run with it.

For his part, Francesco had to deal with another effect of the increased mortality in Pine Deep. He managed a cemetery. He dug the graves.

And he didn't like what was going on at Pinelands Grove, which is what the place was called.

His discomfort with things at work started a few weeks after Lou's funeral. It was an overcast day late in October. The colors of the autumn leaves were muted to muddy browns and purples as the slate-gray sky thickened into an early darkness. A wet wind was blowing out of the southwest, and the breeze was filled with the smells of horseshit and rotting leaves. Francesco was working in the west corner of the Grove, which was almost a mile from the front gate. The Grove was huge, with sections of old plots that dated back to the Civil War and even a few to colonial times. But the west corner was new. Before the Trouble, it had been a cabbage field that belonged to the Reynolds farm, but all the Reynoldses died that night, and the farm went to a relative who sold it cheap just to unload it. Now the only thing that was planted there were dead bodies. Nineteen in the last month. Not all of them from accidents or fires, but enough so that it was a sad place to be.

That afternoon the O'Learys, a nice young couple, buried their thirteen-year-old daughter. She'd been run over by a UPS truck. The truck driver tried to swerve, at least according to the skid marks on the road, but he'd clipped her and then plowed right into a tree. Two dead. Francesco didn't know where the driver was buried. Doylestown or New Hope, maybe. But little Kaitlin O'Leary went into the ground after a noon graveside service. Pretty pink coffin that probably cost too much for her family to afford. One of those sentimental decisions funeral directors count on. And, Francesco thought, Kaitlin was the only kid. She wouldn't need a car, college tuition, or anything else. If buying a pink casket gave her mother even a little bit of comfort, then fuck it.

The family stayed while the coffin was lowered down by the electric winch, and they and all their friends tossed handfuls of dirt and pink roses into the hole, but Mrs. O'Leary lost it around then, and her husband took her away before she had to watch Francesco dump a couple of yards of wormy dirt down on their little girl.

Francesco waited a good long time to make sure nobody came late. Then he used a front-end loader to shift the dirt. He tamped it all down with his shoes and pats from a shovel, put his equipment away, and came back to arrange the bouquets and grave blankets according to the parents' wishes. The garage was by the gate, but he didn't mind the walk. He walked four or five miles a day here at the Grove, and he was okay with that. Kept his weight down, good for the heart.

Except when he came walking across the damp grass toward the grave, he could see that something was wrong.

The flowers were no longer standing in a neat row waiting for him to arrange them. They were torn apart and scattered everywhere. The grave blanket was in pieces, too. And the little teddy bear Mrs. O'Leary had left for her little girl had been mutilated, gutted, its stuffing yanked out and trampled in the dirt.

Francesco registered all of this, but what made him jerk to a stop and stand there was the condition of the grave.

It was open.

Open.

"Jesus Christ," he breathed.

In the time it had taken Francesco to drive the front-end loader back and put his gear away, someone—some fucking maniac—had come up, dug up all the dirt, and left a gaping hole.

Francesco snapped out of his shock and ran to the grave, skidded to a stop, and teetered on the edge, staring down.

The coffin was exposed. Pale pink metal, streaked with dirt. But it was worse than that.

Much worse.

The coffin had been pried open, the seals broken. Inside, there was tufted white silk. There was a photo of the whole family at Disney World. There was a letter from Mrs. O'Leary. All of that was there.

But Kaitlin was not there.

She was gone.

Gone.

God.

4

That was one of the longest nights in Francesco's life. Calling Gaines. Calling the cops.

Answering a thousand questions.

The cops—Sheriff Crow—grilling him, almost accusing him. Gaines looking furious and scared, and giving him looks. Everybody watching as the sheriff made Francesco take a breathalyzer. Their confusion when he passed. No trace of alcohol. All the rubberneckers showing up in crowds like someone sent out invitations.

The reporters. First the local guys, then stringers for the regional news. Then the network TV vans. Shoving cameras and microphones in his face. Hour after hour.

Then the O'Learys showing up.

Yelling at him.

Screaming.

Mrs. O'Leary totally losing her shit. Nobody thinking that was strange, because it wasn't strange. Francesco thought about how he'd feel if this were the grave of one of his kids. He'd fucking kill someone. Himself, probably.

Francesco saw Mike and Scotty and Lucky from the Scarecrow. Some of the other guys, too. Hanging back, standing in a knot, bending now and then to whisper something to each other. Scotty nodded to him once, and that made him feel a little better. Solidarity. He was still one of them, and that wasn't a sure bet at first. Sometimes things cut you out and make you one of *them*, one of the people the guys talk about rather than talk to.

Debbie texted him a dozen times, asking if he was okay, telling him everything was on the news, telling him things would be okay, asking when he was coming home.

It was nearly dawn before the cops cut him loose and let him drive home. By then, most of the crowd was gone. His friends were gone, and the Scarecrow was closed.

Even Gaines was gone. Probably on the phone with his lawyer, worrying about how much of his money he was going to lose to the O'Learys when they sued. And, of course, they would sue. This was America; everybody sued everybody. Might even mean that Gaines would fire him, cut his losses, try to blame it all on him.

The last person left at the cemetery was Sheriff Crow.

"You can go," he said.

Francesco stood for a while, though, staring at the grave.

"Why?" he asked. For maybe the fiftieth time.

The sheriff didn't answer. Instead, he asked a question he'd already asked. "And you saw no one here?"

"Like I told you. I was alone here."

"No kids?"

That was a new question, and it startled him.

"What—you think some jackasses from the college—?"

"No, I mean younger kids. Did you see any young teenagers?"

"No."

"No teenage girls?"

Francesco shot him a look. "What? Like girls from Kaitlin's class?"

The sheriff just stood there, looking at him with an expression that didn't give anything away. "You can go," he said again.

Francesco trudged back to his car, confused and hurt and scared. Sad, too. He wanted to go home and hug his kids, kiss his wife, and check the locks on all the doors.

When he got into his car, he checked his cell phone and saw that he'd missed a bunch of text messages. From Scotty and a couple of the guys. Shows of support. More from Debbie, asking when he was coming home.

And one from Far Danny. He grunted in surprise. The Dannys sometimes texted him, mostly about sports or card games, and always on the birthdays of his kids, but he didn't expect to hear from them tonight.

The message read: *Saw u on the news, cuz. Somebody fucking with you?*

For some reason, it made Francesco smile. He texted back, *Don't know what's happening. Thanks for asking.*

As he was starting his car, a reply message bing-bonged. *Anybody gets in your shit, call.*

Francesco smiled again, started the car, and drove home.

5

Francesco headed down the long, winding black ribbon of A32 with music turned up loud so he didn't have to listen to his thoughts. An oldies station. Billy Joel insisting he didn't start a fire. Francesco not hearing any of the words, because you really couldn't not listen to your thoughts about something like this. His car was bucketing along at eighty when he topped the rise that began the long drop down to the development where he lived.

Immediately he slammed on the brakes.

Two people were walking along the side of the road, so close to the blacktop that Francesco had to swerve to keep from clipping them.

Two people.

A tall man with thinning blond hair.

A teenage girl.

Walking hand in hand.

They heard his car, heard the screech of his tires on the road, turned into the splash of high beams. They stared at him through the windshield.

They smiled at him.

Francesco screamed.

He screamed so long and so loud that it tore his throat raw.

The car began to turn, the ass-end swinging around, smoke rising from the rubber seared onto the asphalt, the world around the car spinning. The world in general losing all tethers to anything that made sense.

Francesco had no memory of how he kept out of the ditch or kept from rolling. His hands were doing things, and his feet were doing things, but his mind was absolutely fucking numb as the car spun in a complete circle and then spun another half-turn so that when it rocked to a bone-rattling stop, he was facing the way he'd come, his headlights painting the top of the rise and washing the two figures to paleness.

Man and girl. They stood there, still looking at him. Still smiling.

Francesco kept screaming.

Screaming and screaming and screaming.

Long after the car stopped rocking.

The man and the girl hesitated; then they took a single step toward him.

Which is when the light on their faces changed from white to rose pink. Behind the car, off behind the humped silhouette of the development, the sun clawed its way over the horizon.

The man winced.

So did the girl.

Wincing did something to their mouths.

It showed their teeth.

Their teeth.

Their teeth.

The man spoke a single word, and even though Francesco couldn't hear it, he saw the shape those pale lips made.

Spoonsie.

Francesco screamed even louder.

And then the man turned and pulled the girl's hand. She, more reluctant, finally turned, and the two of them ran across the road and vanished into the black shadows under the trees.

Francesco screamed once more, and then his voice ran down into a painful wet rasp.

The man and the teenage girl were gone.

Lou Tremons was gone.

Kaitlin O'Leary was gone.

6

Francesco didn't tell anyone about what he'd seen.

By the time the sun was up and he was home and in Debbie's arms on the couch, he was more than half sure he hadn't seen what he'd seen.

Because he couldn't have.

No fucking way.

Right?

That was a long, bad day. After he got a few hours of troubled sleep, Francesco got up, stood under a shower hot enough to melt paint off a truck, dressed, and drove back to the Grove. There was yellow crime scene tape around the open grave, but no cops. The reporters and news trucks were gone, too.

Francesco called Gaines to see what was what, mostly worried about whether he still had a job. Gaines sounded bad.

"Look," he said, "can you work tonight?"

"Tonight?" Francesco hoped his voice didn't sound as bad to his boss as it did to his own ears.

"We . . . we can't let this happen again."

"I—"

"I'm not blaming you," said Gaines in a way that left some doubt about that. "But we need someone there."

Francesco didn't want to mention that he was actually there when this shit happened. He said he'd stay late.

The image of Lou and little Kaitlin O'Leary went walking across the fragile ice in the front of his mind.

"Bullshit," he said out loud.

That usually worked.

It didn't do shit today.

He got back in his car, drove him, went into his bedroom, and got his gun. Debbie was out, the older kids were in daycare or school, and the house was empty. He sat on the edge of the bed and loaded cartridges into the magazine of a Glock nine that Far Danny had given him once.

"Hey, Frankie Spoons, this here's a good piece," said Far Danny. "Totally legal and shit. Not on any watch list."

"Good for keeping your kids safe," added Near Danny. "Long as you're living out in the fucking boonies, you got to be careful."

At the time, Francesco hadn't wanted a gun, but even though they were family, you simply didn't argue with the Dannys.

Now he was glad they'd given him a gift like this.

Then a pang of mingled pain and fear stabbed through him.

Lou Tremons had taught him how to load and shoot the gun.

Feeling strange in more ways than he could describe, Francesco got back in his car and drove to work. There was a storm coming, and the day was so overcast that it looked like twilight and it was only nine-thirty in the morning.

Francesco parked by the shed and began the slow, sad walk back to the grave. But halfway there, he veered to his left into a different section. To where Lou was buried.

After a grave was filled in and the dirt had a chance to settle, Francesco brought in some rolls of sod and filled in the open dirt with green grass. It took a while for the sod to set, for the roots to anchor it to the ground beneath. It had been weeks since Lou was buried, and the grass roots had long since taken.

But as Francesco slowed to a stop by the grave, he could see that there was something wrong.

The sod was wrinkled. There was a distinct bump in the middle.

He squatted down and stared at it, studied it.

He licked his lips, afraid to do what he was about to do.

Then he reached out a hand and pulled at the sod.

It came away like a heavy comforter. The roots were all torn, and below the layer of sod the grave dirt was wrong. It was loose, churned.

"No," said Francesco.

He fell backward and clawed the gun out of his jacket pocket, dropped it, picked it up again, and *bang!*

His finger had slipped inside the trigger guard, and the gun went off by accident. The bang was so loud that he recoiled from it, the gun bucked so hard that it fell from his hand, the bullet hit the granite headstone and whipped backward past Francesco's ear. The sound scared a hundred crows from the trees.

Francesco sat there, his ass on the wet grass, feet wide, eyes wider, heart hammering, mouth opening and closing like a fish.

Above and around him, the world ticked on into the next minute, and the next.

Then something happened.

Something awful.

The sod moved.

It rippled. Twitched.

Francesco absolutely could not move. All he could do was sit and stare.

The grass cover bulged and trembled.

The Glock lay on the edge of the grave, but Francesco could only stare as it rose up and thumped down as something *moved* beneath the sod.

Then a pale worm wriggled out from under the edge of the grass cover. Thick, gray, deformed.

And another.

And another.

Five worms in all, moving through the damp earth.

Only they weren't worms, and Francesco knew it. His mind screamed inside his head that this wasn't happening, that it wasn't true. But he knew.

Not worms.

Worms don't have knuckles.

Worms don't have fingernails.

Worms aren't attached to a hand.

A word boiled up inside Francesco's throat and burned his mouth. He spat it out.

"L—Lou . . . ?"

The fingers stopped for a moment as if *they'd* heard him.

There was a sound from under the sod, under the dirt, muffled and indistinct. Like a voice heard through a closed door.

Like a voice.

Like a name.

Spoonsie.

Then Francesco was up and running as fast as he could.

He didn't remember picking up the gun, but he became aware of it pressed to his chest with both hands. Hiding it because of his mistake? Or clutching it like a talisman? There was no time, no thought, no breath to answer those questions.

His car tires kicked showers of mud and gravel and torn grass as he drove the hell out of there.

7

Francesco spent the whole day at the Scarecrow.

The whole day.

Joey the bartender tried to get him to talk about it, probably thinking it had to do with the big thing last night. And it did, Francesco was sure of it, but he couldn't talk about it. Not now. Maybe not ever.

The pistol was a cold weight between belt and belly flesh.

Joey must have made some calls, because Lucky Harris showed up. Then Mike and Scotty. They clustered around him. Nobody said a word. For hours.

Joey put the TV on, and they watched the news. Watched *Family Feud*. Watched *The View*. Watched the day get older. Outside, it started to rain. There was a low snicker of thunder.

It was late afternoon inside the bar; outside, it looked like the middle of the night.

Scotty was the first one to talk, to try and pry him open.

"Hey, Spoonsie, you okay . . . ?"

Francesco felt his nose tingle and then his eyes and then, before he could get away from the guys and go hide in a toilet stall, he was crying. Really crying. Sobs, shoulders twitching, tears and snot running down his face.

Any other time the guys might have fucked with him. Made fun, handled it like dicks because that's what guys do when emotions get real for anything except the Super Bowl. But not after last night.

Scotty—the closest their group had to a hard-ass, reached out and took Francesco's hand, gave it a squeeze, but didn't let it go.

"We're here, brother," he said softly.

Without wiping his face, without looking up, Francesco said, "I saw that little girl."

And he told them what he'd seen on the road.

Lou Tremons.

Kaitlin O'Leary.

Walking hand in hand. Smiling at him with all those long, white teeth.

Saying his name.

And then . . . the five white worms under the dirt. And that voice down there in the dirt. Saying his name again.

Mike pressed a wad of paper napkins into his hand. Francesco stared at them for a moment unable to comprehend what they were or what they were for. Then he wiped his face and his nose. Mike patted him on the back.

Joey poured some shots, and they all had one.

No one told him he was crazy. No one asked him if he was sure. Maybe if this was another town. Maybe if the Trouble had never happened. Now, though . . . no one tried to tell him that he was wrong or suggest that he'd imagined it.

It was Lucky who asked, "What are you going to do?"

It was unfortunately phrased. What are *you* going to do.

Not *we.*

There's a line. If you stand on one side of it and let a statement like that go uncorrected, then the line becomes a wall. The moment stretched, and everyone at the bar knew that Francesco was suddenly on one side of the wall, and they were on the other.

Lucky tried to fix it without fixing it. "Spoonsie . . . you should just say fuck it. You should call Gaines and tell him to shove his job up his ass."

Francesco shook his head. "I can't."

No one had to ask why. This was Pine Deep, and this was America, and if the economy blew in the rest of the country, then it was going deep throat in Pine Deep. There were no other jobs.

"I got Debbie and the kids," Francesco said.

It was a stupid thing to say. Crazy. Impossible because the town had become impossible. The job was impossible.

But there were no other doors marked *Exit*.

For better or worse, this was his town.

His *family* lived here.

And he had nowhere else to go, nowhere else he could go.

The gun in his belt weighed a thousand pounds.

His heart weighed more.

8

When he was drunk enough so that his legs could carry him and his terror, he staggered into the bathroom, locked himself into a stall, turned and leaned heavily against the door. It took nearly four full minutes to convince himself not to put the barrel of the gun into his mouth and blow his troubles all over the walls.

Inside his head, some maniac had started a slideshow, flashing high-res images onto the walls of his brain.

A pink coffin resting on the canvas straps, ready to go into the ground.

The same pink coffin open. Tufted silk. An eviscerated teddy bear.

Cold dirt on white teeth.

White fingers grubbing through the soil.

Lou Tremons calling his name. On the road, under the ground.

Monsters.

In his town.

"God . . . help me."

And as if in answer to his prayers, he heard the bing-bong alert of a new incoming text message.

How's it going?

It was from Far Danny.

Francesco almost laughed.

How's it going?

Well, fuck me, cuz, I think I'm growing a crop of vampires, that's how it's going. How the hell are things with you? How's the leg-breaking business? Any goddamn vampires in the protection racket?

Those thoughts tumbled through his head, and a laugh bubbled at the edge of his control. He had to fight it back because it was the wrong kind of laugh. The kind you don't ever want to let get started because there's no way you can stop it. That kind of laugh can break something you know can't be fixed.

He stared at the stupid message.

How's it going.

So, instead of laughing, instead of going totally apeshit out his mind, Francesco did something else equally crazy.

He called Far Danny and told him exactly how things were going.

Every goddamn bit of it.

9

Far Danny took it pretty well.

After a bit.

At first, he got a little mad and asked Francesco if he was fucking with him.

Then he asked him if he was drunk.

And he asked if he was crazy.

Francesco said no to the first question, yes to the others, but he didn't take back anything he said. He couldn't. It was out there. He wasn't even afraid of pissing off the Dannys. Things had changed, and getting his ass kicked by his goombah cousins didn't seem so scary anymore.

Far Danny said, "Debbie and the kids? They okay?"

Francesco stiffened. It was already dark outside. He'd been here in the bar all day.

"Oh, God . . ."

10

Francesco ran out of the bathroom with the Glock in one hand and his car keys in the other. Lucky and Scotty and the others yelled and started to make a grab for him, misunderstanding what he was doing, but Francesco blundered past them and headed out into the rain.

He drove badly and way too fast.

He sideswiped a mailbox and tore some expensive stuff off the side of his car, and he didn't give a cold shit about it. The storm was pounding down on the hood and windshield, and Francesco drove as fast as he could all the way out of town, along the wet black tongue of Route A32, into his development, up to his front door, skidding to a sloppy stop and splattering mud ten feet high on the front of his house. Left the car door open, ran onto the porch, banged the door open.

Scared the hell out of Debbie, who was putting supper on the table.

The kids started yelling. The baby started screaming.

Debbie saw the gun in his hand and the look in his eyes, and she started screaming, too.

It took a long time to calm everyone down.

He had to calm down a lot to manage it.

He put the gun on top of the fridge, out of any kid's reach.

He closed and locked the front door. Checked the whole house. Locked and pinned the windows. Took the cross down off the bedroom wall, the one Debbie's grandmother had given them for their wedding. Heavy, with a silver Jesus nailed to it.

Francesco had to lie to make Debbie calm down.

He told her there was an escaped criminal in town. A madman.

She looked at the cross in his hand and then at the top of the fridge, and deep lines cut into her pretty face.

"Frankie," she said very softly—too quiet for the kids to hear—"is this about . . . the Trouble?"

He stared at her, floored.

"What . . . ? How do you . . . ?"

She shrugged. "At the beauty parlor. The girls. We . . . talk."

Outside the rain hammered the door, and the thunder beat on the walls.

An hour later, Lou Tremons kicked open the front door.

11

Francesco and Debbie screamed.

So did the kids. Even the baby, who didn't know what was going on.

Lou smiled. He seemed to like the screams.

He was dressed in mud and rainwater and his funeral clothes. He had Kaitlin O'Leary with him. And three other people. People Francesco had buried in closed coffins because they were supposed to have been too badly mangled in car wrecks or burned in fires. But they looked whole now.

They were smiling, too.

Wet lips, long white teeth. Red eyes.

Debbie screamed again and broke away from Francesco's side, throwing herself between the vampires and her children. Francesco raised the cross, holding it up like a torch against the darkness.

A couple of them flinched. The little O'Leary girl hissed and backed away.

Lou Tremons said with a wicked grin, "Yeah, well, here's the thing, Spoonsie . . . I'm a fucking atheist. If we don't believe in something it can't hurt us, and I don't believe in that shit."

A voice behind him said, "Do you believe in *this* shit?"

Lou turned. Everyone turned.

Far Danny stuck the barrel of a shotgun under Lou's chin and pulled the trigger.

As it turned out, Lou was able to grasp the concept of buckshot.

Francesco screamed.

Debbie and the kids screamed.

Kaitlin O'Leary screamed.

The other vampires screamed.

Near Danny yanked the pull cord on a chainsaw.

He screamed, too. But for him and his smaller cousin, the screams sounded a lot like laughter.

12

Francesco sat on a beach chair between Near Danny and Far Danny.

It was the last day of October.

Halloween.

That night at the house was ten days ago, but it felt like ten years ago. Debbie and the kids were staying with Far Danny's mother in South Philly. Just for a little while. Until things calmed down. Until things got straightened out.

Scotty was gone. After that night at the bar, after what Francesco told them about Lou's grave, he'd driven to a motel of town, then came back the next morning and put his house up for sale. Mike and the other guys were still here, though. But the nights at the Scarecrow were long and mostly silent. No one wanted to talk about what was going on in town.

The Dannys went back to Philadelphia for a few hours then came back with suitcases. They moved into Francesco's house. Near Danny slept on the couch. Far Danny slept in the La-Z-Boy. They'd brought more guns and other stuff.

The bodies of Lou Tremons and the others were back in the ground. Francesco had done that quietly, when no one was looking. The cemetery was a big place, and these days, not even the college kids went there to hang out.

Only Kaitlin's body was aboveground. It was in the morgue. It had been "found" by a motorist on the highway. No one could explain how she managed to get a big piece of sharpened wood buried in her chest. Some kind of post-mortem mutilation by the madman who dug her up. That's what the papers said.

Sheriff Crow came and asked Francesco some questions, but not as many as he expected. And the sheriff had a strange, knowing look in his eyes. He gave Francesco a smile and a pat on the shoulder, and that was the end of it.

Of that part of it.

Now it was ten days after the Dannys had come to Francesco's house.

Ten days after a slaughter that would probably keep his kids in therapy for the rest of their lives. Something to deal with. Something *else* to deal with.

The three of them sat on beach chairs. There was an open plastic cooler between Francesco and Far Danny.

"Beer me," said Far Danny, and Francesco dug into the ice, pulled out a longneck bottle of Stella, popped the top, and handed it to his cousin. He opened a fresh one for himself.

They drank.

Sitting in a row. Three thirty-something guys. Cousins. Drinking beer in a graveyard as the sun tumbled over the autumn trees and down behind the mountain.

The grave in front of them was a new one.

A construction worker named Hollis who'd died when scaffolding collapsed on him. Or so the story went. Lots of injuries, not enough blood at the scene.

"Smart they way they do that," said Near Danny.

"Fucking up the body so you can't tell," agreed Far Danny.

Francesco sipped his beer.

They watched the bare patch of dirt that Francesco had filled in and patted down three hours ago.

They'd brought a wheelbarrow with them. The handles of two shotguns stuck out the back, flanking the plastic grip of the Black and Decker chainsaw. There were other things in the wheelbarrow, too. Practical things. Holy water from St. Anne's. The priest there was a fourth cousin. A Donatella. The boys had bottles of garlic oil and Ziploc bags of garlic powder—the latter from Aldo's Pizza on Two Street. Stuff like that.

There wasn't a lot of conversation.

Francesco had said his thanks. He'd wept his thanks, clinging to Debbie and the kids while looking up at the blood-splattered Dannys. It had all been said. And it was all understood. This was family.

You do *not* fuck with family. Not even if you're an undead blood-sucking soulless fiend. No sir.

To have kept thanking the cousins would have been weak. And even though he was not a strong man, Francesco knew that.

The sun fell away, and the purple shadows flowed over the cemetery.

Near Danny lit a Coleman camp lantern. They had another beer. Far Danny lit a joint and they passed it back and forth.

The dirt trembled.

The joint paused in mid handoff, Far Danny to Francesco.

The dirt shivered and danced as something beneath it moved.

Near Danny sighed, bent forward, grabbed the handle of the chainsaw and sat back with it. Watching the dirt.

Francesco took the doobie and had a nice, long hit. Blew blue smoke out over the grave.

The dirt bulged as something pushed upward. Rising. Coming out.

Near Danny handed the chainsaw to Francesco.

"Yo, Frankie Spoons," he said. "You're up."

Francesco took the chainsaw. But it was Frankie Spoons who stood up with it, jerked the ripcord, and stood wide-legged, waiting for the dead to rise.

A House in Need of Children

1

There was note with the check. It read:

We bought a house and need your help.

My first thought was, *who do I know who needs help moving?*

Second thought was, *who gives an aerial fuck?* My lower back and knees were older than the rest of me, and humping couches and boxes of books sounded too much like a hard-labor punishment for convicted puppy killers, and not how a middle-aged private investigator should spend any part of his time.

My third thought came after I looked at the check. It was made out to me, Samuel Theiss Hunter, and the number of zeroes after the one made my hair sweat. Been a long damn while since I'd seen a check for ten grand.

That's when you start doing bad math. How much of that could I earn before I ruptured a nut or slipped a disk? Not enough. And, let's face it, for ten grand they could hire the front four of the Philadelphia Eagles to move their furniture.

Which meant that's not what this was.

There was nothing on either check or note, however, that explained *what* this was. The handwriting on the note was female, but the name was given as A. Pish on the check, just Pish on the envelope, and the note was signed with an A. Not illuminating.

I wish I had a sidekick. A Dr. Watson to whom I could say things like, "That's not illuminating, old chap." Or whatever Holmes would say. Then I'd amaze him by examining the envelope to reveal that it was a rare type of paper, with ink used only by a rogue band of Carmelite Nuns. Or some such bullshit.

I'm not Sherlock Holmes, and I don't have anyone to talk to but myself, which—admittedly—I've started doing sometimes. Can't blame drink for all those times, either.

So I sniffed the envelope. That's what I do. Sherlock is hyper-observant and does all that inductive reasoning—and, yes, I can be a grammar Nazi sometimes. He does inductive, *not* deductive reasoning—but I have heightened senses. It's not a birth defect. My Aunt Tillie calls it a birth*right*. It's something everyone in my family has as part of a whole package of extras. Comes with awareness that a wolf lives within each one us, always waiting just below the skin. Figuratively and literally.

Point is, I sniff like a motherfucker.

The paper itself told me nothing except that it was paper. I could smell skin oils, though. The most recent scents were female, but not from A. Pish. I recognized the freshest scent, which belonged to Jeri, the letter carrier on my route. Jeri looked like a fashion model who'd spent a lot of her nights and weekends getting drunk and eating fried foods. The bones and the classic beauty were there, buried under hypertension, too much weight, but a lot of laugh lines. I liked Jeri. Sad heart, but a sweet one. She slept over sometimes. We had history.

The other scents of recent vintage were probably different people along the chain of mail handling, from the postman who took the letter out of the mailbox where it was dropped all the way through the Post Office process until it landed in Jeri's bag.

Then I got all the way down to a female scent that I didn't know, which matched the scent on the note and check, as well. Hello, A. Pish. And that's where the frequency of my afternoon changed.

I could smell soap and perfume and all of that normal stuff. I could smell other things, too. Sweat and tears. I could smell lactic acid and urea, and minerals like potassium, sodium, calcium, and magnesium. I smelled dopamine, but not in the amounts that would be present when someone's feeling good. Wrong mix. There was adrenaline there. It wasn't at panic level, but that could mean that something had happened and the immediacy of it was wearing off by the time she sat down to write me a note. The kicker was the presence of a shit-ton of a corticotropin-releasing hormone, which is a peptide that produces feelings of anxiety or dread.

Emphasis on the dread.

I placed the note on my desk blotter, got up, and poured another cup from the ancient Mr. Coffee on the table by the file cabinets. Sat back down and sipped it while I thought about what my senses had told me.

I'm pretty familiar with fear. To someone like me, it's abundantly clear that fear comes in a lot of different flavors. There's the fear of dying, the fear of asking a woman out on a date, the fear of falling, the fear of the dark. Phobias and rational fears. And within each brand of fear there are individual frequencies. It's like a volume control. One is fear of a piece of broccoli between your teeth at a business lunch. Ten is being awake and aware as your car goes through the guardrail and you can see the ground two hundred feet below you with total clarity as you fall.

This was a level of fear that was trying to turn the dial to eleven.

Trying real hard.

Ms. A. Pish had been so deeply, completely, and profoundly terrified that it had changed the chemistry of her sweat, and some of that same chemical soup was in her tears. I could smell those tears. They'd fallen onto the note and the check. Small tears, but there.

We bought a house and need your help.

The envelope provided an address in Black Marsh, a small town on the Delaware, sandwiched between New Hope and Pine Deep.

There was no phone number. The note, the envelope, and a check for ten thousand dollars.

"Okay," I said. Talking to myself. Talking to A. Pish.

2

First things first.

I logged onto the Internet and accessed the database search engines that P.I.s like me subscribe to. Yeah, we can get all sorts of information about you that neither you, nor any law-abiding tax-paying citizen of these United States, wants anyone to have. You worry about the NSA? Fuck. Guys like me get background trace gigs from credit card companies, and no one's scarier than them.

There were a lot more A. Pishes that I would have thought prob-able. Eleven in western New Jersey alone, which is where Black Marsh was. Of those, eight were men. Adam, Alan, Allen, Arnold, Anderson, Andrew, Able and—of all things—Ahab. The remaining three were women. Annabelle, Alicia, and Anne.

None were new listings though, and none in Black Marsh. The note said *we*, which meant Pish could be a married name, though I doubted it. Women use a first initial a lot more than men do, and married couples either use both names or something like *The Pish Family.* A. Pish felt like a single woman. Or a woman who kept her own checking account separate. Or she could be a single mom, and the *we* was one or more kids. Or something. Lots of ways to spin that.

So I researched the property.

And that's where this started to make the hairs on the back of my neck stand up.

The address was 318 Stone Hill Creek Road. Sounds nice. Like a Thomas Kinkade painting. When I pulled up a picture, it fit the name. A large *faux* Tudor-style place with a flagstone path winding between hedges and opening up to flower beds. Old oaks and elms flanking the house, and an actual creek behind it. Gorgeous. The title search said that it was older than it looked, having been built in 1901 by Andrew and Abigail McHenry, who had a large family. Owned by the builder until the 1920s after Mr. McHenry died in a railroad accident near Frenchtown. There was a notice that the place was sold by the estate of the widow, but no additional notes to say why she sold it or what happened to her or her family. Seemed kind of beside the point anyway.

After that, it was sold several times over the last century. That part wasn't odd. The time frames of residency were. It was sold sixteen times in one hundred years. In each case, the owners sold the place within a year. Each time. Total registered occupation was one hundred and eighty-five months, not counting the original owner. The house sat empty for most of the last century. That left it empty for more than one thousand months. Each time the house sold, it was for a number well below market value.

Pretty house like that, ideal location, easy drive to schools. So what was making everyone leave?

I found the most recent notice of sale. Annabelle Pish, 33, formerly of Easton, Pennsylvania. She paid six hundred and ten thousand for the house. The comps on the same street, some of which were smaller, ran well over a million, some as high as two mil.

She got it for, in real estate terms, pocket change.

We bought a house and need your help.

We.

Now that I had a full name, I searched her. And found Ms. Pish on Facebook and Twitter. On LinkedIn, too. She was an artist. Sculpture and portraiture. Apparently someone of note, because she had image folders of gallery shows in Doylestown, Lambertville, Philadelphia, and one in New York.

I found pictures of her, too. Short woman with black hair and blue eyes. Not especially pretty, but nice to look at. I guessed some Italian and maybe some Welsh, with some of this and that. A melting-pot American.

There was a folder marked *Tommy.*

Thomas William Pish, Jr. Born in Newark, grew up in Easton, died in Syria two years ago. He had been Special Forces and an RPG had shot his helicopter out of the sky the first day he was in-country. Never fired his weapon in combat. I studied his face. Blue eyes, freckles, and a scuffle of red-blond hair. He didn't look much like a soldier. He looked like a high school teacher, maybe math, maybe science. A kind face, laughing eyes. Dead now, sent home in a box and buried in Arlington.

Leaving Annabelle to raise Beth, three, and Kara, five.

We.

I drank the rest of my coffee and got a second cup.

We bought a house and need your help.

We need your help.

Annabelle, Beth, and Kara.

We.

So, I closed up the office and drove to Black Marsh.

3

Black Marsh is a small town. Picturesque, quiet, quaint, and forgettable. No one would ever have heard of it had it not been across a small bridge from Pine Deep, where they had all that trouble a few years ago.

I hated Pine Deep. Got into some trouble there myself. And I have about as much desire to go back as I do for getting genital warts.

I drove up Route 611 and then crossed into Jersey at Stockton, meandering through autumn back roads toward Black Marsh. You can miss that town pretty easily. Like a lot of farm towns, it covers a big area in terms of square mileage, but the entire population could fit easily into a high school auditorium. Bemused cows watched me from their side of wood rail fences. A horse decided to try and race me, but since I was driving a ten-year-old Hyundai piece of shit, he won so easily he got bored and stopped to piss on the sunflowers. I tooted at him as I drove past.

This was late October in rural New Jersey. There is no actual number in mathematics to count all of the colors of leaves in the trees. Golds and reds and oranges and purples and browns, and even some stubborn greens. There's a phrase, a *riot of color*. But this was a soccer riot of color. Much bigger and more emphatic. Every tree seemed to think it was in a reality show competition with every other tree, each of them showing off with exuberant ostentation. To a city boy like me, this was always stunning. I don't get out into the country often enough, and there have been years when I missed fall altogether. Now here I was, tooling down a country lane through nature's color palette while the radio blasted old Beatles songs. Could have been a beautiful day if it wasn't for what I was out here to do.

I've been fooled by days like this before. Start out great and they whisper promises all day until they break your heart sometime around sundown. I hoped this wasn't going to be one of those days but, let's face it, my luck tends to run that way.

4

There was a small turnaround in front of the house, and I parked on the arm that was closest to the exit. Not that I was deliberately planning for flight, but there you go. The house was three stories tall and had a two-car garage with one door open to show the ass end of a cream-colored Toyota RAV4 hybrid.

I killed the engine and got out. The last bees of the season were flying with drowsy semi-interest from flower to flower, and a fat spider hung drunkenly in a badly spun web under the curbside mailbox. A hula hoop and a rubber kickball lay in the grass. Over near the elm was a tether pole with a cable long enough for a dog to have the run of the yard without reaching the street.

I sniffed. Dog was a golden retriever. Young. I could smell the kids, too. Soap and laughter and PB&Js. It made me want to smile, because at face value, this place was selling *happy* pretty hard.

Happy people never hire me.

The farther out into the country you get, the more likely it is that people know you've arrived before you knock on the door. It saves having to knock. I walked slowly toward the house and was not at all surprised when the door opened before I reached it and Annabelle Pish peered out from shadows into sunlight.

In person she was prettier than her pictures. Some people are like that. They have a vibrant life force that shines through and amps up your reaction, no matter how ordinary their features might be. This was a classic example of the case. Pish had blue eyes that were almost exactly the same shade as the sky, and there was a crow's wing luster to her thick black hair. Her mouth was made for smiling, and she actually smiled as she said, "Mr. Hunter?"

"I got your note," I said.

She stepped out of the house and offered her hand. "I'm Annabelle. Call me Belle."

"Sam," I said, shaking her hand. Her grip was firm, but her skin was moist. Nervous perspiration. Up close I could see the fragile way in which her smile was pinned to her face. There were lights in her eyes, too. The kind that let me know she'd *seen* something.

"First things first," I said, releasing her hand. "How'd you know to reach out to me?"

"Oh. You were recommended to me by a friend."

"May I ask that friend's name?"

"Mike Sweeney," she said. "He's a deputy over in Pine Deep."

"I know Mike." Though I'm not sure *friend* is the word I'd use to describe what we are to each other. We worked a very bad case a couple of years back, and during that gig we discovered that he and I share some things in common. Sometimes we both go running around on all fours and howl at the moon, if you dig what I'm saying. He's not a *Benandanti* like me and all of my family. He's something else, and quite frankly he scared the shit out of me so much, I didn't want to go sniffing too much into his backstory. Mike is one of the most powerful and dangerous people I'd ever met, though, and despite his being a class-A weirdo and indisputable monster, he is one of the good guys. If you fuck with the people he cares about, he will end you. I might give you a chance to make things right. He won't. He's also a misanthropic curmudgeon of epic proportions and lacks what you might call "social skills."

"You're a friend of his?" I asked.

"We, um, see the same person," she said. And by *person*, I figured it was a therapist. "We got to talking in the waiting room, and we've had lunch a few times. He's very sweet."

"Uh-huh. Mike. Sweet." I had to smile.

"Very sweet. And the kids love him."

"Okay," I said.

"When I told him what was going on here, he suggested I get in touch with you."

I glanced past her to the house and back. "This wasn't something he could handle?"

"He, um, said that it wasn't in his, um . . . area of specialty?" Belle said, posing it almost as a question.

"He's a cop and has some, ah, similar skills to mine," I said, being delicate.

"You mean he's a werewolf?" she said bluntly. "I know."

"Oh," I said.

"Yes," she said.

The two of us standing outside of her pretty house, surrounded by autumn foliage, gorgeous flowers, and bright sunshine. Talking about werewolves. So, that happened.

She studied my face and laughed. "God, I guess that was too blunt."

I held my thumb and index finger an inch apart. "Just a little."

"Sorry."

"I don't have conversations like this very often."

Belle giggled. "No, I don't suppose you do."

We stood there.

"So," I said, "werewolves . . ."

"Yes."

"No," I said, "that was kind of a leading sentence intended to get us somewhere."

"I know," she said, and the smile dimmed perceptibly, taking some of the brightness of the day with it. "Sorry, I . . . I guess I don't really know how to do this."

"Well, let's stick with the werewolf thing. Mike Sweeney just up and said, 'Oh, and by the way, I'm a lycanthrope'?"

Belle crossed her arms under her breasts. "No. Not at first."

"Because that would have been weird," I suggested.

"Because at first, we were seeing the same shrink, and we both thought that either the other person was crazier than us, or we were definitely crazier. You play those kinds of mental games in psychologists' waiting rooms."

"Been there," I said. "I usually figure I'm the weirdo in any pack."

"Move to Black Marsh," she said. "Or better yet, Pine Deep. You probably wouldn't make Top Ten weirdoes."

"Fair enough," I conceded.

She turned and leaned against the doorframe. It was notable that she had not yet invited me in. She was saving that for an appropriate moment, and we both knew it.

"Mike and I started talking," she said. "First about nothing, the way people do. Then one day he was in the waiting room wearing his uniform, and I made a comment about Pine Deep, about the Trouble. I asked if he'd lived there then. He got up and moved to another seat and didn't speak to me for two visits. If either of us was in the waiting room after that, he'd sit as far away as he could."

I said nothing.

"Then one day, when I had a session after his, I came out of the office, and he was waiting for me in the parking lot, leaning against my car. He had a bunch of flowers with him, and he apologized for being mean. The thing is, I didn't think he was being mean. I figured that maybe he'd been in Pine Deep when the Trouble happened—he'd have been in like, ninth grade—and had PTSD, like a lot of people over there have, you know?"

"I heard," I said.

"Mike and I started going out sometimes. Not dates exactly. I'm still not ready for that kind of stuff. My husband was killed in action in Syria. It's a little more than two years, but I guess some things take time. I got my two girls, and that's about as much of an emotional commitment as I'm ready to make. Mike understands that. He has his own stuff he's dealing with." She cocked her head and squinted through sunlight up at me. "But I guess you know all about that."

"He came right out and told you?"

Belle took her time thinking of how she wanted to answer that. "We sometimes sit on my porch and talk halfway through the night. We found that we can tell each other anything. I . . . I've only ever had one person I could talk to like that, and that was my Tommy. I told him everything. Stuff I probably don't even remember anymore. There were no secrets between Tommy and me, and when he died, it was like part of me died, too. No, that's not right. It was like part of me was—"

"Erased?" I suggested, and she nodded.

"Exactly. His death edited part of my life out of my own story." She made a face. "God, that sounds so stupid and poetic—"

"It doesn't, actually," I said. "I get it. I've lost people who were close to me, too. When they go, a part of you actually does go with them. My grandmother used to say that we are the custodians of those we love."

She thought about that and wiped at a small tear, nodding. "I never thought I'd ever be able to talk like that with anyone ever again. Pretty sure I didn't think I'd want to. But Mike . . . he's so open, so nonjudgmental. So gentle."

I thought about Mike Sweeney. He's six-and-a-half foot tall, two-hundred and seventy-five pounds of hard muscle and rubbery hide. Even if he wasn't a werewolf, he looked like he could bite the head off a rattlesnake and spit it in the Devil's eye. For kicks. Not sure I ever saw him smile.

Here's the thing, though. Since Mike is one of the good guys, and because his boss—the town's chief of police, Malcolm Crow—has told me stories of what Mike has done, what he's sacrificed to protect those who couldn't protect themselves, I was kind of happy to know that he had a soft side, and that he had made a friend like Annabelle Pish who was able to reach him. There's a bit of hope in that for all of us, even lone wolves like me.

And I could definitely see why Mike opened up to Belle. She had that rare and special energy that engenders trust and compassion. I still didn't know what was going on out here, but I knew that I'd walk barefoot through glass to help her. Some people bring out the white knight in you, even in rusty, cranky old bastards like me.

"You said Mike couldn't help you?"

Belle's eyes clicked over toward the house. "He tried."

"And—?"

"And the house beat him."

"The 'house' beat him?"

"Oh, yeah, sure . . . didn't I get to that part yet?" she said, pasting on a very crooked smile. "The house is really haunted."

5

So, okay, haunted house.

Never did a haunted house case before.

Never *been* to a haunted house before.

I walked a few paces back and looked up at the place. There was absolutely nothing creepy about this place. Not one thing. No belfry filled with bats. No ghostly faces at the upstairs windows. No ominous creaks or crooked towers or looming gables. If gable can loom. Not sure about that part.

Thing is, this house looked like it was made for building go-carts in the summer, kids having tea parties on the lawn, watching fireflies dance, drinking a cold beer after mowing the grass, planting geraniums. I'm not actually sure I've ever seen a place less likely to be haunted than this house. Stephen King would get writer's block in this place. Goth girls would dress in pastel prints and actually laugh out loud. The best Hollywood gaffer couldn't light this place to make it look ominous. Pretty sure this is where Disney princesses go to retire.

"Haunted," I said.

"Haunted," she agreed.

"How haunted?"

"Very," she said, and she wasn't smiling anymore.

I put my hands in my back pockets and studied every inch of the exterior; then I sighed and came back to where she stood by the front door. "What makes you think it's haunted?"

She shrugged. "I see the ghost all the time. My girls see it. Mike's seen it."

"Oh. And what does the ghost look like?"

She didn't answer at first.

"Belle . . . ?"

She still didn't reply, so I waited her out. I sure as hell wasn't going inside without more information. Finally Belle took a crumpled tissue from her pocket, dabbed at her eyes, and blew her nose.

"When Mike saw the ghost, it looked like his mother."

"Oh."

"When I saw it," she said in a small voice, "it looked like Tommy."

"Oh shit."

"That's who Kara sees, too. She remembers her dad. She was three when he left for the Middle East. She wakes up screaming sometimes because she doesn't see Tommy the way he looked when we took him to the airport." Fresh tears glittered in the corners of her eyes. "She sees him the way he must have looked after that rocket hit his helicopter. All torn up. With . . . fire . . . with his hair on fire and . . ."

And that was as far she could get. She turned away and buried her face in her hands and began to sob. I stood there, not touching her, feeling incredibly awkward and stupid and ineffectual.

"Is that how you see the ghost, too?"

She shook her head, and in the small and broken little whisper, she said, "I see him the way he is now. In his grave. Rotted away . . ."

I turned and looked once more at the house. It was still lovely and prim and orderly, but now there was something hateful and ugly about it. As if its mask had slipped, revealing the face of a *thing* rather than a place. Cruel, monstrous, vile.

Hateful.

I could feel the wolf in my blood come to point, sniffing the air, salivating, feeling the ache in muscles and belly and teeth.

I had no idea if I could hurt a ghost, or if one could ever *be* hurt, but on the other hand, over the last few years I've come up against vampires, demons, and other kinds of creatures. In my experience, if it's supernatural, then it can be hurt by something on its own level. If that was the case, then I decided I was going to tear the fucking heart out of this goddamn place. For Belle and her kids. For her brave husband two years in his grave. For everyone whose lives had been polluted by this house.

You see, that's how it works with me. When I take on a new client, it's like they become part of my pack. I care about them. Maybe it's the wolf in me; maybe it's the human soul. Don't know, don't care. What matters to me is that this thing was doing harm to genuine innocents.

Fuck that.

"Let's go inside," I said.

6

She went in without hesitation.

"It's quiet most of the time," she said. "It's been quiet today."

The short foyer opened into a living room that had comfy cushioned chairs and sofas, a big fireplace, lots of wood beams, and exposed rock. More of a rustic motif than I would have expected considering the outside. Art on all the walls. Some of it was hers—I could tell that because I'm a trained investigator and can read an artist's signature—some of it was from artists I'd never heard of. No prints. Everything was original.

I know a little about art because my first wife worked in a gallery. My take is that there is usually a theme, but it only ever makes sense to the artist, and it's often as simple as 'this is a bunch of fruit'. Critics, gallery owners, and collectors endlessly debate underlying metaphors and what the artist is 'trying to say'. On the whole, a lot of that is horseshit, because it's supposed to be a bunch of fruit.

Her paintings were not bunches of fruit.

They were abstracts and impressionistic pieces, and I could have bet a shiny nickel I could tell which pieces had been painted before she moved here and which were recent. Even if I couldn't smell the age of the paint, which I can.

The oldest pieces were about optimism and a genuine love of life. They were big, with swirls of color that took unexpected but intriguing turns. Then there were paintings that were tighter, darker, painted with sad colors and truncated lines. Even then, though, there were small islands of brighter hues. Belle shouldn't be wasting her money on therapists; she should let her therapist look at her art. I glanced at the older paintings and saw when first one bright splash appeared in the chronology of her art, and then a second. Kara and then Beth, and their proxies-in-color, were constants throughout the canvases painted by a grief-stricken hand.

Then I saw a dozen canvases stacked against a wall, and I went over and tilted them against my thigh one by one as I studied them. The paint here was recent. Weeks and months. Nothing older than a year. Painted here.

They were a balance of her older themes. The colors of hope, the colors of grief, the splashes of joyful colors that represented her daughters. In each, though, there was a smoky, indistinct form; swirling in some, static in others. Belle had added small tints of her happy colors, but they were woven together with the darkest black and the saddest grays. That it was the ghost was obvious, but it was not the intensely ominous presence I expected to find.

The canvas at the front of the stack was the most compelling of all, and it confused me. Structurally it was the least impressionistic and clearly showed a bedroom with a bed, a chair, and a window, outside of which was the big elm. It was far from photo-real, with these items conveyed by suggestion. However, it was how the painting was populated that caught and held my attention.

The ghost was there, seated on the chair, its body sexless and blurred but still painted with blacks, grays, muddy whites, and moody blues. There were also threads of the same colors Belle used to represent her kids. Clustered around the ghost were forms of various sizes. I saw the colors of Beth and Kara, but there were five other smudges, as well, each given their own combination of innocent, bright colors, as if they were other children. The seven smudges of bright colors were gathered on the floor and the bed as if listening to the ghost. Each of them leaned slightly toward her. Drawn to her.

And, I realized, that I was starting to call the ghost *her*.

"I painted that last week," said Belle, and I jumped a foot in the air. I should have known she'd come up behind me—big scary werewolf and all that shit—but the painting had held me totally entranced.

"Sorry," she said.

I pretended it hadn't happened.

"What do you think it means?" I asked.

She lifted the canvas, considered it for a moment, and then moved it to the back of the stack, turned to face the wall. "I . . . I think the ghost wants to take my children from me."

I turned to her. "Tell me about the ghost."

7

We sat in her kitchen and had coffee. Good coffee, too, none of that instant powdered sin-against-God stuff. Once we were seated, Belle told me her story.

"When we moved here, it was supposed to be a fresh start," she began. "Tommy's been gone two years now, and since he's buried in Arlington, we didn't need to stay near his, um, grave, you know? He has no family, and I don't either. It's just me and the girls. I've always loved this part of Jersey, and it's right across the water from Bucks County, and that's been one of the strongest centers for the arts going back to forever, and the arts community is very supportive. I saw this place on Trulia and couldn't believe the price. The realtor was very nice and did everything she could to make me want to buy it."

"Bet she didn't mention the ghost," I said.

"That seemed to have slipped her mind," Belle said with a pained smile. "The Trulia ad is what sold me, though. You know how they put these taglines on certain listings? Like, 'A magical cottage,' or 'Build a life here'? This place had a description I thought was so wonderful at first, but now it scares me."

"What was it?"

She fetched a folded computer printout of the ad. It showed the house in the full flush of summer and written in a lovely script font was this:

A house in need of children!

"Well, holy shitballs," I said.

She explained how she had gotten such a positive vibe when she did her walk-through with the realtor, and when she had worked on the place to redesign the interior and have some work done. The house had been empty for a while, though the various realtors had made sure to keep it secure, clean, and free of families of raccoons. Belle moved in two months after purchase, and everything was quiet for almost the whole first month.

Then the girls started having nightmares. They'd wake up screaming.

Belle thought it was because they moved from the house where they'd always lived to a new place with all new people. Kids were like that. Belle invented new bedtime games to send them off with happier dreams.

It didn't work. The dreams got worse.

Belle let the kids come in and sleep with her.

And the dreams got worse.

It wasn't until the third month that Belle herself started having bad dreams.

In her dreams, Tommy would come into the bedroom, his body withered to a husk, his eye sockets black and empty, withered flesh pulled back from cracked and grinning teeth.

Because the girls were sleeping with her that night, Belle managed not to scream. She wanted to, though. She needed to, but she held it in. For them.

Mother's courage. Geez.

From there it started going south. Tommy began appearing during the day, sometimes sitting at the dinner table. Sometimes coming into the bathroom when Belle was taking a shower. Then he tried to climb into bed with her.

I felt my skin crawl. There had been cases of hauntings where the ghost targeted a woman or a child and made definite sexual advances. There was a movie with Barbara Hershey about one of those cases. Scary fucking stuff. When I mentioned that to Belle, though, she shook her head.

"It wasn't like that," she said. "I thought it was, at first. Tommy would get into bed and try to wrap his arms around me. Sometimes I'd wake up because I felt arms around me."

"Jesus," I breathed.

"But that was all. It was like he wanted to hold me but not to . . . not to . . ."

She couldn't finish it, and I didn't need to hear it.

"Did this ghost ever put hands on the kids?"

Belle's eyes filled with a special light, a bright horror that burned hot as a candle. "All the time. But again . . . it was just to hold them. He never tried anything else."

She called it *he*.

Then she told me about what happened when she asked Mike Sweeney for help. Belle drove the kids to Lambertville and left them with a friend overnight. She and Mike stayed at the house and waited for the ghost to arrive.

It was a no-show, though.

The next night, after Mike went home and Belle was back with her kids, the ghost came back.

So, they repeated the same plan, with the kids once more at a friend's house. No ghost.

"It's the girls," I said.

Belle nodded. "A house in need of children," she said, and the tears began falling again. Two of them, cold as silver.

It was only when Mike stayed over on nights the children were home that he encountered the ghost. He didn't see Tommy Pish because he had never met the man. And even Belle did not think the ghost *was* Tommy.

"My Tommy would never do that to me," she insisted. "And he'd never do anything to hurt our girls."

I believed her.

Mike Sweeney saw his mom. Belle told me that Mike had explained who and, more importantly, *what* his mother was. Or had been. Mike's father, Big John Sweeney, had been murdered by Vic Wingate when Mike was little; and Wingate had gone on to marry Sweeney's widow, Lois. Wingate was a sick, sadistic, abusive son of a bitch who was also the lieutenant and enabler for Ubel Griswold, a monster in every way in which that word could be used. Griswold had moved from Eastern Europe to Pine Deep years ago and had murdered a lot of people. The locals, a bunch of redneck mouth-breathers with KKK leanings, had lynched an itinerant black farm worker for the killings, but Griswold was responsible, and it was Wingate who orchestrated the lynching.

Griswold, you see, was a werewolf. Not like Mike or me. The bad kind, and sadly there are more bad ones than good ones. Wingate had covered up the killings and paved the way for Griswold to come back from the dead. Not as a werewolf, but as a kind of vampire.

I know, it's complicated, but this is supernatural shit, so roll with it.

It's always complicated. In Belarus and Poland, there are plenty of old legends about werewolves who return as vampires. Scary, even to guys like me. The "Trouble" in Pine Deep was all about Griswold raising an army of vampires and trying to start a war on the living, with Vic Wingate as his human aide-de-camp.

It didn't work, which is why we're alive to have this conversation.

Malcolm Crow—who wasn't a cop at the time—his fiancée, Val Guthrie, and a couple of others, including a fourteen-year-old Mike Sweeney, were the pieces on the other side of that chessboard. They were outnumbered and outgunned, but they won. I'm still not sure how. A lot of other people died, and if you watched the news, you know that it still stands as the largest act of domestic terrorism in U.S. history. Not as a vampire apocalypse, but because Wingate had managed to build in a cover story that made it all look like a coordinated attack by white-supremacist militia groups. Urban legend, in this case, has been telling the truth ever since.

During this whole thing, Mike discovered that his real father wasn't John Sweeney but was, in fact, Ubel Griswold. Which made Mike the son of a werewolf.

For the record, it's a gene, not a curse. It may be supernatural, too, but it is definitely a gene. Funny old world.

During the Trouble, Mike's mother was turned into a vampire along with hundreds of others. Eighty-three vampires survived the final battle that killed Griswold, and over the next dozen-odd years, Mike hunted them down and killed them all. Including his mother.

So, yeah, Mike's in therapy.

When he stayed over, his mother showed up. Covered in blood, her limbs torn by tooth and claw. Mike was confronted by the evidence of the murder he had committed. It didn't matter at all that he had killed Lois Wingate to save everyone in Pine Deep. He had torn his own mother to pieces, and the evidence of that act visited him at Belle's house. Must have been horrible.

"Mike freaked out a little," said Belle quietly. "He made me grab the kids and go sit in my car outside. He told me later what happened. He tried to attack the ghost, but it wouldn't fight him. Mike said he could *feel* it, though. It wanted him to leave and tried really hard to scare him away. It, um, changed shape. Becoming his stepfather."

"Vic Wingate?"

"Yes. You know about that, I guess."

"I do."

"The ghost became Vic and the other one. The one who came before Vic."

"Ubel Griswold?"

Belle nodded and didn't repeat the name. She hadn't spoken Vic Wingate's name, either. Some people are afraid of putting a name to certain things. It's like the people in those Harry Potter books calling Voldemort "he who must not be named." They're afraid that the name will call or conjure the evil. I can't really blame them. In my experiences, there's some truth in that.

"Mike tried everything he could," continued Belle, "but he couldn't fight it. He wants me to move, but . . ."

She shook her head.

"What?"

She looked at me, and I saw something flicker behind her eyes. A harder light than I'd seen before. Defiance, anger, and something else.

"What if this thing *is* Tommy?" she said, and now there was an edge to her voice. "What if Tommy is trying to reach us and is . . . I don't know . . . *confused* about how to do it. If we move away, then I could lose that, too. I could lose the last connection I have to him."

Her voice began to quaver a little at the end. One of the problems of having that edge is that it can cut you, too. Strength can be brittle.

I sat back and considered. "Somehow," I said, "I don't think your ghost is Tommy."

"Why not?" she snapped, and then blinked in surprise at how angry and defensive she sounded. The speed and depth of her self-awareness was one of the many good qualities I saw in this woman. Tommy had been a lucky guy, at least for a while. And maybe Mike Sweeney was lucky now. Kind of. She was a great woman to know, but at the same time, she certainly had her share of complications.

"Why'd he have you call me?"

Belle nodded as if expecting that question. "He said you'd ask, and the answer's a little complicated. During the Trouble, Mike got to know a woman named Jonatha Corbiel from—"

"From University of Pennsylvania. Professor of Folklore, sure. I know Jonatha pretty well. She's been pretty useful to me in certain kinds of, ah . . . cases."

She nodded again. "Mike asked her because she understands the supernatural stuff. She's an expert."

"World-class," I agreed.

"Maybe this is going to sound stupid," said Belle, "but Professor Corbiel told Mike that an ordinary werewolf could not fight a ghost because they aren't on the same existential plane. She said, and I'm quoting her exact words, 'a *Benandanti* can walk through doorways closed to others.' Does . . . does that make sense to you?"

"Some," I admitted. "Three years ago, I'd have said you were listening to too many Enya CDs. My personal view of the universe has expanded a tad since then."

"I guess mine has, too. And Mike's been living in that world since the Trouble."

I heard a *thump* in the other room and half-turned. As I did so, I habitually sniffed the air, a thing my grandmother and aunts taught me when I was in a dangerous situation. Our noses absorb and process smells faster than a normal wolf's. A lot faster. I expected to smell little girl-kids, but there was nothing beyond the paint smells of her canvases.

"Oh," said Belle, "it's back."

It. Not *he* this time.

I got up and went into the other room, and my muscles ached to make the change, to drop to all fours and go hunting.

The living room was empty, and for a moment I thought that the sound had been a distortion, a house echo of something else. But my senses aren't wrong all that often.

Belle came and stood beside me. She nodded to her stack of canvases. I saw it, then.

Before we'd come into the kitchen, she had put one painting at the back and turned it around to face the wall. The one where the ghostly image was surrounded by children. Belle's and other kids.

Now the painting was in the front, face out, where it had been when I'd first seen it.

"It happens all the time," said Belle. She stood very close to me, and I could smell her fear. "Every time I try to turn it away or put it in the closet or even in the garage, it's right back there. Sometimes I even find it on one of the walls where something else should be hanging."

"Where are your kids, Belle?" I asked.

"Upstairs."

"Alone?"

"Sure. Nothing bad ever happens during the day unless you count the wasps."

"Wasps?"

"Oh, yeah, we had a nest under the eaves. Mike got it out, but we still get some in the house. I have to keep on top of it, too, because Beth is very allergic. I keep EpiPens in every room. I found two of them this morning. Dead, thank God, but they were on the windowsill in the playroom."

"You need to call Orkin."

She laughed. "One pest problem at a time, don't you think?"

"I guess."

Belle said, "At night the girls always sleep with me."

"Are both of them scared of this thing?"

She gave me a funny look. "Of course they are. We all are."

"Are both of them scared in the same way?"

She chewed her lip. "Like . . . is one more scared?"

"Yes," I said.

"Kara's older. She remembers her dad more, so she's more hurt by it, I think. Beth is little and she sees the ghost in all sorts of ways, but it's not as real to her. I don't think it's much more real to her than the witch in those Disney films. But, yeah, they're both really scared."

I nodded. "Okay, let's go talk to your kids."

8

Belle's daughters were adorable, beautiful, and terrified.

The house had three bedrooms on the second floor. One was the master, the second was shared by the girls—or had been before they began sleeping with Belle—and the third was a playroom. Belle said that her studio was in the attic, which she'd made by knocking the walls out of two smaller bedrooms. The girls' bedroom was clearly the one in the painting, but I went into the playroom and sat down on the floor.

Kara and Beth were surrounded by stuffed animals and dolls, and there was some kind of tea party thing going on. They looked at me with large eyes that were identical matches to their mother's, even though both girls were strawberry blondes. Their dad's gene, I assumed.

Belle sat down with us, letting her presence assure the girls that I was okay.

They looked at me, assessing me with their large, young, wise eyes. The older girl, Kara, lost interest pretty quickly. I'm used to that. But the little one, Beth, stared at me and into me with a truly penetrating gaze that I swear to God I could feel. This one was special, and although I didn't know how, I knew it for sure.

"You're here to talk to Grandma," said Beth. It wasn't a question, and even with her little-girl lisp and high voice, the effect was immediate and chilling.

Kara sighed heavily. "She's always saying stuff like that."

I cut a look at Belle, who had two deep vertical lines between her eyebrows. I mouthed the word *grandma,* but Belle shook her head. New to her.

"Beth," I said, "is your grandma the one who keeps showing up at night?"

Beth nodded. She picked up a stuffed aardvark and poked it in the stomach.

"Are you sure it's your grandma?" I asked.

Beth said nothing.

Kara said, "We don't have a grandma. She died."

Beth's head turned slowly toward her, the way a praying mantis does, though not—thankfully—as far around. "You're stupid."

"No I'm not. We put flowers on Grandma Ellie's grass." I figured she meant that they put the flowers on the grassy grave, but it wasn't a time to be pedantic.

"We got more than one grandma," said Beth, turning back to the aardvark.

Belle very quietly said, "Grandma Ellie was my mom. She died before the girls were born. Grandma Rose was Tommy's mom. She died before I met him. The girls have seen their pictures."

"See," said Kara, "I told you."

Beth nuzzled the aardvark. "Not talking about them."

"Well, we only have two grandmas," said Kara quite firmly, "and they're both dead."

"All of our grandmas are dead," said Beth.

All.

"Beth," I said gently, "do you have *another* grandma somewhere?"

The little girl didn't answer. Not at first. Instead she held the aardvark up to her ear as if listening to what the thing wanted to tell her. She nodded a few times.

"Beth . . . ?"

"Yes," said the little girl.

I licked my lips, which had gone dry. The room seemed colder than it should have been, even though I could feel a steady stream of warm air from the vent. If I wolfed out, I'd have been able to see the thermals in the room, but this did not seem like a good time for that. Kids, you know?

Belle looked very confused and very scared.

"How many grandmas do you have?" I asked Beth.

After a moment she said, "Three." As if that made all the sense in the world.

"Who are they, baby?" asked Belle. "Can you tell me their names?"

Beth took a long time with that. "Grandma Ellie and Grandma Rose."

"And who else?" I asked.

Kara was watching this, and after a short lag had seemed to catch onto the fact that we weren't blowing off the concept of a third grandmother as quickly as perhaps we should have. She sidled closer to Belle, who put an arm around her.

"She's going to make Daddy come back," whispered Kara with a hitch in her voice. "I don't want Daddy to come back. Not anymore. He's all hurt. He's all bloody."

She sounded younger than her little sister. Terror can do that. Drain us of our age, and both the confidence and certainty that came with growing up.

"Beth, honey," I said slowly, "who's your third grandma?"

Again she raised her head and turned slowly, this time to look at me. Those blue eyes were as sharp and penetrating as lasers. "Grandma Abbie," she said matter-of-factly.

"Abbie?" I echoed and glanced at Belle, but she shook her head again.

"Grandma Abbie lives here," said Beth.

I looked around. "Is she here now?"

"She's always here," said Beth. "Sometimes she's asleep, though."

Kara whimpered and pressed closer to Belle.

"Is Grandma Abbie sleeping now?"

Beth smiled. It was sudden and bright and completely unnerving. "Oh, no," she said. "She's right behind you."

I whipped around, turning, rising, and almost goddamn shape-shifting right there in front of the kids. There was something behind me, but it was gone. Not really there. Like a fading wisp of smoke caught in the corner of the eye, gone before I could even get a look at it.

Gone. Sure. But it had been there. In the split second it took me to turn, *it* had registered on my senses. A fraction of a second's worth of input. A smell like old ashes, burned out and gone cold. A whispery sound of heavy cloth. A shimmer in the air. My exhaled breath puffed steam into the air and then faded.

Gone in an instant.

Kara started to cry. "Daddy's here."

Belle pulled her close and reached for Beth, but the little girl evaded her grab. She sat and stared at the empty air behind where I had been sitting.

"Take the kids out of here," I said quietly. "Do it now."

Belle got to her feet with Kara clinging to her like a spider monkey. Beth rose, too, but without haste. She let her mother take her hand, but at the doorway, the little girl looked back at me.

"She isn't afraid of you," she said.

And then they went out.

9

I locked the door, turned, and leaned against it.

The room was empty.

Except that it wasn't.

I waited for a long time, tacitly offering the option of first move to Grandma Abbie—whoever or whatever she was. A silence settled over everything, and I tried to observe and be receptive without imposing any deliberate will on the moment. Sounds Zen, but it's a wolf thing. We react when there's something to react to, and until then, we try not to make assumptions. A quiet forest seldom is. An empty room in an old house isn't always as empty as it appears.

Then I heard a faint buzz and turned to see a wasp squeeze itself through a tiny gap between the top of the window and the frame. I stretched my senses and heard more of them buzzing. Clearly Mike hadn't found the only nest. I watched the wasp crawl onto the frame and then launch itself, dropping a little as gravity pulled it and then compensating with its wings and moving slowly from one side of the room to the other. It passed over the circle of stuffed toys and landed on the opposite wall. Then it vanished.

I went over and saw it had crawled through another tiny gap, this time between the wall and a rafter. I leaned close and allowed my lupine ears to reshape and grow so I could follow the sound. I heard it go all of the way through the wall. Immediately the feeling that there was someone else in this room ended.

Was the wasp a manifestation of the ghost? Did it want me to follow? I had no idea what the rules were here, so I shifted back to normal and went out into the hall. Belle had taken the kids downstairs and out into the yard. Good.

The wall through which the wasp had passed led to the girls' bedroom, and I went in. Same chair, same bed as in the painting, except that the painting had been of one side of the room. There were actually two beds here. The one on my right—the one that hadn't been in the painting—clearly belonged to Kara. The toys and books around it were for an older girl. The other bed was crammed with picture books and lots of stuffed animals. Beth's domain.

I sensed a presence in here as soon as I entered.

So I closed the door, pushed a chair in front of the handle to make sure no one could get in, and then took off all my clothes. I folded them and placed them on the chair.

No, I'm not a perv. Shapeshifting is tough on off-the-rack Kmart clothes.

I changed, going all the way to wolf. Takes me a hot second, and it hurts a whole damn lot. But it changes the way in which I see the world. My senses dial all the way up to levels that are not only above human, but above normal wolf, as well. Werewolf senses are insane, and unless I'm in that form, the input is too much for my brain to handle.

I stood there on all fours and let the room tell me its story. Not just five senses, but many more. Infrared and ultrasonic are the start. I could feel spiritual energy, smell emotions, taste ectoplasmic residue. Like that, and some stuff I've never even tried to label.

I tensed my muscles for the fight I knew was coming. Jonatha Corbiel was right in that the *Benandanti,* the lineage of lycanthropes from which I descend, have been fighting evil of one kind or another since before Etruscan times. A lot of us have been burned as witches or demons. We're neither. We're the Hounds of God, and except for a very few rogues, we've always fought to defend those of our pack from less savory predators.

The room seemed to swirl with colors and energies.

Nothing came at me, though.

Then I saw her.

Not him. Not it.

Her.

She stepped out of nowhere and was suddenly very much there. Very real, very solid. And she looked like my own grandmother.

It was a solid kick in the throat, a punch over the heart.

My grandmother had been the alpha of our family pack for a long, long time. Immensely powerful, beautiful in the way some older women can be. Queenly. Cold and harsh and dangerous, but also loving and funny. She was my world growing up, and she taught me most of what I know about how to be a good person. She and her daughters taught me how to manage the change, how to deal with the realities of what we all were. It's possible that my grandmother was the most powerful werewolf of the last two or three hundred years. Like that.

But tough as she was, age always wins. At ninety-six, she fell sick and died within days. No lingering or wasting away for her. It was as if she said to Death, "Well, stop dawdling and get about your business, boy."

I missed her every day, and now here she was. A skeleton wrapped in dried meat and dripping maggots onto the floor. She stood there, half human and half werewolf, in that transitional state that inspired the legend of the "wolf-man."

It hurt me. It hurt me so goddamn bad, and for a moment I was ten years old again and powerless with my heart cracking down the middle.

"Samuel . . ." she whispered. "My good little boy."

She reached for me with those twisted fingers, white bone showing through where the skin had been eaten away.

I shifted back to human and fell back against the door, naked, weeping, my heart hammering so hard it hurt. Even without my werewolf senses, she was still there. Standing in the middle of the room.

I saw the wasp fly past her, and it swung wide so as not to make contact and then flew toward little Beth's bed. That's when I saw a flicker of something on the rotted face. A curl of lip, and flare of light in the dead eyes.

The wasp suddenly stopped as surely as if it had hit a wall, and it dropped onto the floor. Dead. Bang, just like that. I looked at it and then at the ghost of my grandmother.

"You're not her," I said, my voice hoarse.

She looked at me.

"You're not her," I repeated, slowing it down, leaning on each word.

She said nothing, but then after a long pause, she changed. For a moment, she became a dead man whose flesh was burned and rotted.

"No," I said.

Then she was a beautiful dark-haired woman whose lovely body was crisscrossed with deep lacerations. Mike's mother.

"No," I said again.

She was a fat woman with blond hair up in a sloppy bun and rosy cheeks. No sign of disease or damage, but I knew this person was dead, too.

"No."

A man with a broken neck.

A preacher with a Roman collar holding an empty whiskey bottle.

A wasted woman who held a smoking gun and whose temple ran with blood.

No. No. No.

"Stop it," I said, getting to my feet. I took my underwear and put them on. "Stop doing that."

Several more images came and went, and then, like a slideshow that had come to an end, they stopped. For a moment I looked at a slowly turning column of dust. Not smoke, as I had thought when I saw Belle's painting, but dust. And ash, I think.

"No," I said again.

The smoke curled from floor to ceiling and then it slowly, slowly faded away. When it was gone, a woman was there. Middle-aged, dressed in old fashioned clothes. Farm clothes from a century ago. All black, though. Mourning clothes.

I nodded and said, "Hello, Mrs. McHenry."

She looked at me and then put her face in her hands and began to weep.

"Please," she said between her sobs, "don't take my children away again."

10

I got dressed and sat on the edge of the bed. She sat on the wooden chair by the little drawing desk. She was a tiny thing. Frail and weathered and ruined. The skin of her face was pulled tight with pain, and she sat with her pale fingers knotting together in her lap.

We talked for a long, long time.

I won't tell you everything, because a lot of what she shared with me was private. And private in a way that mattered to her as a ghost and to me as a monster.

I left her there after a while and went downstairs and out into the sun of late afternoon. Belle and the girls were in a small gazebo near the creek. I came and sat down with them, and I told them the story. A version of it.

Abigail and Andrew McHenry built their dream house here and moved in more than a century ago. He farmed and worked as postmaster for the area, and she raised chickens and vegetables and had a bunch of babies. In the last year of World War I, her two oldest sons joined the army and went to fight. They were in the American 33rd Division supporting the British during an attack north of the Somme in what became known as the Battle of Amiens. Both of her sons died. Back home, the news hit the McHenrys hard, but the following year, it all spiraled into total disaster as the Spanish flu swept through parts of New Jersey and Eastern Pennsylvania. The third son and both daughters got sick and died. Andrew McHenry survived, but he was a broken man, and he drank himself to death within a few years. Abigail lived alone in the house into the 1920s until she fell ill and died. Her body was not found for weeks.

Yeah, she died in what was now the girls' bedroom.

When she woke up again, the house was occupied by strangers, but Abigail became confused and thought the children of that family were her own kids come home again. She tried everything she could to be with them, but no matter what she did, the children screamed and screamed, and then the family moved away.

This happened again and again and again. Each time she longed to be with the children in the house. She loved them. She wanted to keep them safe. She would never hurt them.

When Abigail began to slowly realize what she was, she tried to trick the families, to be the people they loved and had lost. It always failed, and I explained to Belle as I explained it upstairs to Abigail. She was dead, and when she took on an aspect other than hers, one pulled from the memories of the people in the house, her nature only allowed her to connect with the dead of that family. In trying to do good and offer comfort, she had become the boogeyman.

Each time the family moved away.

It wasn't a house in need of children.

No.

I had to stop and wipe my eyes. Belle leaned her head against my shoulder, and Beth crawled onto my lap. Kara sat staring at the house, her eyes filled with tears.

"Oh my God," whispered Belle when I was finished. She sat there, shaking her head, a hand over her mouth. "Oh my God."

"Grandma Abbie is so pretty," said Beth.

I hugged her. "You see her the right way, don't you?" I asked.

She nodded. Wise beyond her years. I wondered if that gift would stay with her. "She don't let the wasps hurt me."

Belle's head jerked up, and she met my eyes. I nodded.

"I saw it firsthand," I said. "Those dead wasps? That's Abigail's doing."

"But, why . . . ?" began Belle; then she stopped, and I saw her get it. She turned to look at the house.

"Grandma Abbie won't let anything bad happen," said Beth.

We sat with that for a long, long time.

When the sun began dipping below the level of the trees, Beth slid off my lap and pulled my hand until I stood up. Belle and Kara stood up, too. We walked together back to the house, in through the door, and up the stairs.

There were no monsters up there. No burned faces or rotting skin.

There was an old lady who was happy to see her little ones. There was a lovely mother who didn't need to be afraid anymore.

And there was me.

I left quietly and walked out to my car.

The check for ten grand was in my pocket. I tore it up and threw the pieces into the back seat. There were stars up there and a hint of moonglow that turned the creek to a river of silver.

I turned the car on, put a Johnny Cash CD in the player, and drove home.

The Trouble

Author's Note: This story takes place a few years after the events described in *Bad Moon Rising*, the third book of the Pine Deep Trilogy.

1

Malcolm Crow stepped out onto the porch to see if the sunset was doing anything interesting. He had a coffee cup in one hand and leaned on his cane with the other. His Phillies home-game shirt was untucked and unbuttoned over T-shirt and jeans. His Beretta 92F was snugged into its clamshell holster under the shirt, two full magazines Velcroed into their slots on the nylon rig. As always.

Ready.

Always ready.

Not that sundown threw a switch. They weren't nocturnal. Not most of them, anyway. Some, not all.

For them it was a preference. They could see better in the dark. It was an edge. One of many.

Just as the rounds in the Beretta were Crow's edge. Each hollow-point was filled with a drop of garlic oil and then sealed with wax. An edge that had saved his life. Saved his wife's life.

Crow made sure he kept all his edges sharp. Like the farm fields that surrounded the big old house. Ten thousand acres of hard-necked German white garlic, with scattered patches here and there of elephant, wild, rocamboles, softneck, silver skin, porcelain, artichoke, and purple stripe. The barn was full of it. Silo, hoppers, and grind shed. All filled. Barrels of oil everywhere, large-capacity bins piled to the top with bulbs.

All part of his edge.

Crow fucking hated garlic.

Hated the smell, the taste. But he ate it with every meal. Breakfast, lunch, and dinner. Cloves in his salad, more in the spaghetti sauce Val made fresh every day. He even had a pack of garlic chewing gum in his shirt pocket most days.

There were thirty-six garlic farms in Pine Deep. It was now the second-largest-producing region in the country.

He sipped his coffee. No garlic in that. No bourbon, either, which was a shame. Crow longed for bourbon. Ached for it. Every god-damn day. For years now, and ten times as much since the Trouble.

There may be truth in wine, but there was bliss in bourbon.

That was a downhill road he didn't feel like walking, though. Been there, done that, have the souvenirs. Or scars. Same thing.

Coffee was his drug of choice now. He didn't wind up naked, bruised, and in trouble with everyone he cared about when he drank coffee. He sipped it. Val knew better than to brew decaf for him, even this late in the day.

He laid his cane across the arms of a rocker and leaned a shoulder against the wooden pillar beside the porch steps. The cane was on its way out of his life, the physical therapists assured him. Crow planned to burn it when he got the all-clear. After the night of the Trouble, he'd spent eighteen months in a wheelchair and another alternating between crutches and a walker. The switch to a cane had been against doctor's orders, but Crow had been diligent with his physi-cal therapy. Hours a day in the pool, lots of sweaty sessions with machines, cortisone shots, the works. He was four years into his re-covery, and it was time to retire the cane. He knew he'd always have some pain, especially on humid days. Of which there were many in Eastern Pennsylvania. His hips and thighs had been crushed. It was, according to his doctors, a miracle he wasn't in the wheelchair for life.

Miracle.

Crow thought that was funny as shit.

He sipped the coffee and watched the day end.

The sun was going down in flames, leaving so many deep red

streaks across the sky that it looked like a crime scene. Bloody and gaudy. A bit too lurid to be actually beautiful.

It was impressive, though.

And scary.

Crow believed in omens, but he thought the old "red sky at night" thing was backward. The saying promised:

> *Red sky at night, shepherd's delight.*
> *Red sky at morning, shepherd take warning.*

But that was wrong.

When there was this kind of blood spatter painting the clouds before a dark autumn night, even getting to morning was a sucker's bet.

Inside the house, Val was switching on all the lights. Every single one, in every room.

Soon she'd begin closing and locking the storm shutters.

There was no rain coming.

But a storm?

Sure.

It was coming. Or maybe it was already here. Maybe it had never left.

He thought about tomorrow.

It would be his seventh day in his new job. Mostly a desk job because of the cane. His old business, a craft store in town, had burned when the town burned. For the last couple of years, Val had supported him, and he had his insurance checks and disability. Now he was making a modest wage in a job for which he was physically ill-suited, but which the mayor and his own wife had to admit he was the perfect man for.

Chief of the Pine Deep Police Department.

The local kids called him "Sheriff" as a kind of cool-cat nickname. But he was the chief.

It wasn't why he always carried a gun.

Or maybe it was.

Crow sipped his coffee and watched the sun die in the west and, as he always did, he trembled at the coming of night.

2

Even though he was the youngest and newest member of the Pine Deep Police Department, officer Mike Sweeney preferred the night shift. He also preferred to work his shifts alone, and he was the only officer on Crow's force who was allowed to do that. None of the other officers complained about the arrangement, because none of them wanted to share a car with Mike. He couldn't blame them. Mike knew how he affected people and accepted it as the way it was, and the way it would always be.

Besides, who better to work the graveyard shift than him? It was even funny in its way.

Since midnight, he'd run from the new bridge that crossed the Delaware to Black Marsh down south to the Crestville Causeway in the north, then east to west straight through town. Mike never crossed the bridges, even on his days off, but he preferred to stay inside the natural water boundaries. Pine Deep was essentially an island formed by rivers and canals. It was also massive in terms of square mileage for a town with so few people, and was because it wrapped like a horseshoe around the state forest. More than two-thirds of the town was protected land; the rest was sprawling farms and the town proper.

At six minutes to two, he got a cell phone call from the dispatcher. His heart jumped a gear. There was a special arrangement between Crow and the dispatcher, Staci Silver, and the method of contact depended on the type of report. If it was something that anyone could handle, it was done through proper channels, using the radio, recording the call, and all paperwork neat and tidy.

Some things, Mike knew, were not neat and would never be tidy.

He hit the button. "What's happening, Staci?"

"Shots fired at the McWilliams place. Neighbor called it in."

"And—?"

"Mrs. Sitler was the caller. She said she saw someone she knew in their yard."

Mike waited, bracing against it. There were a lot of names that he could bear to hear. A few that would hurt him. One that would absolutely fucking kill him. He winced and gripped the knobbed wheel.

"She said she saw that kid you used to go to school with. Your friend with the funny pants. The kind with chains on them, like kids used to wear sometimes. You know. *Before.*" She paused. "She said she saw Brandon."

It was a splinter in his heart. But it wasn't the name he most feared. It wasn't his mother's name.

Even so.

Brandon.

Before the Trouble, Brandon Strauss was his best friend. One of only two kids Mike ever thought were real friends. Mike had always been a loner. A lot of abused kids are. He also knew that he was strange. Even by Pine Deep standards.

Brandon hadn't cared much about Mike's moods or his weirdness. Brandon was the school eccentric. He wore jeans set with jangling chains, T-shirts with the names of obscure edgy bands. He had the beginnings of a goatee by the time they were in middle school, and he planned to become a forensic entomologist. His love of bugs—the weirder, stranger, and more disgusting the better—did not endear him to most of their classmates. Mike thought it was cool. Mike liked Brandon because his friend was exactly who he wanted to be and didn't give much of a fuck about what anyone else thought or said. Given time and a kinder world, Mike had no doubt that Brandon would become a scientist and a success.

But they lived in Pine Deep, and kindness was not something sown in the soil there, and few people reaped a harvest of their dreams.

During the Trouble, over eleven thousand people had died. Brandon Strauss had been one of them.

And he'd been a problem ever since.

Mike's throat was dry, but he sucked enough spit from his cheeks to be able to talk.

"Roger that," he said hoarsely.

"Do you want me to call the chief?"

"Not yet. Let me check it out first."

"Mike . . . ?" she said tentatively, making it almost a question.

"I'll be careful," he said, and with far more confidence than he felt, added, "I got this."

Mike made a U-turn in the middle of the empty road, took a breath, and stamped down on the gas. He drove the latest model police interceptor, and it was tricked out with every upgrade in the catalog. Mayor Sarah Wolfe made sure that Crow's department had the latest and the best. From what appeared to outsiders as a weirdly large police force to the high-tech gadgets, vehicles, and weapons, Pine Deep was a model for the twenty-first-century law enforcement. The excessive budget was always defended as a response to the threat of terrorism. After all, as far as the rest of the world was concerned, the Trouble was just that. Terrorism. Domestic white supremacist mania. That's what it said in most of the books and movies made about the town. That's what it said in all of the official Homeland and NSA reports. It's what any of the townies would tell you if asked. The official story was so much easier to swallow than the truth.

He kept his lights and sirens off. Mrs. Sitler was the third-grade teacher in town. Her family owned a small farm that grew a variety of herbs. She also had a border garden of garlic that surrounded her house on all four sides. She was old, a pain in the ass, a busybody, and absolutely nobody's fool. She knew which way the wind blew, and as such, had become part of what Staci called "the network." Those folks in town who had survived the Trouble and didn't pretend that it was something other than what it was. During the Red Wave, she'd stood her ground in the hallway outside her classroom, and while forty-six children and a few teachers huddled under desks, screamed, prayed, and waited to die, she'd fought off the school's janitor and math teacher with a baseball bat.

Mike loved her for that.

If she said that she saw Brandon Strauss, then she saw Brandon Strauss.

Mrs. Sitler wasn't given to hysterics. She came from centuries-old colonial stock. Tough, smart, and uncompromising.

Mike put the pedal down.

The McWilliams place was deep in farm country. They grew corn, squash, and cabbages.

As he drove, Mike began to smile.

At first, he wasn't aware that he was doing it. Then he was, and it scared the shit out of him. That fear did not chase the smile away. If anything, it made it grow and stretch.

He never looked in the rearview to see what kind of smile was on his face. He knew what kind it was. And a line from a fairy tale whispered in his head.

Oh my, Grandma, what big teeth you have.

3

Mike cut his headlights when he was a mile out.

He saw better without them.

The McWilliams farmhouse stood back against a wall of alders. The kitchen light was on, the rest of the house dark. Three cars sat silent at different angles in the front yard—a big red Tundra, a much older half-ton Ford pickup truck, and a sporty four-year-old Infinity that Mike knew had been bought with life insurance money after the Trouble. Faint woodsmoke curled up from the chimney, a warm and homey sight against the failing sun.

Mike rolled to a stop fifty yards from the gravel turnaround in front of the house and killed the engine. He sat for a moment, drumming his fingers on the steering wheel, while he read the scene. He knew more about the place than he learned by seeing it. There was a tension in the air that Mike opened himself up to, tasting it, learning it, feeling the wrongness of it. So, he stretched his senses, trying to define the feeling, to give it shape, to learn its texture.

Then he opened the door and got out. The dome light had been disabled; the hinges oiled. His Glock was in its holster, and he left it there. If this was what Mrs. Sitler thought, then Mike would prefer not to be encumbered by the gun. He had other weapons available.

He walked beside the gravel path, preferred the muffled quiet of the grass as he moved quickly and cautiously toward the front porch. When he was thirty feet from the house, he shifted his angle of approach and went around the house, slipping along the side of it toward the back, where moonlight sparkled off of the glass in the kitchen windows. The rear door that stood inches ajar.

He sniffed the air and took a moment to process what he smelled. None of it was good. But none of it was immediate. Then he straightened from a cautious crouch and stood looking at the red smear on that door handle.

"Shit," he breathed, letting the word hiss almost silently through the tiny gaps of his gritted teeth.

The back door opened into a mudroom. It was empty, so he moved to the inner door that led to the kitchen. Leaning close to the jamb, he sniffed a few times, taking in the scents of what lay beyond the door. People—living people—smelled a certain way. Brandon and his kind had a different smell. Earthy, with an undertone of the predator's stink of rotting meat and old blood.

There was some of that here.

Faint, though. A stain left on the air.

The strongest smell was neither the vibrant aroma of life nor the alien stench of Brandon's kind.

What he smelled was death.

That's when Mike knew what he would find when he opened that door.

He paused, closing his eyes for a moment, feeling so many emotions warring inside his chest. Pain and regret because of what had almost certainly happened here, and of his failure to protect and serve. Mike was many things, but he genuinely was a cop, and this stabbed him. There was also disgust, because part of him was still human, and that part was vulnerable to the atavistic dread of the things that troubled the night. There was anger, because he was very territorial, and this had been done in *his* town. And deeper anger because this was a direct attack on him. It was a statement that the treaty—however unspoken—was no longer going to be honored.

It meant that the Trouble wasn't over.

It meant that it was going to start up again.

He steeled himself and pushed the door open.

It was all there. All carefully presented to make a statement. For him, for Crow and Val. For the people in the network.

The bodies on the floor told him that. The broken lives told him that. The shotgun with its barrel bent backward and out of shape told him that. The wreckage of these lives and the invasion of this home told him that.

The killer did not need to leave him a message. But he did anyway. Written in blood on a wall from which a dozen framed family photos had been swept.

The words were from an old Disney cartoon about the Three Little Pigs. It said so much. The dead family were the pigs. Slaughtered for food. The rest was a challenge.

Directed at him.

Specifically, him.

WHO'S AFRAID OF THE BIG BAD WOLF?

Mike stood in the doorway and stared at it, and beneath his skin, the wolf screamed.

4

The phone rang at twenty-two minutes past one in the morning.

Nothing good ever comes of a call that late. Nothing.

Crow snaked a hand out from under the covers and snatched his cell off the bedside stand and was fully awake before he even pressed the button.

"Crow," he said, no trace of sleep in his voice, even though he'd been way down in the hole seconds ago.

"We got a bad one, chief," said the voice of Staci, his night dispatcher. "A fire at the McWilliams place."

Beside Crow, Val switched on the light on her side of the bed.

Like Crow, she'd learned how to wake up without pause. To be alert. To be ready. She had a hand under the pillow, but Crow shook his head. No need for the Glock she kept there. He put the call on speaker.

"Give it to me," he told Staci.

She did, explaining about the call from Mrs. Sitler and calling Mike on the down-low to investigate.

"You lost me," interrupted Crow; "you said it was shots fired, but now there's a fire?"

Staci paused for a long time, waiting for Crow to catch it. He did. "Ahhhh . . . shit."

"I called the fire department and rolled back up," she said, as if that helped.

"Okay, I'm on my way."

He ended the call, but before he could set down his phone, a text message from Mike Sweeney flashed on his phone.

McWilliams place.

Three down.

Trouble.

Crow's heart tried to freeze in his chest.

He showed it to Val, who mouthed, *Oh my God!*

He texted back:

On my way.

Then he set the phone down but didn't move. Instead, he let Val wrap him in her arms and pull him close. She asked, and he told her.

She pulled back. "Oh my God . . ."

"It'll be okay," he said.

"Please don't lie to me," she snapped. "Promise me you'll be smart about this."

"I promise."

Smart. Val's personal definition of that word fell somewhere between *safe* and *vicious*. Val was a wonderful woman and had the biggest heart, but when it came to anything related to the Trouble, she was merciless. It had taken every single member of her family. It had taken most of her town, and she was even more deeply invested in Pine Deep than Crow was. It was *her* town, and she had fought alongside him to save it.

"Look at me," she demanded, and he did. Val searched his eyes. "Tell me again."

"I swear I'll be smart about this. I'm always smart about this stuff."

"No, you're not. You're a professional smart-*ass*, and that's not the same thing."

He smiled but shook his head. "I'm a smartass most of the time, love. Not about this."

Val kissed him with real heat. That was their rhythm. Every kiss was fifty percent passionate goodbye and fifty percent a demand that he come back home. It filled his heart and broke it at the same time.

He got up, got dressed, checked the action on his Beretta, slapped the magazine into place, pulled back the receiver to put a round in the chamber, and eased the hammer down. Then he blew her a kiss and left the bedroom.

He didn't take his cane.

5

The house burned like a bonfire.

Yellow flames reached up to brush the undersides of the storm clouds, and to Crow, it looked like the sky was the ceiling of hell. He'd seen bad fires here in Pine Deep before. Including the one he started down in Dark Hollow, which had gone on to burn half the state forest and a lot of the town. The black scars of that fire were everywhere in town and seared into Crow's memory.

This fire seemed to ignite old fears in his chest. He did not believe for a minute—not for a second—that this was an accidental fire.

Mike had been sent to investigate a shooting, not an arson.

"Damn it, Mike," Crow breathed as he pulled off the road and thumped over a cabbage patch to get around the fire trucks, ambulances, and police vehicles. One of his patrol officers was handling traffic, and when she spotted his Explorer, she waved him through. He slowed to a stop beside her.

"Mike's up at the house," she said before he could ask. "In back, by the barn."

Crow nodded to the blaze. "They going to save it?"

The officer, Belinda, laughed. "Not a chance in hell."

Crow drove on, circled the burning house slowly, looking at the arrangement of firefighting equipment and hoses, matching them against the inferno. Belinda was right. Not a chance in hell.

He spotted Mike standing alone in the middle of the short gravel road that ran between farmhouse and barn. Mike was no longer the scrawny freckle-faced kid who used to work for Crow at the craft shop. A growth spurt and a lot of hours in the gym had turned the boy into a towering man. Several inches over six feet, packed with muscle, unsmiling. The Trouble had stolen most of the humor and a great deal of the humanity from Mike's face, leaving him quiet, dour, and strange. So, so strange.

He stood with his hands in his back pockets, slowly chewing gum, wearing sunglasses at night. Crow knew that it wasn't because of the brightness of the flames.

Crow parked beside one of the big oaks that anchored the corner of the farm, killed the engine, blew out his cheeks, took another breath, and got out. The big young man waited where he was, face turned toward the fire, muscles in his jaws bunching and flexing as he chewed. He didn't even turn as Crow crunched across the gravel.

"Walk me through it," said Crow as he came to stand next to his adopted son.

Mike nodded, removed his cell phone, queued up the photo stream, and handed it over. "Hope you ate something bland," he said. "This was messy."

Crow accepted the phone with trepidation. There were sixty photos, and each one was taken with the highest pixel setting.

There was a lot of mess; Mike hadn't exaggerated. If anything, he understated the crime scene. The inside of the house looked like a spilled paint box except that all of the colors were shades of red. It was on the floor, the walls, the ceiling. It glimmered on the stainless-steel handles of a vast old farm stove, gleamed on the three water glasses on the kitchen table, sparkled on the silverware laid out for a meal that would never be eaten, and shimmered on each and every one of the thousands of drops of bright-red blood that splattered the floor and up in wild patterns on the walls. The light from Mike's flash had danced along the blood patterned on the outstretched leg of a woman who lay partly hidden by an overturned chair. And on the other parts of her that were across the room. And on the table. And hanging from the overhead room fan. At least Crow thought those were all parts of Dora McWilliams. It was hard to tell. There were parts of her husband, too. And their seven-year-old daughter.

Parts.

Nothing more than that.

Crow had seen a lot of crime scenes and a lot of photos of murdered people. He knew the difference between knives and icepicks, meat cleavers and machetes, chainsaws and swords. He saw none of that here. There were no tool marks of any kind. The flesh at every point of damage was ragged.

Torn.

Ripped by sheer force and without any artificial aid.

Crow stopped when he was a third of the way through and closed his eyes for a moment. "God damn it," he breathed, then shook his head. "Even so, kid, you didn't have to burn the fucking place down. This could have spread and—"

"It didn't spread. You think I don't know how to do this after all this time? Give me some credit, man. Like you always say, this isn't my first rodeo."

"It was stupid and reckless. We could have kept a lid on the forensics and—"

"No, we couldn't." Mike used a fingertip to blot a tiny drop of spittle at the corner of his mouth. "Go to the last picture and tell me if I jumped the gun."

With trembling fingers, Crow scrolled through the images of butchery until he found one that was different. Writing on the wall. He spoke the words aloud.

"*Who's afraid of the big bad wolf.*"

"Yeah."

"Shit."

"Yeah."

Crow cut him a look. "That's not your mom."

"No."

"Shit."

"Yeah," said Mike. "There wasn't time to clean that off the walls. That's why I lit a match. We can call this a home invasion that went south. Killers torched the place on the way out. We can sell it. We have before, one way or another."

"Not really keen on Pine Deep becoming the arson capital of Pennsylvania."

Mike looked at him. "You like the alternatives better?"

"Fuck."

"Yeah."

For a few moments, the only sound was the roar of the fire and the muffled yells of the firefighters trying to contain it. It was clear they were going to let the house burn down. Keeping the trees and fields from burning was the obvious plan. The fire chief spotted him and began walking over, shoulders hunched, head low, a study in frustration. Probably some grief there, too. Everyone knew everyone in Pine Deep. Every loss was personal.

While they were still out of earshot, Crow asked, "It's Brandon, isn't it?"

"Yeah."

"Fuck."

"Uh-huh."

"We're going to have to go break the truce."

"Kind of think they already did that, boss," said Mike.

"Fuck."

"Yeah."

Crow said, "We're going to have to go into the state forest and find him." He paused, then corrected himself. "To *hunt* him."

"No," said Mike.

"What?" Crow asked, looking at him again.

"*I'm* going to have to go hunt him."

Crow kept his balled fists at his sides. "Fuck," he said again. Really meaning it.

Mike nodded slowly. "Yeah."

6

Conversation overheard at the Pine Deep Shop-N-Save.

Mrs. Peters: "Shame what happened. The McWilliams and all."

Mrs. Sitler: "Lord protects those who protect themselves."

Mrs. Lucas: "What's that?"

Mrs. Sitler: "It's all about common sense, isn't it? It's all about taking steps."

Mrs. Lucas: "Steps? I don't understand. Dora McWilliams was in church every Sunday. Always had her daughter with her. Fred went at least once a month."

Mrs. Peters: "Not about that."

Mrs. Lucas: "Then what—?"

Mrs. Sitler: "They had near four hundred acres of squash and cabbages and all sorts of greens and not so much as a square inch of garlic."

Mrs. Lucas: "Garlic doesn't stop your house from burning down."

Mrs. Sitler: "Maybe not. But it might keep you being in it when it burns."

7

Crow and Mike sat in the young officer's cruiser in a deserted spot at the end of Dark Hollow Road.

Once upon a time, that secluded clearing was the town's lover's lane. The Passion Pit. Since the Trouble, it had been abandoned. No one but a fool came out here, especially not to neck. When a place is tied to savage mass murders, it tends to cool the ardor of even the horniest young lovers.

The engine was off, the motor ticking as it cooled. The sun was high and bright, but the trees grew heavy here and there with a dense canopy of green leaves. Here and there, they could see the blackened stumps of burned trees, but the fires had sparked a riot of growth. Bees flitted among the flowers that grew in glorious profusion along the edge of the drop-off. Starlings and grackles chattered in the trees.

"It always amazes me how fast the forest bounced back," said Crow. "Kind of renews your faith in the world."

Mike looked at him. "Sometimes you scare me, man."

"What? How?"

"You see all this, and you think it's a sign of Mother Earth healing herself and cleansing the woods of all the spooky badness."

"It is."

"You're fucking nuts. Trees don't grow this fast. They don't. And, yes, I've read all the reports about growth spurts following forest fires and how the soil becomes enriched, blah, blah, blah. It's all bullshit." He leaned forward and tapped the inside of the windshield. "This is camouflage. This is *them* twisting nature to help them hide."

"You don't know that."

"Yes, I do. I can *feel* it. You want to sit there and tell me I can't? That I'm wrong? That of the two of us, you're the one who's more in touch with the way this stuff works?"

Crow said nothing.

Mike sighed.

Finally, Crow said, "Play it again."

"Why?"

"Because I want to hear it again."

Mike removed his cell and punched the button to replay the voicemail he'd gotten a few hours after the fire. The caller made no attempt to disguise his voice or his identity. Why should he?

"*Hey, dude,*" said the voice of Brandon Strauss, "*how's it hanging, Iron Mike?*"

A pause and a short laugh.

"*That whole truce thing? Yeah, well, it's for shit. No one I know is getting fat sucking on deer and raccoons. And I guess your mom's tired of sucking on me.*"

Another laugh, and in the background, Crow could hear another person laugh. A woman. He'd known Lois Wingate his whole life. He'd been close with her when she'd still been married to Big John

Sweeney, though when John failed to make the turn on Shandy's Curve and Lois cried herself into Vic Wingate's arms, they'd fallen out of touch. He knew her voice, though. He knew her laugh.

"*So, I guess we need to work this out, you dig?*" said Brandon's voice. Still a teenager's voice. Forever a teenager's voice. That wouldn't change, and maybe it was the only part of Brandon that would never change. His face and voice, always young, always a lie. "*So, let's us have a little chat, mano-a-mano.*"

"He always got that wrong," muttered Mike. "He still thinks it means man to man. That's so Brandon."

"*So tomorrow down in the Hollow. High noon, 'cause you pussies think that makes you safe. So lame. Come alone. You and me, winner takes all.*"

There was more laughter as the call ended.

"You can't possibly believe he's going to be down there alone."

Mike shrugged.

"We need to do this right. I can get six, eight guys, and we can go in there and clean them the hell out. Like we should have done a couple of years ago."

"Really? When exactly? When you were still in a wheelchair, or when you were hobbling around on a walker? When exactly was the right time? And before you answer me, Crow, tell me how the hell you expect to haul your ass down that drop-off? You can't walk a mile without sitting down and chewing Advil like they're Skittles. No offense, man, but you can't do this."

"Oh, sure, no offense," growled Crow. He jerked open the door and climbed out. Mike cursed under his breath and got out, too, and he glared at Crow across the hood.

"Don't start that poor-me shit, man," he said. "I know it's fake, and you know I know. You're just pissed off that you can't do it."

Crow started to reply, but Mike's expression softened, and he touched Crow's shoulder.

"Listen, I love you, man. You and Val, you're the only real family I ever had. The only family I care about. My mom . . . well, you know how I'm going to have to play that out, either today or some-day. And I'm pretty sure you know that this isn't my first time down in the Hollow."

"Yeah," said Crow quietly, "I know. I saw your chalkboard."

Mike nodded. After the Trouble, when all of the dead were counted, there were eighty-four people missing. Some townies, some tourists. Their bodies were never found. Soon after, the animal population in the area began dwindling. Every once in a while, a person would be killed, usually in a bad farm accident or car crash. The kind of accident that makes it impossible to tell if there are bite marks.

But Crow and Mike knew the score.

After each of those incidents, one of the missing eighty-four would turn up. Always dead, always killed in a random traffic accident. Hit and runs. Mike was an artist when it came to making things look like what they weren't.

In his room, which was built onto the back of farmhouse where they all lived, Mike had a chalkboard hidden inside a cupboard. The number *84* had once been written there but had long since been wiped out and replaced by another number. The most recent number was *27*.

Crow never spoke openly about it to Mike, and Mike never brought the subject up. Month by month, though, he grew stranger, darker, and less . . .

Crow fished for the word.

Human.

Which, to be fair, Mike really wasn't anyway. He hadn't been since the Trouble. Mike had a very complicated parentage. Lois had been impregnated, but not by John Sweeney. There were other, much older forces at work in the young man's life. Ugly, twisted forces, and they burdened Mike with a nature and with personality elements that had to be very carefully managed. His rage was one of those elements, but it was by far the least threatening.

"You think this is pushback for your, um, extracurricular activities?" asked Crow.

"You know what I think," said Mike.

"You're really that sure?"

"We wouldn't be out here if I wasn't."

Mike took some gum from his pocket, offered it Crow, who

shook his head. Mike put two pieces in his mouth and chewed in silence for a moment.

"Are there really only twenty-seven left?" asked Crow.

Mike shot him a look. "Where you been? That was like three
months ago. It's twenty-one."

"Jesus Christ."

Mike shrugged.

"How do you know they haven't recruited more?"

The young man smiled. It was a strange smile that made him look
much older than his nineteen years. "They couldn't take that risk.
Not and stay off the radar."

"You call what happened last night at the McWilliams place staying off the radar?"

"No, I call that a two-minute warning."

"Jesus fuck."

"What can I say? We both knew it might come to this. The whole
Network knew. We've *talked* about this happening one day. That's
why I have to go down there and find out."

"Against all of them?"

"I can handle myself."

"Really? Come on, kiddo, even if you've done this much damage
to them, it's been what, one at a time? Two? You go down there, and
it's you against twenty-one of them."

"Maybe," said Mike, "but I don't think so."

The smile lingered as Mike opened the rear door of the cruiser and
pulled out an oversized black canvas equipment bag and set it down
on the grass. Crow came and stood with him. Inside the bag were
dozens of loaded magazines for Crow's Beretta, a combat shotgun
with a drum magazine, flash-bang grenades, and two katana. Crow
grunted as he realized that one was his own sword.

"I took it from your closet," said Mike. "Thought you might
want it."

"I thought you made it clear that I was too much of a gimp to go
down there."

"You are," said Mike, handing it to him. "But you don't think
they're only planning to ambush me, do you?"

They studied each other for nearly half a minute as the blackbirds

sang in the trees and the sun burned overhead. Then each of them
began stuffing their pockets with extra magazines. Crow limped
with Mike to the edge of the drop-off. It was a steep slope that could
only be navigated safely with rappelling gear. Mike didn't have any.

"You don't have to do this," said Crow. "We'll find another way
and—"

"There *is* no other way, man. This has been coming at us for five
years, and you know it. If I don't go down there now, then they're
all going to come up here. You want to see another Red Wave? You
want the Trouble back?"

Crow said nothing.

Mike held out a hand and they shook, then each pulled the other
into a ferocious hug.

"You're *my* son now," said Crow, his voice breaking. "You goddamn well come back home."

Mike Sweeney said nothing. He pushed Crow back, gave him a
smile that was a heartbreaking echo of the boy he'd once been. Then
he turned and jumped over the edge.

He had no rappelling gear.

He didn't need it.

Crow watched with a mixture of awe and horror as Mike dropped
to hands and feet and ran on all fours down the hill.

"God almighty . . ." breathed Crow.

8

It took five minutes to get to the bottom of the hill. When he reached
the bottom, he stopped all at once, letting his body become part of
the hill, the trees, the shrubs, the moment. His muscles ached from
the things Mike had made them do in order to run down the slope.
Once he was sure that he was alone and, for the moment, safe, he adjusted his clothes and tried to listen to what was going on inside his
head.

He was grouchy and sometimes dismissive with Crow, but that

was because he knew he had to deflect his adopted father's fears.
Valid though they were. In truth, he had his own fears. Being who
and what he was did not make him fearless, and it didn't make him
less afraid. Because of what he'd become during the Red Wave, Mike
Sweeney knew that pain, injury, and even death were far from the
worst things that could happen to him in Pine Deep.

Especially down here.

The air down in Dark Hollow was thick and damp and smelled of
rotting vegetation. Swirling columns of gnats towered above any
patch of standing water. In the mud, he could see the whipsaw trails
left by snakes.

It was an unpleasant place. Not even the hardiest hiker or deep
woodsman could love Dark Hollow. No one could. It was the kind
of place that had been born bad, the way some people are. Places can
be like that. Maybe something in the soil, or maybe there was some
act of horror committed here so long ago that only the rocks and dirt
and trees remember. A poison that even the forest fire Crow had
started five years ago had been able to burn away.

And it got worse deeper into the woods.

Mike did a quick equipment check and then moved off. For the
first few hundred yards, he kept to the game trail at the bottom of
the hollow, but then he veered off into the brush, moving slower but
being quiet. Keeping his eyes open and taking in everything that
smell and hearing could bring to him. His senses were very keen, and
he could no longer remember or even imagine what it was like to
have normal senses.

And even with that, they managed to ambush him.

9

Crow stood at the edge of the drop-off and strained to hear. The
shadows down there were too deep to be able to see anything, but he
hoped to at least hear something that let him know Mike was okay.
They had satellite phones with signal boosters and earbuds, but

Crow didn't use it. This wasn't a time to be chatty. Not while Mike needed to focus.

The sun shifted from directly overhead and began clawing its way toward the west, toppling long tree-shaped shadows in Crow's direction. A cool wind snaked its way through the trees, pulling moisture and foul smells up from the hollow. It made Crow feel suddenly very alone and very small.

He shivered and tried to tell himself it was just the wind.

Just that.

Until it wasn't that.

No, not at all.

"Nice day for it," said a cold voice behind him.

10

Mike kept expecting a formal confrontation at one of the clearings, and he was certain he knew which one. Deep into the hollow was the place where Crow had set his fire using gasoline sprayed from borrowed exterminator's backpack tanks. That would be the logical place, especially if this was about starting a new Red Wave. That's where all of it began.

It was where Ubel Griswold was buried.

It's where that great monster had died. Twice.

The first time had been years and years ago, back when Crow was a kid and Griswold hunted for fresh meat in the farms and fields of Pine Deep. Back when Griswold was a creature similar to what Mike had become.

Similar, but not the same. No sir, not the same at all.

Griswold had been a psychopathic man, and when his hunger was on him, he became a four-legged predator of nearly insatiable appetites. He'd slaughtered his way through the population of the town while managing to keep the truth of his identity and his guilt hidden. Only a few knew who and what he was.

Vic Wingate had been one. The Renfield to Griswold's Dracula. Except Griswold hadn't been that kind of monster at the time.

That happened after a second man discovered Griswold's secret. Oren Morse, an itinerant bluesman nicknamed the Bone Man by the local kids. It was Morse who'd put it all together; he was the one who knew enough about the shadows in the world and could make sense of what was happening in town. And it was Morse who had chased Griswold down here into Dark Hollow. It was Morse who had used the neck of his own shattered blues guitar like a dagger to end the reign of terror. It was Morse who'd pushed Griswold's body down into the mud, where he hoped it would rot and be damned.

And the townsfolk, tricked by Wingate into believing that it was Morse and not Griswold who had been the killer, lynched him.

Then, thirty years to the day, the killing began again.

Only this time, Griswold did not use his own hands or claws or fangs to tear the life from his victims. His body had rotted down in the swamp, and all that was left of him was a presence, a spiritual evil that was far more powerful than anything that had troubled these woods before. Griswold drew the evil and corrupt men and women of the region toward him. He transformed them into fiends who craved blood and who worshipped him as a god.

Then he turned them loose on Pine Deep.

Eleven thousand people died.

Crow, Val, Mike, and a few others fought to save the town. The others fell one by one, and in the end, it was just the three of them who stood their ground as Griswold rose from his own grave, forming a terrible new body, rising as a newborn god of pain and darkness.

Crow, Val, and Mike had won that fight. Somehow, impossibly, with fire and sword, garlic, and the stingy grace of a perverse universe, they'd won.

Hundreds of Griswold's army died that night.

Hundreds.

Leaving eighty-four.

And now, twenty-one.

The swampy clearing where Griswold twice died had to be the only place grand enough for this kind of confrontation, Mike was sure of it. It would be like the floor of the Circus Maximus. Brandon and he would square off, and then a bunch of others would come in to steal away any chance of a true duel. All of that was to be expected, and Mike felt that he was as prepared for that as he could be.

Except.

Except . . .

A figure stepped out of the shadows between two thick pines. Not particularly tall, not strongly built.

Not Brandon.

Mike stumbled to a clumsy stop as if he'd been punched in the chest, and for a moment, everything else was slapped out of his mind. His plans, his predictions for the encounter, tactics and strategies. Everything. Instead, he gaped at the figure, eyes and mouth wide, heart slamming around in his chest, bashing into the walls of his chest like a ship's gun come loose from its lashings.

He thought that he'd be ready for this. For five years, he'd rehearsed this in his mind. Worked out what to say, how to act, what to do. Had it all planned.

But that was gone.

In an instant. Just gone.

Instead, he felt his knees buckle. He was only dimly aware of his kneecaps thudding into the muddy ground. The forest seemed to tilt and swirl around him in a nauseating vortex. Tears burned in his eyes.

The figure smiled at him. Soft, loving, so familiar.

"Michael?" she said.

That one word was a knife in his heart.

He said, "Mom . . . ?"

11

Crow whirled, snatching his pistol from its holster, bringing it up into a two-handed grip, cocking the hammer back, pointing, his finger slipping inside the curve of the trigger guard.

Brandon Strauss stood fifteen feet behind him.

He no longer wore the jeans with the chains on them or the obscure rock-band shirt, but he still looked fourteen. His clothes were torn and stained with dark brown splotches that Crow knew had probably started out red. Stolen clothes from a person whose blood and life had likewise been taken by force.

Brandon smiled at him. He was still the same height, a few inches shy of six feet. Tall for his age back then. His eyes were no longer the same. Once they had been distinct from each other—one blue-gray, the other blue-green; now they were different from any human eyes. They were black and bottomless, without sclera or iris. Like the soulless eyes of a great white shark. With just as much humanity and compassion.

The smile was on Brandon's mouth. If Crow couldn't see those eyes, and if he didn't know the story, he might have accepted that smile at face value. But this was not a face on which true humor belonged.

"Nice day for it," said Brandon.

Crow licked his lips. "Let me guess," he said thickly. "Trap?"

"Trap," agreed Brandon. "Big honking trap, too."

He snapped his fingers, and six others stepped out from between trees or behind bushes. One even rose up on the far side of Mike's cruiser. Five male, one female. None human.

Crow knew three of them. Townsfolk who'd gone missing during the Red Wave. He recognized the other three, though. Tourists reported missing. All of them part of the missing eighty-four.

That left fourteen.

Down in Dark Hollow. Where Mike was.

Brandon nodded, clearly following Crow's thought process. "Doing the math?"

"No, my mind's just wandering," said Crow. "Trying to recall how many blow jobs I got in high school."

"Cute."

"Plentiful," said Crow.

They smiled at each other.

"Is there a script for this?" asked Crow. "Maybe some banter? A few threats? How's this work?"

"No, not really," said Brandon. "Mostly this is us letting you know that we're done with the whole 'live in the woods and let bygones be bygones' bullcrap. That's so yesterday."

"I pretty much figured that."

"Right."

"But you've been pushing that for a while now, kid. And Mike's been pushing back pretty damn hard. Last I heard, the count was sixty-three to zip, with Mike running touchdowns all over your skinny ass."

"Hey, not mine, man," said Brandon. "I don't call the plays. That's for her highness, the Grand Imperial Queen of all the Damned."

"Two pop culture references in one sentence. I'm impressed."

"Thought you'd appreciate that."

"I do. Classic *Star Wars* and Anne Rice. Dated, but let's pretend you're not that far out of the loop. We'll call it retro."

"I'm good with retro."

"So," said Crow, "if you're not here to banter, and you're not running the fang gang—"

"*Fang gang*," said Brandon, chuckling. "I am so getting that on a T-shirt."

"—then why are we having this little conversation?"

Brandon shrugged. "Wanted to say hi. Shoot the shit. Maybe do a little stalling, but that's pretty much it."

"Stalling to make sure Mike walks into another trap?"

"Yeah, I guess. That and some other fun stuff we have going on."

Crow forced his mouth to keep wearing his own smile, but those words stuck an icy sword through his guts.

"What . . . other stuff?"

Brandon's grin brightened, and a few of the others laughed. Two of them exchanged high fives. They were having a great time with this.

"What other stuff?" repeated Crow, though he was absolutely sure that he knew.

"You really want me to tell you?" asked Brandon, laughing as he said it. "Do you actually want to know how bad this is all going to get?"

"Yes," said Crow. He couldn't hold the smile in place, and it fractured into pieces and fell away. "Tell me."

He hated that it sounded like what it was.

Like begging.

Brandon nodded, lips pursed, hands clasped thoughtfully behind his back. "You know," he said slowly. "I was going to tell you, 'cause I thought it would be funny. But the more I think about it, the more I think it's a cheap shot. Besides, the quicker this is over, the sooner I get to go play. There might even be a pint or two left in ol' Iron Mike if I hurry."

12

Two miles away, down the winding stretch of Dark Hollow Road and across a broad field that had once been green with corn, a farmhouse sat baking under the midday sun. Val Guthrie-Crow sat on the steps of the front porch with the parts of a motorcycle engine. The bike, a 1926 Harley-Davidson JD that once belonged to her great-grandfather, stood in the front yard, stripped down to a frame and wheels. Val was carefully cleaning ninety years' worth of smutch off of the bearings. She'd been buying replacement parts for years and was pretty sure she could restore it completely. She'd already restored a Triumph Scrambler and a 1961 Harley-Davidson FLH Panhead.

She loved her bikes. Her everyday ride was a V-twin Indian Model 841. Ugly, clunky, with awful suspension, but she loved it. Her father had given it to her for her eighteenth birthday.

A long, long time ago, it seemed to her.

She was thinking about her dad when she heard the floorboard behind her creak.

13

Mike Sweeney's mother stood in hazy space just outside a pool of sunlight. Careful not to step into the glare because she was one of the kind who could abide the light. Like Karl Ruger had been. Like some of the strongest of them were. The shadows were bright, though, almost glowing, and Mike could see bits of pollen and motes of dust swirl around her like stardust.

She was so beautiful. She looked the way he remembered when his dreams and memories were being kind to him. Slightly built, thin, with dark hair and eyes that were filled with kindness, with love and caring.

Her clothes were filthy, but the stark light made them seem almost ethereal, like the garments of some fairy queen from the movies. A Galadriel of the shadows.

"Michael," she said softly, "oh my baby, Michael. How beautiful you are. Look how big and strong you are."

"Mom . . . ?" he said again.

No, there wasn't any real way to prepare for this.

No way in hell.

And this was hell, of that he had no doubt.

All around them, the woods seemed to rise up, to become bigger, denser. A fortress of brown and green, strung with vines as tough as ropes. Figures appeared in the gloom.

The others.

Her new family.

Her *kind*.

"Mom," he said, still on his knees, "you have to stop this."

"Stop what, honey?"

"Stop *this*. You can't do this anymore."

She gave him a quizzical half-smile. "Do what anymore, Michael? You're not making sense. What is it you think I'm doing?"

He shook his head. "We had a deal."

"Deal? I don't remember ever making a deal. I gave no promises."

In the woods, the others laughed. Not loud. Low and mean. In on the joke. She held up a hand, a tiny gesture, and the woods fell instantly silent. Mike saw it, heard it.

These were her people.

He tried to count them without looking like he was. Familiar faces, every one of them. He'd studied the files of every single one of the missing eighty-four.

But something was wrong.

There weren't enough of them here.

Including his mother, there were only ten here.

Where were the others? Where was Brandon?

"Mom," he said, "we had a truce. For five years. You stayed here and you left the town alone, and we left you alone."

"Except you didn't leave us alone, Michael. You've been very rude to my friends. You've been so mean. So nasty."

He shook his head. "I only went after the ones who went hunting outside of here."

She cocked an eyebrow. "You're going to kneel there like a bad boy in church and lie to your own mother?"

"It's not a lie," he said, though he was lying. They both knew it. Everyone knew it.

"It was you who broke the *truce,* Michael. You."

"I only hunted the ones I knew had killed people during the Red Wave. I didn't go after anyone who turned and just came down here. Not one."

That was true enough, though he knew in his heart that sooner or later, he'd have come hunting for all of them.

Sooner or later, he would have come hunting for his mother.

She took a step toward him. Still avoiding the light but bathed more completely in the diffused glow. Steam rose in soft tendrils from her skin, and she gave him a small, sad smile. "Oh, Michael, my sweet boy, why does it have to be like this? Why can't you just *join* us? You're my son. And you are your father's son."

Mike leaned forward, pressing his palms into the muddy ground, fingers splayed. Then he slowly balled them into fists. Tears broke from his eyes and ran hot and fast down his cheeks. "My father was Terry Wolfe," he said, and there was a growl in his voice. "He died trying to save this town."

"Your father was our master, Ubel Griswold," she corrected. "He was a god. He was a gift to us, and he would have raised us to glory."

"No," said Mike, shaking his head slowly back and forth. "No. My father was Terry Wolfe. Griswold killed him, and I killed Griswold. I gutted him like the pig he was."

The figures in the shadows hissed, and they all moved forward a few steps, eyes blazing with dark fire, fingers hooked, mouths open to show their wicked white teeth.

"Don't say such things," gasped his mother. "You must not. Oh, my baby boy, you must not say such horrible things."

"Fuck you," he said, as the tears fell from his chin to be sucked into the greedy soil. Even the dirt here was hungry for life. For pain.

"Michael," said his mother, her tone suddenly confidential and urgent, "you can still be a part of this. It's almost too late, but there is still a chance."

"A chance for what?"

She took another step forward and knelt in front of him. Her fingers were cool when she brushed away his tears.

"For us to be a *family* again."

"Family—?"

"Yes. *He* is not dead, Michael."

Mike's head snapped up, and he stared at her. "Wh-what?"

"He *can't* die, don't you understand that? He is eternal. That parasite they called the Bone Man didn't kill him. All he did was destroy a shell, a husk. But our lord shed that skin and made a new body for himself, and on the night of the Red Wave. He *will* rise again. He will always rise again."

"How?" he asked, and the word burned his throat. "*How?*"

"Blood," she said. "And pain and life. All of his children that you killed? They were bringing offerings to him. They were preparing the way. As I am. It's a new world, Michael. Vic failed him. Karl Ruger failed him. But I . . . I won't. I'll be the priestess of his new church, Michael. And you can join us. Instead of being drowned when the Red Wave rises again, you can be with us. One of the saved ones, one of the *chosen* ones, one of his angels."

Mike stared at her. "That's why you stayed here all this time. Not because you were afraid to come out. Not because the rivers and canals around the town were a barrier. You stayed because you were trying to *raise Ubel Griswold from the dead*?"

She bent forward and licked the last of the tears from his face. "Yes. And I want you to be with us. Please, *please*, Michael . . . be with us."

Mike Sweeney sat back on his heels, wiped the last residue of tears from his cheeks, sniffed, nodded, took a ragged breath, and touched the satellite bud nested into his ear.

"You get all of that?" he said.

14

"Yeah," said Crow, touching his ear. "I heard everything."

Brandon frowned. "What?"

Crow took his pistol in one hand and held up the finger of his other. "Hold on, Brandon, I really have to take this," he said.

"Take what? What are you talking about?"

"Hey, can't you see I'm on a call?"

Brandon half-smiled. "Is this some kind of—?"

"Shh," said Crow. "Geez, some people. Mike, you were saying?"

Brandon and the others looked around as if expecting Mike Sweeney to step out of thin air. One of the others gave him a *what the fuck* look, but Brandon could only shake his head.

Crow said, "You were right, kiddo. God damn it, you were totally right. This is all about that ratfuck Griswold."

That made Brandon and his followers stiffen.

"You watch you goddamn mouth," snarled Brandon, "or I'll—"

Crow shot him in the face.

15

Val Guthrie-Crow didn't bother to turn around.

She knew what had come sneaking over the porch rail. She knew what had come up behind her on stealthy feet.

Just as she knew what was inside the house, behind drawn sheers.

"Mrs. Sitler?" called Val. "Any old time—"

The last word was obliterated by the god-awful din of a shotgun blast.

Val flinched as something hot and wet slapped against the back of her neck. She pawed at her skin, and her fingers came away red.

"God damn it, Emma," she growled as she threw down the engine part and shot to her feet. Behind her, a young man lay sprawled. Half of his face and one arm had been torn to rags by deer shot. Blood spread out around him in wild splash patterns.

"You watch your mouth, young lady," snapped Mrs. Sitler as she leaned out of the window. Blue smoke curled up from the twenty-gauge she'd laid over the sill. "It was your idea to sit right there. Oh—wait, he's not done."

Val looked down at the creature. His mouth was shattered, but in his delirium, he tried to bite the air with his broken fangs. Val reached under her sweatshirt and pulled out the Glock 26.

"Oh, don't waste the bullet," cautioned Mrs. Sitler. "The garlic oil will do for him."

Steam rose from the dozens of wounds drilled into the man's skin.

"It's okay," said Val. "I know him."

She leaned close and touched the barrel to the man's forehead.

"He killed Missy Sykes."

She fired.

The bang echoed off the side of the barn.

A moment later, there was the chatter of automatic gunfire as two of Crow's deputies opened up with M4s.

Val stood on the porch and peered off toward Dark Hollow.

"Be smart," she whispered to the wind.

Then she turned and walked down the steps toward the pale-faced creature who was running in terror from the hollow-point rounds. It was a woman. A stranger. One of them. The woman raised her hands. Not in surrender but as if to plead for mercy. Woman to woman.

As if there were any kinship of that kind left.

It made Val so angry.

The anger made a cold heart go colder still as she walked toward the woman.

She raised her pistol.

There was no expression at all on her face as she pulled the trigger.

16

Brandon saw it coming. He spun away, trying to dodge something that even his speed could not evade. He was fast, though. Crow had to give him that.

The bullet caught him on the cheekbone as Brandon turned. Blood and pale flesh and bone flew outward in a spray as the young man hurled himself in the opposite direction.

Crow pivoted to fire again.

And his bad leg buckled.

Not completely, but enough. The bullet punched a hot hole in the air one half inch from Brandon's skull. The young man screamed and flung himself forward, diving without plan or caution toward the edge of the drop-off.

Snarling in pain, Crow fired again and again.

Maybe hitting him as he vanished over the edge.

Then the others were coming.

Six of them. Roaring like lions, slashing at the air with black fingernails as they rushed forward.

The trunk hood of Crow's car popped open, and a deputy— sweaty, wild-eyed, scared as hell—sat up with an assault rifle clutched in two trembling hands. He fired, blowing through an entire magazine in seconds. Then he stood there, staring blankly at the two figures who had seemed to fly apart inside the storm of bullets. There was red everywhere. A cloud of pink mist swirled in the air.

The other four rushed at Crow.

"Reload, goddamn it," he bellowed as he once more took his Beretta in both hands.

He fired.

Fired.

Fired.

Fired.

17

Lois Wingate recoiled from Mike as if he'd struck her. She got to her feet and backed away from him.

"What are you doing?" she demanded. "What are you saying? Who are you talking to?"

Mike, still on his knees, opened his jacket to show the satellite microphone clipped to his shirt.

"You didn't raise me to be stupid, Mom," he said. Meaning it to sound flip, but it came out broken and filled with thorns that cut them both.

"What do you mean?"

"I mean it's over," he said. "This was all a setup. When Brandon left me that message, Crow and Val and those of us who *remember* what happened, we planned this. I told them what was happening."

"You couldn't," she protested. "You couldn't *know*."

He felt an ugly smile form on his mouth. "You said it yourself. I'm my father's son. Of *course* I know. I felt it. Why do you think I've been hunting you? All of you? How could I *not* know?" He slapped the sat-phone. "And now everyone knows. Crow, Val, the rest of our network. Everyone."

She laughed. "Crow and Val are dead."

"No, they're not. I just *spoke* to Crow. And Val has a whole army with her at the farm. Come on, Mom, you can't be this dense. You were always smart, even if you let Vic beat the crap out of you all the time. You think I'd come down here without taking precautions? Did you and Brandon actually believe that I'd come down here and leave my friends and family defenseless?"

"I'm your family, Michael."

He could feel fresh tears burn in his eyes. "No!" he yelled. "No you're not. My mother died five years ago. Karl Ruger and Ubel Griswold killed her. Vic Wingate *fed* her to them, and she, them. You're not real. You're a ghost. A monster." A sob broke in his chest, and he caved forward and beat the ground with his fists. "My mother is dead. God . . . God, I wish you were her. I wish my mom was still alive. I wish . . . I wish . . ."

The sobs wouldn't stop. Or the tears.

All around him, the shadows deepened as the rest of the missing eighty-four closed around him.

"Michael," said the thing that wore his mother's skin. "I—"

"No," he begged. "Don't you say it. Don't you dare say it. You're not my mother. You're a monster. That's all you are. A . . . monster . . ."

He looked up and saw her eyes change, losing all color, all white. Becoming black wells. If the eyes are the windows of the soul, then he looked into her eyes and beyond into a world that was pestilential and dying. A world that was so corrupt and vile that it consumed it-self, consumed all light and life.

When she spoke, it was no longer his mother's voice.

She spoke in a voice like thunder.

Like *his* voice. Like Griswold's.

"You have no idea what you have done," she said, and that voice shook the trees. "You have no idea what I am."

There was no trace of her now. The lie was gone, taking with it the last hope that he would ever find his mother. He'd found the thing that had killed her. The thing that pretended to be her, and in doing so, defiled her and her memory.

With the lie revealed, it took away something else from Mike Sweeney.

It took his humanity, too.

He said, "No, you have no idea what *I* am."

And his voice was a greater thunder.

His voice was a roar.

His voice was a *howl*.

When he launched himself forward, it was not a man rising from his knees. It was not a man at all.

It was a wolf who leaped and snarled and slashed and tore.

18

Night fell slowly over Pine Deep.

There was no moon at all, and the stars littered the sky like cracked chips of diamond. They sat on the porch. Eleven of them. On chairs, on folded blankets, on the steps, on the porch rails.

A few in uniforms, some in ordinary clothes.

Mike was in sweatpants with a bathrobe draped around his shoulders. His clothes never made it back up the hill with him, and no one commented on it.

They passed around a bottle. One of many. Everyone drank except Crow, who drank coffee. Everyone had guns. In holsters, tucked into belts, laid across laps.

No one said a word.

Not a word.

As night fell slowly over Pine Deep.

Ghost Creepin' Blues

1

It wasn't Jennifer or Jenny. It was Jinnifer. With an I. Or Jinn. She liked Jinn. She spelled it that way most of the time; though when she was writing about herself—something she always did in third person—she used a different spelling. Djinn. Like in the Arabian Tales.

Djinn.

That's who she was to herself.

Her mom said the misspelling—Jinnifer—was intentional.

"It's pretty," Mom said. "It's different. It wasn't a mistake, sweetie."

But Mom was high a lot of the time. She was probably high when she went into labor. She was high when she wrapped her car around a tree that one spring. Djinn overheard a doctor tell Aunt Kay that being high probably caused the accident and also probably saved her life. Limp as a rag doll, he said.

Mom was always high.

Ever since Dad died, she was high, and that happened seven months before Djinn was born. That's what Aunt Kay said.

"Don't hate me for telling the truth, honey," Kay said once when they were driving from Pine Deep to the clothing outlet stores in New Jersey to get last year's fashions for next year's school term. "Your mama was getting high ever since the Trouble. She was high when she met your daddy, Jimmy Lee Howard. He was a sweet boy and handsome as they come. But he was always stoned. Started on it after his father was killed and never could give it up. Him and your mom . . . well, they started getting high together. Pot and then some crack. Other stuff. Rocket fuel for love, your mom always said. High as kites, both of them, and crawling all over each other. Maybe it wasn't *love* how you came about, sweetie, but you came out all right."

Aunt Kay tried hard to be nice, but she was a terrible liar.

The truth, as far as Djinn could figure it out, was that both her parents were high on something, and they'd had sex. Djinn even wondered if Mom, already a junkie and needing a fix, made some kind of barter. Which would make an awful situation that much worse. But . . . that was something Djinn would never quite know. Mom said that it was love, but never met her daughter's eyes when she said it. And Dad rode a hot spike into the big black nowhere a day after Mom told him she was pregnant.

Mom was pretty much high from then on.

High.

Though that word always bothered Djinn. What a weird thing to call it when someone was hitting rock bottom.

Mrs. Copley next door said that Mom was lucky. Another strange word. Lucky because she was still alive after all those years. Lucky Mom was alive after three overdose close calls. Lucky that the accident hadn't killed her—that one or any of the other fender benders. Lucky another crackhead hadn't murdered her.

There was nothing lucky about Mom.

Nothing.

Aunt Kay liked to tell Djinn about how Mom had been before the Trouble. Before her first family had all died. Djinn only knew them from photos. A husband—tall, handsome, with a kind smile and great hair. Three other kids. Half-siblings who had been two, four, and seven. The older one, the girl, even looked like Djinn. Same brown hair and green eyes. And grandparents—three of them. Mom's parents, Bob and Addy; and the mother of Mom's first husband, Claire.

All gone.

Swept up in the Trouble. Consumed by it.

Most of the websites and books about that time said it was white supremacists who laced the town's water supply with LSD and other drugs and then began attacking everybody who had the wrong skin color, prayed in the wrong church, or was wrong about their own sexual identity. That was the official story. They said that the white racist militia got high on their own drugs and simply started killing everyone, even white people.

A total of 11,641 people died that day. Most of them tourists in town for that year's Halloween Festival; but a lot of Pine Deep residents were lost, too. Whole families were wiped out, or families trapped on both sides of death and grief. It was the worst hate crime in American history unless you counted the Civil War. That's what they thought in Pine Deep High, and in Black Marsh, Crestville, New Hope, Doylestown, and other local towns.

Other websites told a different story. There were all kinds of conspiracy theories about weird cults, devil worshippers, and other weird stuff. Some even said it was vampires. That made Djinn smile, because she watched reruns of *The Vampire Diaries* all the time. Damon Salvatore was her dream boyfriend. Those blue eyes? Djinn sipped her iced tea and smiled.

No, she thought, *it wasn't vampires. Not here in Pine Deep. I mean . . . come on.*

Djinn read all the stories. She talked about it with her friends. Everyone seemed to believe something different. Djinn was still working on what she believed. She was no fan of the white supremacists. Mom dated a few now and then. If *date* was even the right word. Slept with. Got high with. Whatever. Of all the guys who seemed to pass through her mom's life, assholes like that tended to be the ones most likely to make a pass at her, at Djinn. Or grab her ass, stare at her boobs. Make comments. When they were in the house, Mom seemed to be both blind and deaf. She swore she never saw anything like that. When Djinn insisted it was true and begged Mom not to bring guys like that around, there was always an argument. A bad one. Mom started screaming, maybe loud enough to drown out her own insight, her own thoughts. Twice Mom had slapped Djinn. Not recently, but some memories stay fresh. She could still feel the blows, still remember the burn, still see the red handprints. Sometimes she even caught looks of horror and regret in Mom's eyes, but there were no follow-up conversations. Ever.

Djinn wondered how much the Trouble mattered; in what ways it factored into the process. What she didn't know is how much Mom actually saw that day all those years ago, or *what* she had seen. The fact that Aunt Kay said that her sister was "different before all that mess" influenced how much Djinn blamed her mother for what had happened since.

Unlike a lot of other kids in school, though, she wasn't obsessed about the Trouble itself. That was a horror story from before she was born. All that really mattered to her was the fact—the truth— that Mom was messed up because of whatever happened. She started getting high and, except for some short time in county jails and five attempts at twelve-steps or rehab, she was still high.

Djinn knew she always would be.

All that mattered to Djinn, because Mom had been high all through her pregnancy. Mom had experienced placental abruption; her placenta separated from the uterus, and Djinn nearly died. She delivered at thirty-four weeks and weighed four pounds, six ounces. And to cap that all off, Djinn was born with neonatal abstinence syndrome—born addicted and going through withdrawal even as she struggled to stay alive.

The doctors and social workers and school counselors gave her some version of "the speech" at least forty times. Djinn would likely be vulnerable to addiction her whole life, much more than regular kids. She had to watch for addictive tendencies. And there were all kinds of risks of psychological crap, especially during adolescence.

Djinn was sixteen and she could write a book on all that psychological crap. Depression, panic attacks, spiraling, paranoia, and even what Aunt Kay called "dry drunks," where she felt high herself, even though Djinn had never touched anything like crack. She hadn't even sipped a beer. Fear of what it might do to her, and how that could lead to her personal apple falling pretty close to Mom's tree. She even had flat-out hallucinations now and then. Mostly then. They weren't common. Two or three times a year, tops.

Fun.

That was her life.

It sucked.

Mostly.

But not entirely.

There were times she had auditory hallucinations. That's what a therapist called them. If it was because the wiring in her head was askew, then that part of it was cool. The sounds she heard every once in a while were music. Not the same song over and over again, but the same kind of music. Blues. Very old blues. Classic stuff, which Djinn knew about only after humming some of the pieces to a friend at school who was really *into* music. Djinn's best friend, Gidge, recognized the melodies right off.

"That's 'My Love Will Never Die' by Willie Dixon," Gidge said, and then explained who Willie Dixon was. Classic blues songwriter and singer from the middle twentieth century. The second song was "Seventh Son," another Dixon song that was covered by everyone from Mose Allison to Peggy Lee to George Thorogood and the Destroyers. None of whom Djinn had ever heard of before that day. Gidge dragged her home after school that day and played all kinds of blues songs. Son House, Big Mama Thornton, Muddy Waters, John Lee Hooker, Blind Lemon Jefferson, and many others . . . and then played cover versions by rock and rollers like The Doors, Cream, Led Zeppelin, and even The Rolling Stones. Gidge took it as her mission in life to shift Djinn from emo and EDM to classic blues and classic rock, and it worked pretty well.

Now, when Djinn had one of those auditory hallucinations, she often recognized the tune. The most recent was three weeks ago when she lay in bed at night, her window open—she kept it open summer through winter—and the plaintive strains of the classic Robert Johnson song, "Hellhound on My Trail," floated to her on the chilly night wind.

Djinn knew that she was nothing special. Not in terms of being messed up. The newspapers ran all sorts of articles about how Pine Deep had one of the highest rates of addiction per capita. Highest PTSD per capita, too. Mostly it was people who lived through the Trouble. The ones who said it wasn't *just* white racist assholes. The ones who double-locked their doors, hung strings of garlic over every window, who always left lights burning, and who never went out after dark. There were lots of those. And what the news called the Second Wavers—kids like her, who inherited that fear and paranoia, and a lot of the addictions. Hiding inside a needle or a crack pipe or a bottle.

There were posters for twelve-steps in school and everywhere in town. Even the disposal paper placemats at the Scarecrow Diner had ads for them.

Djinn managed her inherited addictions, though. They weren't her big problem. It was the hallucinations. She heard that blues music even when she was with other people. When it was clear *only* she heard the songs.

Only her.

That was a prescription for preferring isolation, for wanting to keep her own company. Sure, she knew she was crazy, but there were worse kinds of crazy. She knew that firsthand every time she walked past Mom's picture on the mantle.

Djinn sat on the middle step of the porch, a bottle of Snapple between her bare feet. Dozer—all eight pounds of him—asleep beside her, snuggled against her hip. Dreaming Yorkie dreams. Maybe dreaming of being a mastiff or a pit bull.

There was no music on the breeze, but there were lots of crows gossiping in the trees; lots of interesting clouds to look at. The afternoon was warm, but the breeze was cool, and Djinn felt okay.

Mostly okay.

Their house clung to the edge of the Wilderness of Weeds. That's what Aunt Kay called it. Before the Trouble, it was the Bergstrom Farm, which had been farmed since 1744. Djinn once tried to do the math on that—a farm with 6,000 apple trees with a standard yield of 700 to 800 apples per year for 262 years. Her math was never great, but it was more than a billion, she was pretty sure.

And now the trees were mostly gone. A blight had rotted them the same year as the Trouble, like it did a lot of the farms. Some crops had come back—pumpkins, corn, garlic—but some never did. They could grow apples in Black Marsh and Crestville. Not in Pine Deep. At least, not on any farm Djinn knew about. All those acres were overgrown with weeds and weed trees like wild maples and scrub pines.

Djinn's house was not the one Mom had lived in before. That one burned, like a lot of homes. Burned, like a lot of people.

Mom got some insurance money, and Aunt Kay bullied her into buying a small place and putting money into a trust that would pay the mortgage. The place was small, but not awful. It was clean because Djinn cleaned it. The hedges were a bit shaggy, but Djinn would get around to them.

The day was too nice to worry about that, though.

She idly scratched Dozer's furry belly and watched the clouds. They were the big white ones, and she could see all kinds of shapes in them. That one over the fence looked like a dragon rolling on its back, feet in the air and tail curling. The little one was an opossum, and it was sneaking between the dragon and another that looked like a leaping sailfish. She never took photos of them, preferring to be totally in the moment. The iPhone owned too much of the rest of her life. The clouds were little gifts from the day, and they were just for her, just for now. Even the clouds that just looked like clouds were fun. Djinn loved watching their shadows glide like purple waves over the heads of the wild grass.

Then she saw the man.

He was just *there*.

All at once.

He stood thirty feet away, facing away from her. Looking across the road to the drop-off that tumbled down to Dark Hollow. At first, she thought he was a scarecrow, because he was that skinny and ragged. His clothes hung on his thin frame and flapped softly in the breeze. He wore a battered and stained Phillies baseball cap, turned backward on a retro Afro that was disheveled and nappy. A pair of dirty canvas gloves were tucked into a rear pocket. Across his narrow back was slung a beautiful guitar, the tuning keys angled toward the dirt. His arms hung loosely at his sides, and she could see brown skin that looked almost gray.

A thrill of fear lanced through her, but it did not find any real target and faded quickly, leaving behind it only curiosity. There was something familiar about the man. But it was one of those odd familiarities, as if she knew him from somewhere other than real life. TV? A movie? She considered that but discounted it. No. It was more like someone glimpsed in a dream. Her dreams were like that—incredibly vivid, with lots of specific details, but always composed of people, places, and things she did not know pasted over normal elements from Djinn's waking reality.

Dozer jerked awake as input from his canine senses finally poked through the veil of sleep. He looked around, his confusion making his tiny body tremble, but when he caught sight of the stranger, he shot to his feet. His muzzle wrinkled, but only for a moment. Then Dozer leaned against Djinn and whined softly.

"It's okay," said Djinn, laying her hand gently on his back.

The dog looked at her and then at the man with the guitar. The dog's trembling faded and stopped. Djinn realized her own tension, and even her surprise was easing. And that was odd, because this man *was* a stranger, and he was in her yard.

"Hell—" began Djinn, but her throat was oddly dry, and she stumbled, getting only half the word out. She coughed her throat clear and tried again. "Hello . . . ?"

A breeze swirled some stray leaves along the dirt road.

"Can I help you, mister?" she called.

He began to turn but paused, still looking at the woods. She could see the side of his face. He looked like he was in his thirties and had both a sense of youth and great age about him—the way some people who lived hard sometimes have. Like Mom's face in pictures. Like a lot of people in town who'd lived through the Trouble. Like that cop, Chief Crow, and his cute sergeant, Mike Sweeney. They had it. And it was the kind of thing Djinn saw in people who felt compelled to move to Pine Deep because bad luck and trouble made them feel at home.

It was like the look in her own eyes when she looked in the mirror. Really looked. Not when she was putting on eyeliner or brushing her hair, but when she looked into her own eyes deep enough to *see*.

"Help me?" asked the man. There was a lot of Deep South in his voice, even in two words.

"Are you lost?" asked Djinn.

He turned all the way now. His face was calm, his eyes dark and complex.

Dozer wagged his little tail.

"I know where I am," said the man.

"Oh. Okay," said Djinn. "Sorry." She wasn't sure where to go with things like this.

He took a single step toward her. It was not in any way threatening; there was no sense of intrusion about it. He looked a bit shy and hesitant, even confused.

"You're Jimmy Lee Howard's daughter," he said. "Aren't you?"

That gave Djinn a little jolt. "You knew my dad?"

"In a way," said the man. "I knew *his* dad. I was living here when he got killed. That was a shame, because he was a good cat. Treated me like I was a person and not a skin tone.

I saw Jimmy Lee later on, all grown up. He was running with a pretty girl. Can't recall her name, but you got her face."

"I guess I do," said Djinn. Then she frowned. "I thought Grandpa Howard died back in the seventies, when my dad was little. You don't look anywhere near old enough to have known him."

The man with the guitar gave one of those smiles that looks like a grimace. "Guess I'm a bit older than I look."

He left it there.

She said, "Were you here during the Trouble?"

"The Trouble . . . ? Oh. Yeah. Sure," he said after fumbling around for a moment, "I was here. I was here for all of it."

"Was it as bad as people say?"

That chased the last of the man's smile away. His eyes seemed to go dark, and he turned away and stood for a few seconds looking toward the drop-off down to Dark Hollow.

"It was bad," he said.

Djinn watched him looking at the forest.

"Was it what they said it was?" she asked. "White racist guys starting some kind of Civil War?"

He gave a small, dry laugh. "It was a bit of that, sure."

"A bit . . . ?"

"Bit of that," said the man, nodding in agreement to his own words. "Bit of other things, too. Wasn't a good time for anyone."

"Glad you weren't hurt, then," she said, surprising herself with the comment. When the man turned an inquiring look to her, she added, "Being African American, I mean. With those racists and all . . . ?"

It trailed off as a question.

The stranger sighed and reached back to lay a hand on the neck of his guitar. He did it the way a Catholic would touch a crucifix. Like Aunt Kay did with hers.

"No one came through that without some dents," said the man. "We all got our scars." He paused and looked at her. Into her eyes, and she endured it for as long as she could.

"What?" she asked.

"You got some scars of your own, don't you, miss?"

She almost said that she didn't have any scars. But it was a lie. Her scars didn't show, but they were there. The stranger nodded as if she'd answered.

"My granny had a word for it," he said. "For people who have certain kinds of scars. Some that show, some that don't. All of them part of who we are. They remind of us of what we've been through and how that changed us. Who we became as a result. You understand what I'm saying? Children of the Storm Lands."

Djinn silently mouthed that phrase.

Children of the Storm Lands.

Then she nodded. "I guess so."

"Some of us are too scared to admit the scars are there, 'cause it would mean thinking about how they *got* there. I know that dance real well. Black boy growing up in the Deep South? Walking across America, dodging the draft so I didn't have to die in someone else's war. Living rough in order to live at all. Came North looking to get away from that. Went to Philly. City of Brotherly Love, except they didn't much love the Brothers back then. Went out to farm country looking for some peace, maybe some day labor working the fields. Guess what I learned? Pennsylvania has more Ku Klux Klan groups that any other state."

"They taught us that in school," said Djinn. "People joke that everything between Philly and Pittsburgh is Pennsyltucky. Guess they aren't wrong. It's pretty awful sometimes. Been worse lately. There was a shooting at a Baptist church in White Haven. A black church. Some teenage asshole with an AR-15 killed nine people. Guy posted a bunch of hate stuff online. Nazi stuff, and White is

Right. Taking America Back. Stuff like that. Happening more and more often."

The man sighed and shook his head. "Hate don't ever go away."

"No," she agreed. Little Dozer whined softly.

Djinn and the man stayed silent for a moment, both clearly feeling the weight of that bit of shared understanding.

"Children of the Storm Lands," she murmured.

"There's a lot of us 'round here."

"In Pine Deep?"

"Yeah. A bit more than the average, I suppose," said the man. "But there's plenty most places, too."

She studied him. "What's your name? I mean, if it's okay to ask."

"Always okay to ask," he said. "My name's Oren Morse."

"Really?" she said, brightening. "Then you must be related to the Bone Man."

He said nothing.

"Don't you know about him?" Djinn wondered. "He lived here a while back. Before my time."

"The Bone Man," echoed Morse, his voice barely a whisper.

"Sure," said Djinn. "There're all sorts of stories about him. Was a . . . I mean . . . he *worked* here as a migrant worker. Worked for the Guthrie family just over there." She gestured to the massive farm that shared some of the border of Dark Hollow Road with her own home. "Bunch of those white militia creeps killed him back in the seventies. They blamed him for a whole slew of murders that were really done by this German guy. I forget his name . . ."

"Ubel Griswold," said Morse, and in the trees, the crows fell silent. Djinn glanced up but made no comment about that.

"Right! My Aunt Kay said that there were all these urban legends about that *other* Oren Morse. The Bone Man. They said that he haunted the town."

"Is that what they said?" he asked distantly.

"But there's a whole section of the history book we had in seventh grade where Chief Crow was interviewed. He *knew* the Bone Man when he was a kid and said that he'd saved the chief's life from that Griswold freak. Chief Crow said the Bone Man was not only innocent of the murders, but he was a real hero."

"I don't know about 'hero'," murmured Morse.

"There's a statue of him in Pinelands Park. A plaque, too."

Morse shook his head. "Well, that's something I think I need to see."

"So . . . you *are* related to him? I mean, you have to be. Was he your dad? Or . . . granddad . . . ?"

The stranger shoved his hands in his back pockets and looked across the road again. He did not answer the question.

Djinn waited, and as the seconds passed, the hair on the nape of her neck began to slowly stand up. Gooseflesh pebbled her forearms. The crows in the trees were talking again, but softly. Whispering. Djinn's mouth went dry, and fear began to swirl inside her chest. Dozer felt it, too, and he stood up again, the fur all along his spine as stiff as a hairbrush.

"Mr. Morse . . . ?" Djinn asked slowly.

He said nothing.

"You're *him*," she said. "Aren't you?"

He said nothing.

"You're the Bone Man . . ."

Oren Morse took his hands from his pockets and pulled his guitar around front. Without turning to look at her, he began to play music. Blues. Of course it was blues. Djinn recognized the melody.

"Ghost Creepin' Blues." An old song by St. Louis Bessie. Djinn fished inside her head for the lyrics, and while the Bone Man played, she softly sang . . .

> *Mmmmmm, something cold is creepin' around.*
> *Mmmmmm, something cold is creepin' around.*
> *Blue Ghost is got me, I feel myself sinkin' down.*
>
> *Black cat and a owl, come to keep my company.*
> *Black cat and a owl, comes to keep my company.*
> *He understands my troubles, mmm, and sympathize*
> *   with me.*
>
> *I been in this haunted house, for three long years today.*
> *I been in this haunted house, for three long years today.*

> *Blue Ghost is got my shack surrounded, oh Lord, and I can't get away.*

That was all she knew of the song, so she hummed the rest as he played. The crows fluttered their wings and cawed softly on the breaks between stanzas.

Morse finished the song, but the last few notes he picked were soft and slow, and it let the song kind of drift away on the breeze. For some reason, Djinn turned her head as if she could actually see it move from her yard across the road and over the edge and all the way down to Dark Hollow. The shadows there at the edge, crouching beneath the canopy of trees, were inky dark.

Morse walked a few steps over to the stump of a tree that was all there was left from an ancient oak that hadn't survived a big storm three years back. He sat down wearily, his knees popping. He gave a long sigh and set his guitar on end, the body leaning against his thigh. Djinn watched him. She kept trying to be afraid, but the fear wouldn't come.

"Are you real?" she asked.

He looked puzzled. "Real?"

Djinn tapped her head. "I got some bad wiring."

"Bad how?"

She shrugged. "I hear things sometimes. See things once in a while, too. I'm not crazy. Just broken. Mom was a junkie, and she was high all the time she was carrying me."

Morse nodded. "Seen a lot of that. Bad wiring don't define a person."

"Maybe, but that doesn't mean I'm normal."

"Normal is overrated," he said, and they both smiled at that.

"So . . . are you real? Or am I having a *moment.*" She leaned on that word, giving it deeper meaning.

"I'm real."

Djinn nodded. "But you are the Bone Man, right?"

"I guess I am."

"And you died."

"I did."

"So . . . are you a ghost?"

Morse cocked his head to one side as the crows in the trees began chattering more loudly. His face was seamed, but more with care and hard use than age.

"I guess I am," he said. "If I'm anything."

2

A ghost.

They sat with that.

"I hope this is really real," said Djinn.

He nodded.

A couple of butterflies flitted past, bobbing and weaving like boxers. Dozer watched them, his little tail wagging. The Bone Man reached out a callused hand and then held it still, and after a moment, one butterfly landed on the knuckle of his thumb. A moment later, the second one alit on the second joint of his index finger. Their wings folded and unfolded slowly, and then they sat still.

"That's so cool," said Djinn. "Do they always do that?"

The Bone Man shrugged. "Sometimes."

They smiled at the butterflies. They smiled at each other. The crows hushed their noise. A soft wind blew past them and stirred her hair and the folds of his loose shirt.

"I heard of a book once," she said. "It was called *Ghost Road Blues*. Written by this reporter guy—Willard Fowler Newton. They made it into a movie, too. *Hellnight*. It was all about vampires and werewolves and ghosts. I never saw it, though."

"Uh-huh. That's the guy."

"Did you know him? Mr. Newton?"

"Not exactly," said the Bone Man. "But I know who he is. I saw him."

"People said that book was all made up. Lies. My teacher said Mr. Newton was just trying to make a buck by making up stupid stories."

"Uh-huh."

She waited.

"Well . . . ?" she asked.

"Well what?"

"Was it all just lies and made-up stuff? Silly conspiracy theories?" Instead of answering, he asked, "What's your name?"

"Jinnifer. With an I. But I go by Djinn." She spelled it.

"Like the demon."

"I guess."

"I like it," said the Bone Man. "Well, Djinn, what do *you* think happened? Do you think it was just white supremacists and all that?"

"I . . . don't know . . ."

"Do you believe in vampires and werewolves and ghosts?"

She looked at him. "Unless I'm having a moment, I guess I'm talking to a ghost right now."

"Guess you are," he agreed. "But what about the rest?"

Djinn shook her head.

"What's that mean?" he asked. "That you don't believe or don't know if you believe?"

"Both, maybe."

He nodded, accepting that. "You know what they mean when some people talk about the 'larger world'?"

"Yes," she said. No hesitation.

"Do you believe in the larger world? The world unseen? Spirits of the air? Demons and monsters, ghosts, and all the rest?"

Djinn scratched Dozer's neck and stared at the drop-off for nearly a full minute before she answered.

"I guess I do," she said. "Either that or I really am crazy."

"You don't seem crazy to me."

"Not a lot of people would agree with that."

"People can think whatever they like," said the Bone Man. "I believe what I know and know what I believe."

Djinn thought about that and nodded, liking how that fit into her head.

"They killed you, didn't they?" she asked. "The KKK guys, I mean."

"They weren't in the Klan, but same difference," he said. "They knew I didn't kill all those people back in the seventies. Most of 'em knew it, I mean. Some didn't, but they also didn't much care. White people were dying, and I was as black as everything they hated."

She chewed her lower lip for a few seconds. "Was it bad? Dying, I mean?"

"It was bad."

"Did it hurt a lot?"

He nodded. "And it lasted a long time."

"Oh my God," she breathed. She felt the burn of tears in her eyes. "I'm so sorry."

Morse looked at her.

"I don't know as any white person ever said they were sorry about what happened to me. Sure, Crow and Val and some of their friends were sorry. Val Guthrie's dad, Henry, was sad. But if they ever said so out loud, I never heard it. Not blaming them, you understand. They *felt* it, and that's a lot. That's more than a lot of brown people ever get. But you said it to my face. You said it with tears running down your cheeks." He paused and smiled a gentle, powerful smile. "You'll never know how much that means. That's powerful, Djinn. That's actual magic right there."

As if his words were a spell that conjured the wind, a stiff breeze blew past them both. It was very cold and very wet. It smelled of mold and sickness and wrongness.

The shiver that cut through Djinn was so strong it hurt. Dozer whined and pressed himself against her, his little tail curled up under his body, ears down, eyes filled with fear. The Bone Man turned into the breeze. He shivered, too, but he stood his ground, staring across the street to where a wall of crooked brown weeds hid the lip of the drop-off.

The wind blew and blew and then stopped. Just like that.

"Wh-what wuh-was th-that?" stammered Djinn through chattering teeth.

The Bone Man took a few steps toward the road.

"I guess that's why I'm back," he said. "I think Ubel Griswold just sent his regards."

3

They stood at the edge of the drop-off and stared down into shadows. The girl and the ghost. The little dog was back in the house, hiding under the bed.

The trees that grew near that edge were sickly and twisted, with bark lumpy with blight and limbs hung with hairy vines. Djinn never liked standing there, because no matter where the sun was, its light never touched this spot. Not even in the winter when the canopy of leaves had withered and blown away. She stood with her arms wrapped around her chest, hugging herself for warmth that was not on offer.

"What do you really know about him?" asked the Bone Man.

He spoke in a pale whisper. It wasn't a respectful church whisper. Or even the kind of whisper people use at a funeral. There was no respect for the living or the dead in his tone. There was fear, and there was hate.

"You mean Ubel Griswold?" asked Djinn. She winced because that name felt bad in her mouth. Different than when she'd said it before while sitting in the sun on the porch steps.

"Him, yes," said the ghost. "What'd they teach you in school?"

"That he was an immigrant," she said. "That he started a small cattle ranch on the other side of Dark Hollow. That he was kind of weird and quiet and didn't have many friends. Mostly those white racist guys. I forget their names."

"Vic Wingate," said Morse. "Eddie Oswald, Jimmy Polk. A few others. Crow's dad was one of 'em."

She gaped at him. "Really?"

"Yeah. Crow's a good guy, but his dad was an asshole. Used his fists on his kids. A lot."

"Chief Crow's not like that."

"Some apples fall a long damn way from the tree," said Morse, "and I guess the wind was blowing when he was born. Crow—Little Scarecrow I used to call him when he was a kid—had his issues, but his heart was always in the right place. Talk about children of the Storm Lands . . . he's a charter member."

"He has kind eyes."

Morse smiled. "He does. And his sergeant . . . Mike Sweeney?"

Djinn perked up. "What about him?"

"He's one of us, too. He grew up hard and turned out strange, but if he has your back, then you're good."

"He's cute, too," said Djinn, almost under her breath. "I mean *really* cute."

The Bone Man studied her a for a moment as if he was about to make another comment about Mike Sweeney, but he left it unsaid.

"You said this was why you came back," prompted Djinn. "What'd you mean?"

"I killed that black-hearted son of a bitch," said Morse bitterly. "That's why his boys lynched me. I . . . came back when Griswold came back."

"He came *back*?" cried Djinn.

The Bone Man nodded. "That was what the Trouble was all about. Griswold wasn't no serial killer. Not in the way people think. He was a monster. An *actual* monster."

"A vampire?"

"You sure you want to hear this?"

A dusty farm pickup came along the road. The driver tooted the horn. It was Buck, the assistant foreman for the Guthrie place. He slowed and leaned out the window. "Hey, kiddo . . . we got a whole bunch of corn and some peppers in the kitchen garden. Val told me to say you can come over and grab what you want. There's some baskets by the cellar door."

"Oh . . . that's great," said Djinn, brightening. "Thanks, Buck. Tell Val I said thanks, too."

"You'll love it. Best corn in a couple seasons. Grab as much as you can carry. Bye now!" He sketched a wave and headed off toward the junction with Route A32.

"Seems like folks like you," said the Bone Man.

"They know we're broke," said Djinn. "They're just being nice."

"Or," said Morse, leaning on that word, "maybe they actually like you."

She shrugged and shook her head, letting the topic go. Then she looked over the edge for a moment. "You asked if I wanted to hear what you had to say? Well . . . I guess I kind of have to."

"Why d'you say that?"

"Because why else would you have come to see me?"

The ghost nodded. "Yeah. Not sure if it's God or just whatever makes the larger world work, but it does move in mysterious ways. No doubt about that."

"Yeah."

They stood for a few silent moments.

"Griswold was a werewolf," said the Bone Man.

Djinn actually jumped. And screamed, though it was a stifled, high-pitched *yeep* of a scream. She stared up into the Bone Man's face, her eyes as big as saucers.

"Get the fuck out of here," she cried. "Are you actually serious?"

"As a heart attack," he said. "Didn't come all this way to mess with some teenage white girl's mind. I mean . . . I'm dead and all, but I'm not some kind of prankish poltergeist."

"But . . ."

"There are lots of kinds of ghosts," he said. "First time I came back, I had no idea what I was or how any of this higher realm jazz worked. Had to work it through, learn by doing and shit. Wasn't even until that folklore professor lady came to town that I got a bead on what kind I was."

"Folklore . . . ? Oh!" she said. "You mean Jonatha Corbiel-Newton. From U of P."

"That's her."

"She married the guy who wrote *Ghost Road Blues*. She's always on those History Channel shows they run around Halloween. One of those talking heads."

"Uh-huh."

"She told you what kind of ghost you were?"

"Nah," said Morse. "Just kind of picked it up from her. Hard to explain how that works."

"Osmosis?" suggested Djinn, and Morse grinned.

"I guess that's as good an explanation as any. As for me . . . I'm what people like her call a *crisis apparition*. You may think this is funny, Djinn, but I'm actually no expert on all this," he said. "I just know what I picked up, and in some cases, I know what I know . . . and I'm aware that don't make a lot of sense. Then again, this is Pine Deep and, I guess, this is the world. It don't always have to make sense."

"I get it," she said.

"So, this whole crisis apparition thing . . . sometimes it's only a vision. Someone who is running headlong toward some bad shit sees something that lets them know things are going south, you dig? Like someone's going to die, or *they're* going to die. Or a big accident. There are all these tales going way back. Generals seeing angels before a battle, and people seeing a ghostly iceberg in the water before the Titanic even launched. All sorts of things. Sometimes they see something; other times it's a call from a dead relative, or the smell of something burning. Lot of different ways. Mostly it's nothing to do with ghosts," he said. "Except when it is. For me . . . I was nothing but bones in a box in some grave over in Crestville, and then all of a sudden I'm standing right next to my own grave. Even my guitar was there."

"Wait . . . your guitar is a ghost, too?"

Morse laughed. "Weird, ain't it?"

"Really weird," said Djinn. "Not sure why that freaks me out more than the rest."

"Well, I ain't got to the freakiest part yet."

"Shit."

"Y'see, when Ubel Griswold came to Pine Deep and set up as this bullshit gentleman farmer, he wasn't raising cows because he likes to barbecue. Nah. He was trying to lay low and establish himself, and he was hunting and killing his own livestock."

"You mean . . . as a werewolf . . . ?" she asked.

"Uh-huh," agreed Morse. "Some folks think he was actually trying to go straight, that maybe after being a monster over in Europe that he came to the States for a fresh start. And that raising cattle to kill was his way of doing some kind of monster twelve-step."

"But you don't believe that?" asked Djinn.

"Hell no. He was just trying not to shit where he lived. Who knows how many people he killed when he went out of town on business? You know how many people go missing every year in this country, even back then?"

"I do know, actually," said Djinn. "We learned about it in school. It's a lot. It ranges between half a million up to just under seven hundred thousand. Every year."

"Goddamn, that's worse than I thought," said the ghost. "But you see my point. A killer like Griswold—even if he wasn't a were-wolf—could be ranging two or three counties on moonlit nights, killing whoever he wanted and just not leaving any clues, or maybe not even any bodies."

"That's . . . terrifying."

"Damn right it is. Scares me, and I'm already dead."

It wasn't meant as a joke, and Djinn didn't laugh.

"Then there was that Black Autumn, where a blight killed a lot of the crops and most of the livestock. Griswold's, too. All of them. Not sure why he didn't keep hunting far from home. Maybe he just went a little crazy. Crazier than normal, I mean. He started attacking people in town. Killed them and tore them apart to hide the evidence of teeth and claws. Dismembered them. Killed Chief Crow's older brother, Billy. Killed Val Guthrie's uncle. Killed a lot of folks."

"And nobody knew that's what it was?"

"Well, hell, girl, it's not like *werewolf* is the first thing that comes to mind," laughed Morse. "Even here in Pine goddamn Deep."

"Oh. Yeah. There's that."

"But I figured it out," said the ghost.

"How?"

"I saw him. Saw the man turn into a wolf, and saw that wolf go after a kid."

"Chief Crow?"

"Yeah. I was able to help that boy . . . though if all the ruckus didn't cause people to come running out of their houses with guns, I think Crow and me would have been lunch."

"That's disgusting," said Djinn, wincing. "No . . . it's scary as hell. But also disgusting. Is scary-disgusting a thing?"

"In Pine Deep? Yeah, that's sure as hell a thing."

The Bone Man kicked a pebble over the edge of the drop-off. It seemed to fall a long time, and when it landed, the sound it made was too soft and wet. There was something nasty about it.

A couple of neighbor kids came by on their bikes. "Hey, Djinn!" they yelled.

"Hey," she said, waving. She and the Bone Man watched them whizz past.

Djinn cocked her head and gave him a speculative stare. "Why you?"

"Huh? Like in why they lynched me?" he asked. "Those cracker assholes didn't need any reason 'cept that I'm black."

"No, I get that stuff . . . and we can file that under scary-disgusting, too," she said quickly. "And for the record, I'm having this conversation with a ghost, so I'm borderline freaked out. Maybe more than that."

"Weird for me, too," admitted Morse. "But what was it you wanted to know? You asked 'why me'?"

"Yeah, a lot of people were killed back then. All the people Griswold killed when he was a . . . I mean, when he was all wolfed out. They didn't all come back as ghosts. But you did, and now you're back again. So . . . why you?"

The Bone Man turned away for a moment and walked along the rim, leaning out now and then to look down even though the gloom down there was too dark to see anything. Though Djinn wondered if his senses were still human or not.

"I don't really know," he said, stopping a few feet away, his back to her. "I guess maybe because I took some action. I mean, I knew there was something wrong about those killings back in the seventies. No one else seemed to know, but I kind of did. Maybe it's from growing up down south, where we tend to believe a whole lot of weird stuff. I mean, knew something about werewolves from tall tales of the *loup garou*. Lycanthrope stories told by folks whose ancestors came over from France. But not so tall when you come to think on it, because I saw the real deal." He turned toward her and shrugged. "I'm not sure I believe in that karma stuff, but I think once you touch that larger world, it touches you back. Leaves a stain, maybe. Or a mark. Whatever. Since then, I been kind of a guardian. A watcher."

"A watcher? Like in Buffy?"

"Who's Buffy?"

"Oh. After your time, I guess," she said. "A show about a teenage girl destined to be a vampire slayer. She has this stuffy older guy looking after her and teaching her. He was a Watcher. Part of this group who are always looking for monsters to fight."

He grunted. "I don't know about that. And I ain't part of no group. I've always been alone, ever since I left town. Only *group* I was ever with were the Guthrie family, and the kids who hung around with the daughter, Val. Little Scarecrow was part of that group. They treated me like family. Actually, gave a certified damn about me. My skin color didn't seem to mean a goddamn thing to them. All they saw when they looked at me . . . was me. When I got killed, it was old Henry Guthrie who cut me down and saw that I was buried right and proper. Had words read over me, gave me a nice headstone. Most wouldn't have done a tenth as much. So . . . well, maybe my karma—if that's even the right word—got tied to theirs, and since they always seemed to be at the heart of things, maybe I still have work to do. I don't know, Djinn. I really don't. Though . . ."

His voice trailed off.

"What?" asked Djinn.

"I never know how I know some things. What'd you call it? Osmosis? Maybe it's that, but as I was telling you about being someone who was tied to this town because I was tied to the people, I got this feeling that I'm right. That it is what happened. And that is weird as hell, even for me."

Djinn nodded. She looked up at the sky and saw that the clouds had thickened, though she did not smell rain on the breeze.

"How did you kill Ubel Griswold?" she asked.

"Wasn't easy, that was for damn sure." The Bone Man touched his guitar again. "I chased him through the corn and chased him down this slope right here and caught him just as he was starting to change. We had us a knock-down brawl, and I smashed him upside the head with this here guitar, and then I stabbed him with the broken neck. That did it. But . . . if I'd been two minutes later, he'd have torn me all to hell."

"What did you do?"

"I sunk his dead ass in the mud of a bog that's down there. Figured I'd let the worms have their way with his ugly ass."

The cold breeze whipped past them again, and Djinn gasped when she thought she heard the faint hint of laughter as the wind moved through the trees. The Bone Man heard it, too, and he frowned.

"But I did it all wrong," he said. "I thought *killing* him was enough. But . . . like I said, I'm no expert. Turns out there's all kinds of werewolves. Some are like the kind you see in movies, but there are a lot of other ones. Strange-ass versions. There's *vukodlak*s from Serbia and *jé-rouges* from Haiti; the *lobison* from South America and the *nagual* from Mexico. Tons of them. If I'd known that before, I'd have maybe read up on it some so I knew how to kill it proper and make sure it never came back. Hindsight's a bitch, though. The kind of werewolf Griswold was turned out to be one of the worst."

"What was he?" asked Djinn, terrified to ask but needing to know.

"A *pricolici*. Those are ghosts, more or less. They are the souls of the dead who rise from the grave to prey on the living. Sometimes they possess someone so completely that the personality of their victim is just *pushed out*, and afterward the *pricolici* owns the body like it's theirs. When they do that, they can change their shapes. Since the *pricolici* looks like a wolf anyway, into wolves or wolfmen. But that's not even the worst part."

"Do I want to know?" she asked, cold sweat beaded on her face.

"Probably not, but we're in this now," said the ghost. "You see, I killed the body that this monster stole, and I buried him in the swamp before he could just take over someone else. So, the werewolf part of him rotted away and the worms had him. But the spirit of that evil motherfucker . . . it lived on. If *lived* is the right word. Endured, returned. Whatever. It became a kind of vampire. And I'm not talking about Christopher Lee in a cloak."

"Christopher Lee?" she asked, confused. "Count Dooku? Saruman . . . ?"

He stared at her blankly. "I have no idea what that means."

"Christopher Lee was an actor. Real deep voice. He was in *Star Wars* and *Lord of the Rings.*"

"Don't know what *Star Wars* is, and last I remember, *Lord of the Rings* was a series of books. Wizards and elves and shit. No, I mean the guy who played Dracula in a bunch of movies. Anyway, point is, Griswold wasn't a *physical* vampire. He was more of a presence." Morse looked around, up and down that lonely road. "I think there's something about Pine Deep makes bad things worse."

"That I can believe," said Djinn.

"The kind of vampire Griswold became like a field of negative energy. A kind of spiritual infection. He could call certain kinds of people to him and turn them into vampires. Didn't take no bites or blood swapping or any of that shit. He maybe drove them to do things that got them hurt, and just when they were about to die, he did some kind of magic to keep them alive as vampires. These were the actual vampires that killed all those people here in Pine Deep."

She turned more fully toward him.

"Why are you telling me about all this?" she asked. "I mean . . . why me?"

Oren Morse met her gaze but was silent a long time.

"Because this is in your blood, Miss Djinn," he said.

"My . . . ? What's that supposed to mean?"

"You know much about your daddy? About Jimmy Lee Howard?"

"Some. Why, are you going to tell me he was a vampire, too? Or a werewolf?"

"What? Oh, hell no. Not Jimmy Lee. Maybe I should have asked . . . what do you know about *his* dad? What's it called? Your maternal grandfather?"

Djinn thought about it. "Not a lot, really. Mom never talked about him," she said. "Aunt Kay just said he died."

"And she never told you how?"

"Not really," said Djinn, uncertainty creeping into her voice. "She didn't like to talk about it. And . . . to tell you the truth, I didn't want to know all that much. I mean . . . let's face it, I don't have a lot of family pride. Mom and Dad were junkies. Mom's family all died during the Trouble, except for Aunt Kay. We don't exactly get sentimental about family. No one tells happy stories at Christmas or any of that shit."

The Bone Man nodded. "I guess I can see that. None of those stories ended well. Lots of people dying before their times. Lots of mistakes made after. The kind of mistakes people make when they realize there's no rule book for dealing with grief."

"Why did you ask?"

"For the same reason I came to see you today, Djinn."

She took a half step back. "Why? What's wrong? I mean . . . what did you say you were? A crisis apparition, for God's sake. Are you here to tell me I'm about to die? Oh shit, that's it, isn't it?"

There was a rising note of panic in her voice, but the Bone Man raised his hands, palms outward in a calming gesture. "Hey, whoa, whoa now . . ."

Djinn was shaking again, even though the cold wind from Dark Hollow was not blowing at that moment. "I don't want to die," she said. Begging, pleading.

"No," he said in a soft voice. "No, Djinn . . . this isn't about anything like that. I'm not here to tell you anything about you dying. Just the opposite, trust me. I want you to live a long time. It would make me happy as hell to see you clock out somewhere after your hundredth birthday, surrounded by a whole crowd of kids, grandkids, great-grandkids, and all that. So . . . no. That's not why I'm here."

She looked at him through her tears and terrors. "Then . . . why *are* you here?"

He offered her a kindly smile. "Maybe the better question is why can you see me?"

"You're standing right in front of me," she said with more edge than she intended.

Morse shook his head. "Those kids on their bikes didn't see me. That guy who works for Val Guthrie didn't see me."

"Oh. Great. I can see dead people."

"Why'd you say that like that? In a whisper?"

She rolled her eyes. "It's a movie line. *The Sixth Sense* . . . ? Came out a million years ago?"

"Might come as a big surprise, kid, but I'm dead. I don't go to the movies a lot, you dig?"

She stood there, fists balled, unsure of what to say next. Despite his assurances that he wasn't here to warn about her impending death, he was still there. A dead guy. A ghost. Talking about werewolves and vampires. Literally the things that went bump in the night.

Finally, she said, "Maybe this is me being crazy."

"What?" he asked.

"I said I have hallucinations. Stuff I hear. Sometimes stuff I see."

"How do you know any of those things were hallucinations?"

She blinked. "What?"

"I know I'm here. I know you can see me and other people can't," he said. "I know that I'm real to you because I'm actually real. A ghost, okay, I'll give you that, little sister, but . . . real."

"You know what's not real?" she asked. "This conversation. It's surreal."

He nodded. "It is that."

There was a sound, and they both looked up. Above them, filling every branch of every tree, were birds. Crows and starlings, grackles and blackbirds. All of them as dark as night; their feathers so black that it was hard to pick out any definition. Like looking at shadows in the shapes of birds instead of real animals.

"I . . . I didn't notice them before," said Djinn.

"They weren't there before."

"But I didn't hear them land or anything."

"Maybe they didn't want you to," said Morse.

"What? Are you saying they're ghosts, too?"

One of the birds, a ragged old crow, opened its mouth as if to utter a caw, but there was no sound at all.

"They're not ghosts," said the Bone Man. "And they are very much alive."

"Then I don't understand. What are they?"

The ghost walked over to the closest tree and reached up a thin hand. He scratched one of the birds softly. It ruffled its feathers and allowed it.

"I call them nightbirds," said Morse.

"Wait, you've seen them before?"

"Yeah. They were around when Griswold was running on all fours biting people," he said. "And they were there in the days leading up to the Trouble."

"Are they . . . crisis apparitions?"

"Nah. They're . . ." He paused. "Tell you the truth, Djinn, I don't know exactly what they are. All I know is that they're on our side."

"How do you know?"

He shrugged. "I just do."

The old crow repeated that silent caw.

"Why are they here? What do they do?"

"I don't know what all they can do," admitted Morse, "but I'll tell you one thing . . . they don't just show up for no good reason. They taught me some stuff before. They were there when I first woke up a month before the Trouble. When I stepped out of my grave, there they were. And they were there when Mike Sweeney died."

"Wait!" she cried. "Mike's dead? Holy fuck, what happened? I just saw him the other day."

"Shh, calm down. It's okay," said the Bone Man. "Mike's fine. I meant when he died during the Trouble."

"I . . . I . . ."

"Don't look for it to make sense, kid. This is Pine Deep. Weird shit happens on any day that ends with a Y. Those birds helped Mike and they helped me, and that kept us in the game. That helped us fight. That helped us stand tall and be true." He withdrew his hand and nodded up to the old crow. "But . . . I got a feeling you ain't here for me, are you?"

The birds looked at him but made no sound.

Oren Morse nodded. "Yeah. I get it. That's what I thought."

"What?" asked Djinn. "What do you—"

Suddenly that icy wind blew past, harder and more vicious than ever. It hit Morse so hard it staggered him, and it brought with it that sound of laughter. Cold, harsh, ugly. Djinn did not like the sound of that laughter at all.

"Ubel Griswold," she said, not making it a question.

The Bone Man fought for balance, but the wind seemed to hit him harder than it did Djinn. "The fuck, man . . ."

"What's wrong?" cried Djinn.

He held up his hands, and they both looked at them.

They both looked through them.

"What's happening?" demanded Djinn. "What's he doing to you?"

Oren Morse winced as if he were in pain. The birds squawked but did not flee the trees. Djinn stepped in front of the Bone Man, putting her body—small and slim as it was—between the fury of the parasitic thing buried in the mud down in Dark Hollow and the scarecrow of a dead man. The wind whipped through the strings of the old guitar, tearing discordant noise from it.

"I can't stay," said the Bone Man.

The wind blasted Djinn, but she dug in, leaning into it, teeth clenched, glaring hatred at the thought of Ubel Griswold.

Slowly, slowly the assault faded.

It seemed to take hours to stop.

But then the air went dead still.

Djinn wheeled toward Morse. He looked gray—clothes, hair, skin, shoes. And the trees—with all their birds—on the other side of him were visible through his chest and face.

"I asked you what you knew about your granddad," he said, and his voice was as thin and faint as the rest of him. "But we got sidetracked."

"I don't care about that," she breathed, her face cut with lines of worry. "What can I do to help you?"

The old crow cawed audibly this time. Not loud, but there.

"I ain't got much time," said Morse. "Not sure how I know that, but it's what it is. So you got to answer me, Djinn. What did they tell you about how your granddad died?"

"They just said he died when he was young. Twenty-something. My dad was only two. Why? What does this have to do with him? Or me? What's all of this mean?"

"Djinn . . . your granddad was one of Ubel Griswold's first victims," said Morse, and the words slapped Djinn to a shocked silence. "The beast got him. Ripped him up. Tore his life and all his days out of him. Left him with nothing. No chance to become a proper father to his boy. No chance to be a husband to his wife. No chance of ever seeing his granddaughter grow up to be a strong young woman. Griswold stole all of that from him."

"No . . ." she whispered.

"Yes. Griswold killed him, and he tore a hole in everyone in his family. Your daddy grew up in the shadow of that. He grew up scared and paranoid. He tried to be strong, but he wasn't. Somehow what Griswold did stole that from him. It polluted his life, 'cause that what that monster motherfucker *does*. He doesn't just take lives. That's food but it's not fun. No, he ruins lives. Has for more years than anyone can count. He's been ruining whole families for a long damn time, Djinn, and he destroyed almost all of yours."

"Almost? I'm messed up in the head," she said, fighting fresh tears. "Dad . . . Mom . . . all of us. He won. That son of a bitch won."

"No," snarled the Bone Man with such force that it silenced everything—the birds, the movement of the leaves in the trees, the sound of traffic out on the highway. Even the crickets went silent. Morse had faded so much that the last rays of sun slanted down through a hole in the gray sky and passed right through him without deflection or diffusion.

Morse took a step toward her. He moved like a bundle of sticks, awkward, unbalanced. He fought to stay upright. Only his eyes were filled with power. They were so fierce, they exuded actual heat.

"You listen to me, Djinn," he said sternly. "Ubel Griswold hasn't won. Not yet, and goddamn it, not ever. I beat him once. Crow, Mike, Val, and their friends beat him when he came back. It cost them a lot. Griswold had taken so much from each one of them. Val's whole family. Crow's brother. Any chance Mike ever had of being normal. Griswold stole all that . . . but they made a stand, and they beat his ugly ass."

He took another wobbly step.

"Djinn . . . that monster killed your granddad, and whatever dark magic he has keeps clawing at your family. Whittling it down. Killing the ones who can't fight back. Killing the ones who aren't damaged enough to know scars are like armor. But you know who *has* kicked his ass?"

She stared at him. Her lips formed the words but, like that old crow, they were soundless.

And so, Oren Morse said it. "The children of the Storm Lands kicked his ass. Me, Val, Mike, Crow . . ."

Djinn reached out to touch his shoulder, but her fingers passed through him as if he were smoke.

"You're crazy," she said. "What you're saying . . . what you're asking . . . I can't do it. I'm sixteen. My head's broken. I'm crazy."

His smile was so gentle. Like a father's.

"You may be crazy, Djinn," he said, "I'll give you that. But your head isn't broken. You don't see things that aren't there. You never have. Same with what you hear. The difference between you and the guy in that pickup truck and the kids on those bikes—and maybe everyone you go to school with who thinks you're damaged goods—is that they see what's there. But you see what's *really* there. Behind the veils. In the shadows. On the air. That's not you being broken. That's you being split open like a caterpillar's cocoon. You're already here, Djinn. You got power you ain't even unpacked yet. Each and every scar on you, body and soul, is yours. Your power, your understanding—it's all in those scars. And most important of all, my girl, your eyes are wide open, your ears hear just fine."

"I can't fight him . . . that's insane. I don't even know how to throw a punch."

"Yes, you can. You can see, don't you understand? You have the sight. He can't hide from you. Not ever. Whoever fights alongside you will need you to be their eyes. You see, and I think you know. Be that, Djinn. Be exactly that and be more." Like the Cheshire cat, his body was nearly gone, but his smile—and his gentle eyes—lingered. "What you need to know, you'll learn, or figure out, or ask."

"Ask? Ask who?"

"Maybe Mike Sweeney," said Morse. "Maybe Val or Crow. And there's this new guy who lives here now. Monk Addison. Maybe look him up and ask him."

"They'll think I'm this weird, stupid kid."

"I don't think so," said the fading shadow of the ghost. "You go up to Mike Sweeney and you tell him the Bone Man said hello. You go right into the police station and tell Chief Crow the nightbirds are following you. Yeah, you tell him I said . . . I said . . . oh . . . damn . . . this feels really . . ."

Those last few words were as faint as a whisper. She blinked her tears away, and when her eyes were clear, she was alone. The Bone Man was gone.

She sat down hard on the grass, put her face in her hands, and wept.

It was awful. Sobs torn from a deep place like that always hurt. It burned her throat and sent lances of pain through her ribs. It abraded the skin around her eyes and made the day so ugly. So very ugly.

And it lasted a long time while the cold wind began to blow again and the nightbirds watched in their silent vigil.

4

It took a lot for Djinn to stop crying.

It cost so much for her to get to her feet.

Thoughts—random, broken, unfinished, raw—tumbled like debris in the path of a tornado. She looked around and even the colors of the day seemed off, like this was a bad copy of the day she knew and painted with cheap materials.

There was no sign at all of Oren Morse. Not even footprints in the dirt. She strained her ears to hear if there was music on the wind.

Only the cold mockery of a faint laugh rode the wind.

The loss of that music made her mad. The thought of Griswold still alive after all that everyone had done made her anger go cold. Very, very cold.

She turned toward the drop-off. The darkness down there seemed to roil and twist.

Djinn leaned all the way out, hocked a good one into her mouth, and dropped the spit down into the darkness. She did not even exert the energy to spit it. She did not want to give him even that much.

The nightbirds rustled as they huddled close to gossip in small whispers.

Djinn looked around again. The day was the same, but the world was different. She could feel that down to her marrow. Something impossible but real had happened. Djinn was absolutely certain. She flexed her muscles and squeezed her hands into fists and wondered if this came with superpowers.

But nothing happened. She could not fly, did not burst into flame, commanded no lightning, nor felt she could leap tall buildings.

"Okay," she said, testing her own voice. "Same old me. One hundred and nine pounds with no bulging biceps and no magic hammer. Shit."

The wind kept pushing her. Trying to anger her. Trying to scare her.

Djinn turned her back on the drop-off to Dark Hollow.

With slow yet purposeful steps, she walked across the road and through her garden gate and up her porch steps. She lingered with the screen door half-open, looking back at the woods across the street.

He was down there. In the dark. In that wormy bog.

Then she caught the eye of that old crow. Despite the distance, the shadows, and the masses of birds, she saw that crow as clearly as if it stood on the porch rail.

"Okay," she said, nodded.

Griswold was down the hill.

The nightbirds were between him and her.

Djinn smiled at the birds. Then she went inside.

No one was home, so she climbed the steps to her bedroom. Opened the door. Went inside.

Saw the old guitar standing against the bed.

Djinn picked it up and sat down on the bed with it. The guitar was completely solid, and somehow, she knew it always would be. It was hers, after all, and she was alive.

Hers now.

She brushed her fingers down the strings. She had no idea how to play the guitar. Before or then. But, she decided, she would learn. Maybe Gidge would teach her.

Djinn sat there for more than an hour. Thinking about everything. The gray clouds boiled black and threw an ocean of water down on Pine Deep. Djinn got up and fetched a plastic bucket and put it under the usual drip, doing this mostly on autopilot. The clock on the wall was a kitschy gift from Gidge—one of those black cats whose eyes clicked back and forth with the seconds, as did its bushy tail. Djinn stared at it for a while, until her own eyes began to move like that, and she shook herself out of it.

All that time, her mind was working. All of her emotions were in full gear, screaming at her in tones of fear, anxiety, doubt, wonder, joy, hate. Fury.

And a coldness that was different from the bitterness of that breeze from the hollow.

It was more than two hours since coming inside that Djinn fished her cell phone out of her jeans pocket. Didn't have to look up the number. Three digits. Everyone who's ever been in trouble knew it.

"Pine Deep Police," said an old woman's voice. "What's your emergency?"

"No emergency, ma'am," said Djinn. "Can you put me through to Chief Crow?"

"Miss, this line is for emergency use only."

"Sorry. Please let me speak to Chief Crow."

"You'll have to call back on our non-emergency number."

"Can't you just—?"

The woman read off the numbers, and the line went dead.

Djinn breathed in and out through her nose a few times; then she dialed the other number. The same woman answered the phone. "Pine Deep Police, how may I direct your call?"

"I'd like to speak with Chief Crow," said Djinn. "Please."

"May I ask what this is about?"

"No," said Djinn. "It's a family matter."

"I beg your pardon?"

"Tell him someone from the Storm Lands is calling," Djinn said. "I think he'll understand."

"If this is a prank, young lady," scolded the operator, "let me remind you that there are serious penalties for making crank calls to the police and—"

"And you're going to piss him off if you don't give him the message."

She had no idea if that was even remotely true. She heard a sound and glanced around to see a line of crows perched on her windowsill.

"Tell him that," said Djinn.

She nodded to the crows.

There was a silent four-count of nothing, and then a familiar male voice came on the line. "This is Chief Crow," he said. "With whom am I speaking?"

"I . . . really don't know how to make this make sense," blurted Djinn. "Please don't hang up on me."

"You said something about the Storm Lands," said Crow, his voice lowered and confidential. "What did you mean?"

"Maybe you're going to hang up on me," said Djinn. "Maybe my home number and address are showing up on your computer screen and all that TV stuff. Maybe I'm getting myself in trouble, but . . ."

If she expected Crow to interrupt, she was surprised. He waited her out in silence. Her gambit of mentioning the Storm Lands had given her that much, at least.

"I met someone today, Chief Crow," she said. "He said he used to call you Little Scarecrow."

In a small, fragile voice, Crow said, "What did you say?"

"Chief," said Djinn. "Something bad is coming. The nightbirds are in all the trees by the drop-off to Dark Hollow."

"Oh my God," breathed Crow.

"But I need to say something to let you know that not all of it's bad. Listen to me, okay?"

"Okay," said Chief Crow.

"That man I met today . . . he wasn't able to stay. He wanted to, but he couldn't."

"Tell me," whispered Crow.

"The Bone Man sends his regards," said Djinn, and she heard Crow gasp. "I think *he's* coming back. You know who I mean. The other guy. The one down in the Hollow. He's trying to come back. The Bone Man wanted you to know. So you can prepare, I guess. So you can get ready. You see, I can hear him. And I think if I have to, I can see him. And . . . Chief . . . ?"

"Yes . . ."

"I think maybe I can help," she said. "I think I need to. But . . . no, that's not right. I think I want to. Hell, I think I was born for this."

Outside in the trees, all of the nightbirds raised their heads and cried out at once. It shook the rain-soaked branches. It echoed all the way down the side of the slope and into the mossy wet bog that was Dark Hollow.

There, beneath tons of wormy dirt, Ubel Griswold turned over in his sleep. The dream that he long had dreamed changed. It went wrong. And in the throes of that dream, he groaned in immortal terror.

Acknowledgments

I've been writing stories about Pine Deep for the entire length of my fiction career, and there are some folks who have offered tremendous help along the way. Most notably my literary agent, Sara Crowe of Pippin Properties; Michaela Hamilton, my Kensington editor and the fairy godmother of the Pine Deep Trilogy; my original webmaster, Jeffrey Strauss, and his son, Brandon, both of whom came to bad ends in that creepy little town; my colleagues, staff, and students at the Writers Room of Bucks County and, later, the Writers Corner; the board of directors of the Philadelphia Writers Conference and the Pennwriters Conference; the members of the Liars Club: Don Lafferty, Jon McGoran, Keith Strunk, Merry Jones, Janice Bashman, Dennis Tafoya, Kelly Simmons, Edward Pettit, and the late and much-missed L.A. Banks.

Visit our website at
KensingtonBooks.com
to sign up for our newsletters, read
more from your favorite authors, see
books by series, view reading group
guides, and more!

Become a Part of Our
Between the Chapters Book Club
Community and Join the Conversation

Betweenthechapters.net

Submit your book review for a chance to win exclusive
Between the Chapters swag you can't get anywhere else!
https://www.kensingtonbooks.com/pages/review/